DEC 2 6 2007

D0498409

THE AFFECTIONATE ADVERSARY

THE AFFECTIONATE ADVERSARY

CATHERINE PALMER

THORNDIKE PRESS

An imprint of Thomson Gale, a part of The Thomson Corporation

Detroit • New York • San Francisco • New Haven, Conn. • Waterville, Maine • London

LIBRARY OF CONGRESS CATALOGING-IN-PUBLICATION DATA

Palmer, Catherine, 1956–
   The affectionate adversary / by Catherine Palmer.
     p. cm. — (Miss Pickworth series ; #1) (Thorndike Press large print Christian historical fiction)
   ISBN-13: 978-0-7862-9830-3 (alk. paper)
   ISBN-10: 0-7862-9830-8 (alk. paper)
   1. Wealth — Fiction. 2. Gossip — Fiction. 3. Pirates — Fiction. 4. England — Fiction. 5. Large type books. I. Title.
PS3566.A495A69 2007
813'.54—dc22   2007027443

Published in 2007 by arrangement with Tyndale House Publishers, Inc.

Printed in the United States of America on permanent paper
10 9 8 7 6 5 4 3 2 1

To Becky Nesbitt and Anne Goldsmith, who have guided and supported me for so many years. Thank you for reacquainting me with Miss Elizabeth Bennet, Mr. Darcy, and the joys of Jane Austen. If only you lived nearby, dear ladies, I might persuade you to follow my example and take a turn about the room. It is so refreshing!

Looking at the man,
Jesus felt genuine love for him.
"There is still one thing
you haven't done," he told him.
"Go and sell all your possessions
and give the money to the poor,
and you will have treasure in heaven.
Then come, follow me."
At this the man's face fell,
and he went away very sad,
for he had many possessions.

Jesus looked around
and said to his disciples,
"How hard it is for the rich
to enter the Kingdom of God!"

Mark 10:21–23

ACKNOWLEDGMENTS

Many thanks to the people who encourage and support me as I write. I'm grateful to my husband, Tim, for editing my books before I send them to Tyndale House. Kathy Olson, my beloved Tyndale House editor, thank you so much for the work you put into each manuscript. Anne Goldsmith and Becky Nesbitt, bless you for acquiring my books and guiding me along the way. Ron Beers, thank you for your vision and your faithfulness. Karen Solem, I'm grateful for your advice and efforts as my agent. To everyone at Tyndale — marketing, sales, editorial, warehouse — thank you for being a part of God's work. Bookstore owners, managers, salespeople, may God bless you richly for your service. And to my Lord Jesus Christ, thank You for redeeming me. My life and my words belong to You. Make of me what You will.

ONE

The Indian Ocean
April 1814

Through the salty mist that blurred the lens of his spyglass, Charles Locke watched the pirate ship draw near. A large, stout vessel, it boasted thirty guns and more than a hundred hands.

For two days, the captain of the privately owned clipper on which Charles sailed had taken pains to elude the pursuers, tacking first to the south and then heading due west toward the mainland of the African continent. His efforts were to no avail. The pirates bore down on the *Tintagel,* hounding their prey on the waters of the Indian Ocean — their familiar hunting ground.

"Have ye arms, Mr. Locke?" One of the ship's boys joined Charles at the rail. A ragged, scrawny lad of twelve, Danny Martin had attached himself to Charles early in the voyage — polishing his boots, laundering his shirts, bringing down a tray of tea in exchange for a few coins.

Charles enjoyed the young orphan's company. From this child — who made the *Tintagel* his home and the life of a sea captain his dream — he had learned much about the ocean, her ships, and the world's ports of call.

"We be in range of the pirates' cannons now," Danny declared, his gray eyes earnest. "It cannot be long afore they attack. The cap'n bids me ask what means of protection ye have, sir."

"Nothing more than a pistol," Charles told the boy. "Captain Heald knows I am a merchant, not a soldier. Yet I am a fair shot and I can handle a sword. Tell him I shall be happy to —"

"Take these." Danny handed him a brace of pistols and a small dagger. "They be from the cap'n's own closet. He says ye must do your best with them, sir, for he has no others to spare."

"But our ship's guns outnumber theirs, and the *Tintagel* is larger. Surely we can defeat such untrained savages."

The lad's narrow face grew solemn as he studied the approaching vessel. "The *Tintagel* be no warship, Mr. Locke. We have fewer hands on board, and them chaps be pirates from the Malabar Coast of India — the most fearsome of all. They ply the waters from their homeland southwest to Madagascar, north to the Gulf of Aden, and back to India again. They've not had formal trainin' at the Royal Naval Academy, no, but they be masters at fightin', sailin', and sinnin'. We'll be thankin' God if we come out of this alive."

His anxiety increasing, Charles thought of the chest of gold coins secured with locks and seals in the bowels of the *Tintagel*. Charles's father had labored many years as the steward of a grand estate in Devon, and much of that gold had been his reward. Though loyal to a fault and greatly admired by the duke who was his employer, James Locke had little respect for the man. He had considered the duke uncouth, immoral, and unworthy of the lofty rank to which aristocratic lineage had elevated him.

But James had worked in silence and had kept his opinions to himself. Upon quitting his position at last, he had combined a lifetime of frugal investments and carefully hoarded funds with the substantial sum that the duke had settled upon him at retirement. This total he had turned into the gold coin with which he intended to build the foundation for all his hopes and dreams.

And James had entrusted the gold to his only son, Charles.

Together, they had conceived of an enterprise that they believed would surely ensure the family's financial well-being for generations to come. Never again would a Locke labor under the charge of some slothful, profligate, pompous, and fatheaded aristocrat. Charles was to take the gold to China and purchase chests of the finest teas available. During his absence, his father would secure a warehouse in London from which to trade the tea. Both men would labor to recruit investors, for they intended one day to own a merchant ship, a tea estate in China, and a thriving business in London.

Pirates? Such a calamity had never entered their minds. Charles and his father had plotted out each move they must make to ensure success. They factored in every risk imaginable and chose to trust the Almighty. It was perilous to invest all their money in one product, they had acknowledged. Most traders carried manufactured goods, gunpowder, shot, and cannons to Oriental ports. They returned with silks, muslins, ivory, spices, sandalwoods, and other exotic products.

But Locke & Son, Ltd. would build an empire on tea. Tea alone. For what Englishman could start his day without a pot of the hearty brew? What Englishwoman would consider welcoming callers unless she laid out her finest china, silver, lace, and, of course, the best tea she could afford? From the vegetable mongers in the markets to King George himself, every soul in the realm drank several pots a day of the welcome amber liquid. Who better to provide it for them than James and Charles Locke?

Charles gritted his teeth now as the *Tintagel's* captain barked out orders in preparation for battle. The clipper's hands raced back and forth, arranging the guns in batteries on both sides of the vessel. Although the cannons could only be aimed straight ahead, they were deadly. Divided by size, the small-caliber guns fired eight-pound balls. The large-caliber weapons launched twenty-four-pound shot.

"Look, sir; she be pullin' broadside of us to attack!" young Danny told Charles as the pirate ship tacked into position. His voice rang with excitement and fear as he pointed a skinny arm at the battery of cannons facing the *Tintagel.* "The waves be high, and they will miss with some of their shot. We shall miss too. I doubt we can outlast them, sir." Danny's gray eyes met his. "Save your weapons until they board us, Mr. Locke."

"You speak of our defeat as a foregone conclusion," Charles called out as Danny started away.

"Now be the time to address your Maker, sir, for ye may soon be standin' afore the gates of glory!"

Sarah Carlyle, Lady Delacroix, dipped a silver spoon into her tea and gave it a stir. As she gazed from her deck chair upon the fair scene of lapping waves and sapphire sky that stretched out before her, she could not imagine herself any happier. Her quest had succeeded admirably.

In China, Sarah had encountered the most admirable woman of her acquaintance, a teacher whose efforts to spread the gospel of Jesus Christ had met with much success. In Burma, a young missionary couple had welcomed Sarah into their hearts and home. In India, she had spent three weeks in the company of missionaries laboring to translate and print the Scriptures as well as to minister in body and spirit to the unsaved. While most of Africa remained darkened by sin and its villainies, Sarah had every hope of sponsoring those who would take the light of salvation to the green shores of that continent.

As she took a sip of steaming tea, Sarah

closed her eyes and allowed a sense of well-being to flow through her. God had permitted her to endure many hardships in order to teach her the truths she now embraced with wholehearted devotion. She thought of her late father, Mr. Gerald Watson, an ambitious and ruthless opium merchant, who had taught his three daughters that while money might buy power, it could purchase neither respect nor honor. Position and esteem belonged to those born of aristocratic lineage, Mr. Watson had insisted — men such as George Carlyle, Lord Delacroix.

Determined that his descendants might experience the privileges of the peerage, Sarah's father had arranged the marriage of his eldest daughter to the penniless baron. She and Lord Delacroix were married for less than a year before her husband's unexpected demise in a carriage accident. Before his death, the dissipated and impoverished baron had taught his much younger wife that the admiration and deference due the aristocracy were worth little without the money to enjoy them. Yet Sarah — who now lived with the privilege of title her father had desired and the wealth her husband had coveted — had discovered that neither of these two gleaming grails brought happiness.

Ambition had made her father heartless, while poverty had bequeathed her husband insecurity and self-loathing. A quest for position and money brought out unpleasant qualities in everyone she met, Sarah had learned. Women fawned over her with words of false admiration in hopes of earning the privilege of an invitation to be seen in her company. Men fairly stumbled over their own feet as they scrambled to win a place on her dance card, the favor of her presence in their opera box, or — the grandest prize of all — her hand in marriage. And what had all this wealth and admiration given her? Nothing but false friends and utter loneliness.

Sighing deeply, Sarah opened her eyes and gazed out at the endless expanse of turquoise sea. The *Queen Elinor's* white sails billowed overhead as the wind propelled her across the Indian Ocean toward England. Toward home and family. Yet only in the past months of solitary travel had Sarah discovered true joy.

Her Savior had been so right when He told His disciples how difficult it was for the rich to enter the kingdom of heaven, she reflected as she took another sip of tea.

16

When a wealthy young man had asked Jesus what he must do to be saved, the Lord had told him to sell all his possessions, give the money to the poor, and follow Christ. Jesus — and He alone — had taught Sarah the truth. She must cast off the privileges that came with her position in society. She must divest herself of the wealth that weighed like a millstone about her neck. She must give up everything she owned, all that she might claim as hers, and surrender to the crucified and risen Christ.

Traveling throughout the Orient, Sarah had done just that. And how happy and free she now felt. Not only had she disbursed large sums to various worthy recipients, but she had identified various other causes that would help her be rid of the remainder of the vast fortune with which her father had saddled her. Upon returning to England, she would resume her philanthropic quest. Orphanages, schools, printing presses —

"Sail, oh!" A cry from the crow's nest scattered Sarah's contemplative musings. "Sail, oh!"

"Where away?" came the response from below.

As the bearings were called out, Sarah rose from her chair and hurried to the ship's rail along with everyone else who had been lolling about the deck. Endless days of looking at nothing but the sea brought on a strange, hypnotic torpor, and all were eager to break its spell.

"Is it a friendly vessel?" Sarah asked a young man who was studying the horizon through his spyglass. Clad in the regimentals of the Royal Navy, he and several other officers aboard were responsible for protecting the *Queen Elinor,* one of the most reliable barks in the East India Company's vast merchant fleet.

Sarah leaned her elbows on the rail and peered at the ship in the distance. "Can you make out her flag, sir?"

"Dash it all, I can hardly hold the glass steady with these infernal waves tossing us about so."

"Dear me. You address the sea with much vehemence, my good man. Are these particular waves truly worthy of your linguistic efforts?"

The officer glanced at her. "Oh, Lady Delacroix," he gulped, straightening to attention and squaring his shoulders. "Forgive my poor manners, madam. I thought perhaps another of the passengers had spoken. Uh . . . would you . . . would you care to look through my spyglass?"

"You bestow your fine manners on some

and save your ill ones for others, do you?" she asked with a smile. "For myself, I think it best to attempt politeness to everyone."

"Yes, Lady Delacroix. Of course. You are absolutely correct."

"I am glad to see that we concur, sir. And now if you would return to your glass, I should very much like to know what sort of ship shares our corner of the ocean. I hope it is not pirates."

The poor fellow threw out his chest and fairly barked his response. "Madam, I assure you that any East India Company vessel is more than prepared to defend itself from such marauders. You must have no misgivings on that account."

Sarah laughed. "And why do you suppose I booked passage on just such a vessel? But please, sir, do look through your spyglass ere we both die of curiosity!"

He snapped to obey, but before he could report, the good news rang out. The ship flew an English flag! No one could make out more, and speculation fluttered like seagulls across the deck. Pirates sometimes hoisted friendly flags to deceive unsuspecting ships. Could it be an enemy in disguise? Was it a vessel of the Royal Navy perhaps — a man-of-war patrolling the coastal waters? Or might it be another East India-man?

And suddenly news of greater import descended. The clipper was cloaked in a veil of smoke. It must be engaged in a sea battle! But where was the opposing vessel? A mixture of shock and thrill raced around the deck.

"Our captain alters course," the officer noted grimly. "The wind is at east-northeast, and we tack to larboard."

Sarah glanced at the wheelhouse. "We go to assist the English clipper?"

"Aye, madam," he confirmed as the sails began to shake. "It must be so, for the captain brings the *Queen Elinor* eastward, and soon we shall head to wind. With more rudder, he will have her facing southeast."

Sarah gripped the rail as the full-rigged bark performed the elaborate maneuver and then began an agonizingly slow trek toward the besieged clipper.

"She is definitely engaged," the officer reported while observing the conflict through his spyglass. "I fear the English ves-sel is aflame. And now I make out another ship . . . just starboard . . . aye, there she is. . . . Great guns and ghosts — 'tis pirates indeed!"

"Sail, oh!" came the cry from the crow's

nest. "Sail, oh!"

Now the captain emerged from the wheel-house, and the young officer excused himself and hurried to join his fellow Royal Navy men who were forming ranks beneath the mainsail. The ship's mates scrambled to prepare the *Queen Elinor,* while ashen-faced passengers huddled together near the galley in earnest discussion of the situation.

Still at the deck rail, Sarah tightened the bow on her bonnet. Difficulties, she had learned, were to be expected in the life of every Christian. And thus, with the smell of gunpowder stinging her nostrils, she began to pray.

His vision blurred and his head throbbing, Charles crouched behind the splintered stump of the foremast. Early in the pirates' attack, a broken spar had tumbled down, dashing him to the deck. He had struck his head on a pyramid of iron cannonballs and was rendered senseless. How long he lay unmoving on the deck Charles could not say. But he had returned to consciousness only moments before a pirate missile struck the base of the *Tintagel*'s soaring mast.

The timber had wavered for an instant before crashing to the deck, bringing fore-sails, gallant sails, and studding sails down in a tangle of canvas and rope. At the sudden imbalance, the deck dipped seaward, and the great clipper nearly capsized. Charles had clung to an armful of soaking canvas, only releasing it as the mast slid into the deep, and the ship righted itself in a dizzying swoop of wet wood and crashing waves.

Bloodcurdling howls rose from the pirates as they realized the *Tintagel*'s hopeless position. They unleashed a barrage of ordnance from their cannon — chain shot, bar shot, canister, and deadly langrage. Composed of nuts, bolts, nails, and scrap iron, a langrage ball hit the deck and exploded in every direction. Men screamed as shrapnel tore into their flesh.

Charles stared in stunned shock at the carnage.

What once had been a scrubbed and orderly vessel now took in water at the bow and burned like a funeral pyre at the stern. Sailors lay groaning in pain or gasping for a last breath. Many had been tossed into the sea, some had leapt to their deaths, while others were crushed beneath the falling mast. Those men who still labored at the *Tintagel*'s cannon shouted encouragement, but few remained to heed it.

Charles staggered toward the nearest gun

and scanned the deck for young Danny Martin. The boy had vanished along with so many others, leaving the clipper eerily empty. Reaching the poor man who vainly tried to load the cannon's muzzle, Charles clapped him on the shoulder.

"My good sir," he said, "allow me to assist you."

"Aye, but see how they shoot their grapnels at us now!" the fellow cried as the pirate ship's cannons launched an array of iron barbs across the narrow expanse between the two vessels. Charles knew the grapnel hooks carried ropes that would tie the ships together. It would not be long before the enemy would board the *Tintagel.*

His leg a bloodied mess, the sailor struggled to lift a ball. "Oh, God, where be Ye now? Shall Ye leave us to perish in the deep?"

"Take heart." Charles took the shot from the man's hands and thrust it into the cannon's mouth. "God has not abandoned us. Here, you must have this pistol, sir. Protect yourself."

"Bah! What good is a pistol? Look — their boats now hoist and swing away. They shall be upon us in moments!"

From the pirate ship, six smaller barks filled with well-armed men were lowered to the sea. Bellowing insults and taunts, they rowed toward the foundering clipper. There were too many of them, Charles realized, and far too few left to defend the *Tintagel*. The attackers came too fast, too furiously, and there was little hope for salvation.

But he would not give up his life and his dreams so easily. "Come, where is your tinderbox, man?" he demanded. "We are not dead yet."

The two worked to light the fuse, and in a moment, the ball burst from the gun with a blast of black powder that knocked them both to the deck. Charles rolled onto his knees just as another round of langrage hit the *Tintagel* and exploded. Shrapnel flew. Wood splintered. Bolts and nails burrowed into the railings and the deck. A shard of scrap iron tore a hole through the chest of the man Charles had just assisted. He stared at Charles with lifeless eyes before toppling in a heap.

As a knot of disbelief and terror formed in his throat, Charles wiped the sweat and blood from his eyes. Now the pirate boats bumped against the hull of the *Tintagel*. Boarding pikes arced over the rail and buried their pointed iron heads in the splintered wood of the deck. Charles grabbed one of the seven-foot poles and yanked it loose. But he quickly saw there were too many to dislodge them all. The Malabar pirates were already climbing ropes attached to the pikes.

As Charles drew his pistols, they came. Swarming up and over the railing like so many ants, the pirates poured onto the *Tintagel*. Clad in every color of the rainbow and with gold chains and jewels hung about their necks, they carried cutlasses, flintlocks, axes, muskets, knives, and granados. The few seamen who were still able now unleashed the last of their weaponry. Balls flew, swords hissed and clanged, men cried out in pain.

Unable to still the trembling in his hands, Charles took cover behind the wheelhouse. A giant of a man with a great black mustache and a red turban spotted the Englishman, drew his saber, and rushed forward. When the pirate was nearly upon him, Charles pulled the trigger — and missed his target by a foot. With a roar of rage, the marauder continued his charge, pausing only to replace his saber with a brace of pistols drawn from a leather sling across his chest.

As the pirate resumed his headlong plunge, Charles caught a glimpse of Danny from the corner of his eye. The lad was hidden inside a coil of rope near the capstan, yet his head protruded as he helplessly observed the massacre unfolding before him.

"Danny!" Checking the two pistols he yet carried and unsheathing his knife, Charles called to the ship's boy. "Danny, 'tis Locke here! Take my knife!"

"Mr. Locke! Look well behind ye, sir!" Danny screeched the words as the pirate took aim at Charles.

Having only the two pistols remaining — and thus only two shots — Charles dropped to the deck and scrambled toward the capstan. A massive device used to heave the main topsail aloft, its long wooden bars provided little protection. As the pirate fired, a ball ripped through Charles's sleeve, nicking his arm.

"Danny!" He tossed the knife to the boy at the very moment that another beefy buccaneer began to hack at the coil of rope with an ax.

A second ball hit the back of Charles's leg, and he fell. Drawing his pistols, he rolled and fired. One shot went wide, but the pirate took the second in his right knee. With a snarl of pain, the man snatched another pair of pistols from the sling on his chest. Urging Danny to save his own life,

Charles ducked behind the rope coil and began to crawl across the deck, his useless leg trailing behind him.

He would die now, he realized. This was how his life would end. His fingers gripped the wet wood as he pulled himself toward the rail in a hopeless attempt to escape the pirate. If he went overboard, he would drown. The ocean was too wide. Too deep.

One death or another.

His father's gold would go into a pirate's treasury. To hedonism and lust and drunkenness. All was lost.

Charles grasped the ship's rail and tried to heave himself into a standing position. But as his head cleared the wooden bar, the pirate lighted a granado and tossed it at him. The hollow iron orb filled with black powder glanced off the stump of the mainmast and burst into deadly pieces. One ripped through Charles's arm. Another cut across his shoulder. The shock wave deafened him, lifted him from the rail, and tossed him into the sea.

Water swept into his nostrils and poured down his throat. As he sank, Charles looked up toward the surface of the water. For an instant, he thought he saw heaven.

Two

"These poor souls . . ." The captain of the *Queen Elinor* walked across the deck. "All dead. All lost."

Sarah held her handkerchief in a clenched fist as she watched the man survey the devastation of the English clipper *Tintagel*. Too late, the rescue vessel had arrived upon the scene of the sea battle. By the time the *Queen Elinor* sailed into position near the beleaguered ship, the pirates had killed nearly every man aboard, stripped everything valuable, and sailed north toward the Malabar Coast.

Hoping to save those few yet living, the captain had chosen not to go in pursuit of the pillagers. Instead, his sailors had boarded the foundering clipper, put out fires, transferred the dead and dying, and salvaged what remained of the captain's logs and journals. Those men who had survived the pirate attack were taken to the *Queen*

Elinor's mess hall, where a small hospital had been hastily set up. Tables became beds; every passenger donated blankets and bedding. The ship's physician hurried from one patient to the next, occasionally shaking his head in dismay.

Sarah Carlyle had assisted in the recovery, first tending to the living who were brought aboard and then laboring with the other women to stitch a pair of cannon balls into each length of canvas that must become a dead man's shroud. Once the captain had conducted the brief funeral service, the canvas would be sewn into place, starting at the feet.

The afternoon had flown by in a race against time and heat, and at last no more could be done. The *Tintagel* was left to its inevitable sinking as the *Queen Elinor* drew away to a safe distance. In preparation for the burials, the captain ordered the sails adjusted so that some were full of wind while others were laid back, thus rendering the ship motionless. The top gallant yards were set acockbill to signify both death and burial, and list lines were put out of trim to speak of grief. The entry port on the starboard gangway was opened to windward.

The crew, under immediate command of the boatswain, gathered to witness the rite.

Sarah stood to the side with her fellow passengers as the petty officer cried out, "Ship's company . . . off hats!"

Determined that the dead must all lie at the bottom of the sea before the blistering equatorial sun rose the following morning, the captain stepped forward and spoke quickly. " 'Dear God, we commit these bodies to the deep,' " he read from his book of prayers, " 'to be turned into corruption, looking for the resurrection of the body, when the sea shall give up her dead, and the life of the world to come, through our Lord Jesus Christ; who at His coming shall change our vile body, that it may be like His glorious body, according to the mighty working, whereby He is able to subdue all things to himself. Amen.' "

He then motioned the ladies to gather up the shrouds and follow him. By now, Sarah retained no distinction as a baroness. Grateful to be regarded as an equal by the other passengers, she took an armful of canvas and joined the women at their labors.

Recruited to record information that might assist in contacting the families of the deceased, the boatswain accompanied the captain as he began his walk down the row.

"No identification papers," the captain stated. "Red hair. Scar on left cheek. No jewelry or personal effects. Death by injury to the head. Lord, have mercy upon the soul of this poor man; amen. Ladies, the corpse may be shrouded. Gentlemen, assign the earthly remains to the benevolent arms of the sea."

Her gown wet with seawater and blood, Sarah bit her lower lip in a futile effort to hold back tears as two women knelt to hastily stitch the canvas into place. In all her travels, she had never witnessed a sight so gruesome, so sad, so utterly grim as this.

The pirates' actions astounded her. Such inhumanity! Such wickedness! Such barbarity! And why? All for the ill-gotten gain of riches.

The Lord's message to her was again made clear, Sarah realized as she followed the captain down the row. She must do all in her power to rid herself of the evil of material wealth. Not only must she become as poor, humble, and reliant upon God as the birds of the sky and the flowers of the field, but she must teach others to do the same. Christ had stressed this truth again and again, yet few were those who heeded His teachings.

"Black hair. Beard. No teeth." The captain spoke in a low rumble. "Tattoo of an anchor on the right forearm. No personal effects.

31

Death by . . . I am uncertain of the cause. Lord, have mercy upon the soul of this poor man; amen. Ladies, the corpse may be shrouded. Gentlemen, assign his earthly remains to the benevolent arms of the sea."

As the sailors tipped a table set up at the entry port on the starboard gangway, each body slid into the sea. One. Two. Three. Four.

"Brown hair," the captain said. "No scars. No tattoos."

"There's a neck chain, sir. With a key." The boatswain handed him the small gold trinket.

The captain motioned that this be recorded. "No other personal effects," he continued. "Death by . . . hmm . . . he has several wounds."

"This one were pulled from the water, sir. Drownin', I would guess."

"Drowning then." The captain nodded. "Lord, have mercy upon the soul of this poor man; amen. Ladies, the corpse may be shrouded. Gentlemen, assign his earthly remains to the benevolent arms of the sea."

Touched by the gentle expression on the dead man's face, Sarah started to kneel. But another woman fell to her knees to begin the shrouding. Offering up a prayer that God might comfort and bless the family of the dead man, Sarah stepped to the next body.

"Brown hair," the captain said, then amended, "curly brown hair. Scar on the left shoulder. Tattoo of a mermaid on the chest. Death by —"

A cry pierced the evening pall. "He is alive! Captain, the man moved! I swear it!"

The lady who had been stitching the shroud of the kind-faced man now stood back and clutched her skirts tightly around her legs. As the captain and others crowded around the still form on the deck, she babbled on.

"My needle, sir. I was putting in the last stitch, and I felt his breath! And he moved his lips! He yet lives!"

As Sarah stepped to the captain's side, she could hear the men grousing about addlepated women and their wild fancies. Kneeling near the boatswain, who had laid his cheek near the man's nose, Sarah picked up the cold arm, set it upon her lap and began to stroke it up and down as if somehow she might bring him back to life with her touch.

"I feel no breath," the boatswain announced. "I fear 'twas just the lady's imaginin'. He is drowned."

"Allow me to test him," Sarah whispered.

Taking her needle, she pricked the soft skin inside the man's forearm. He made no move. Praying for some response, she touched the sharp steel tip to the inside of the man's nostril. Nothing. At last, she opened her chatelaine bag and slipped a tiny mirror from it. When she held the glass beneath his nose, a pale white fog clouded it for the briefest instant.

"Alive!" she proclaimed. "Captain, this man indeed lives."

Instantly, the seamen burst into action. One ran for the physician while two fell to their knees and began to push upon the man's chest in an effort to expel water from his lungs. Yet another began to pray loudly as the captain gave orders to retrieve blankets and a pallet. Sarah drew back and continued rubbing the chilled arm as she silently pleaded with God to spare this life. Two of the attending ladies tugged off the man's boots just as the physician appeared.

Determined to accompany the pallet belowdecks, Sarah was gathering her skirts when the captain touched her shoulder. "Lady Delacroix," he said "you have done more than enough here. I beg you to retire and attend to yourself. I shall order the first mate to see that water is heated and a bath drawn for you. I insist you take nourishment and rest."

"Sir, you must do no such thing!" she replied, rather more forcefully than she intended. Calming herself with a deep breath, she continued. "I am honored to serve my Lord and my fellow man in this way. Please permit me to assist the physician. There is nothing I should rather undertake at this moment."

"Then I shall not stop you. But please, may I ask you to take this man's neck chain into your safekeeping? Clearly, he was a passenger aboard the *Tintagel,* for his attire attests to some measure of standing above that of the common sailor."

"Certainly, Captain." Sarah accepted the gold chain with its attached key and slipped it into her chatelaine bag. "And now, if you will excuse me . . ."

"Thank you, my lady. I assure you, your kindness aboard my ship will never be forgotten."

Sarah picked up her skirts, gave a brief curtsy, and hurried away. She had done nothing more arduous than any of the female passengers aboard the *Queen Elinor,* and it pained her to be distinguished from them. Once there was a time when Sarah had accepted the solicitous compliments of others, for she had believed the admiration of her rank and person to be sincere. No more. She now saw through such falseness, and she could not abide it. Though her title as the dowager Lady Delacroix must linger, she would do all in her power to dispel its effect.

With some difficulty, Sarah negotiated the steps leading to the galley below. Her wet petticoats felt as though their hems were lined with bags of sand, and the delicate stitching of her slippers' seams had given out earlier. Never mind if her toes were wet and her ankles cold, she thought as she hurried down the lamplit corridor. She was warmer and better clad than many aboard this ship, and she had no cause to complain.

By the time she arrived at the long room in which the sailors took their meals — now the makeshift hospital — the rescued man had been laid out on a table and covered with blankets. A quantity of water had been expelled from his lungs, the doctor informed Sarah, and he now breathed more easily.

"Speak freely with me, Dr. Winslow," she addressed the physician. "As far as I am able, I mean to assist these men in their recovery." She held up a hand. "Do not protest, sir. I shall not be denied."

"If you insist. But you will see things here that are not meant for a lady's eyes. These men are all gravely ill. I do not expect many to live."

"Nevertheless, I shall do my part. Now tell me what you know of this man. I must know the extent of his injuries."

"I fear he cannot survive," the physician confided. "There is much danger from his intake of water. Pneumonia, fevers, and ague all lurk in wait to attack the lungs of one who has nearly drowned. As for his other injuries, they are most severe. It appears the gentleman was wounded by more than one ball. His leg is fractured here below the knee. Such grave damage may necessitate amputation, though I shall do all in my power to save the limb. And here, a ball passed through the shoulder. Another has lodged near the elbow, and it must be removed if he is to retain mobility. Finally — though certainly not the least of my concerns — is the injury from an explosion of langrage or perhaps a granado. He will be much scarred from this, and the danger of suppuration is great."

Sarah's heart ached as she absorbed the full extent of the man's unhappy condition. As the physician began to work over him, washing and probing wounds, she wondered how such a one had come to be aboard an English clipper in the Indian Ocean. What had led him so far from home and safety?

Taking a rag, she dipped it into a pail of water and began to wash his pale face. Such a noble nose and fine square chin he had. He was recently shaved, and his hair had been cut into a style common among well-to-do men. Perhaps he was an aristocrat. Or a merchant. Or maybe he was a missionary, like those wonderful gentlemen Sarah had met on her journey. Perhaps eager to spread the gospel of Christ, had this man been sailing to some foreign land where he would reside for many years? What would he think when he learned that the ship in which he now reposed was returning him to England?

She glanced down at the myriad injuries that mottled and marred his broad chest and well-muscled arms. Had he fought valiantly when the pirates attacked? Or had he cringed and hidden? Had he battled until the moment he was thrown overboard? Or had he leapt into the sea in desperation?

When the physician and an assistant began to move the broken bones of the man's leg in order to set them into place, the poor fellow cried out. As though he were emerging from a nightmare, his eyes flew open, unblinking and filled with terror. He stared at Sarah; then he clenched his teeth and squeezed his eyes shut again.

"There, there, sir," she said softly, running her palm over his forehead. "You are safe aboard the *Queen Elinor*. Dr. Winslow tends your wounds. Pray, my dear man. Pray that God may heal you."

Again the man's lids slid open, this time more slowly. His gaze fastened on Sarah. "My father," he gasped. "Tell him . . ."

"You will see your father again," Sarah whispered. "You must rest now. Take in breath and refresh your lungs."

"Tell my father . . ." He grimaced in pain. For a moment, she believed he had fallen unconscious again. Then he groped for her hand, found it, and carried it to his chest. "Tell him I tried."

"Of course, sir. What is your father's name?"

"James Locke. London."

"Yes, James Locke. I shall not forget it."

"I tried. Tell him that."

"He will know. I promise you."

As he swallowed, the tendons in his neck stood out. "Is Danny dead?" he rasped.

Sarah glanced at Dr. Winslow.

He shrugged. "The injured often speak nonsense. I advise you to make no promises, madam. Nor must you take seriously his ramblings."

She took a small ivory comb from her bag

and ran it through the injured man's wet locks. So dark brown it was nearly black, his hair formed a shocking contrast to the blue of his eyes. Sarah watched the salty water fall in droplets onto the table. This was a fine man, she thought. God could use such a creature — once so hale and handsome — to His own glory. If he had intelligence, education, humor, and curiosity, he would make a godly tool for the Lord's work. She must pray in that direction.

"Danny?" he mumbled. "Danny?"

"Rest yourself," she cooed as she finished combing out his hair. "The future of all men lies with God. Whether alive or dead, Danny is in the presence of the Lord."

The blue eyes opened wide again, shimmering like sapphires in the lamplight. "Is the lad dead then?"

"I cannot say, Mr. Locke. I have never met Danny."

His brow furrowed, as if he would begin to weep. "Dead. A boy of twelve."

Sarah glanced at Dr. Winslow. "Was such a youth brought aboard, sir?"

The doctor shook his head. "More to the point now, madam, I must see to my other patients. Will you not retire to your cabin and allow my assistants to aid in treating the survivors? You are very pale, and I urge you to refresh yourself with food and rest."

"But you have not removed the ball from this poor man's elbow. I shall stay here during the surgery, sir."

"That must wait until later. I have more urgent wounds to attend first. The leg is set, and God willing, it may begin to mend. Salt water, though painful, has a curative effect, and we must rely upon its powers for the minor injuries while we use our medical skills upon the serious ones."

Sarah let out a breath of frustration as the physician moved away. What hope had these poor men aboard such a dank and ill-fitted ship? In London, the world's finest medical care could be found — and it was rarely good enough. In the countryside, doctors were scarce, and so apothecaries plied their trade in various liniments and tinctures that hardly ever worked. Those few practitioners of medicine who chose to spend years away from home and family as ships' doctors must be considered the least successful of the lot. Their aim, it was rumored, too often involved the pleasures to be found at ports of call rather than upholding the Hippocratic oath.

No matter whether incurred on sea or shore, an injury often resulted in suppuration and the victim's demise. Death, in fact, seemed to Sarah as common as life. At a young age, she had lost her mother to an unnamed illness. Five years ago, her father had died of pneumonia. Her husband, too, was dead. He was killed instantly when a horse ran amok and toppled his carriage.

Reputable physicians tried bleeding, applying various tonics and plasters, and even surgeries in an effort to heal their patients. But success was uncommon. It was no wonder that Sarah's father had made a fortune in the sale of opium and its derivatives, for easing pain proved far more successful than curing its cause.

As Dr. Winslow had confessed, not a single one of the men who lay moaning in this galley could have much hope of recovery. Sarah touched the key and chain inside the cloth bag she wore. Was Mr. Locke married? And if so, why had he not mentioned his wife? No, it was his father who haunted him at his darkest hour. Were the man to perish, Sarah must know more than his father's name and city of residence. She laid the back of her hand against his cheek and stroked upward to his temple.

"Sir," she said, leaning near his ear, "may I be so bold as to ask your name?"

At that, his eyes opened. He reached up, and with a cold finger he touched her cheek.

"I am Charles Locke," he answered. "Charles Locke of London."

With her free hand, she pressed his palm to her face. "And I am Sarah. Sarah Carlyle."

"Miss Carlyle." He turned his head toward the fingers that lay upon his temple. "I thank you."

"I am . . ." How could she correct him at a time like this? To insist that he call her Lady Delacroix seemed ridiculous. She despised titles and all that went with them. "I am Mrs. Carlyle," she finished. "I am a widow."

"Mrs. Carlyle, your hand is soft. You smell of lavender."

With a start, Sarah drew back from the touch of his palm upon her cheek. But he held her other hand pressed firmly to his temple.

"Stay here," he said, his voice firm. "Pray for me, Mrs. Carlyle. And after I am dead, tell my father —" his lips tightened as he fought emotion — "tell him I tried to do his will. Though I failed . . . tell him I tried."

Standing over the wounded man, Sarah knew a tenderness she had never felt in all her life. It swept over and through her, welling up in her eyes as tears that brimmed and spilled down her cheeks.

"Mr. Locke," she managed to whisper. "Trying is all that matters, for the results of our efforts always lie in the hands of the Almighty."

For an instant, his blue eyes opened again. "Mrs. Carlyle," he addressed her. He did not speak again.

Of the one hundred and thirty-three men aboard the *Tintagel,* only eleven lay alive in the makeshift hospital inside the galley of the *Queen Elinor.* The faces of the dead came to Charles as he slept. The captain. The first mate. The boatswain. Merchants. Steersmen. Helmsmen. The ship's boys. Danny Martin.

Anguish pouring through him at the memory of the lad whose cheerful hop-skip across the deck had become so familiar, Charles knotted his fists. "Danny," he murmured.

A cool hand instantly covered his forehead, and again he smelled lavender. Opening his eyes, he saw that she was there, as she had been so many long days. Mrs. Carlyle. How could he have survived without her?

"Are you hungry, Mr. Locke?" she asked now, as she always did. "I have a hearty soup just here. It is quite warm and good, for I ate a bowl of it myself at luncheon."

Charles closed his eyes. He knew fever raged through his body, for he could feel the heat inside his veins as his blood rushed through his head and pounded inside his ears. His leg throbbed with pain. His arm was paralyzed. His chest flamed.

Now she was singing a hymn, something his mother used to hum while she knitted beside the fire. Mrs. Carlyle's voice lifted through his agonizing torpor. Sweet, clear tones with none of the affectations young ladies often used to impress their listeners. She was a songbird, a lark, a gift from God.

She sang day and night. Even when he could not see her, he heard her voice. Sometimes she went away — to sleep, he supposed, or to attend the other patients. But always she returned to his side, took his hand, wrapped his senses in soothing lavender, and raised him from the fire with her song.

He loved her. This much Charles knew. More than anything in his life, he loved Mrs. Carlyle. He loved her gentle smile. Her soft touch. Her lovely voice. He loved her eyes — deep brown eyes with long black lashes and brows that swooped like the wings of a dove across her forehead. He loved her nose, a pert and proper nose, with just the hint of pink along the bridge. He loved her mouth, full and beckoning lips that mesmerized him as she spoke or sang or fretted.

His physical pain mingled with the agony of knowing he had lost everything. Lost the gold. Lost young Danny. Failed his father. Somehow squandered all hope of the future he had once dreamed possible. But Mrs. Carlyle was near. In that, he could die a happy man.

"The rains passed us to the east," she was saying now, as though they conversed over a tea table. "The captain said he expected a squall, but we had not a single drop. Though our freshwater stores are low, I am pleased at the storm's passing. I am not fond of a tossing sea."

"Mrs. Carlyle, will you marry me?" Charles asked her. Every day, he asked. Many times a day. She always said the same thing.

"No, Mr. Locke, I shall not marry you. Please do be reasonable." With a sigh, she reached into her bag to retrieve a book. Quite often, she read Shakespeare's sonnets to him. Sometimes it was Milton. But usually, she chose passages from a small volume of the Psalms. Each time she read the words of Scripture, her voice softened and mellowed, as though she were drinking the comfort she found therein.

Today, instead of a book, she held up something smaller. "This chain was taken from your neck," she told him. "The captain gave it to me for safekeeping. Mr. Locke, I must be so impertinent as to ask if you are married. I should be remiss if I failed to inform your wife of your condition immediately upon our arrival in London."

He studied the links of gold and the key lying in her palm. "I have no wife," he said at last. "That is my father's chain. He gave it to me at our parting. Father to son."

As he spoke the words, Charles closed his eyes in painful memory. The chain was many generations old, a rare treasure forged by some unknown craftsman. Each Locke father had passed it to his eldest son. And on down the line to him. The last of the line. The only son of James Locke. And he had failed them all.

From slave to serf to farmer to tradesman and finally to steward of a great estate the Locke men had labored, climbing slowly and painfully through the ranks that society had imposed upon them. In Charles Locke reposed the dreams of all those who had come before him, all who had toiled on the land and served others in the quest for

47

freedom from such bondage. At last, with James Locke came the single opportunity — enough gold to build a fortune. And James had passed the chain, along with the key to the box of coins, to his son. No longer servants, the Lockes would become masters. They would not plow the dirt or wash other men's floors. They would not tally another's gold. No — they would count their own money now.

James had entrusted all this grand hope upon his only male progeny. And Charles had failed. The chest of gold had gone to a pirate band. Sea rovers. Thieves who would squander it on drink and women and baubles.

"Keep it," he told the woman, pushing her hand away. "I do not want the chain or the key. I have no need of either."

" 'The Lord is my shepherd; I shall not want,' " the voice beside him said. " 'He maketh me to —' "

"No!" Rearing up from his pallet, Charles leaned across and bellowed in her face. "No! No more Psalms, Mrs. Carlyle."

Stunned, she drew back as if he had hit her. "Mr. Locke!"

"God took it from me! Took it all. I shall not praise Him!" As he shouted, two men came and pressed him back onto the pallet.

"Leave off reciting Bible verses! No more!"

"Be still, Mr. Locke!" Dr. Winslow's face appeared before him. "You will wake the other patients." He turned to Mrs. Carlyle. "Dear lady, I beg you . . . leave us now. You can see the effects of the fever for yourself. I must remove the leg. The surgery cannot be delayed."

"Please, sir," she begged. "Another day."

"Another day and the infection may spread to his chest. If the heart is attacked, he cannot live."

"But without his leg, he may be too disheartened to go on. Sir, you see how heavy his spirit lies within him."

"He has lost all, madam. As you have told me, his young companion perished at sea, and his father's gold was stolen. What reason does he have to live?"

Her beautiful eyes appeared in Charles's vision now. Brown, dark with unshed tears, they searched his face as if seeking answers he could not give. She closed her eyes, and her lashes formed shadows across her cheeks.

"He has not lost everything," she said in her soft voice. "He wishes to live, Dr. Winslow. Of that I am convinced."

"Because he asks you to marry him? Madam, surely you see this is the rambling of a man consumed with ague."

"Of course I understand that!" The dark eyes flashed. "But it is evidence of human feeling. Though he may be fevered, he has an awareness of life. He mourns his lost friend, and he thinks of his future. He smiles when I sing to him, and he fights to recover his health. He battles the ague just as he battled the pirates. You must not remove his leg, sir. Not yet."

The doctor let out a hiss of frustration. "I shall not debate the matter with you after today. If his fever has not broken by morning, the leg must come off."

As Dr. Winslow vanished from Charles's vision, a tear slipped from the corner of Mrs. Carlyle's eye. She flicked it away like an annoying fly. "Mr. Locke, you are to recover your health at once. I implore you. I command you. If you do not, you will lose your leg and perhaps your life. Dr. Winslow has amputated one survivor's arm and a leg from two others already, and every man his knife touches is dead within the week. Now, if you are sensible in the least, you will obey me and rid yourself of this ridiculous fever. Do you understand, sir?"

He reached out and took her hand. "Will you marry me, Mrs. Carlyle?"

"Mr. Locke, if you can muster the will to

recover, I shall consider it."

Smiling, he relaxed onto his pillow. This was a happy thought indeed.

THREE

After spending much of the past two months in the galley tending injured passengers, Sarah thanked God when the last of them was able to go on deck into the fresh air and sunshine. She did not care for the ship's dark, smelly hold, and the constantly swaying lamps made her dizzy. Gimbaled, the lanterns safely pitched about with the movement of the waves and did not tip over. But Sarah knew that one careless passenger or a single drunken sailor could set the entire vessel aflame. This fear plagued her despite her best intentions.

Now at an outdoor tea table once again, she observed the white cliffs of Dover with gratitude. It could not be long before she must set sail again, and she intended to make the most of her short time on the blessed firmness of land. Six months, perhaps a year at the most, would allow time to put the affairs of her estate back in order.

With her parents deceased, Sarah felt responsible for her two younger sisters. Mary had wed John Heathhill, an upstanding gentleman who had inherited eight thousand pounds, and she enjoyed enough financial security to reside in comfortable circumstances. Prudence, who was as silly as she was beautiful, had yet to fix her mind upon any one of her many suitors. As Prudence was utterly dependent on the charity of her eldest sister, Sarah had allotted her a thousand pounds a year. Unless their situations had altered since their last letters, the two young ladies lacked nothing. All the same, Sarah had decided to settle the sum of ten thousand pounds on each of them.

Such a generous gift would elate Mary, who had a propensity for hosting balls, grand dinners, and other affairs that put her into the company of the smart and fashionable among London society — the *ton,* as they liked to call themselves. Prudence adored the countryside. Her endowment would allow her to marry well and afford the home of her dreams outside the city.

Thus only one person of any concern to Sarah remained. As the last living heir to the Delacroix family legacy, George's nephew, Henry Carlyle, had inherited the title, the London house, and the country manor. But the new baron was in no better monetary condition than had been his uncle before him. Because Sarah had brought her father's fortune into her marriage, it had reverted to her upon her husband's death. Though some funds had gone into refurbishing the two homes, the actual barony remained nearly penniless.

Lord Delacroix, whom Sarah had met on several occasions, had impressed her as among the most foolish and reckless cads of her acquaintance. Duty called her to consider settling some few thousand pounds upon this wastrel, but she had not made up her mind how much. It had been her father's money, after all. Now it was hers — and thus, without question, it belonged entirely to God.

Sarah poured herself a second cup of tea and was reaching for the sugar when a man's hand suddenly appeared around her shoulder and lifted the bowl. She glanced up with a start, but her surprise quickly vanished in the warm glow of recognition that flooded her chest.

"Mr. Locke," she said, taking the sugar from him. "You have come to tea. How delighted I am to see you. Please do sit down, sir."

"Thank you, Mrs. Carlyle." Leaning his cane against the table, he seated himself in the chair nearest hers. "You are lovely, as always."

She smiled, more pleased at the compliment than she wished to acknowledge. "And you have more color in your face today. I believe yesterday's promenade about the deck did you much good."

At this, his expression sobered. "A week of regular exercise has done little for my leg. I now walk with a limp. It is as simple as that."

"A week is nothing, sir. A month or two will tell you more." She poured him a cup of steaming tea, dropped two lumps of sugar into it, and then gave it a stir. The ship had run short of fresh milk since its last port of call on the coast of West Africa, and Sarah missed its mellowing effect in her tea.

"A week is enough to know," he replied with a sigh. "My left arm is useless, and the leg is permanently maimed. I doubt that I shall ever ride again. As for the pain, I fear it may abide the rest of my life."

"Nonsense. You are far too grim, Mr. Locke. If you could see what great progress you have made since your arrival on the *Queen Elinor,* you would be more cheerful. You may recall that you were so near death that we nearly stitched you into a shroud and tossed you overboard. And not long after that, Dr. Winslow was determined to amputate your leg. Had you not rallied, he would have succeeded despite my best efforts to protect you from his knife. No indeed, you are a miracle, sir. I fully expect that you will regain all your former strength and live a long life of service to the Lord who has preserved you."

One corner of his mouth lifted as he regarded her. "I have never known an unhappy word to proceed from your mouth, Mrs. Carlyle."

"You have not known me long enough, then. I assure you, I have spoken many unhappy words in my past, and no doubt many are yet to come. But I am of the firm belief that God is with us through every storm, and how dare we complain?"

"I dare very easily. Two months ago, I set sail from England with the aim of establishing a profitable tea trade upon which to build my fortune. Now I return to those same shores, penniless and crippled. If that is not reason for discontent, I must declare myself not only poor and weak but of unsound mind."

"Once upon a time, sir, I thought you might be quite out of your mind. You raved and muttered and groaned such nonsense as to keep the entire company awake at night. But see how well you are recovered. Just as you have regained your senses, so you will return to health."

He took a sip of tea and gazed out upon the shimmering white chalk cliffs. Sarah knew she was perhaps too hopeful, yet she could not bear to see this man in such a mournful state. During his convalescence belowdecks, she had often witnessed his glorious smile as she sang to him or discussed the affairs of the ship. Until he attempted to stand and walk, Mr. Locke had been a gentle, kindly sort of person. She had enjoyed his company immensely. Now this dark passion had erupted, and she tried to understand how it had been brooding all along in the depths of his soul without her knowledge.

"I believe," she ventured, "that your father will be delighted to see you. Perhaps he has heard of the attack on the *Tintagel* and presumes you dead. Think how happy he will be to learn you are alive!"

"My father is ruined and I with him. There can be no happiness in that." He set down his teacup and raked his fingers back through his thick dark hair. "Our hopes sailed away with those marauders. Their theft of my chest ends our dream of an enterprise built on this very product. Tea."

Sarah studied the brown-red beverage in her cup and tried to think how anyone could place all his hopes and dreams in such an unsubstantial thing. "Tea is tea," she said. "But God is the master of all the earth, and in Him should you place your future."

"As you do."

"Of course. I have seen enough of the world to know that nothing in it has value beyond what use God may make of it. Including myself. You must give yourself to Him heart and soul, Mr. Locke, and then you shall see what He does with you. Perhaps your injured leg and arm may matter little to you then, except that they bring Him glory."

"Bah!" He hurled the delicate china cup to the deck, where it smashed to bits. Growling in pain, he pushed himself up from the table, took up his cane, and made his way to the rail, dragging his left leg across the damp deck.

A ship's boy was at Sarah's side in an instant. "Madam, I shall report this incident immediately. The captain will have that man taken down to the galley. Or to the brig."

With a laugh, she held up a hand. "Good heavens, no, William, for Mr. Locke's ill humor does not frighten me in the least. When you have swept up the cup, do bring out another, please. It is teatime, after all, and England is in sight. What happier moment could there be?"

As the lad dashed away to fetch a broom, she shook her head. No matter how common and familiar she had tried to become aboard the *Queen Elinor,* the passengers still treated her as her rank demanded. It was so dispiriting. She longed to be simply Mrs. Carlyle, as the injured men called her. They knew her only as the woman who had looked after them, bathed their wounds, sung to them, and insisted they be given the best of the food aboard the ship. Mr. Locke, in fact, had come to speak so openly with Sarah that she considered him far more than a mere acquaintance. He was a dear friend. A companion. A man she had come to care for. Perhaps his anger was a necessary part of his healing. She felt glad he trusted her enough to voice it so openly.

Charles Locke stood at the rail now, the tails of his coat flipping in the brisk breeze and his brown leather boots planted solidly on the deck. Though he limped, the man stood tall and straight, as though nothing could cripple the sense of pride within him. His shattered elbow gave him much agony, yet he squared his broad shoulders in an expression of defiance. Everything about him bespoke strength and vitality. Determination. Confidence. Courage.

Saddened that his physical limitations had so disheartened him, Sarah rose from the table and made her way to his side. From their conversations, she knew he had been educated at Cambridge. His father had been employed as the steward of a duke's estate in Devon, and neither man was without resource. Though their gold had been stolen, they had their life, their health, and their sharp minds. No doubt they soon would rebuild their fortune and make themselves comfortable enough.

"I do believe this is the loveliest sight imaginable," Sarah said, leaning her elbows on the rail and knitting her fingers together. "Is not England the dearest isle in all the world? See how the seabirds kiss the water and the sun paints patterns on her cliffs. When I think of all that is contained in this one small place, I am astonished. The cities of London, Leeds, and York. The bustling harbors at Portsmouth, Dover, Liverpool, and Hull. The Pavilion at Brighton, the castles of Northumberland, the churches at Canterbury and Staffordshire. The streams, the moors, the rolling hills, the lake country.

Oh, is it not an embarrassment of riches, Mr. Locke!"

A wry chuckle rumbled from his chest. "More so than Burma, China, and India, Mrs. Carlyle?" he asked. "I recall many a conversation in which you sang the praises of the Orient."

"Aye, yet none can compare to our beloved England. I am so eager to set foot in my own house again that I can hardly keep my toes still."

She could feel his eyes as he studied her face. Sarah knew she had never been considered a great beauty, and she had no doubt that Mr. Locke found her appearance wanting. On this long journey, she had abandoned the trouble of pinning up her hair in plaits and ringlets. Nor did she wear her finest gowns and jewels. Instead, she chose simple cotton dresses and wound her hair into a bun at the nape of her neck. Only the curls at her temple testified to any knowledge of feminine fashion.

She did not mind that a man might find her plain. Sarah had decided as much long ago. She wanted to be plain, that nothing might stand in the way of the truth she prayed would shine through her life.

"And who will greet you upon your arrival in London, Mrs. Carlyle?" he asked.

"Your sisters, Mary and Prudence?"

"I hope so. Pru now stays in my house, and Mary's home is nearby. I shall send for her to call upon me at once. I am eager to hear what has transpired in their lives since my departure."

"You will have much with which to acquaint them, as well. You told me you had compiled quite a list of places that were to receive the benefaction of your father's legacy. A printing press in India. A hospital for blind girls in China. A mission in Burma. I believe the world is soon to be much better for your presence, dear lady."

"Neither my presence nor my father's money can change the world. Only the saving power of Jesus creates true and lasting change. You do believe this yourself, do you not, Mr. Locke?"

"Certainly. I am a Christian, and my father and I attend church together every Sunday. Yet I cannot say the effect of my faith upon my behavior has been the same as yours. You are . . . a bit obsessed."

"Am I?" Now it was Sarah's turn to laugh. "Obsessed? Such a word! I prefer to call myself convinced. My conversion — and with it the experiences of my childhood, youth, and marriage — has taught me that nothing retains any value outside of faith and obedience. Certainly not a firm stride, or a steady hand . . . or even a chest of gold."

At this last comment, Sarah feared she had gone too far. But the man at her side did not respond in anger. Instead, he fixed his gaze on the green shores in the distance. Overhead, the snapping of ropes and canvas mingled with the cries of seagulls and terns. The salty air of the ocean now became laden with the fertile smell of plowed fields and blooming meadows. Land beckoned.

By the next morning, Sarah would bid Mr. Locke farewell. Perhaps he might wish to call on her in London, though she expected they both would be far too busy for such social niceties. This sojourn aboard ship must end, and with it their easy companionship. Sarah knew of no other option, for her commitment to her cause was resolute. And yet, she would miss this man. Perhaps more than she had ever thought possible.

Nights when she had lain alone in her cabin and toyed with the gold chain and key she now wore about her own neck, she had permitted her thoughts to wander too freely. Often, they had marched directly to Mr. Charles Locke, and there they stayed until she forced them onto more sobering matters. On the day of his rescue, she had considered him nothing more than a poor, ill man who must be treated with as much tenderness as possible. But as time went by — as they talked and laughed and passed the idle hours together — she had come to think of him differently.

At the sight of her entering the galley each morning, his handsome smile lifted her heart and set it to dancing. His hand on her arm sent tingles to her elbow. Then to her shoulder. And up to her neck. She had thought how much she would like to know the touch of his fingertips on her skin. How very warm his arms would feel around her. How breathtaking would be the pressure of his lips against her mouth. . . .

And that is when she always remembered her husband. Cold hands. Brief kisses on her cheek. Separate beds. With that lonely chill came the equal bleakness of a life of parties, gossip, and endless empty flatteries heaped upon her until she nearly suffocated. She had no desire to repeat such misery. Ever.

"Mrs. Carlyle." The voice beside her was hushed, barely audible above the splash of waves against the hull. "Please may I call you Sarah?"

She swallowed as Mr. Locke took a step that brought his shoulder against her own. Such liberties could not be taken lightly.

Yet, when would they see each other again? Why not for this one brief time permit the walls of etiquette to topple? To act as they were. As friends.

"Yes, Charles," she whispered. "Today . . . now . . . you may call me Sarah."

"And may I take your hand in mine?" Before she could answer, he slipped his fingers between her clasped hands and drew one of them into his own. "Beautiful Sarah, in these past two months, you have become to me the very dearest of women. You have cared for me. You have comforted me. You have encouraged me when I supposed nothing could ever give me hope."

"I am . . ." Her heart thudded so heavily that she was not sure she could think of a single appropriate thing to say. "I am . . . happy. Happy to have helped."

"I understand you have many plans, Sarah. You have sisters, friends, your dreams of traveling the world."

"As have you," she continued. "You and your father will rebuild your own dreams. I am sure of it."

His fingers tightened around hers. "You believe in me, though you know my every weakness."

"Sir, I hardly think you weak in any way. On the contrary, you are the strongest man

I have ever met. You fought nearly to your death aboard the *Tintagel.* And then you battled infection and the threat of permanent injury. Now you will go forward with your honor and your intellect intact, and you will boldly create a happy life for yourself. How much stronger could one be?"

"Is it possible, dear Sarah, that you do not find me terribly tedious?"

"Tedious? Upon my word, to me you are a marvel. I have never known anyone so handsome or so —" She clamped her mouth shut. One more heedless moment and she would confess things she had not acknowledged even to herself. Swallowing down her mortification, she spoke a single word. "Kind."

His laugh sent spirals of joy through her heart. "Handsome and kind am I? Well, Sarah Carlyle, I believe I can better that, for I find you beautiful and kind and charming, delightful, witty —"

"Enough!" Sarah reached out and cupped her free hand over his mouth.

He caught it at once and kissed her palm. His eyes closed, he pressed his lips to her fingers, then to the back of her hand, and finally to her wrist.

"I cannot bear the thought of parting from

you, my darling Sarah," he murmured, his cheek so close to her own that she could smell the shaving soap he had used that morning. "The idea that I might fail to wake to the soft glow of your brown eyes or fall asleep to the scent of lavender on your skin is unbearable. I love you, Sarah. I cannot imagine living my life without you. Please, I beg you, Mrs. Carlyle, will you marry me?"

So stunned as to be rendered utterly speechless, Sarah stared at Charles. Marry him? Could he mean this seriously? So many times he had asked — pleaded with her in his delirium. She had denied him again and again, of course. But now, surely now, he was fully sensible. He knew what he said. He meant every word. This amazing, wonderful man wanted her to become his wife!

Yet how could such a thing ever be? He intended to build a trade. She would do nothing less than return to the Orient to disperse her fortune. Though he knew she had inherited some income from her father, he could not have any idea the vast scope of it. He did not know her as a baroness, as Lady Delacroix. He could not envision the incredible wealth, power, and prestige that would come to him as her husband.

In this way, he made the perfect mate. For

once, she had met a man who loved her for who she was.

But how could she reveal the truth? His love would turn to greed. He would forbid her to give away the money and live as Christ demanded. His patience and kindness would end, and his visions of riches would take their place.

"You must allow me time, sir," she said softly. "I had not expected . . . I never thought you might love me."

"You do not reject me at once? Then I have hope." He took both her hands into his own, enfolding and clasping them warmly. "My dearest lady, do you love me? Tell me the truth, and I shall be content."

Sarah looked into his blue eyes, amazed at the radiant love she saw shining there. "I care for you, Charles," she told him. "I confess, I think of you in a way far different than I have ever thought of any man. You are all that I could ever want in a husband. But . . . love . . . ? I cannot say I know the true meaning of earthly love."

"Then let me teach you, for one glimpse of your face inspires such passion inside me that . . ." He shook his head. When he spoke again, his words were heated. "What hindrance can there be to our union, Sarah? If you believe in me, as you say you do, then you must trust me to care for you and our children. Give your father's money to charity, and see how I shall fight my way back to health and financial success. I can do this, Sarah. With you by my side, I can do it. For us."

Pursing her lips, she turned her head lest he see the tears welling in her eyes. "It is not so simple. There are . . . complications."

"Your sisters will become my own, dear lady. I cannot doubt that I shall adore them as you do. Perhaps my father's home may not be as large as that of your late husband, but in time, I can purchase a good house for us. You will have a lady's maid, footmen, servants. You will wear fine gowns and mingle comfortably in society."

"Heaven forbid," Sarah muttered. "You mistake me, Charles. Such accoutrements of wealth are hardly my aim."

"But you have said you believe I can create happiness for myself. I beg you to become a part of my life, and I shall make you happy as well."

"Charles, please . . ." Sarah drew her hands from his. "I must have time to consider your offer. I am not the young girl I once was, and I do not proceed in any matter of great import without carefully weighing the implications."

"Not a young girl? You cannot be more than five and twenty."

"I am exactly that — and old enough to have experienced two lifetimes of woe. Believe me when I tell you that your offer of marriage holds many attractions for me. But I must pray, Charles. I must seek counsel from my Lord. I cannot and shall not give you my answer until I have done so."

Pulling away for fear that he might continue trying to convince her — and succeed — Sarah gathered her skirts and hurried to the steps that led belowdecks. As she fled to her quarters, she lifted her fingers to her lips, pressing them there as he had done.

With one true kiss, she would be lost to Charles Locke. One reckless moment, and he might carry her away. A single touch, and she would abandon all her resolve. She must not permit him near again. Yet how she longed for his embrace.

FOUR

Though he had been pulled from the sea with nothing to call his own, Charles was given a frock coat, waistcoat, trousers, shirt, and cravat from the captain's personal wardrobe. Only his boots remained from the fine set of garments with which he had departed London months before. On this day, as the *Queen Elinor* sailed up the Thames, Charles polished the brown leather to a high shine.

Would she have him? Dare Sarah Carlyle take the risk of being wed to a man she had known such a short time? A crippled pauper who by his own admission had nothing to offer her save a raft of promises and dreams? She must set aside all reason to take him on, Charles knew. Yet how could he make his way forward without her?

He would return to his father empty-handed, their plans erased by a band of sea rovers. But if he could bring back Sarah to become his wife, the journey would have been worth the loss. She was a treasure beyond compare. Her lovely form and bright brown eyes would inspire any man. Her faith in him, her stalwart certainty that he could achieve his goals, meant all the world to Charles.

Standing from the bench where he had shined his boots, he checked that his coat lapels lay flat upon his chest and his shirt collar stood firmly upright against his neck. Sarah had to love him. She must. He would do everything in his power to win her heart. No sacrifice could be too great, for he had seen inside the woman something that would complete him. She held the key to his success and happiness, and without her beside him, he could not imagine going on.

Breathing a prayer to the Almighty for strength and courage, Charles gritted his teeth and took a step toward the rail. Sarah stood with the other passengers as the ship sailed along the banks of the Thames, where wharves and warehouses teemed with laborers ready to greet each new vessel. His heart thudding, Charles took up his cane and forced his weakened leg forward. He *would* lift it from the deck. He *would* stride like a man again. And he *would* have Sarah Carlyle.

As he moved into position beside her, she spotted him and caught her breath. Her face broke into a brilliant smile. Cheeks pink and eyes shining, she greeted him warmly. "Good afternoon, Mr. Locke. I feared I should not see you at all today."

He tipped his hat. "I was much occupied this morning, madam. If I may have a word with you in private, I shall present a summary of my thoughts."

Glancing over his shoulder, she nodded. "The tea tables are empty, I see. Everyone waits at the rail, for we are expected to weigh anchor in less than half an hour."

"Time enough." He took her elbow and led her to a chair beneath the awning that had been erected to protect passengers from the equatorial sun. As he seated himself, Charles took a folded sheet of paper from the breast pocket inside his coat. "Before I present to you any repetition of that offer which yesterday caused you such bewilderment, Sarah, permit me to explain myself further."

Lowering her eyes, she folded her gloved hands together on the table. "Charles, you must allow me to speak."

"Hear me first, Sarah; I beg you." The expression in her eyes told him what he had no desire to hear. He must convince her now. He must. "It is true that the chest of money upon which my father and I intended to build our fortune is lost. But as you said yourself, I am not without resources. On this page, I have listed my assets and my options. You know that I was educated at Cambridge, and it is likely that I shall find beneficial employment with any number of respectable establishments. Or I may choose to study further — in the law or in finance. My uncle works at the Bank of England, and I am certain he can assist me in joining him there. No matter what position I take, I am certain to rise in the ranks, and my salary will grow. But see now how I have outlined several other viable options for my future."

Charles ran his finger down the paper on which he had detailed every possibility. "For example," he went on, "it is likely that my father may know of investors who might be willing to embark on another tea venture — even without the basis of capital that was stolen from us. We are not wholly unconnected, for the family my father served as steward has many reputable friends and acquaintances. These gentlemen have access to financial resources at minimal risk to themselves. They are, in fact, eager to hear of various ventures that might seem foolhardy to some. On such as these are great fortunes built."

"Charles, please," Sarah implored, her eyes meeting his. "Whether you work in a bank or direct a tea enterprise matters not to me."

"Yet you have not seen the whole of my plan." He turned the paper toward her. "My father's house on Threadneedle Street sits alongside a piece of valuable land that is currently available for purchase. Once I am established in trade, I intend to buy it. There I shall build a warehouse. I also expect to extend the dimensions of the house itself, for I know that a man of property requires abundant space for his family's comfort. Entertaining associates in one's home is necessary to a successful merchant or banker, and several drawing rooms will —"

"Charles, stop at once," Sarah cried, clapping her hands over her ears. "I do not care for banks or warehouses or drawing rooms. Business ventures and grand houses have no meaning to me whatsoever."

"Then what is it that you desire? Tell me, Sarah. I am determined to have you and to make you happy."

Her eyes brimmed with tears as she gazed at him. "Oh, Charles . . . if only you knew how very happy you make me already. Your love for me is a blessing I never expected in all my life. But I cannot accept it."

A hardness came over him, filling his chest with steely resolve. "What objection can you have? What barrier can stand between us? Tell me, and I shall overcome it, Sarah. I am not deterred by anything you will say, for my love is too strong to be denied."

As the tears welled in her eyes, she slipped her hand into her bag and withdrew a white handkerchief. Pressing it to her cheeks, she attempted without success to stem the flow. "I have made a promise," she mumbled into the wad of fabric. "I am . . . committed to a vow."

"You are attached to another man?" He slumped back in his chair momentarily. The very idea was unthinkable. He leaned forward again and took her hand. "Already engaged? Break it off! I shall see that it is done without embarrassment to either party, Sarah. Surely you do not doubt I can accomplish such a thing. Who is he? Tell me his name at once, and I shall make arrangements directly we go ashore."

"It is not a man," she sniffled. "Not an attachment. I have made a vow. I am determined . . . absolutely committed in my heart . . ."

"Sarah." Unable to bear the sight of the

woman so distraught, Charles folded her hand in both of his. "Sarah, please —"

"Do not touch me!" she exclaimed, pushing him away. "I cannot marry you, Charles, and you must accept it. I am not able to spend my life as your wife, for I have another occupation to attend. Not only that, but I abhor everything that you most desire."

"What can you mean?"

"This!" She snatched up the sheet of paper on which he had penned his plans. "Trade and enterprise and schemes to make money are nothing to me. In fact, I deplore any goal of financial gain. My sole object in life is to rid myself of such earthly encumbrances and devote my whole being to the pursuit of heaven. It is God I wish to please, not man. I do not want a house or servants or fine gowns. I cannot abide a husband who desires to spend his days laboring to increase his wealth."

She handed him the page. "Forsake your assets and your material pursuits, Charles. Abandon your dreams. Join me in my mission to reduce myself to nothing more than a vessel that God can use for His glory. Then — and only then — can I become your wife." Shaking her head, Sarah buried her face in her handkerchief.

Charles stared in such shock and dismay as to be nearly overwhelmed. Forsake what few assets he had left? Abandon his dreams? What could she possibly mean?

"Sarah, speak plainly," he insisted. "If you wish to give away your father's legacy, I support your endeavor. You must follow your heart in this matter, and I would by no means suspend your efforts to be obedient. If God leads you to support various ministries and missions, then you must do so. Act with my blessing and encouragement. And be assured that without hesitation, I shall do all in my power to restore to you a lifestyle befitting your place in society."

"That is precisely what I do *not* want!" she cried. "You cannot possibly understand the suffering I have known, Charles. My greatest joy has been this journey, for at the Christian missions in Asia I found people who truly live the teachings of God. I wish to be poor. I wish to have nothing. If I wear rags and sleep in a hovel, I shall be content. Any man who would have me as his wife must feel the same."

"This is absurd. Surely you cannot mean to divest yourself of every last farthing and live as a beggar."

"Indeed I do."

"But why? Did not God place ambition in

the heart of every man? Surely it cannot be wrong to work hard and improve oneself to the end of providing for a wife and children."

"Is that ever enough? No, Charles, for you have said as much yourself. When you find work, then you intend to purchase land, and then build a warehouse, and then add rooms to your house, and then hire servants."

"Aye, and buy a ship and establish a trade and live as well as I possibly can. Is that a sin?"

"Yes, it is. It is greed. And greed leads to corruption. And corruption ends in utter depravity and evil. Again and again, Christ spoke against such wickedness."

She drew down a ragged breath and pushed herself up from the table. "If you wish to marry me, Charles Locke, you must divest yourself of every ambition and surrender every dream. You must leave your father, your house, your possessions, all that you have and desire the most. You must accompany me on my missions of ministry, and you must be willing to abandon all earthly glory in exchange for the joy that only heaven can bring. Will you do this, Charles? Can you?"

Rising to face her, he rested one hand on

the table for support. "Sarah, be reasonable, I beg you. Do you love me? If you do, then marry me. At this moment, that is all that matters."

"You will not give it up, will you?"

"My ambition? No, and why should I? I was not born with a brain and two strong hands only to live as a beggar on some street in China."

"We are told to take up our cross and follow Christ. We are instructed to sell all we have and give everything to the poor. That is the teaching of our Lord and Savior."

"Perhaps I do not know Him as well as you, Sarah, but I cannot believe —"

"You cannot believe, and you do not believe," she said hotly, tears streaming down her face again. "And that is why I can never marry you, Charles. My mind is settled. Please do not speak of it again."

So saying, she spun away from him and ran across the deck to the stairs that led below. He frowned at the empty chair. Beauty, intelligence, wit, joy — everything he could desire in a wife. And more. She had believed in him. She had told him he could succeed. He would recover. He would follow his dreams. But *she* was his dream!

Where had such a reversal originated? Once she had told him that she believed he could be healed and do anything he desired. But she now insisted that he surrender every goal in life. Who had planted such ideas in her brain? such ravings? such mournful recitations of misery and the need for abandonment of all human pleasure?

His hopes dashed, Charles limped across the deck and leaned on the rail. He was a man without health. Without wealth. And without love.

Yet he would not succumb to doubt and fear. He would survive. He must.

"Sarah, I am sorry to be the bearer of bad tidings," Mary said, "but you are an absolute idiot."

"Sister!" With a cry of exasperation, Sarah rolled her eyes. "How dare you say such a thing?"

"I agree with Mary," Prudence announced in a calm voice. "Dear Sarah, your whole life stretches before you, and what do you mean to do with it? Give everything you own to the poor. Forsake the one man who truly loves you. And go to India to live as a beggar. There can be no other way to look at the situation: you are quite out of your wits."

"I am perfectly sane, and I should very much appreciate the support of the family I hold dear." Sarah crossed her arms and leaned back in the silk-upholstered chair.

Two evenings after Sarah's arrival in London, the three sisters were gathered for dinner at Trenton House, the family residence. Situated on the exclusive Cranleigh Crescent in Belgravia, the residence had been their late father's pride and joy. At the start of each social season, London's *ton* raced from their country manors back to the large, ornately furnished town houses that lined Belgrave Square and its adjoining streets. Sarah's father had coveted a home in Belgravia, but Mr. Watson's heritage as a tradesman had relegated him to nothing better than the ancestral family house on Gracechurch Street in Cheapside.

Only after Lord Delacroix became his son-in-law had Mr. Watson been welcomed into the *ton,* whereupon he promptly purchased Trenton House, just across the crescent-shaped park from Delacroix House. He filled it with the finest of furniture, carpets, draperies, and art. He hired a phalanx of servants to heed his every whim. And then — at the very peak of the power, wealth, and influence he had so craved — he died.

Newly married to Lord Delacroix at the time, Sarah had taken on the responsibility of maintaining her father's household, along with the baron's London home and his country estate at Bamberfield. After her husband's death, she had considered selling Trenton House, but her youngest sister still needed a place to live. During the two years of Sarah's absence abroad, Prudence had presided over Trenton House. Now she was eager to surrender her duties, for they had proved more onerous than she expected.

On Sarah's return to London, Prudence had begged her elder sister to live with her at the imposing edifice on Cranleigh Crescent. Henry Carlyle, the new baron, was living at Delacroix House, after all, and he was not likely to welcome the dowager Lady Delacroix into a home he had come to call his own. Delighted to be with her sister, Sarah had sent her trunks to Trenton House, where she and Prudence eagerly greeted Mary for dinner.

"First of all," Sarah informed her dear sisters who had just pronounced her quite out of her mind, "I do not intend to give everything to the poor. In fact, I mean to settle a sum upon each of you."

"Ooo, how much?" Prudence cried, leaning forward. Her green eyes lit with a bright fire. "The thousand a year you gave me is certainly sufficient, but you received the whole of the legacy, Sarah — which I must tell you I never did think was fair."

"Sarah is eldest, and it is hers by rights," Mary stated. "Besides, she endured much more suffering than we did — and she deserves the money. Father could hardly have settled any great sum on you, Pru, for you are too foolish to manage it properly. I rely on my dear Mr. Heathhill to look after me — though I certainly could not object to any addition to my husband's accounts." She, too, leaned toward her sister. "How much, Sarah?"

Sighing, Sarah gazed at her sisters with a mixture of love and exasperation. Mary, younger than she by little more than a year, was a small, pretty creature with pert features and a heap of brown hair studded with every manner of jewel and ribbon to be found in the marketplace. She adored expensive gowns and enjoyed attending the events her society offered. Mary had informed Sarah that in the past two years, she and Mr. Heathhill had attended court at St. James's no less than five times — an astonishing honor.

In contrast to her sister's petite frame, Prudence enjoyed the benefits of ample feminine curves and features equally sumptuous. Her olive green eyes seemed to fill her whole face, and her lips wore a natural pout that had enchanted men from the moment she was allowed out into society. At every ball, her dance card filled before the musicians struck the first note. At picnics, she could hardly be seen for the sea of eager gentlemen swarming her like bees around a glorious flower. Even at church, Pru attracted so much male attention that she was obliged to linger a full half hour after her sisters had gone away to luncheon. Flattered and admired by one and all, the young lady could hardly think beyond the next beau who sought her favor. And she hardly tried.

"I believe ten thousand pounds should do you each very well," Sarah stated. "I shall have my steward draw up the papers to that effect directly."

"Ten thousand! Oh, thank you!" Mary exclaimed, leaping from her chair and throwing her arms around her sister. "I am delighted at this news, and I assure you I shall make good use of every tuppence!"

"Aye, buying bonnets and slippers." Prudence giggled. She joined Mary, kissing Sarah lightly on the cheek. "You are a dear sister, and I thank you for remembering us. This evening when you began to talk about your journey, I confess, I feared you must be so much altered that you had forgotten

Mary and me altogether."

"I am altered," Sarah said, as the two women returned to their seats. "But I am not changed in the way you might assume. I have learned so very much about the world. About life. About myself. We are blessed indeed, sisters. Do you know that parents in China pierce out the eyes of their young daughters in order to make them more successful beggars? In the town of Ningpo, an Englishwoman named Mary Ann Aldersey runs a school for these poor blind girls."

"Good heavens, Sarah." Mary picked up her fork and knife. "Must you speak of such things as we are trying to eat our dinner?"

Sarah studied her sister in dismay. "If you cannot bear to hear this, Mary, how will you fare when I tell you of the widows who burn to death on their husbands' funeral pyres in India? Or the children who grovel —"

"Please, Sarah! I beg you. I can hardly swallow."

"Do I err in giving you and Prudence such an allowance?" Sarah retorted. "While I speak of the world and its many needs, the two of you think only of yourselves. Neither of you can bear to hear of the suffering of others."

"We can hear of it," Prudence protested.

"But why bother? There are wars in France and America. Starving people in India. Poor blind girls in China. Certainly all of that exists, yet there is nothing we can do about it now. Not at dinner. Not ever. We are only young ladies, after all. Even if we gave away our ten thousand pounds and more — as you mean to do — one woman cannot make any real difference to the world, can she, Sarah? Not even you."

Staring down at her plate laden with rich beef tenderloin, fresh vegetables stewed in butter, and a thick slice of white bread, Sarah reflected on her sister's words. If she gave away every last penny of her father's legacy, would the world be changed in any material way? Probably not.

Despite all her silly and frivolous ways, Prudence had spoken the truth. Yet the rich young ruler of Scripture had not been instructed to surrender his wealth in order to save the poor. No, it was to save himself that he must do it.

"You are right to settle ten thousand on Mary and me," Prudence spoke up as she blotted her lips on a napkin. "I mean to purchase a country house with my money. I want to have horses."

"In Burma," Sarah informed her, "some

people are so hungry they would eat your horses."

"Well, that is quite enough!" Mary tossed down her napkin. "By chance you were born first of the three of us, Sarah, and we all know that Father chose to use you very ill. Neither Pru nor I can deny your suffering, and certainly you have earned the right to do as you like with his money. But I should appreciate it if you would keep your miserable tales to yourself. Moreover, if you have half a heart, you would remember that Father worked very hard to build his fortune, and if he knew you were giving it all away, he would be most unhappy. By all that is sensible, he ought to have settled it upon the one of us who could be bothered to find herself a decent husband."

At this, Prudence audibly caught her breath. "Mary," she said in a hushed voice. "Sarah had nothing to do with marrying Lord Delacroix. You know that."

Mary's eyes narrowed. "You could have refused him, Sarah. Everyone knew what sort of man he was."

"I did not know," Sarah said in a low voice. "Father did not know. The baron said he wanted an heir. He assured Father he would see to it that the title passed to a son. How could anyone doubt him?"

"I doubted him and so did my friends. Delacroix had no interest in women. He spent his days at the gaming tables and his nights at taverns in the worst parts of London. The baron was a sot. I never saw him sober. Not once. He was drunk the day you married him and drunk the day he ran his carriage off the road and into the river. Honestly, Sarah, you are so blind."

"And now the barony has gone to his nephew," Prudence put in, her eyes wide. "He is fearfully handsome, Henry Carlyle, the new Lord Delacroix. Have you seen him lately, Mary? His hair is as gold as anything and all in curls. He might be thought feminine but for his chin. Oh, the cleft! Right in the center, exactly as it should be, and such a jaw. He is certainly man enough for my taste, and I have been honored to sit beside him several times at dinners. Although he was known as a roué in years past, he is now thought to be one of the most elegant gentlemen in his society, and this naturally makes him desirable to the ladies — as does his eligible status. But, dear me, he is no wealthier than his uncle before him. He has only Delacroix House and the country manor at Bamberfield to his name. Sarah, will you not settle something on him, poor man, for he ought to get himself a good wife."

Still unnerved at the memory of the baron to whom she had been married, Sarah could hardly concentrate on Prudence's chatter. Her sisters had not changed in the least since she left them two years before. Mary was selfish and absorbed in her own affairs. Pru cared for little but the attentions of men and her own fascination with riding, boating, picnicking, and everything else that could be done out of doors. Neither would hear of the world beyond the small realm in which they reigned supreme.

"I should think two thousand a year would do Lord Delacroix rather nicely," Prudence was saying. "He cannot object to that."

"Two thousand pounds *a year?*" Mary scowled. "That is absurd. He would live like a king, and he deserves no such luxury. His father, his uncle, and all those Delacroixes before them were wastrels, as you said yourself. Better to give the baron a lump sum and be done with it, Sarah. What do you think? Would he be happy with five thousand?"

"I think —" Sarah blinked, trying to force herself back to reality — "I think that the subject of money brings out the worst in everyone I know."

"Well." Mary sat back in her chair and

glared at her sister. "If Pru and I refuse to discuss your beggars and you will not talk about money, then what subject is left to us?"

"I should like to know more about the man on the ship," Pru spoke up. "Sarah, did you really reject a suitor because he would not abandon everything for you?"

"Not for me. For God."

"But it was *you* who made the demand of him, was it not?"

Sarah had to nod. "I thought it important."

"Was he handsome, sister?"

The blue eyes that had so entranced Sarah now swam before her. "Yes, he was," she said softly. "Most handsome indeed."

"And he fought pirates? That is utterly dashing of him! I should never be able to reject a handsome man who could fight pirates and who loved me with such a passion as to beg for my hand in marriage. And wounded, too. Oh, Sarah, that is so romantic!"

"His wounds were not romantic in the least. A ball broke his leg and tore the muscle —"

"That does it for me," Mary exclaimed, pushing back from the table. "I shall never be able to finish my dinner now. Would that

91

you had married your crippled pauper and gone back to India with him."

The silence in the dining room was broken only by the arrival of the pudding. As the servants circled the table taking away plates and silver, setting out bowls, and serving the steaming custard, Sarah reflected on all that had gone before her. Her childhood, her marriage, her widowhood, her journey to Asia. Charles Locke. And now London and her sisters again. If she could, might she alter anything in her past?

Truly, Sarah had not heard of her husband's reputation for drink and gaming. Although she barely knew the baron, she had been ordered to wed him. Conditioned to obedience and believing the marriage would bring contentment to her father and sisters, she had entered into the union in the hope that bearing children would fulfill her. But despite his promises to Sarah's father, Lord Delacroix had made no effort to consummate their union. Sarah was as much a maiden as she had been on her wedding night.

The marriage had been a mistake. Had she made as great an error in not accepting Charles's proposal?

"Where does he live?" Prudence asked as the servants left the room. Her voice was softer now, kinder. "Perhaps Mr. Locke will call on you, Sarah. You might at least continue your friendship."

"He cannot live anywhere near Belgravia," Mary said. "If Mr. Locke's father was a steward and they have lost all their savings, they can have little to call their own."

"They live on Threadneedle Street." Sarah eyed Mary. "Very near to our old house in Cheapside. We are no better than the Locke family for our fine address. Our father was a merchant, and nothing can undo that. Or should. Rank matters very little in the grand scheme. Nor do riches."

"You will soon see to that, will you not? Sarah, how can you think of giving away all that Father worked so hard to earn?" Mary asked.

"And how could you turn down a man who loved you so deeply?" Prudence heaved a sigh. "Do you know . . . this sounds very like a dilemma that might be set out in a letter to Miss Pickworth in *The Tattler.* A poor but handsome suitor in love with a wealthy widow who wishes to give away her fortune. You ought to write to Miss Pickworth, Sarah, for she gives good counsel."

"Miss Pickworth does not exist, Pru," Mary admonished. "That is a fictitious name for a frivolous advice columnist, and I cannot think why all of London is so enraptured by it."

"She is a real woman, no matter what her true name," Prudence argued, "and she is very wise. Miss Pickworth knows everything that is happening in the *ton,* for it appears she attends every ball and reception, though no one has any idea who she is! And people write letters to her, listing all the details of their terrible circumstances and begging her for help. And she pens the most humorous and yet brilliant answers ever heard! She would tell you exactly what to do about your dear Mr. Locke, Sarah, for she knows everything about love. Miss Pickworth would understand the importance of true devotion. I have thought of writing to her myself. I am not loved for anything that matters."

"Never discount beauty," Mary said. "Now you are beautiful and wealthy as well, Pru. What more could you want?"

"I could wish for a man to love me for who I am and not for what I look like or how much income I can bring to the marriage. That would be true love indeed."

A lump rose in Sarah's throat as she remembered Charles Locke's shoulder pressed against hers, his ardent avowal of love, his presentation of a plan to offer her security and contentment the rest of her life.

But what of her commitment to God? What of her certainty that only poverty could lead to true joy?

"I do not believe love can bring happiness, Prudence," Sarah said. "Not even true love."

"Really? But there is nothing I should like better than to meet a man who would love me truly and eternally."

"For myself," Mary put in, "I believe wealth is the real measure of one's potential for happiness. Love hardly matters in the end, Pru, I assure you. Passion is fleeting, as you must sadly learn when you find a husband. No, sister, I should much rather have money. If one is rich enough, nothing can stand in the way of making life the best it can possibly be. And therein lies the true source of pleasure."

Sarah lifted her dessert spoon and slipped it into her custard. "You are for wealth, then, Mary. And Pru is for love. But I have decided that only God can bring real purpose and joy to life."

"Aye, by giving me a handsome husband!" Prudence quipped. "What can be wrong with that?"

"Nothing," Sarah replied, "and perhaps

He will. But I can see the possibility of peace and joy only if I divest myself of all earthly bonds. That is why I shall give the greater part of Father's legacy to the needy. And that is why I turned down Mr. Locke's proposal."

Prudence tossed her head. "And that is why — as I am certain Miss Pickworth would warn — you are doomed to roam the world on a creaky old ship, dodging pirates and sleeping with beggars until you are old and alone and eaten up with some awful disease. Then my darling husband and I shall whisk you back to England, where Mary will have to spend her money on a good doctor to make you well again. Never mind that if you would come to your senses in the first place, we could be spared such rigors altogether. There!"

As Prudence waved her spoon in the air in a final flourish to her recitation, both Sarah and Mary burst out laughing. With a giggle, Pru returned to her dessert. Upon her last visit to St. James's, she declared, she had met the most fascinating gentleman of her acquaintance, and she insisted on telling her sisters all about him at once.

FIVE

"You must go and make of it what you can." James Locke handed his son the card that had arrived in the morning post. "It is very likely you may encounter a gentleman who would be interested in investing in our tea company."

Charles scanned the invitation to the formal reception and then set it aside. Since returning to London a fortnight before, he had done little but listen to his father's schemes and plans. James had been devastated at the news of the pirate attack and the loss of his gold. Though relieved to find his son alive and in reasonable health, he could not seem to accept the truth: Locke & Son, Ltd., no longer existed.

The few men who had invested in the enterprise immediately demanded the return of their money. Plans to lease a warehouse until one could be built had to be scrapped. All hope of freedom from the mundane and servile existence that had been the Locke family's lot for generations was gone.

Charles sighed. "Father, may I state with all due respect that you are too much fixed upon the past. We no longer have your gold. We are not proprietors of a tea company. That dream is at an end."

"Nonsense!" James smoothed down the fringe of graying hair that remained at the back of his head. "We must think. Think carefully."

"Sir, we have repeatedly considered all our options. Without financing, the situation is hopeless."

"But that is the key!" The older man swung around, his blue eyes aglow. "We must secure investors once again. I have earned a respectable reputation in the city, and you are young and healthy —"

His jaw clamped shut as his gaze fell upon Charles, whose injured leg extended on a footrest at the end of the chintz-upholstered chair he occupied. As on board ship, Charles had continued to endeavor to exercise the injured limb in an effort to return it to its former usefulness. His efforts were of little avail, for the limp remained. His arm was hardly better. The shattered elbow continued to cause Charles much pain, and the wound where a ball had passed through the muscle atop his shoulder refused to heal.

Such physical maladies might be enough to discourage any man, yet Charles knew his ill humor rose from another source. He could not stop thinking about Sarah Carlyle. After refusing his proposal of marriage, she had vanished belowdecks, and their paths had not crossed again.

Charles felt not the faintest hope of winning her hand — she had made it plain she did not even wish to see him again. Where she lived, he could not know, for there must be at least a hundred Mrs. Carlyles in the city of London. He could not call on her, thank her for helping so much in his recovery, wish her well — anything. Their brief friendship was at an end. He must accept this, yet he did no better than his father at acknowledging the truth.

How was it possible that Sarah had rejected him in such a way? Even now he could hardly believe she had been serious in demanding that he surrender his plan to establish a trade and provide for a family. And in exchange that he accept a life of poverty! Who on this earth would welcome penury and the suffering that must accompany it — hunger, disease, isolation, homelessness? What rational woman would not long for a secure future with a warm home, children, and a husband she loved?

But Sarah did not love Charles, and this was the cruelest memory of all. She had tended him, cared for him, done all in her power to restore him to health. They had talked together, laughed, shared their hopes and dreams. And yet she could not love him. Why? Did she mourn her dead husband? Was she repulsed by the injuries that had crippled him? He could not make it out. And even if he did understand every aspect of the matter, nothing could change the inevitable fact: she would not marry him.

Charles pushed himself from the chair, took up his cane, and walked across the room to the fireplace where his father stood. Laying a hand on the other man's shoulder, he spoke in a low voice. "Father, you must accept the situation. I am not the man I was. The gold is gone. The enterprise is ended." He waited a moment in silence, watching emotions pass like shadows over his father's face. Anger. Sadness. Determination.

"I have been thinking a great deal of my mother," Charles added gently. "She was wise, you know. We both respected her immensely, and we took her advice to heart. Consider what she would say to all this,

Father. She was a true Christian in word and deed, very much like —" he shook his head — "like you and I ought to be. Mother would impart good counsel to us now, as she always did. She would say that honor ought to come before all else. She would urge me to seek honest employment —"

"Honest, yes. But would she have you work in a bank?"

"And why not? You were the duke of Marston's steward, and Mother admired you for it. I inherited your talent with finance, Father. You have said yourself that my ability to balance ledgers and keep accounts is equal to your own. Is there any dishonor in my seeking employment with a bank? Or as a steward —"

"Never! You will not toil for some cabbage-headed aristocrat, as I did. You are better educated and more capable than I was. I shall not sit by and watch my only child, my dear son, spend the best years of his life as I wasted mine. How many thousands of pounds did that reprobate spend on gowns and jewels and slippers for his ridiculous wife? I labored day and night to balance the duke's insatiable appetite for balls and dinners with the income he derived from those poor tenants who labored on land he never even bothered to visit! Did he care about his sheep? his mill? the small village that — ?"

"Father, I know how you suffered under that man's excesses." Charles had heard such diatribes against the duke of Marston all his life. His father's feelings were justified, of course, yet now was hardly the time to rant. "If you do not wish me to seek a position as a steward, I shall honor your request. But why not the bank? It is a respectable profession that will provide a satisfactory income. With the gold lost and only a small sum left in your account, you will need my financial support in the years to come, and I fully intend to give it. Think what Mother would say to this."

"Your mother perished for lack of good medical care! And why? Because I was nothing better than a steward to a pompous, self-possessed cretin! I had insufficient funds to see that my wife received the best treatment during her illness. Do you suppose I wish for you to bear such a shameful burden? Unthinkable! No, Charles, I shall not hear of you taking a position at a bank or as a steward. Not until we have exhausted every other avenue." He snatched up the invitation. "The duke of Marston's son does you a great honor in asking you to attend his reception, for this is the high event of the social season. With his elder brother missing and presumed dead in America, Sir Alexander is likely to inherit his father's title and estates. You ought to oblige him. No doubt he has heard of your misadventure at sea and longs to amuse himself and his friends with your tale of woe."

"Father, I cannot tolerate such censure of Sir Alexander. He and I played together as boys, and I am certain our friendship stands as it was."

"Then go to the soiree and make some good use of the man! He will have cronies who may be interested in our enterprise. They all have money enough to waste on balls and such frippery! Perhaps you can convince one of them to finance us."

"Father, I deplore dancing, and I am no more fond of mingling with the aristocracy than you are. Do see reason here. If you object to my taking some common employment, then I must join a regiment. As an officer, I shall earn the respect of my peers and the income to satisfy our requirements."

"The army? Would I have you marching off to war against the French or those rebellious Americans? Certainly not! As well you might pursue the pirates in an effort to reclaim our gold! You returned to me barely alive, crippled, and in pain. Should I now wave you off to some foreign battlefield and have you killed?"

"If you are so determined to make a fortune, then perhaps I ought to go after the pirates," Charles retorted. "I could sail to the Malabar Coast and raid every pirate stronghold in search of your chest of gold. Would you be happy then, Father? Is that the only thing that could satisfy you?"

"Charles!"

"Is this tea enterprise more important than health and security, Father? Is it so essential that we rise above our humble roots? Perhaps we are both wrong in our thinking. I have heard it said that God would wish us to rid ourselves of all earthly treasures and practice charity."

"Who told you such nonsense? Was it that woman on the ship? That . . . that silly creature —"

"Mrs. Carlyle, yes. And I cannot believe my mother would have disagreed. What is truly important in this life, Father? Should we become as rich as those repugnant aristocrats you so abhor? To what end? That we might host our own balls and purchase gowns and slippers enough to clothe a harem?"

"Upon my word, you are altered! Altered, indeed! Come here, my dear boy." James

Locke stretched out his arms and took his son into a rough embrace. "Oh, Charles, I do not mean to cause you such distress. You have suffered greatly, and I am sensible of your unhappy condition."

Drawing away, Charles hobbled to the window and lifted the curtain aside to look onto the bustling London street. "I love her," he murmured. "I love her dearly. With Sarah beside me, I might have accomplished all our aims. But she would not have me. If I am altered, Father, it is not enough. I am still the man I was, for I could not bow to her wishes. I could not become the man she wanted me to be. I refused her — and then she refused me. And now it is done."

"Then turn your sorrow into joy again." James joined his son at the window. "Go to the Marston event and speak to your friend. Tell Sir Alexander of your adventures and acquaint him with our loss. Perhaps he will recall his fondness for you and seek to assist you. Remind those gentlemen you meet of the end of the East India Company's monopoly. Assure them of the abundant dividends an independent tea enterprise must earn. If you can find one investor — even one — willing to capitalize us, we shall be on our feet again. Locke & Son, Ltd., will become a reality."

Letting out a deep breath, Charles faced his father. He took the invitation and scanned the information it contained. "I shall do as you ask," he said. "But I assure you it gives me no pleasure."

"How can you know such a thing? Perhaps you will meet an enchanting young lady!" James fairly skipped across the room to pen an acceptance to the reception. "There must be many such women eager to hear how you battled pirates. Such a tale! You must seek out the wealthiest of the lot and entertain her with your saga. You are too handsome not to win the heart of more than one woman."

But Charles wanted only one woman. Sarah Carlyle held his heart, and he could not imagine how to take it back again.

The duke of Marston's London house faced directly onto Cranleigh Crescent in Belgravia. As Charles descended from his carriage, he noted that every window was lit. Hundreds of candles must be burning within, for each room in the house would be occupied on such a grand occasion. This reception was of such renown that it must be attended by everyone who was anyone in the *ton,* and the gowns and jewels on display might put the regent himself to shame.

Arriving in droves, the young ladies and gentlemen greeted one another with laughter and happy cries — as if they had not seen each other at one ball or another nearly every evening of the year's social season.

Setting his cane firmly on the walk, Charles stepped toward the grand staircase that rose to the massive front door of the duke's house. Though he could never compete in lineage or wealth with the other guests, Charles knew he was as educated, respectable, and welcome as anyone. His acquaintance with Sir Alexander and his elder brother, Ruel Chouteau, the marquess of Blackthorne, had been of long duration. The three had attended school together as boys. They had been classmates at Cambridge. As adults, they had continued their association through letters and the occasional social call.

Charles had been dismayed to hear that while traveling in America, Lord Blackthorne reportedly had been killed by Indians. Scalped, it was said. He certainly hoped the rumor was false, for the marquess had been by far the more capable of the two brothers and certainly the best candidate to take on the responsibility of their father's duchy. Yet it was Sir Alexander who had befriended the family steward's son.

Sir Alexander had been little different from young Danny Martin, the ship's boy who had hop-skipped so happily across the deck of the *Tintagel* as he did his errands. Thin and sunburned, with skinned knees and a mop of golden hair, the young Alexander had spent many hours with Charles — fishing, riding, or pretending to be knights of King Arthur's famous Round Table. Charles reflected on the passing of his own boyhood and the sad end of the lad he had known aboard ship. Now Danny was gone, and Alexander had become a man — very likely the heir to the title and wealth of his father, Lord Marston. Charles was grown, as well, and he bore the heavy burden of his father's wishes and his own hopes and dreams.

But tonight was not one for sadness. He had come with a mission, and he intended to make the most of the event. James Locke was right. Perhaps Charles would meet a lovely young lady who might distract him from his woe over the rejection by Mrs. Carlyle. He might even make the acquaintance of a woman of wealth who could find love for him in her heart. If so, he would make the tea enterprise a reality and fulfill his own longing for a happy home.

To that end, Charles had dressed in his

finest tailcoat of black wool with split French cuffs and a high collar. He wore a blue waistcoat of striped Valencia, cream-colored kerseymere breeches that ended just below the knee, and a pair of leather gloves. New black shoes provided good support for his injured leg and set off his white stockings. As a final flourish, he had tied a silk cravat at his neck, set a cocked hat upon his head, and taken up an ebony cane with a silver knob. Restoring his wardrobe had further strained Locke & Son's dwindling assets, but James had insisted upon it. At least Charles knew he dignified his rank, such as it was, and he would not bring any shame to his friend.

Now as he labored up the steps, several acquaintances greeted him. He had seen none of this social set since departing London five months before, but he might have been away no more than a fortnight. Everyone expressed great sympathy over his recent misadventure and urged him to join them at their dinner table. But none offered to assist him or waited while he made the difficult climb.

Once inside the house, Charles was swept into the crowd of partygoers as though an ocean wave had overcome him. The fragrance of French perfume and burning candles swirled above his head. Gowns of blue, gold, green, pink, and silver flounced about. Frothy lace spilled from men's collars, and ribbons tumbled over extravagant mounds of ladies' coiffures. Music swelled and pitched amid the hubbub. Footmen helped remove fur-lined cloaks. Gentlemen doffed top hats and overcoats. Servants navigated the shifting currents. They bore drink-laden silver trays, which they dipped now and then to some passerby or another.

Disoriented, Charles made his way across the foyer to the main ballroom. After a moment standing in a queue, he was shown toward the reception line. A footman took his card.

"Mr. Charles Locke," the servant announced to the evening's hosts.

"Locke! How very good of you to come!" Sir Alexander grinned broadly as he welcomed Charles. As cheerful as ever, the young man was eager to show off the lovely woman at his side. "May I introduce you to my fiancée, Gabrielle Duchesne, daughter of the comte de la Roche? My dear, this is Mr. Charles Locke, of whom I have told you so much."

"I am honored to meet you," Charles said, bowing deeply in response to the lady's curtsy. Considering the current turmoil with

France, he was surprised that his friend would choose a Frenchwoman as a bride, but Sir Alexander's choices in life had often been less than judicious. "I had no idea you had taken such a bold step, my good man. Madam, may I assure you that you are engaged to marry the finest gentleman of all my acquaintances."

"There, Gabrielle, what did I tell you?" Sir Alexander beamed with satisfaction. "Of course Locke ought to have been sent an invitation. He is my dearest and oldest friend in the world. But, Locke, what is this news I have heard of you? Were you truly attacked by pirates and nearly killed?"

Aware that the line of greeters behind him was growing restless, Charles tipped his head at his host. "Indeed I was, and I shall give you the entire account at your leisure. And you must tell me news of your brother and your sisters."

"Most certainly," Sir Alexander replied.

Moving on, Charles greeted the young man's parents, Laurent and Beatrice Chouteau, the elderly duke and duchess of Marston. They asked after the health of his father and then seemed eager to pass him along down the queue in favor of other guests. They had not changed. Nor had Sir Alexander, for he was as affable as his father was arrogant. But apparently Sir Alexander's fiancée had not wished to include the son of a former steward on their invitation list, and whether a friendship could survive that sort of censure was doubtful.

Determined to make the most of an opportunity that might be his last, Charles spotted a gathering of gentlemen among whom he could claim several acquaintances. At once, the tale of his sea voyage was seized upon as the topic of interest. With as much heartiness as he could muster, Charles recounted the pirate attack. Like moths drawn to light, ladies gathered around, eager to know every detail. They gasped and fanned themselves as the story progressed to its climax.

"Blown overboard by exploding langrage!" a woman exclaimed. "Upon my word, I am all astonishment! My dear Mr. Locke, how have you possibly recovered your health enough to come here tonight?"

"I was pulled from the sea by the crew of the *Queen Elinor,* which had come to our rescue," Charles told her. "The captain took one look at me and declared me dead. The women passengers began to stitch my shroud. At the very last moment possible, I gave some small signal of movement."

"And your awakening startled all on board!"

Everyone in the group turned to see who had made such a bold addition to the tale. The young lady who had spoken gasped, "Oh, dear!" and covered her mouth with her hand.

Charles cocked his head inquiringly at the woman, whose large green eyes, full lips, and well-turned figure became her exceedingly. She blinked and gave an embarrassed shrug. "I believe I have heard the story before," she offered in a low voice.

"From whom, may I ask?" Charles queried.

The lady's cheeks blazed bright pink now, and she glanced to the side as if searching for someone who might come to answer his question in her place. "I heard it from . . . from round about," she said. "You are Charles Locke, are you not?"

"I am. And may I ask your name, madam?"

"This is Miss Prudence Watson," one of the men spoke up. "She is sister to Lady Delacroix."

The young lady now appeared ready to burst into flame, such was the glow on her face. She fanned herself wildly, scattering bits of ostrich feathers about like ashes on a breezy evening. Charmed by her beauty and bemused by her discomfiture, Charles elected to ease the poor woman's unease.

"Indeed, my unexpected return to consciousness caused quite a shock," he confirmed. "From the deck I was taken into the charge of the ship's doctor. My leg received adequate care, and my other injuries gradually began to heal. And that is the sum of it. I am well enough to return to society and resume the task of building my tea enterprise. The value of tea, as anyone may assume, can hardly be overestimated. With Parliament's action to remove power from the East India Company and to open trade with the Orient, the future of independent tea entrepreneurs must be healthy."

As he spoke of his company, the sea of listeners began to drift away. The green-eyed young lady vanished, as did most of the other women. The onset of dance music drew the men, leaving only a handful of those who had once attended to his tale with such eagerness.

Charles pressed on, hopeful of interesting any possible investor. But before he could go into detail about his plan, one of the gentlemen mentioned another of Parliament's actions — that of declaring King George incompetent and placing his son into power as prince regent. This brought a round of response both positive and negative from those gathered, for in his five years of power, the regent had garnered a vast number of both friends and enemies.

Though he tried to concentrate on the discussion, Charles could not help scanning the shifting crowd in the room. He had been fascinated by the pert Miss Watson, and now he wondered where she had gone. Her sumptuous beauty was the sort that drew men into rash, heedless deeds of derring-do meant to impress the object of their affection. Though appreciative of a woman's graces, Charles had never been overly drawn to that kind of lush and bounteous female charm.

No, it was Miss Watson's knowledge of the events aboard the *Queen Elinor* that intrigued him. How had she heard about his ordeal? And why — on realizing she had divulged her prior knowledge — had she reacted with such dismay? Someone must have recounted the story to her. Someone who had been on the ship.

The very idea that the *Queen Elinor*'s captain, the ship's doctor, or one of the naval officers was in attendance compelled Charles. If he could speak to such a person — someone who had shared with him that life-altering event — he might find some peace at last. He had nearly lost his life. And he had most definitely lost his heart. But not even his father could fully comprehend the magnitude of the experience that had occurred at sea.

"The regent is said to be quite a reader," one of the men was saying. "Can you imagine that? I understand he admires the novels of Jane Austen."

Covertly searching the room for the green-eyed woman, Charles forced himself to participate in the conversation at hand. "Upon my return from sea, I purchased one of her novels," he commented. "It is a comic account and truly brilliant in its wit. The regent has a great affinity for humor, I am told."

"Yes, but I can hardly believe he would ever bother to open a book," someone else said. "I supposed all his time was taken up with his plump little mistresses."

There! Charles spotted Miss Watson near the punch bowl. A cluster of men leaned forward to offer her and a female companion a total of seven cups of the pink beverage. Miss Watson laughed at their enthusiasm and coyly laid her head on her friend's shoulder.

"I believe Miss Austen's novels offer just

the sort of entertainment the regent would enjoy," Charles commented, even as his focus remained on the women across the room. "Her characters are endearing. Some are silly enough to bring a chuckle to the reader, while others are sober studies of human nature at its —"

The woman beside Miss Watson turned, and Charles caught his breath. What? In *this* company? Impossible! But how could he be mistaken? He stepped to one side in an effort to see through the constantly moving crowd. Brown hair. Brown eyes. A sweet, generous smile and a fair complexion.

His heart stumbled.

"I say, Locke, are you feeling ill?" one of the men asked. "A row of chairs is set up against the wall if your leg is —"

"That woman," he cut in, gesturing with his chin. "The one who accompanies Miss Watson. Who is she?"

The gentlemen turned as a group.

"The woman in the blue gown? Why, that is Lady Delacroix, of course."

Charles leaned on his cane. Lady Delacroix? Absurd! He knew this woman well. Had seen her many times. She could only be one person.

"Are you absolutely certain of her identity?" he repeated.

"Of course, Locke. She is widow to the late George Carlyle, Lord Delacroix, and aunt by marriage to Henry Carlyle, the current baron — though the latter is her elder by several years. See how she talks with him and her sister?"

"Miss Prudence Watson is her sister?"

"Lady Delacroix has two sisters. Miss Watson there. And Mrs. John Heathhill — dancing with her husband."

Though he had been told a different name, Charles knew he was gazing at Sarah Carlyle. *His* Sarah. Sarah from the ship who had nursed him back to life and given him reason to hope again.

But this Sarah was much altered from the gentle, humble woman he had met on the *Queen Elinor.* Gone were the simple cotton gowns and loose knot of hair. Gone were the bare fingers that had so tenderly ministered to his wounds. Gone were the simple expression and natural, clear complexion of the woman he loved.

This creature — this Lady Delacroix — wore a shimmering blue silk gown dripping with lace, pearls, ribbons, flounces, and beads. Her hair sat high on her head in a mound of artful braids, ringlets, and curls. Her cheeks were powdered and her lips stained red. White kid gloves covered her hands and skimmed up her arms to her elbows. Dangling sapphire earrings, a gold necklace, and a tiara that glittered with diamonds accentuated the vision of this creature of incredible bearing and stature who glided through the crowd, nodding at one person and then another.

"It cannot be," he murmured. "And yet it is."

"You speak of Miss Watson's beauty?" someone asked. "Her loveliness often renders men speechless. I am married these twenty years, and yet I must say it is difficult to think beyond the lady when she is about."

"You would do well to set your sights elsewhere, Mr. Locke," another added. "A hundred eager bachelors stand ready to heed her beck and call. She can have any of them she chooses, for she has not only her sumptuous features of which to boast, but she is tied to the Delacroix name."

"And that elevates her to high society, of course," Charles murmured.

"More than that! Through her sister, Miss Watson is likely to bring an ample dowry to her marriage."

"Lady Delacroix married into wealth, then."

"Hardly. Her husband was a pauper. It

was her father, a highly successful opium merchant, who left his eldest daughter such a vast legacy. Lady Delacroix ought to be the object of your quest, Mr. Locke, for her riches might finance three tea companies, a fleet of ships, and enough warehouses to line the Thames for more than a mile."

"Is that so?" Charles muttered, recalling his darling Sarah's conversations with him about her father's money. She intended to give it all to the poor, she had told him. She wanted to build schools and printing presses and hospitals. She looked forward to being poor herself. No better off than a beggar.

But look at Lady Delacroix on this night. In direct contrast to her words, she floated through the ballroom like a queen. Her sparkling jewels and elegant laces vied for attention. Her very posture bespoke fortune and class. Everything about this creature belied Charles's certainty that he had known and loved her as Mrs. Sarah Carlyle aboard the *Queen Elinor*.

"I fear Lady Delacroix is unlikely to take notice of you, Mr. Locke," one of the men commented. "I am told she is quite content with her situation in life and does not intend to permit another husband to intrude upon it. Who could blame her? As eldest daughter of the late Mr. Gerald Watson, she has all the money she could ever want. And as the dowager Lady Delacroix, she possesses the effects of her late husband's good reputation and place in society."

"Thus she has immense power, prestige, and influence," another added. "Lady Delacroix lacks nothing, and she makes her disdain for suitors well-known. As if to avoid all society, she has been abroad these two years past and is only lately returned to her family and friends. No, Mr. Locke, were I a bachelor, I should make every attempt to win the hand of Miss Watson. Lady Delacroix herself, I believe, is unattainable."

Unwilling to quell the urge to confront this proud and indifferent creature the men described, Charles excused himself and stepped away. As he started toward Lady Delacroix, he recalled Sarah Carlyle's rejection of his marriage proposal. How her words had reverberated through him again and again as he sat in painful loneliness in his father's house. But now he understood that although she had wept tears enough to convince any man of her innocence, her message on that day aboard ship had been filled with deceit.

"I do not care for banks or warehouses or drawing rooms. Business ventures and grand houses have no meaning to me whatsoever,"

she had insisted. *"I deplore any goal of financial gain. My sole object in life is to rid myself of such earthly encumbrances and devote my whole being to the pursuit of heaven."*

What rot! Look at her now, laden with "earthly encumbrances," Charles fumed as he strode through the crowd toward the object of his ire. How dare she cite religion as an excuse to be rid of him? Sobbing as though her heart must break, she had told him of her devotion to her faith and her aim of poverty.

"It is God I wish to please, not man," she had assured her wooer, the words dripping with piety. *"I do not want a house or servants or fine gowns. I cannot abide a husband who desires to spend his days laboring to increase his wealth. I wish to be poor. I wish to have nothing. If I wear rags and sleep in a hovel, I shall be content. Any man who would have me as his wife must feel the same."*

Utter tripe! Of course it mattered not to Lady Delacroix whether Charles Locke worked in a bank or built a tea enterprise. She had no need of his pathetic efforts to provide her with security and comfort. How she must have laughed to herself as he told her how he planned to add rooms to his father's house on Threadneedle Street and to erect a warehouse nearby. What amusement she must have taken in his pitiable list of assets and options. When she had a world of riches and honor spread before her, she had surely thought his small chest of stolen gold a paltry thing.

His fury mounting with each step, Charles followed the woman and her sister across the ballroom. As they neared the dance floor, the flaxen-haired Lord Delacroix tipped his head and left them to join another group. With much obsequious bowing, an elderly gentleman greeted the two ladies. They paused for a moment, accepted his salutations, and then moved on. A young friend in a feather-tipped turban stopped them momentarily and said something amusing. They giggled and hurried away.

Charles edged around the double lines of dancers and passed the portal to the dining room, where the evening's repast was being set up. At last Lady Delacroix was within his reach. As he approached, she suddenly halted, opened her fan, and whispered something to her sister. Then with a last glance about the room, she slipped through a pair of tall, glass-paned doors and vanished.

Six

Such a relief! Sarah leaned against the stone wall, tilted her head to the starlit sky, and drank down a deep breath of fresh air. Since her return to London, she had attended three dinner parties and two balls, and she had made an appearance at St. James's court. This evening's reception at Lord Marston's house was certain to go on until well after midnight. She had never felt so exhausted in all her life.

Boating on the Ganges and trekking across China were nothing to this endless social whirlwind! Caught up in it at once, she had been hurled headlong into her former life. Gowns had come out of trunks. Furs had been aired. New gloves and slippers fitted. Jewels taken from locked boxes. And hats . . . oh, the hats. Sarah could not remember when she had been forced to examine so many bonnets, so much ribbon, so many faux flowers, leaves, and bits of shrubbery.

Mary would not hear of her sister going out in society in a hat that was two years behind the times. And so the three sisters had traipsed from one milliner's shop to another. They sorted through ribbons and laces for daytime, feathered turbans for evening gatherings, and bonnets with narrow poke brims and every sort of adornment imaginable until at last the perfect array of headwear had been procured.

Prudence had insisted that something must be done with her eldest sister's long hair. And so Sarah had been made to sit immobile while her brown locks were trimmed, curled, and set atop her head to reflect the current rage for Grecian style. Sarah informed Mary and Pru that she had visited Greece, and no one there wore such ridiculous ringlets and braids. But they would hear of nothing less than converting their dear sister into the very image of a classical goddess from some ancient urn.

Closing her eyes as she leaned against the cool wall now, Sarah heaved a rueful sigh and tried to think happier thoughts. She pictured the deck of the *Queen Elinor* and her favorite chair, which had given her a stupendous view of the ocean. She thought of tossing waves and salt-sea smells and the snap and creak of ropes and sails. And then her thoughts wandered, as always, to the face of Charles Locke . . . the pressure of his arm against hers . . . the brilliance of his eyes reflecting the blue of the water . . . the corners of his mouth tipped up in a gentle smile —

"Excuse me, madam." The voice was too close for comfort. "May I be so bold as to interrupt your reverie?"

"As a matter of fact," she began, intending to whisk away the offender. And then she focused on his face. Instantly, her blood sank to her knees, and she gripped the stone behind her for support. "Charles . . ."

"Good evening, Mrs. Carlyle. Or perhaps I should say — Lady Delacroix."

Too startled to respond, Sarah could do nothing but stare in disbelief. She had expected never to lay eyes upon the man again. But here he was. Not two paces away. Tall, square-shouldered, his sapphire eyes aglow in the starlight — it was truly him.

"How —" she shook her head — "how are you here?"

"By invitation, of course. The Chouteau brothers were my close companions in childhood. I grew up alongside Ruel and Alexander at Slocombe House in Devon. Lord Marston employed my father as steward of his estate." He set his hands at his waist, disdain curling his lips. "Did you dismiss everything I told you as swiftly as you dismissed me, Lady Delacroix?"

"But I did not think . . . I hardly expected . . ."

"No, I can see that. You supposed I would return to London and try to rebuild my life, while you rushed back to your society and all its perquisites."

Disconcerted, Sarah touched the diamond-and-pearl pendant that hung from a gold chain about her neck. This was Charles, and he was angry. Why? Because she had rejected him? Because she had not expected to find him among the *ton?* What was wrong?

"I am surprised to see you," she tried. "But that does not make you unwelcome, sir. Indeed, I am pleased to find you among Lord Marston's guests. It is you who appear unhappy at this chance encounter."

"Unhappy, no. But I am as astonished as you. During our previous acquaintance, you led me to believe your name was Mrs. Sarah Carlyle. You were a pious young widow bent on ridding yourself of all earthly possessions. Tonight I find myself in the presence of Lady Delacroix, whose enjoyment of her wealth and standing is clear to all."

"Is it?" she said, offended at his accusing tone.

"I believe that pendant with which you toy might be sold for enough money to build a school for blind girls in China," he observed. "Or to purchase a printing press for a needy missionary in India. Has divesting yourself of such trinkets proven too tiresome to undertake?"

"Upon my honor, you are presumptuous, Mr. Locke!" She tilted her chin. "You know nothing of my intentions, and you have no assurance of where I take my enjoyment. If you believe it is in baubles such as these, you are mistaken. Perhaps it is *you* who dismissed me from your thoughts, Mr. Locke, for I once told you exactly what I believe. As for my name — I would have you know that my late husband was George Carlyle, Lord Delacroix. I did not deceive you there, for I am in every way Mrs. Carlyle."

"By your society, you are known as Lady Delacroix."

"When we met, you were not my society. You were a badly injured man pulled up from the sea and nearly tossed back into it for dead. I took it upon myself to assist the ship's doctor in tending to you and the others who had been taken from the *Tintagel*.

In such circumstances, I felt no need to insist upon proper forms of address, nor did I see the necessity of correcting the situation later."

"No necessity — though I believed myself to be in love with a common woman of typical means and a kind heart?"

Sarah clenched her teeth as she struggled against the unseemly retorts that formed on her tongue. How dare he! She had given hours of her time, nearly wearing herself out in caring for him and the other men. And now he stood before her in accusation — because she had not given him her formal title?

"You believed yourself to be in love with Sarah Carlyle," she said at last. "But you were too proud and full of self-pity and ambition to heed her message. Is that not true, Mr. Locke? You supposed Mrs. Carlyle to be a common woman of normal means who intended to give her father's riches to the needy. That woman begged you to join in her mission, but you could not love her that much."

"That was it, then? A ruse to dupe a suitor into believing he must love you enough to abandon every hope and dream in his heart? every effort toward security and comfort? Once you had an avowal of poverty, what

129

then? Do you make a habit of toying with men, Lady Delacroix?"

"I did not play you for a fool, sir. Our conversations were genuine and honest, as were my feelings for you. I am now as I was then. But who are you? I believed the Mr. Locke I met aboard the *Queen Elinor* to be a kind and well-mannered gentleman. I found him brave and wise and caring. He grieved a boy named Danny who had been lost at sea, and he honored a father who had given his all to a bold but ill-fated enterprise. That Mr. Locke was earnest and intelligent and, above all, considerate of the feelings of others." Sarah pulled herself up straight and met his steady gaze. "You, sir, are a brute!"

Unwilling to hear another word from his mouth, Sarah lifted her skirts and hurried back into the ballroom. She must escape this place! Flee these people! How could he have come here when she had worked so hard to put him out of her thoughts? How dare he accuse her of such infamies — toying with men, delighting in her wealth, deceiving others? It was too much!

"Sarah?" Prudence caught her sister's arm. "Where are you going? What is amiss? You are near to tears!"

"I must go home at once, Pru. Help me

find a footman to call our carriage. And tell Lord Marston that I —"

"Lady Delacroix — are you unwell?" Her nephew by marriage, Henry Carlyle, stepped to her side and took her arm. Known as Lord Delacroix now, he had taken up residence in his late uncle's London house. A reputed cad and as penniless as the previous holder of the barony, Delacroix was nevertheless an elegant man who was ever solicitous of Sarah and her two sisters.

"Perhaps we should send for a doctor," he said, speaking over Sarah's head to Prudence, who was attached to her other arm. "I fear your sister may swoon. She is very pale!"

"No, I beg you. I do not need a doctor at all." Sarah allowed them to hurry her across the room to an alcove, where Delacroix quickly emptied a settee of three drowsy matrons.

"Sit down at once, dear lady," he said, kneeling and taking her hand. "Permit me to send for some punch. Perhaps the chill air has upset the delicate balance of your humors."

"Sarah, what has happened?" Prudence demanded as she dropped onto the sofa beside her sister. "You are as white as ashes!"

"I am all right, truly. But I must go home, Pru. I cannot bear another moment of this jarring music and all these candles and everyone moving about —"

"Who talked to you just now? Was it *him?*"

"Why did you not warn me that he was here?"

"It *was* him! Oh, Sarah!"

"Who?" Delacroix demanded.

"The man from the ship. The one she loves!"

"I do not love him!" Sarah tried to stand, but her sister and the baron both pushed her back onto the cushions. "I do not! He is rude and arrogant and impossible!"

"She adores him," Prudence confided to Delacroix. "His name is Charles Locke, and they met on the *Queen Elinor.* He was wounded fighting pirates, and she nursed him back to life, and it was terribly romantic. He asked her to marry him, and what do you think? She turned him down! He wanted to establish a tea trade with China, and she said that any man who would marry her must agree to live as a pauper! And he said he would do no such thing, so she rejected him. It was mightily tragic, though she never expected to see him again, for he is poor and could have no place in our society. But here he is!"

Wishing she had been swept away by an ocean wave, Sarah blotted the tears that insisted on trickling down her cheeks. "Prudence, for mercy's sake, lower your voice," she commanded. "And as for Mr. Locke, I assure you that what I felt for him once is utterly gone. He accosted me outside, insulted me, accused me of all manner of horrid things, and . . . oh, Pru! Please send for the carriage before I make a spectacle of myself!"

"If the man insulted you, he must be made to answer for it!" the baron announced. "Does he know who you are? Your rank! The esteem and honor you are due! Does he know he insults Lady Delacroix herself?"

"Oh, please, sir," Sarah sniffled, "spare your flatteries."

"But how dare he treat you so ill?"

"Precisely because he did not know I was Lady Delacroix — not until tonight. Aboard ship, I neglected to inform him of that fact. But I do not believe my omission should earn such ire."

"Of course not!" Prudence said. "Insufferable lout! Sarah, you are losing your earrings, and your face powder is all streaked.

You must stop weeping at once. Here, let me pat your cheeks. Delacroix, I beg you to find my sister Mary and tell her the situation. She and her husband can make our apologies to Lord and Lady —" She gasped. "There he is now! Charles Locke! He is making his own departure from the duke. He is fearfully handsome, Sarah; I warrant you that. No wonder you fell madly in love with him. I should have done the same in your place."

"Prudence, I am *not . . . not* in love!" A fresh wave of dismay came over Sarah as she watched Charles bowing before the duke and his wife.

"I shall fetch him and make him apologize," Delacroix said.

"You will do no such thing!" Sarah caught his arm. "Let the man go. He is better off as far away from me as possible!"

"Are his eyes blue?" Prudence asked. "Oh, sister, he is uncommonly dashing."

Sarah gave a cry of disbelief. "Can you think of nothing beyond handsome faces, Pru? Upon my word, you are as shallow as a tea saucer!" With that, she stood from the settee and smoothed down her skirt. "I shall summon the carriage myself if neither of you will do it for me. And as for Mr. Locke, take a last look at his blue eyes, sister, for that is all you will ever see of him again."

As Sarah started forward, she saw Charles striding through the crowd toward the foyer. He kept his gaze trained steadily ahead until, at the last moment, he halted and focused directly upon Sarah.

She held her breath. His eyes met hers, searched them, burned into them. And then he turned away again and left the room.

"Your ill humor does you no credit, young man." James Locke pointed a finger at his son. "You had better tell me what truly occurred at Lord Marston's reception and be done with it! Did the duke speak of me with little regard? If so, I care not. The old cabbagehead! Let him say what he will. He matters nothing to me. I served him well, and now I am shed of him. Good riddance is all I can say to that!"

"Lord and Lady Marston kindly asked after your health, Father, and that is all the conversation we had," Charles said. "They have a more amiable intent toward you than you do toward them."

Rising from the chair beside the fire, he took up his cane and used its tip to part the curtains over the window. It was a fine afternoon, and he ought to be about the town in search of employment. Surely such activity would be a welcome escape.

Since the reception, his father had done nothing but lament the failed attempt to secure a patron. Observing his son's dark mood, he had convinced himself that Charles must have offended every single member of the English aristocracy. Or that he had been shunned by someone of consequence. Or that he had been so caught up in dancing that he had forgotten to try to win a backer for their tea enterprise. Any number of theories had been tossed out, and Charles had denied each one. But when he refused to give the true reason for his unhappiness, his father decided to try them all again.

"The rain has stopped, and the sun is out," Charles announced. "I shall walk to the bank and make my inquiries."

"Was the regent at the reception?" James asked. At Charles's lack of immediate response, his face broke into an expression of utter astonishment. "He *was* there! Aha! What did you say to him, Charles? Did you mention our tea scheme? Was he displeased? I believe he may have connections to the East India Company. Investments, you know. Perhaps you should have said nothing to him at all."

"The regent was not in attendance." With

a sigh, Charles reached for his hat and coat. "Father, may we not move forward to some more productive discussion? The reception is ended, and I must seek employment if we mean to keep eating. I am convinced that the bank will happily take me on."

As he donned his hat, their only servant stepped into the room. She bore a small tray on which lay a white card. Her hand was trembling as she extended the card toward her master.

"Who can this be?" James asked as he scanned it. "I am not acquainted with a Henry Carlyle, Lord Delacroix. Fanny, are you certain this is not a ruse? Lord Delacroix indeed! It must be some charlatan."

His heart stumbling, Charles snatched the card from his father's hand. "It is no ruse. Fanny, please show in Lord Delacroix." He jerked off his hat and tossed it onto a table. "Say nothing, Father; I implore you. Allow me to converse with the gentleman, and afterward I shall explain everything."

James gave a snort of unhappiness and muttered something under his breath as the door opened again. His heart hammering, Charles set his cane aside and squared his shoulders. Fanny squeaked out the introduction and then fled as Lord Delacroix stepped into the sitting room.

Shorter than Charles, he was nonetheless an imposing figure with a broad chest and a stocky build. His head of golden curls might have given him a delicate cast, but Delacroix wore such an air of regal male superiority that no one could mistake him for anything but a member of the peerage. Standing just inside the door, he haughtily accepted his hosts' polite bows and made them a curt response. Then he strolled across the carpet, flipped the tails of his coat behind him, and seated himself on the chair nearest the fire.

Charles glanced at his father, who clearly did not know whether to kneel in homage or throw the baggage out on his ear. Delacroix's silence made it obvious he would not be the first to speak, and thus the task fell to Charles.

"Good afternoon, sir," he ventured, taking a place on a chair nearby. "To what do we owe the honor of your visit?"

The baron's eyelids lowered as he turned to Charles. "I believe you know very well the nature of my call, sir. Two days have passed since the evening in which you insulted Lady Delacroix, and she has yet to receive your written apology."

Charles lifted his chin. "I am the one deserving of an apology, sir. The lady in question deceived me. She used me ill, and I reproached her for it."

"Lady Delacroix is incapable of such infamy, sir. She is as mild and sweet and innocent of wrongdoing as any child. Since the evening of the Marston reception, she has been unduly melancholy. Her sisters fear for her, and I am most concerned. She hears nothing that we say to her. Instead, she packs her trunks and insists she will take passage on the first ship to the Orient, though she has been back in England less than a month."

This news dismayed Charles. He could not deny the painful encounter at the Marston reception. His hurt at being rejected by Sarah had combined with righteous indignation upon seeing her in such grand regalia. Together, they had ignited the flame of his rage, and he had callously lobbed one fiery accusation after another at her.

But she had deserved his fury, had she not? Everything about Lady Delacroix belied what Sarah Carlyle had told him aboard the ship. She could not possibly be both women, and so she had deceived him. What else might one deduce?

"She returns to Asia?" Charles asked. "To what end?"

"You know very well to what end, for she

told you herself!" Delacroix leapt up from his chair and began to pace the room. "The lady is determined to rid herself of her father's legacy! She has settled a goodly sum upon each of her sisters, and she has willingly resigned to me any interest of hers in my uncle's properties. Hour after hour, she consults with her stewards, solicitors, and bankers. She writes letters, sends them off to Burma or India or other such forsaken places. And then she writes again. Nothing her sisters or I can say have any effect upon her. She is bent upon this madness, and I hold you responsible!"

"You hold Charles responsible for this lady's erratic behavior?" James Locke burst out. "What on earth can my son have had to do with it!"

"Father, please," Charles said; he stood to face their guest. "If Lady Delacroix wishes to divest herself of her legacy, who are you to stop her? You have called her mild and innocent. If so, she can have no nefarious purpose in her desire to be free of the encumbrances her father strapped upon her."

"Encumbrances? Mr. Locke, the dowager baroness is among the wealthiest in all of England. Her father was a trader in opium, laudanum, and other derivatives of that

140

medicinal plant, and he left his eldest daughter a fortune. Not a small fortune. Not a middling fortune. A great, vast, and magnificent fortune! He saw her wedded to my uncle with the aim of uniting his money to the Delacroix lineage. But Lady Delacroix bore no children before her husband's death, and now she means to distribute every tuppence in her possession to beggars in China!"

"You are concerned, then, that Lady Delacroix has failed to satisfy her father's wishes. Is that it, sir? In our conversations aboard the *Queen Elinor,* she and I discussed many things. Your deep affection for her father was not among them."

Delacroix swallowed. "Well, I believe everyone should do his part to honor his parents. Your own father must surely agree."

"Of course," James concurred. "Charles, by this man's account, you do owe the baroness an apology. She may have failed to give you her true identity, but that is a sin of omission and certainly forgivable. You, on the other hand, insulted and demeaned her to the extent that you have driven her to utter despair. She not only flees her familial responsibilities, but she gives away her money. Surely she has lost her senses!"

"You are mistaken, Father," Charles countered. "Her mind is quite sound. Mrs. Carlyle, as I knew her, claimed that her life had been one of suffering. Certain events in her childhood and marriage had brought her much unhappiness, though she did not give me the specifics of these. She had concluded that her only hope of true happiness was to live as she believed God intended. The Bible, she told me, describes the life of a true Christian as one of poverty. A man must divest himself of all worldly possessions, take up his cross, and follow Christ. The same holds true for a woman."

The two men stared at Charles as though he had been speaking in Hindi. He knew how they felt, for he had not understood Sarah's mission at all. Even now, he could hardly agree that she was correct in her understanding of Scripture. Yet what had become clear to Charles was that Sarah may not have deceived him on board the *Queen Elinor* after all. Not in what truly mattered to her.

Perhaps it really was possible that she cared nothing for her so-called "great, vast, and magnificent fortune." Despite her jewels and fine gown, maybe she really did want to give away everything — and even now, as he and Delacroix stood arguing, she was preparing to do just that.

The diamond-and-pearl necklace Charles had so maligned at the reception might mean nothing to her, he realized. No wonder she had taken such offense at his accusation. Perchance she *would* sell it to build a school in China! Her silk gown and coiffed hair held no joy for her. Those who bowed and curtsied before her might actually bring her no pleasure at all. Unlike everyone Charles had ever known, maybe Sarah really did not want to be rich, and so she would give the money away. Perhaps she had not desired her aristocratic title, and so she had discarded it in favor of her real name.

Sarah Carlyle. That was who she was — and that was the woman he had loved with such desperation.

"I shall go to her," Charles said. "I can make no apology — written or spoken — until the lady explains herself to me."

"Very well," Delacroix agreed. "I shall take you to her at once. You must assure the baroness that you meant her no insult. You must encourage her to abandon her travel plans and to make her home in England for a year or two at least. Above all, Mr. Locke, you must stop her from giving away all that money!"

Charles paused in reaching for his hat. "Stop her from giving away her money? And how am I to do that when it is the aim of her life? Surely you cannot mean for me to bring Lady Delacroix further unhappiness."

"No, of course not, but she is mistaken in her understanding of how things ought to be!" Delacroix declared. "You must try to correct her. Help her to see that her fortune may be put to productive use here in England. She will listen to you, Locke, for I believe — indeed, her sisters swear it is so — that she truly cares for you. We are all of us most distraught over this inexplicable and misplaced affection. And you must agree that such a match is insupportable. Nevertheless, Lady Delacroix's high esteem for you coincides perfectly with her disdain for wealth and position. The material point is that she *can* do better in all ways, and she *will* do better. You must convince her of this!"

The ignominy inherent in the man's words provoked an ire that spilled through Charles's chest in a flood. "Upon my honor, sir, I am no peasant! Lord Marston's son is my close companion, and I am far from —"

"Sir, take no umbrage at my words!" Delacroix cut in. "I do not mean to disparage you or your friends. But surely you are a reasonable man and can see that Lady Delacroix is far above you in rank and privilege.

144

Any connection between you is impossible. Believe me, were such an attachment at all imaginable, her sisters and I would assist you in securing her hand at once. Yet I do not expect you to expend your efforts on our behalf without recompense. Certainly not! If you can convince Lady Delacroix to accept her lot in life and to understand that she may use her privileged position to the benefit of others here in England, then you may be assured of our support in your proposed enterprise."

"Charles!" his father cried out. "The tea company! He speaks of financing our trade!"

Immobilized, Charles studied the golden-haired aristocrat who stood before him. Lord Delacroix was right. Any formal attachment between Charles and one of the wealthiest women in England would be unthinkable. Marriage was impossible. Although he was a gentleman, he could claim no aristocratic lineage and no fortune. Without one or the other of these, he had nothing upon which to base a claim to an elevated woman's affections.

Perhaps Sarah did care for him, but she had told him herself that she did not love him. She did not know what love was. Charles had to admit that not even the strongest affection could lead her to make a match so unfortunate. She would have to be a fool, and she certainly was not that. In fact, he could not be completely sure that her determination to give away her wealth was as ludicrous as he and others had claimed. Since debarking the *Queen Elinor,* he had searched his Bible for teachings on wealth and the quest for material gain. Many passages supported Sarah's contention that the love of money was the root of all evil.

On the other hand, how could a reasonable person even think of giving away all his possessions? How could anyone possibly expect to find happiness as a pauper? Charles was as close to that station in life as he ever hoped to come, and he certainly was not elated by it. In fact, just the opposite. Lack of wealth and social stature had penalized him and every member of his ancestry.

Perhaps, as Christ had told the rich young ruler, ridding oneself of wealth could bring eternal life. But it certainly could not bring any joy in this earthly life. Sarah was wrong in her understanding, and the image of her standing bereft on some street corner in Calcutta — miserable, hungry, and desperately unhappy — clutched at Charles's heart.

Delacroix's offer held more than a little attraction. If Charles could speak humbly to Sarah as a dearly cherished friend, perhaps she would agree to disperse her money in a more reasonable fashion. Perhaps she would keep some of it for herself and award greater sums to her sisters and friends. And then — if Delacroix was a man of his word — a reasonably large measure of it would be entrusted to Charles.

Why should he not receive enough money to build his tea enterprise? He had suffered much pain over Mrs. Sarah Carlyle. If his words could mollify the baroness and enrich him, then all the better for both of them.

He donned his hat and took up his cane. "To your carriage, then, Lord Delacroix," he said. "For I believe we shall be just in time for tea."

Seven

The lady's maid pushed a pin into Sarah's hair, grazing her scalp and eliciting a yelp of pain. "Have a care, please, Anne!"

"Beg pardon, my lady." The maid dipped an apologetic curtsy. "This braid will not stay in its place."

"Then put it in another place, I beg you."

"But, madam, this braid is meant to cross the other one that I have just pinned up. Miss Watson says that the butterfly clip must go at the exact point where the two braids cross or the style will be imperfect."

"I am not Miss Watson, Anne, and I am perfectly happy to abandon the butterfly clip altogether. In fact, I should be quite content to put the whole lot of my hair into a bun at the back of my head as it was when I arrived in London."

In the mirror, Sarah could see the young maid's bottom lip begin to tremble and her nose turn pink. Oh, dear. Now she had offended poor Anne, who wanted nothing more than to please her mistress and be rewarded with her wages at the end of the week. The young woman had come to London from her home in Nottingham just as Sarah returned from her travels. Anne Webster was no ordinary maid, for her father had been a noted rector, and his daughter was educated and well mannered. Had the Reverend Webster not assisted his parishioners in smashing the lace machines that threatened their livelihood, he would not have been thrown into prison, and his daughter would not have been faced with a precarious future.

As it was, Sarah felt blessed to have Anne's assistance. Though untrained in the art of hairstyling and not completely familiar with the requirements of a lady's maid, Anne Webster was a capable and resilient young lady. More important, she was pleasant natured and eager to learn. In fact, not many days had passed before Sarah had made up her mind to do all in her power to improve Anne's lot in life.

"I do very much like the way you style my hair," Sarah told her in a softer voice.

The maid brightened considerably at this compliment.

"I believe I am quite plain, though," Sarah

continued. "My hair and eyes are plain, and my heart is plain as well. I do not mind at all. Plainness can be a great attribute, Anne, for vanity is a wicked trap."

"If you please, madam, I do not think you plain. You are attractive in the ways that matter most. Miss Watson is not plain either, for she has many virtues." Anne's eyes nearly crossed as she worked to insert the butterfly clip between the two braids. "She is lovely and also kind."

"That is true," Sarah conceded. "My sister is beautiful outside and in. I cannot think of a happier combination of merits or a better person upon whom to bestow them. God is wise indeed."

"There!" Anne said. "Now for the beetles!"

The maid reached into a tray of enameled and gilded insects. Such baubles were all the rage in London this season, Sarah had learned to her dismay. As Anne took out a small blue beetle, a soft knock at the door announced another maid.

"Yes, come in," Sarah called out. "We are nearly finished here. Has my sister arrived for tea?"

The plump maid hurried forward and made a brief curtsy. "It is not Mrs. Heath-hill, my lady. Two gentlemen have come. It is Lord Delacroix and his friend Mr. Charles Locke."

"Who?" Sarah pushed up from her dressing table, knocking the blue beetle from Anne's fingers and upsetting three vials of *eau de parfum.* "But I do not wish to see Mr. Locke! Lord Delacroix has done this. Oh, I cannot believe it. Insufferable man!"

"Do you speak of Lord Delacroix as insufferable, madam?" Anne asked.

"Yes! No! Both of them! How dare they conspire against me in this way!" Sarah clenched her fists in frustration. She would have no choice but to greet the men. But, oh, how infuriating!

Since the encounter at the duke's reception, Delacroix had not ceased in insisting that Charles Locke must be made to apologize for his rude accusations. Prudence and Mary had agreed with him. Nothing Sarah would say could mollify any of them, and now it had come to this! She would have to see Charles again and look at him . . . and remember . . . and regret. . . .

"Polly, please tell the two gentlemen I shall be down momentarily," she said, her stomach in knots. "Instruct Cook to put on more tea. And take the men's hats but not their coats, for that will show them that I mean for them both to go away as soon as possible."

"Madam?"

"Oh, take their coats, too!" Hands fluttering, Sarah rushed to her closet and flung open the door. "Anne, where is my sister? I must make Prudence do all the talking, for I cannot bear to hear what either of those thoughtless louts has to say. Oh, dear, this pink shawl I have on is far too happy for him. Where is Pru?"

"Your sister went into the garden to cut lavender," Anne replied. "Shall I send for her?"

"No, but make certain she is in the drawing room before me, for then she will have engaged the men in conversation already. What do you think of this blue shawl, Anne? Is it not more severe than the pink?"

The maid blinked. "It is very nice, my lady."

"Nice? Then what of this brown one? It is dull enough, I think. Yes, it will do nicely."

"You wish to appear dull, madam?"

"Very dull. And severe. And disinterested. Perhaps the gray one would do better?"

"The brown is quite severe. And terribly dull."

"Good." Sarah tossed the filmy pink lace shawl she had been wearing onto a chair and pulled the brown one over her shoulders. "What do you think now, Anne?"

The maid pursed her lips. "You look very . . . dull?"

"Excellent." Sarah paused for a moment, trying to calm herself. She ought to pray. This was the time she needed God's guidance the most. He had allowed Charles Locke into her life for a purpose, and that purpose was clear. The man had been intended as a test. Could Sarah keep to her resolve? Would she be obedient to her understanding of biblical truth? On the ship, she had successfully warded him off. At the reception, God had revealed the man's true nature to Sarah. And now she must face him with solemnity and grace, dismissing him from her heart once and for all.

"If you please, madam," Anne spoke up, "may I suggest that perhaps Mr. Locke has come to apologize. You told me how he had offended you, and it would be proper for him to ask for your forgiveness."

Sarah shook her head. "Charles Locke may have come to make amends, but it is not of his own volition. Lord Delacroix conspired with my sisters to force the man to publicly confess all his wrongdoings. I have heard them plotting, for they have conducted all their schemes in my presence."

"Schemes?" Anne asked.

"Delacroix declares that Mr. Locke must be *made* to apologize. Prudence concurs. She believes that if I forgive him, then I will be more cheery. Mary thinks that Mr. Locke ought to be thrown in jail —"

"Oh, dear! His offense cannot be as bad as that, can it?" The maid swallowed and lowered her head. "Forgive me, my lady. I should not have interrupted."

Aware of the devastating effect that Anne's father's imprisonment had had on that family, Sarah took the young woman's hand. "No, no. It is all right. My sister Mary is always too quick to censure. I have prevailed upon everyone to be sensible. I shall be well enough, I assure you, once I am on my way to India again."

"Yes, madam. I shall send for your sister."

The maid's expression told Sarah that Anne felt exactly as everyone else did. The very notion that Sarah would return to the Orient had sent her sisters into a greater furor than ever before. Now Charles Locke had been dragged to Belgravia to humble himself before her. As Anne hurried out the door to make certain that Prudence was settled in the drawing room with the gentlemen, Sarah dropped to her knees by the chair near the wardrobe. Taking the filmy pink shawl into her hands, she bowed her head and pressed the lace fabric against her eyes.

"Make me an instrument of Thy peace, dear Lord," she prayed. "Help me to forgive Charles, if he has come for that purpose. And please make him go away again quickly, for I have withstood him as long as I possibly can. As for Pru and Mary and Delacroix, Father, please help them to understand that I do not take away the money to do harm but to bring joy. Let them understand that earthly wealth means nothing, but that all our treasures must be laid up in heaven. In the holy name of Jesus, I pray, amen."

She made to rise but sank down once again. "If he looks handsome, Father, can You please help me not to notice, for I am very lonely without him, and I have missed our conversations terribly, and I know that You wish me to be satisfied with You alone, which I am trying to do. But I must tell You, it is very hard when he looks at me with his blue eyes . . . and his very nice mouth . . . and —"

"Lady Delacroix? Oh, pardon me, madam!" Anne began backing out of the dressing room.

"It is all right, Anne. I am coming now." Sarah rose, gathered her skirts, adjusted the brown shawl, and hurried toward the door. "Is my sister in the drawing room?"

"She is, my lady. And the two gentlemen. Mr. Locke is fearful dashing, if I may say so, madam. Were I you, I should wear the pink shawl."

Sarah paused. Then she drew the brown shawl closer around her shoulders and stepped into the corridor.

The moment she entered the drawing room, Charles knew he was lost to her again. Mrs. Sarah Carlyle had returned. Dressed in a plain shawl, a simple white gown, and a pair of kidskin slippers, she gave little indication that there ever had been a Lady Delacroix. How beautiful she was. How gentle and lovely and perfect.

As she stepped forward to greet him, Charles could hardly restrain himself. One look into her soft brown eyes, and he would fail in his mission. A touch of her fingertips, and once again he would fall to his knees and beg her to marry him.

Hang Lady Delacroix and the money and society and every other obstacle that stood in their way! Let him hold her and love her and cherish her forever!

"Good afternoon, Mr. Locke," she said, dipping a slight curtsy. "I see you have discovered Trenton House. You are welcome, of course."

Hardly giving him a glance, she headed for the settee upon which her sister sat, and Charles found himself bowing to thin air. On her way across the room, Sarah tipped her head at Lord Delacroix, who also made an empty bow, and then she seated herself so close to Miss Watson that their shoulders touched. Picking up an embroidery hoop, Sarah took the needle and began to stitch a monogram as though her very life depended upon its completion.

"I made so bold as to invite Mr. Locke to accompany me in calling upon you," Delacroix spoke up. "He informed me that he wished to speak to you, madam."

Sarah's brow furrowed as she focused upon her embroidery. "I did not know the two of you had become such fast friends. Upon our last conversation, Lord Delacroix, you said you had never met Mr. Locke."

In the ensuing silence, Charles knew he could keep still no longer. "Lord Delacroix called at my house for the first time today," he told her. "He made clear that I had caused you pain with my words at Lord

Marston's reception, Mrs. . . . Lady Delacroix. I felt I must express my regret to you in person."

"I see," she said, awarding him with a brief glance and the hint of a smile. "How very kind. I accept your apology, Mr. Locke, if indeed that is what it is. There. I do hope we may not keep you overlong, for I believe you must be a busy man. Mary comes to tea, does she not, sister? I wonder what can be keeping her."

Charles knew he had been dismissed. So, that was the end of it. Sarah had no feeling left for him, and she wanted him out of her house and her life. He could hardly blame her, and it was no wonder she felt angry.

But he was wrong there, Charles realized. Sarah's anger had been vented at the reception, and now he merited only her cold disdain. He should go.

Yet Delacroix had commissioned him with a task. He was to mollify Sarah. Calm her. And then talk reason to her. He must try to convince her to abandon her goal of spending all her father's money on missionary endeavors. But how could he proceed? She refused even to look at him.

"Mr. Locke, my sister tells us that you and she had many conversations aboard the *Queen Elinor*," Miss Watson said in an affable tone. "I understand you were very friendly together."

"She was of great assistance to me," Charles confirmed, feeling as though they were speaking of someone absent from the room. "I should never have recovered without your assistance, Lady Delacroix."

Sarah stitched in silence, swallowing now and then as if something were lodged in her throat. Charles could hardly make himself sit still any longer. Obviously he could have no influence on her, and she was wishing him gone with every fiber of her being.

"Were you not to have your arm amputated if not for my sister?" Miss Watson spoke up. "I think it very good of you to save it for him, Sarah."

"Leg," Sarah muttered. "It was his leg."

"Oh, it was a leg you nearly lost, Mr. Locke! Even worse!" Miss Watson let out a breath. "I cannot imagine losing any part of myself. I should go mad at once. I am fond of riding, you know, Mr. Locke, and I believe it must be quite impossible if one were missing bits and pieces of oneself. Do you like riding, sir?"

"Yes, madam. It is a favorite occupation of mine."

"Well, then! We must all go into the country and stay a week or two at your estate, Delacroix. We could ride, make picnics, and take long walks. I can think of nothing I should like more than to visit Bamberfield House. What do you say to it, Sarah?"

"I am much occupied at the moment, sister," she answered. "This morning I booked passage to India. My departure is less than a month from now."

"Less than a month? Sarah, you have hardly been home a fortnight! What can you mean by sailing off again? Do you care so little for us? for Mary and me?"

"You know I adore you both, Pru," she spoke in a low voice. "I have settled you very well, and now I must see to other tasks."

"Do you suppose that all we want from you is a settlement?" By now, Miss Watson had raised herself to a fine flurry of emotion. Her bright pink cheeks and sparkling eyes fairly glowed. "You are the only sister that Mary and I have besides each other, and we cannot bear to see you go away again so soon!"

"You have many friends," Sarah said.

"But we want you! Speak to her, Delacroix. Tell her she cannot go!"

"I am hardly in a position to order your sister about," Delacroix said. "But I do understand Miss Watson's dismay. By departing after such a short stay, my lady, you deprive our society of its finest ornament."

"Oh, good heavens, Delacroix," Sarah cried. "What is it you want of me? Have I not settled enough upon my sisters? Or do you feel yourself bereft of income, too? Very well, then, I shall speak to my solicitor directly and see that you are given enough per annum to live comfortably. But do not flatter and cajole or I —"

"Madam, I believe your sister is sincere in what she says," Charles broke in. Unable to bear Sarah's distress and ill humor any longer, he stood. "At Lord Marston's reception, I observed Miss Watson for some time, and I believe her attentiveness toward you is due to honest affection. She is younger than you by several years, and she has neither mother to instruct her nor father to guide her path. Her sister, Mrs. Heathhill, is much occupied with her husband and home, as any good wife must be. If Miss Watson begs you to stay in England, her desire arises from a sincere need for your assistance and company."

"Mr. Locke," Sarah said, rising from the settee, "you know my sister far less well than I do, and her motives cannot be understood by you in the least."

"I know that both she and Lord Delacroix are greatly concerned about your state of unhappy restlessness. When I saw you last, your agitation was obvious."

"And why not? You were abusing me to my face, sir!"

"For that I have voiced regret, and you have forgiven me. Or so I thought."

She pursed her lips and looked away.

Charles took a step toward her. "Madam, I realize I offended you greatly that evening and without reason. By your appearance and air at the reception, I misjudged you. I condemned you. I sentenced you. And I took it upon myself to exact your punishment. It was wrong of me, and if my apology has been inadequate, I make it again. Forgive me, please."

Sarah turned away and walked to the window. "I have forgiven you, sir. Now you are no longer needed here."

"Perhaps not needed, but Lord Delacroix called upon me because I am wanted. Neither he nor your two loving sisters can understand the passion that drives you. They have some little hope that I may be able to assist in the situation, for they are greatly concerned for your safety. For your health. For your well-being."

"For my money!" she hissed, swinging

around. "That is what they want. That is what everyone wants. You most of all, I do not doubt. Now that you know who I am, you see a way to finance your tea scheme. Well, I shall not do it, sir. The money is God's, and to Him it will go!"

"Do see reason, madam," Charles implored, crossing to her. "No one wishes to rob you. No one wants to take away what duly belongs to God. But here in England are many destitute and hungry people. The ill and needy throng the streets of London and languish in poorly heated cottages throughout the countryside. Build schools in this country, dear lady. See to the needs of the blind and lame in England. Do not take the joy of your presence from those who love you so very dearly. As for Miss Watson, her need for your wisdom and guidance is great indeed. Can you at all accept my words?"

She held up a hand to stop his approach. "Stand back from me, sir. I hear you, of course. But I trust you no more than I trust any other man."

"What have I done to make you doubt me so? Aboard ship, I frankly told you all my feelings. I did the same the night of the reception. On both occasions, I misunderstood certain aspects of your identity. But I have never mistaken your true character. Nor have you been misled in mine. Why do you distrust me, then?"

She faced him. "How can I not? I know your true motives. You made your choice, Mr. Locke. You chose your tea company."

Feeling as though he had been struck once again by a musket ball, Charles bowed his head. "I did."

"And you would choose it again."

He nodded. "I confess, I would. I believe it is a man's duty to employ himself usefully and productively. For myself, I have always held to the worthy aim of building a successful trade. I should be ashamed to sit idly by while others labor to better themselves. Nor could I endure the disgrace of reducing myself to poverty. God gave me these hands, this mind, and the will to work. To the best of my ability, I shall strive to establish a successful enterprise, increase my material worth, provide for myself and my family, and one day leave behind a substantial legacy. I cannot deny it, nor shall I make any attempt to deceive you in that regard. My statements on the *Queen Elinor* were honest and, I believe, honorable. I have not changed."

"Then your aims are not my own, and you comprehend me no better than do my sisters or Lord Delacroix. The things of God are foolishness to the world. To everyone, it is unthinkable that I should give away my inheritance. Prudence, Mary, Delacroix — and now you — all go to great lengths to dissuade me from what appears senseless. Perhaps even insane."

"I do not think you have lost your mind," Charles said, turning to the window in an effort to keep the other two in the room from hearing. "I believe you are just in your desires, my dear Sarah. There is much reason in what you propose. In fact, since our words aboard ship, I have searched the Scriptures myself in an effort to understand what God teaches on the matters of wealth and social advancement."

"You have?" Her brown eyes misted as she stepped closer. "Oh, Charles. How do you get on?"

"With difficulty. I find much contradiction, for in one passage God blesses those He loves with land and crops and great wealth. Yet in another passage, Christ points to the birds of the air and the flowers of the field and tells us to trust God to feed and clothe us. Once, Christ praises the man who takes his talents and multiplies them, and He censures the one who buries his money. But elsewhere, Christ orders His disciples to go out to preach with only the clothes on their backs. It is a theological matter not easily understood, Sarah, and I wonder that you have worked it all out for yourself. If indeed you have."

"I have had no need to work it out, for I have seen it enacted before me like a great, tragic pageant. My father gave his all to gain wealth and prestige. My husband did the same. Both are dead. What good did their labors do them? None at all. What have money and the name Delacroix done for me? Nothing good whatsoever. How one makes use of wealth is not a theological matter but a practical one. Christ clearly instructed us not to lay up treasures on earth but only in heaven. That is what I mean to do, Charles."

"Then why not do it in England? Your poor sister is nearly mad with anguish over you. And Lord Delacroix suffers great concern for your well-being. Stay here and relieve their agonies. Surely you cannot find Scripture that insists your money go to beggars in India."

She looked down at her hands. "I do not wish to stay in England."

Unable to hold back, Charles touched her arm. "Sarah? Why can you not stay? Why must you run away again from those who love you?"

"Charles, please go now; I beg you. I have heard what you say, and you may assure Delacroix and my sisters that I do take their feelings into account. You have accomplished your aim in coming here. Please . . . please . . . leave me in peace."

"Dearest Sarah," Charles said, "do not think ill of me when I tell you that your presence gives great pleasure to many. You believe that your sisters' primary desire has been the size of their share in your father's estate. You suspect that Lord Delacroix and your society want your company only because it may somehow benefit them. But you are mistaken in this. You have much to offer your family and friends. I knew you once when your character was unhindered by the trappings of wealth and prestige, and you saw my honest response."

Unwilling to leave her until he had said all that pressed him, Charles lifted his chin. "I loved you, Sarah. My feelings are unchanged. Though you choose to believe I am capable only of selfish actions, I know my heart. I adore you, as do many others. Stay in England, then, and accept the genuine affection due you. If, as you say, you cannot trust me, then permit me to prove myself to you. Allow me to be your friend, and you will observe my constancy. But if you can no longer bear to see me, I shall say nothing more and be gone from your life forever."

Lifting a hand, she tucked a tendril of brown hair behind her ear. Her eyes, which had softened as he spoke, now focused on the bustling street outside Trenton House. Now she turned to him. "How am I ever to know the difference, Charles? How can I tell what distinguishes genuine affection from false flattery? How can I be sure that the words and actions directed to me arise from real compassion and not from concealed greed?"

She shook her head in frustration as she continued. "In London, I am not Mrs. Carlyle. I am Lady Delacroix, and I am expected to dress and behave accordingly. Everyone here knows of my fortune, and how can they remain unaffected by it? I must attend this ball and that dinner. I must call on this countess and that marchioness. I must go to court and make my presence felt among the royals at St. James's. Laces and silks and satins will always adorn my gowns. The jewels my father and husband bequeathed me are required to be worn. Everywhere I go, I shall appear as Lady Delacroix, and I shall be Lady Delacroix.

And then all my hope of happiness will be lost forever."

Charles contemplated Sarah's words, knowing she spoke the truth. The *ton* would be unable to see beyond her title and wealth. Even Lord Delacroix, who had professed such prodigious care for Sarah, had made it clear to Charles that his greatest worry was her determination to rid herself of her father's money. He wanted a share of it. Her sisters wanted their portion.

And Charles? He wanted the money, too, of course.

How could he deny it? He had come to Trenton House intending to apologize, to convince Sarah to stay in England, and eventually to receive compensation for his efforts from Delacroix. Charles was no better than the rest of them. Though he did love Sarah as much as before, the knowledge of her fortune had affected him. Could he ever see her again without thinking of it? Could any friendship between them remain untainted?

Unresolved on the matter, he bowed. "I cannot teach you how to discern truth from falsehood," he said. "I can only beg you to remain in England. And now I must take my own leave of you. May God be with you wherever you go, dearest, loveliest lady.

Good day."

Without waiting to hear her speak again, Charles turned away and made for the door. His chest ached from the strain of the encounter. Though he had made the journey without his cane, he now felt the need for its support.

Had he spoken the truth to Sarah, or had he lied? Did he love her for who she was? Or did he desire her money? Could she find happiness in London, or was she better off roaming the world and dispensing the gifts with which God had blessed her?

He made his brief farewell to Miss Watson and Lord Delacroix and then stepped into the foyer. As he donned his hat and coat, Charles knew he must not see Sarah again. He must leave her as he had loved her — pure and untainted by any wrongful desire. If he came into her presence once more, he would be assailed by the same sins that so beset all who tried to love her — covetousness, greed, jealousy. He was not good enough for her. He never could be.

EIGHT

"It is quite unfair! I never have seen the man, and you have seen him twice." Mary fanned herself crossly. "And do not look at me askance, husband, for I have every right to judge for myself whether Mr. Locke is handsome."

"He is terribly handsome," Prudence said. "No one could ever contradict me in that."

Sarah poured out her third cup of tea and tried to endure the annoying chatter of her sisters. Not five minutes after Charles Locke went away, Mary and her husband had arrived at Trenton House. The conversation immediately took a shrill turn as Prudence admired and esteemed their recent guest, while Mary pouted at having missed yet another opportunity to evaluate the man herself.

Mr. Locke was all the talk of the *ton,* Mary informed the others, for his adventure with the Malabar pirates had inspired and amazed everyone at the Marston reception. All the gentlemen thought him brave for having fought so boldly. Indeed, they came very near to actually envying his grievous wounds. All the ladies considered him prodigiously tall and well formed, as handsome a man as ever was seen, and certainly not beneath their interest despite his father's having been nothing more than old Lord Marston's steward.

"I found him rather dark," Delacroix observed. His own heritage had disposed him to the fair complexion and blond hair of his Saxon ancestors — never mind his decidedly French title. Sarah observed that her nephew by marriage had outfitted himself today in an elegant gray tailcoat with two rows of pearl buttons, a fine high neckcloth, and a pair of silk breeches. His appearance had put to shame Charles's common black suit with its green waistcoat and straight trousers. Perhaps Delacroix had intended it that way, for he now seemed determined to malign the man he had so lately claimed as a friend.

"Did you not find Mr. Locke uncommonly tan, Miss Watson?" he asked.

"He has been at sea, sir," she retorted. "Of course he is tan. He will get over it, no doubt, though I do think his being so brown shows his eyes to good advantage. They are very blue, Mary."

"Oh!" She crossed her arms. "Why could we not have arrived sooner? But of course my husband *must* speak to his butler on matters of great import."

"Yes, I must," John Heathhill spoke up. "We are near to an insurrection among the footmen due to the many dinners my dear Mrs. Heathhill has insisted upon hosting in these past weeks. Our attendants have had so few nights off as to put them at the verge of revolt."

"They are all drunkards," Mary said. "If you had employed better footmen, Mr. Heathhill, they would understand that your wife must give dinners during the season. The servants will all have time away when we go into the country again."

"I think we should go into the country next week," Prudence spoke up. "Delacroix will have us at his house at Bamberfield, will you not, sir? And you must invite Mr. Locke to be one of the party, for then Mary may observe him herself and cease complaining that she has been treated unfairly."

"I should be very happy to open the country house to our party," Delacroix concurred. He turned to Sarah. "What do you say to it, madam? Will you accompany us to Bamberfield, or do you still mean to pack yourself off to India?"

Sarah set her cup back into its saucer. How could she explain what had come over her during her conversation with Charles? It had been strange and wonderful — almost as though God had spoken to her through him.

In Charles's eyes, she had read real concern. His face had been consumed with her, as if he could not bear to turn away for even a moment. His words rang with honesty and truth. Everything about him — from the touch of his hand on her arm to the tone of his voice — had given Sarah clarity concerning the most troublesome aspect of her situation. Through Charles's behavior toward her, she at last had realized how to distinguish genuine affection from flattery. She must simply look steadfastly at the one who spoke. Who could meet her eyes and yet deliver a stream of falsehoods? Who could gaze into her face without revealing ingenuousness?

Peace had descended upon Sarah even as Charles walked away from her. He did care. He would not lie to her. Though he could not give himself to her aim of poverty, yet he could be her friend. And that was enough. More than enough.

"I believe I shall stay in England for a while longer," Sarah informed the gathering. "I should very much like to spend Christmas at home. And I have missed the arrival of spring these past two years. Perhaps I shall delay my journey until next summer."

"Sarah!" Prudence threw herself from her chair onto her sister's neck. "Oh, I am so happy to hear this news! Good for Mr. Locke! He has convinced you to stay with us after all. There, Delacroix, what did I tell you? She adores him, and nothing he can say is ever wrong."

"Prudence, upon my word, you are too silly!" Sarah exclaimed. "Mr. Locke merely discussed my situation in a reasonable manner, and I began to understand the sense in what he said. That is all."

"It was his blue eyes," Prudence told Mary. "Wait until you see them. They are the color of sapphires. No, that is too dark, for they have a sort of glow. Like that ribbon on your gown. But brighter. The butterfly in Sarah's hair is the exact shade. Turn your head, Sarah. Look, Mary. Can you imagine? No woman could resist him if he gazed at her the way he gazes at Sarah."

"I fear I cannot see what such a man finds to like in your appearance, my dear sister,"

Mary observed. "You looked as ordinary as a pumpkin when you came back from your journey. And despite all my efforts, you are no better today. That shawl is hideous! Is it not appalling, Mr. Heathhill?"

"I imagine Mr. Locke gives little attention to Lady Delacroix's shawls, my dear Mrs. Heathhill," her husband replied. "No doubt he is enthralled by her elevated position and awed by the rumors of her vast wealth. You must give my wife little heed, madam, for she is convinced that appearance is everything — no matter how I try to teach her to look beyond it to the real worth of a person."

"Are my elevated position and vast wealth the sum total of my real worth, Mr. Heathhill?" Sarah asked. "If so, I shall soon have no value to you whatever."

"Then you mean to carry on with your charity?" Delacroix asked her. "I had hoped Locke might have talked you out of that as well."

"No, sir. I am unchanged in my resolve."

"I am sorry to hear it. No one who really knows you can fail to value your keen wit, your kindness, and of course, your beauty. But certainly your advantages in life add greatly to their effect."

Sarah smiled. "Wealth then, must be the

greatest cosmetic of all, for until my father's death, I was considered no beauty at all. Now I find I am the ornament of my society."

"You are that, madam," Delacroix said, "though I assure you that you have always been among the loveliest women of my acquaintance."

"How happy for me," Sarah informed him brightly, "for I shall take great comfort in that knowledge when I am poor. No, I have not altered my aim of reducing myself to indigence. Nor have I changed in any way other than deciding that I might stay in England until next summer. But if my sisters can talk of nothing beyond Mr. Locke's fine eyes, I may be forced to go sooner than that after all."

"Oh, dear, let us plan our country outing, then," Prudence spoke up quickly. "We must go away tomorrow, for it promises to be a fine day."

"Tomorrow?" Mary cried. "Upon my word, Pru, I cannot leave town on such short notice."

"Too many dinner parties," her husband muttered.

"We must simply wait until next week. Shutting down a house is not an easy matter, as you will learn when you are married.

I should think next Tuesday will be soon enough. And, Delacroix, what would you say to adding several others to the party? We have only three men now, and that is not enough to play at whist."

"Three?" he said.

"You, my husband, and Mr. Locke, of course. You cannot fail to invite the man, for I insist upon judging his eyes for myself. And take care to ask one or two ladies who can sing. I cannot fault my sisters' skills at the pianoforte, but oh! Prudence cannot hold a high note, and Sarah's range is far too low for all the best songs. I should think the Dalrymples would add nicely to our company. He is so clever at charades, and she is tolerable at whist. Now, the Borough-tons are a lovely couple. She sings like a bird. He drinks too much, true, but she quite makes up for it with her voice."

"Mary, before you invite any or all of these people," Sarah said, "perhaps you ought to seek out the opinions of others already included in the party. I prefer a quiet gather-ing, and I imagine Pru will wish to spend her time out-of-doors rather than singing and playing cards. As for Mr. Locke, I prefer that he not come at all. You would gawk at him, Mary, and Prudence would flirt, and I should not be in the least comfortable in his presence."

"Because you adore him," Prudence teased. "And he adores you still. Sarah, you really ought to write to Miss Pickworth in *The Tattler.* I know she would give you good advice, for everyone admires her wit. In yesterday's column, she counseled a poor woman who had written in about her husband — a 'dastardly duke' and his 'moneygrubbing, malevolent mistress,' as Miss Pickworth called them. Sadly, the duchess believes herself in love with the man, though he clearly wants little to do with her. What do you suppose Miss Pickworth suggested?"

"No one cares, Prudence," Mary retorted. "Except that she does have the most unnerving way of revealing the foibles and flaws of the *ton.* I consider her nothing but a malicious gossip."

"Of course Miss Pickworth is a gossip! And the very best sort, for no one who is truly silly can escape her censure. She advised the despondent duchess to remember that mistresses are temporary, but wives are permanent. The duchess is to do all in her power to expose the mistress for what she is, and then she is to go away with her husband on a tour of the Continent in order to rekindle their lost passion."

Mary snorted. "Lost passion indeed. What

sort of duke would marry for love in the first place? Miss Pickworth — whoever she is — had better lay down her pen and cease her inane ramblings at once."

"You fear she may expose you to ridicule, Mary. One of your brilliant parties may become a hot pot of scandal."

"I never invite scandalous people to my parties," her sister snapped back.

"Nevertheless, we should all take heed of Miss Pickworth's prose. Sarah ought to write to her about Mr. Locke. Admit it, sister. You are both violently in love, and nothing but the greatest restraint can keep you apart."

"Nonsense!" Sarah scoffed. "Mr. Locke and I are as different in every way as two people possibly can be. He has dreams of a tea-shipping enterprise that will afford him a grand house and a full complement of attendants. I mean to shed all such trappings."

"He is a tradesman," Delacroix added. "She is a lady. His father was a steward. Her husband was a peer. He resides in Threadneedle Street. She makes her home in Belgravia. They have little in common. Miss Watson, you ought to encourage your sister toward a man more suitable."

"And whom would you suggest, sir?" Prudence asked. "You are a rover, as everyone knows, and your friends are cads. I have been out in society all season, and though I find plenty of men handsome enough to wear on my arm, yet none are worthy of Sarah. She is religious, as you well know, and she means to give away her money if we cannot prevent it. Who could ever desire such a creature but Mr. Locke, who loved her before he knew her as Lady Delacroix? He is the only gentleman fit to have her, and I mean to see that he gets her as soon as may be."

"Prudence!" Sarah exclaimed. "You speak as though I am a prize to be won — and an unwelcome prize at that. On the contrary, I believe I am moving toward the sort of perfection that God requires in each of us. He will be pleased with me, and that is what matters."

"But Mr. Locke —"

"Mr. Locke and I are completely unfit for each other. I shall have you know that I intend *never* to marry, Pru, so you may put such nonsense out of your head at once. As you rightly say, no one would want me, or could want me, in the condition in which I mean to place myself."

"Some impoverished minister might," Mary suggested. "Honestly, Sarah, you are too pious, as I have told you many times.

Keep your money, and find your happiness where you can. If you are deceived in marriage, what of it? Let your husband have his little amusements, while you make your own pleasures. Surely you would not be the first or the last wealthy woman to manage it."

"Thank you for your kind advice, sisters." Sarah stood. "I prefer to live single all my life rather than marry a man who cannot love me as I am. And as you now all know, not even poor Mr. Locke from Threadneedle Street can do that."

Taking up the embroidery with which she had begun the afternoon, Sarah excused herself and made for the garden. Let them sort it all out for themselves, she thought as she stepped onto the stone portico. They found her ridiculous and infuriating and unfathomable. But she knew her heart.

As Charles descended the steps at Lincoln's Inn in the Borough of Camden the following Monday, he reflected with satisfaction — though not with total joy — upon the situation in which he now found himself.

Since boyhood, he had cherished the dream of establishing a profitable enterprise. As he matured, he liked to picture himself as a sort of benevolent conqueror, one who would dominate in his chosen field — yet bring benefit and comfort to those beneath him. While still in school, Charles had learned of the Parliament act abolishing the East India Company monopoly and opening trade to the Orient. He had conceived the idea of building a trade based upon tea, and he had increased his vision from a simple London street shop to include warehouses, ships, and plantations in China.

Upon hearing his son's plan, James Locke had embraced it at once, for it meshed beautifully with his own aims of promoting Charles to the wealth and prestige that neither he nor his ancestors had enjoyed. James endorsed the entire idea, admired it in every way, and saw to it that his son was given the education such an endeavor would require. At Cambridge, Charles had pursued every course of study that could advance his goals. Finance and accounting interested him greatly, but he also attended lectures in literature, philosophy, science, and civic law. The allowance settled upon James Locke at his retirement had provided the final building block for the platform from which to launch the tea plan into reality.

Charles had sailed for China with every high hope in the world. And then the pirates attacked. The gold was stolen. He was injured. The journey to the Orient was disrupted. All but his life was lost.

At last accepting the harsh truth that his original plans must be set aside, Charles had made use of his convalescence to reexamine his education and interests. Determined to overcome his recent setbacks, he elected to plot a different course in life. The tea company must be forgotten, at least for the time being. His father refused to believe that banking would elevate Charles to the financial and social stature deemed essential to success. Thus, Charles decided to become a barrister-at-law.

The Friday after calling on Sarah Carlyle, Lady Delacroix, at Trenton House, he had taken a carriage to Lincoln's Inn to make his application. One of the four Inns of Court in London from which barristers were called to the bar, the law school was situated advantageously just across the road from the Royal Courts of Justice. Based upon his previous excellent marks at Cambridge and a recommendation from Laurent Chouteau, the duke of Marston, Charles was interviewed and accepted into the law school forthwith. He understood that this new venture would put him into debt and must certainly bring hardship to his father. Yet he became wholly resolved upon it.

He could not have the woman he loved. His chosen career was closed to him. His physical health remained compromised. But, lest he begin to wish he had gone down with the *Tintagel,* Charles chose to attack doubt and despair with all the courage he had displayed against the pirates. He would learn to live without Sarah's sweet smile to uplift him, without her unwavering faith to bolster him. He would set aside — but not utterly abandon — his dream of a successful trade. And he would rise to a position of rank and privilege that would bring pride to his father and honor upon his lineage.

As Charles attended his first lectures at Lincoln's Inn on this bright Monday in midsummer, any uncertainties that might have remained were erased. He had chosen wisely. Within the year, he would be admitted to the faculty of advocates. For a circuit or two, he would hold briefs in the Court of Session, where he would either defend or prosecute the accused. Not long thereafter, he would serve as junior counsel in making appeals to the House of Lords. Five years from now, he would be called to the English bar.

In the meantime, Charles would continue his friendship with Alexander Chouteau, younger son of the duke of Marston. If, as all supposed, the older son, Ruel, truly had been killed in America, Sir Alexander would one day assume the duchy from his father. Acquainting himself with politicians, Charles would make every effort to be seen in society, and he would bolster his reputation by writing and publishing scholarly works. He would familiarize himself with international law and gain experience in the prize courts. This course of action must lead successful merchants to retain him as legal counsel. With all this, it could not be long before his influential friends in society, politics, and the trades would secure him a seat in Parliament.

In such an event, Charles would settle his debts, secure contentment for his aging father, bring worthy bills and legal measures before the House of Commons, and — at long last — found the trade upon which he might make his fortune. With his wealth and reputation secure, perhaps then he would seek to complete the only emptiness remaining in his life.

Sarah would be living in China or India by that time, and so many years would have elapsed that he surely must have forgotten her altogether. Another woman would touch his heart and please his eye. He would satisfy her requirements in a husband. They would marry and begin a family. And all would be well.

Taking comfort in the vision of his happy life, Charles could not have been more surprised to find Henry Carlyle, Lord Delacroix, awaiting him outside the gates of Lincoln's Inn that very afternoon. Wearing an expensive wool suit, a glossy beaver-skin top hat, and a pair of shiny black leather boots, the man stood beside his carriage. The vehicle boasted gold fittings and glass windows, was attended by a pair of liveried footmen, and was pulled by a team of pure white geldings. It completed an image that caused men to gawk and brought gasps of admiration from women passing on their way to market. For a gentleman Charles knew to be living on little more than the glory of his title and the kindness of his uncle's widow, Delacroix certainly took great pains to look important.

"How do you do, Lord Delacroix?" Charles addressed him, bowing deeply.

Delacroix responded in kind. "I am well, Mr. Locke. And you?"

"Most content, sir. By your discovering me at Lincoln's Inn, I must assume you visited my father this morning."

"Indeed, and I found him in high spirits.

He is most pleased with your improving health and your decision to pursue a career in lawmaking. And when he learned the reason for my call, his delight increased all the more. I wish to invite you to join our party at Bamberfield, my country house near Reading. It is not far, and you are welcome to accompany us by coach. One of our number is most particularly insistent upon your presence in our number."

Charles's hand tightened on the books he carried. "I cannot think who you mean."

"Miss Prudence Watson is determined to ride out with you once we are come into the country, for she informs us that you enjoy nothing better than a fine horse and a pleasant day."

"Miss Watson?" Charles pictured the lively young lady with her sumptuous curves and bright smile. He frowned. "I fear she exaggerates my enthusiasm for the sport. Do give her my thanks for the invitation, and inform her that were I otherwise unoccupied I might accept it. As it is, I am obliged to attend lectures at the Inns all this week and the next."

"Then you must join us for the weekend." Lord Delacroix held up a hand. "Do not protest, Locke, for your objections are all in vain. Your father already informed me that you have no previous obligations."

"Other than to study." Charles gestured at his books. "My time will be much occupied in reading, sir. I assure you of my gratitude, but I absolutely cannot leave London even for a day."

Delacroix pondered a moment. "Sir, may I be so bold as to ask that we might speak together in private? Come, I see a teahouse just at the corner. Let us walk there together and confer on this matter."

Though he would have liked to protest, Charles could see no polite way to decline further discussion. But if Delacroix believed that he could say or do anything to persuade Charles to spend an entire weekend in Sarah's company, he was sadly mistaken. Sarah's lovely serenity, her pure heart, her genuine speech, and her tender care of all those she encountered had so endeared her to him that he could not imagine finding any woman to take her place in his affections. To be in the same room with her and bear the knowledge that she would never be his was unthinkable.

As they approached the teahouse, Charles felt he could only be perfectly honest with Delacroix. "Lest you suppose you can alter my opinion, sir," he stated, "I assure you that I will never accept your kind invitation.

I cannot be comfortable in any situation in which Lady Delacroix is present. Nor can I imagine that she has approved my participation in your outing to Bamberfield. You must understand that our acquaintance is of a most peculiar nature. From our first meeting, an unexpected intimacy was forced upon us — an intimacy from which it is now necessary, yet impossible, to retreat."

"Intimacy?" Delacroix scowled at the term. "What can you mean by this?"

"Sir, the lady was my nurse, my maidservant, my caretaker. She bathed my wounds, combed my hair, sang to me, listened to my fevered ravings, and soothed my angry spirit. She heard my confessions. She witnessed my rage. She bore my sorrows. In every way she did for me what I could not do for myself. Not for me only, I assure you, for she was available to all the injured who had been rescued from the *Tintagel.* And yet . . . between us there grew some special affection. We became more than acquaintances. More than mere associates. We were companions, you see. Friends."

"You came to love her, I understand," Delacroix said, holding out his arm to permit Charles to enter the teahouse first. "She informed her sisters that you proposed marriage."

Charles clenched his jaw as he removed his hat and stepped into the dimly lit room. If the proposal was indeed known by Sarah's sisters, everyone in London must now be aware of it. People would think him a fool — as he had been — to expect marriage to a woman of whom he knew so little. Yet how could anyone understand those precious days he and Sarah had spent together on the ship? Such warm companionship was rarely experienced even between a husband and wife. Bereft of it, he could hardly endure its absence. But Sarah had made her decision clear, and he knew her well enough to believe that nothing could change it.

The two men found a round table near the back of the room, where gentlemen sat about smoking pipes, sipping tea, and discussing everything from profitable commerce to the latest political scandal. Serving maids in white mobcaps and aprons bustled to and fro, pouring hot tea into cups for those who preferred it so, or into saucers for those from the old school. Much slurping and laughing and murmuring filled the chamber, and Charles welcomed the scent of sweet tea that permeated the walls and drifted around the thick, black beams overhead. The only light came from small, deep-set windows with diamond-paned glass and oil lamps that had stained the ceiling a dark, sooty brown. The tearoom was the ideal place for philosophizing, hatching schemes, and plotting villainy.

"I did propose marriage," Charles admitted, seating himself across from Delacroix. "I was summarily rejected, and that was the end of it. I care deeply for the woman I knew as Sarah Carlyle, but I fully comprehend that I can have no enduring friendship with Lady Delacroix. I am most sincere in assuring you that my presence at your country house would be difficult for both of us. Uncomfortable. Even reprehensible."

"But think what you say, sir." Delacroix leaned forward and lowered his voice. "Your unique and intimate friendship is a great asset. Though she is indifferent toward you in the matter of marriage, yet you do have influence over her. Before your visit to Trenton House, she was determined to return to Asia and distribute her fortune willy-nilly. No sooner had you departed Trenton House than she informed us all that she meant to stay in England until next summer."

Charles absorbed this news as a maid poured tea for himself and Delacroix. Lumps of sugar in a bowl and fresh hot milk in a creamer stood ready to be added. As he stirred, Charles pondered Delacroix's words. Sarah must have been swayed by their discussion to accept that her sisters truly loved her and would miss her companionship. She saw that she had no need to rush away. Perhaps she even believed she might find charities in England that would satisfy her requirements. But this did not indicate any special affection for Charles himself, nor did it lead him to believe that either of them could be comfortable together for an entire weekend.

"I am pleased to have been of some service with my recent visit," he told Delacroix. "I apologized to Lady Delacroix and was forgiven. Though I found it challenging to present arguments for her staying in England, you tell me she has accepted my reasoning. Good. Yet you asked one thing of me that can never be accomplished. I assure you, sir, that she will never be moved from her decision to distribute her fortune to the needy."

"Perhaps not now. But with the passage of time . . . and a change in circumstance . . . she may be persuaded."

"Speak plainly, Delacroix. I am not accustomed to intrigues."

The gentleman leaned back in his chair, turned his cup one way and then the other, and finally focused on Charles. "You are forthright, are you?"

"Absolutely."

"Excellent. Then I shall be frank also."

NINE

Charles studied the dark clumps of damp tea leaves at the bottom of his white cup. Upon these fragments plucked from a green bush, heated, fermented, dried, packed in chests, and shipped ten thousand miles across the ocean, he had meant to make his fortune. All his hope had been built upon so small a thing. Tea had become essential in England, and the demand was growing. Ladies drank it in drawing rooms; children in their nurseries; maids and footmen below stairs; and men in their clubs, their libraries, and their tearooms.

In every kitchen of the realm, teakettles whistled upon stoves. Teapots brewed the savory beverage while sandwiches, scones, and tarts were piled on plates to be served with it. The tea industry kept sailors and shipbuilders employed, potters and silversmiths busy, lace makers tatting away, and sugarcane plantations thriving.

Until recently, all this activity had been generated by the great machine of trade known as the East India Company. But now — only now — did common men have the opportunity to profit from the tiny brown leaves.

"Would you like more tea, sir?" a maid asked, holding a strainer over Charles's cup.

"I would indeed," he said, thinking how very literally he had meant it not so long ago. Tea, tea, and more tea. It was all he had wanted. All he had dreamed of.

As the maid poured Charles's cup full of rich, amber-colored liquid, Delacroix began to speak. "An acquaintance of mine was in attendance at Marston House when you outlined your plan to establish an independent tea-import company. At my gentlemen's club the following day, he related your idea with much enthusiasm. Among our party at the club was a man with whom you have a close friendship — Alexander Chouteau, son of the duke of Marston. Sir Alexander spoke highly of you, Locke, and he insisted you would make good on any endeavor to which you put your mind."

"I am honored to hear it," Charles said. "I should certainly say the same of him."

Delacroix smiled. "Sir Alexander and I are of a mind to invest in your tea company,

Mr. Locke. What do you say to that?"

The baron's words sent a jolt of surprise down Charles's spine. He had gone to the reception with the aim of finding investors, but he had considered the effort a failure. Was it possible he had succeeded after all? Pausing a moment before answering, he evaluated the proposal in light of all he knew about both men.

"I am honored at your interest, of course," he told Delacroix at last, "but there is not to be a tea company. As you must have heard, the gold intended to capitalize it was stolen when my ship fell prey to pirates in the Indian Ocean. To establish an enterprise such as the one I envision must require a substantial investment from its founders. And, sir, if I may be so bold, I confess that your financial situation is well-known to me."

"You have heard aright. Save my two properties and their contents, I am without means. Sir Alexander, of course, is a wealthy man and will have more when he inherits. But if I am able to secure a sum equal to his proposed investment, we are prepared to unite in underwriting your company."

Charles took a lump of sugar and stirred it into his tea. "May I inquire how you mean to secure such a sum, sir?"

"That is where you may play a part in your own fate, Locke." Again, the young man leaned forward. "Use your influence to help me win Lady Delacroix as my wife."

If Charles had been surprised before, now he was utterly astounded. "Your wife? You expect me to convince her of such a thing? Upon my word, that is an extraordinary suggestion in view of the fact that she flatly refused my own marriage proposal."

"Though I highly respect you, Mr. Locke, we can hardly be called equals. Lady Delacroix was once persuaded to wed her fortune to a title, and I believe she will come to see the value in it again. My influence and connections are great. The life I can offer her must be far more palatable than that she made with my uncle. He was much older and of a difficult — even inhospitable — nature. His character and reputation were nothing to my own, sir. My uncle was much taken with gambling and drink, and his marriage cannot have been a success. As you know, they had no children, and not long after his death, Lady Delacroix embarked upon this ridiculous quest."

Delacroix took a swallow of tea as if needing to steady himself before he continued. "I believe — as do many of my colleagues — that she was unhappily wed, and that this led her to think she must give away her fortune. But if she were married to me, she could only be happy. I am but three or four years her elder, and — I flatter myself — I am much admired in our society. Certainly I can woo her with great success and can make her life pleasant. In time, and with gentle coaxing, she may be convinced to abandon the aim of ridding herself of her fortune. Even if she is not, my position as her husband will permit me access to her funds, and with these I shall invest in your enterprise."

Charles could hardly suppress the strange mixture of laughter and anger that filled him. How incredible that this man believed himself capable of winning Sarah's hand! How preposterous to think that Charles could or would assist in such a match! The proposal was close to bribery. Yet it was so far-fetched as to be ridiculous.

Unwilling to give offense — though he had been greatly offended himself by Delacroix's oration — Charles occupied himself by adding another lump of sugar and a dollop of milk to his tea. Surely the man could not seriously believe Charles had so much influence over Sarah. She knew her own mind, and she had never hesitated to speak her opinions. Yet Delacroix would not have made the effort to seek him out unless he and Sarah's sisters believed that Charles could be of assistance.

Had he been correct in assuring Sarah of her sisters' love? Miss Watson, it seemed obvious, truly cared for her eldest sibling. But Charles had never met Mrs. Heathhill, nor did he have any idea of her feelings toward Sarah. And what of Delacroix? Clearly, he was interested only in the money his marriage would bring. He had said nothing of Sarah's beauty or intelligence or kindness — all the things Charles loved so dearly.

He agreed with Delacroix's reasoning in some ways. Both men had concluded that Sarah's unhappiness with her title and fortune resulted from her marriage to Lord Delacroix. Both felt certain she deserved a better life. Both decried her plan to travel to dangerous foreign realms and to divest herself of her property. She ought to stay in England, marry well, and find joy in a husband, children, friends, and perhaps charity work.

Charles was incapable of providing Sarah with such a life — by her own statement and by Delacroix's. That truth could not be denied even by Charles. Sarah rejected him because he was unwilling to surrender his ambitions. Delacroix rightly insisted that if she were willing to keep her money, Charles was far too poor and his status was much too low for him to stand up with her in society. She would be subjected to gossip and ridicule. He could bring her no prestige, no title, no fortune, no real connections — nothing of worth that she did not have already. Nothing . . . save that he loved her desperately.

But Sarah was not romantic. In fact, she craved the most unromantic life imaginable — that of a pauper. Could Charles change her mind? Ought he even to try?

He studied the gentleman who sat across from him. Though not wealthy, Delacroix had other advantages. He was young, strong, and of sound mind. With his golden curls and fair complexion, he was surely thought handsome by the ladies. His title made him a peer and gave him lands and houses enough to keep a wife content even if she did manage to give away all her fortune. The sale of Delacroix's London home or a parcel of his country estate would bring more than enough to provide for a family. And if Sarah would retain her fortune, she would enjoy the comfort of the two residences she had known as the previous Lord Delacroix's wife. There was much to be said for the security and pleasure to be found in the familiar.

"Come, Locke," Delacroix spoke up, "the decision cannot be so difficult. You know your plan for a tea company is a good one. All you need is solid backers. I am offering to join Sir Alexander in providing you that. How could you do anything but agree?"

"I ponder the Lady Delacroix's future far more than my own, sir. As you see, I have settled upon a new way to make my way in life, and I am content in my chosen path. But what of the lady? Can you bring her happiness? Can you make her content?"

"How can I fail? I assure you, Locke, I am not without charms and wit enough to please a woman. Along with two good houses, an array of social pastimes, and my excellent friends and acquaintances, I offer her the many satisfactions she will take in our marriage. No doubt we shall have children, and every woman can take comfort in that. I enjoy fine foods, stimulating conversation, and various entertainments. Dancing, cards, shooting — in all of these I am quite accomplished. I shall treat my wife with kindness and respect, and I have no doubt that these efforts on her behalf will win me her affection. What objection can there be?"

"There must be some, or you would not be seeking my assistance."

Delacroix's high spirits sobered instantly. "Any lady save this one would be delighted to marry me. But I am reluctant to make any proposal to her under the current circumstances. She remains adamant in her determination to remain unwed."

"Perhaps you would get on better if you were religious."

Delacroix set his cup in its saucer with a loud clink. "Locke, do not trifle with me. I am as religious as the next fellow. I am a perfect gentleman in every way. The trouble does not lie with *me* but with *her*. Surely you are not too blinded by your affections for her to see this. She is . . . unreasonable."

"Out of her wits?"

"Thinking unclearly. You seem to have some effect upon her, and so I ask you to influence her in my direction. In exchange, I shall be more than happy to see you comfortably situated. Your own success will be as assured as mine. I doubt you will ever have such an opportunity again, sir."

Charles stared down at his teacup. To voice his concerns would draw ridicule. *Do you love her? Does she love you? Will you see into her heart and understand her dreams? Can you hold her and keep her warm and make her believe she is all the world to you? Will you listen to her talk of God, and will you study Scripture in order to better understand her and to walk with her in faith? Can you ever care for poor blind girls in China as she does? Will printing presses that spread the gospel mean as much to you as they do to her? Do you accept that she cares nothing for jewels and gowns? Do you know how little she enjoys the society you find so amusing? And will you sacrifice all that brings you such pleasure in order to please her?*

Impossible. Charles could never ask such questions aloud. Nor could he ever encourage Sarah toward any man who would do less for her.

"What is your delay, Locke?" Delacroix demanded. "Win her over to me, and you shall have all you desire. What causes you to hesitate?"

"I am not confident in my ability to persuade her to marry you. She will not give up her aims."

"How can you be certain? In a single conversation with you, she changed her mind and elected to remain in England rather than roaming the world. Surely in a weekend you can bring her to reason concerning the advantages of marrying me."

"A weekend? I most sincerely doubt that."

"At least make a start at it. Why not? Come to Bamberfield as my guest and Miss Watson's particular friend. Go riding with the young lady. Who could resist Miss Watson's charms? Perhaps you will even win her for yourself! She is no small prize — a fortune of ten thousand pounds, I am told."

"Why not you, then? Surely that is enough to keep you happy."

"I am hardly likely to settle for a woman with ten thousand pounds when her sister is worth far more than ten times that amount. Come, sir, be reasonable. What harm can two days in the country do you?"

Charles stood from his chair and bowed. "Delacroix, I am much obliged to you for your confidence in me. Yet I am undeterred. As I stated from the beginning, I am unable to accept your kind invitation. And now I must take my leave."

"Hang you, man!" Delacroix leapt to his feet. "Are you such a fool?"

"I prefer to think of myself as a man of honor." Without waiting for a reply, Charles set a few coins on the table and left the tearoom. He would not see Delacroix again. And just as well.

"Three days of rain and nothing to do but play whist or embroider screens." Prudence gazed out the window through which only a low gray mist and an even grayer sky could be seen. "We ought to have stayed in town. At least then we might have had callers. The Pembertons' dance is tonight, you know, Sarah. They always have dances or balls on Fridays, and we are always invited. But now we shall be forced to do nothing more interesting than play at cards or charades. If I have to partner with Delacroix one more time, I shall scream. Every time I play a card differently than he would, he makes me the object of his scorn."

The three sisters had gathered in the great drawing room at Bamberfield House. Sarah was laboring at the watercolor still life she had been painting all week. She was grateful to have the calming influence of her lady's maid, Anne Webster, at her side. The young woman had come from town with some of the other servants, and now she sat nearby, ready to provide fresh water for the paintbrushes whenever needed. But Sarah knew that Anne also listened in silence to the conversation at hand, and more than once while assisting Sarah with her wardrobe or bath, she had boldly offered her thoughts on one subject or another. Though in another house such audacity might have gotten Anne sacked, Sarah enjoyed her company, especially when her sisters grew particularly tedious.

As the rain drummed on the windowpanes and Sarah painted, Mary stitched a fire screen. Prudence could find nothing to do but lament her misfortunes, for she despised being indoors and could find little to entertain herself.

The women expected Lord Delacroix and Mr. Heathhill to come down to tea soon. From their talk at luncheon, Sarah understood that the men had spent the rainy morning cleaning their guns and discussing the merits of pheasant shooting. In this regard, she was happy to have been born a female.

"Why not read a book, Pru?" Sarah suggested. "My late husband never took the trouble to go into his library when we were staying at Bamberfield, but I assure you it is well stocked with the classics."

"Homer and Virgil? I should much prefer a novel. If Miss Jane Austen could only write faster, we should all be the better. She is by far my favorite author, though I like Isabella Kelly well enough. Has either of you read her book, *The Secret*?" Prudence lowered the curtain over the window again as she turned to her sisters. "I adored it. Berthaline is an orphan, you see, and she desires as a father none other than Lord Glenclullen — the man her female hostess calls base and depraved. How lamentable it is that poor Berthaline has no parents, and Lord Glenclullen is a criminal! I thought I should never stop weeping."

"You are too silly," Mary informed her sister. "To weep over a novel!"

"It is not silly, for the circumstances Berthaline faced were nearly as difficult as Sarah's. We both saw how Father treated her, Mary, sending her away to that awful school. Then she had to wed the baron, which was a travesty from the beginning. And now she loves a man she cannot marry."

Prudence paused a moment, then she leapt up from the window seat and hurried across the room to a small desk. "Do you know what I am going to do?" she asked as she pulled out a sheet of paper and dipped a pen into the inkwell. "I shall write a letter to Miss Pickworth on Sarah's behalf. I shall tell her everything that has befallen our dear sister, and then we shall await her advice in *The Tattler.*"

"Upon my word, you must do nothing of the sort!" Sarah exclaimed. "Everyone would know the letter was about me."

"I shall disguise all the particulars," Pru-

208

dence said, scribbling furiously. "But the essence of the situation will be clear. I am convinced that Miss Pickworth will tell us exactly what to do."

"There is nothing to be done," Mary said, "for Sarah cannot continue her friendship with Mr. Locke. He is beneath her."

"Prudence, do come away from that desk," Sarah urged as she returned to her painting. "Mary is right. Mr. Locke is in the past."

"He would not be in the past if only he had agreed to come to Bamberfield with us. Honestly, I cannot think why he —"

"Mr. Locke?" Sarah looked up from her box of watercolor paints. "Surely he was not invited here."

The glances exchanged between Prudence and Mary told their sister that Charles Locke had indeed been invited to join the party at Bamberfield House. Prudence quickly turned back to the desk. "Anyway, he is not to come," she said as she continued writing. "There is nothing more to say on that."

"There most certainly is," Sarah retorted. "Who invited him?"

"First, Delacroix called on Mr. Locke," Mary informed her. "And then Pru sent a letter most particularly requesting his presence for this weekend."

"Two attempts to secure him? And twice rejected? Upon my honor, I am all astonishment at your audacity! Pru, you and Delacroix both know how I feel about Mr. Locke. What were you thinking?"

Prudence glanced over her shoulder at her sister. "Only that we should be more lively with a charming gentleman in our party. Oh, come, Sarah. You know you would enjoy his company, too. You are very dull these days."

"That is true, sister," Mary said. "The only time you have smiled since returning to London was just after Mr. Locke called on you at Trenton House. You informed us you meant to stay in England after all, and at dinner that night you were positively aglow. But as the days went by, you sank back into your black humor. Now you might as well be Marianne mourning that dastardly Mr. Willoughby in *Sense and Sensibility.* Why do you not make yourself happy again?"

"Because Sarah cannot go outside to walk in the fresh air," Prudence lamented. "And because Mr. Locke is not to come. And because all we can do is play at charades with Mary's somber husband and Delacroix!"

"Why did Delacroix invite Mr. Locke?" Sarah demanded. "It was wrong of him, and I shall speak to him on that account directly."

"Excuse me, madam," the lady's maid spoke up, laying a hand on Sarah's arm. "I see a carriage outside. It comes down the drive even now."

"Who can it be?" Sarah asked. "Anne, go to the window and tell us if you recognize the livery."

"Is it a fine carriage?" Mary inquired of the maid. "Perhaps one of my friends calls upon us."

"No, it is plain," Anne reported. "Two horses, a single footman, no livery at all."

"It must be him! Mr. Locke!" Prudence exclaimed, rising from the desk and racing to the window. "It *is* him! He has decided to come after all! Oh, Mary, now you will see his blue eyes. Sarah, do not look so cross. You know you are as glad as any of us to have him here, for I told him how glum you were and how we all feared you would change your mind again and go off to China."

"Prudence!"

"At any rate, he is only come for the weekend, for he wrote that he must return to London by Monday to attend lectures at

Lincoln's Inn. He is to become a barrister, you know."

Revelation upon revelation. Sarah hardly knew what to think or how to feel. But there could be no time for reflection — in moments, he would be among them. Mary took up her needlework. Prudence snatched a book from the nearest table and pretended to read. As her maid returned to her side, Sarah dipped her brush into the blue paint. All were silent, gracefully seated, and properly occupied as a footman opened the drawing-room door to make the announcement.

"Mr. Charles Locke," he called out, and they rose in unison.

The man himself entered, bowed, and scanned the room. As the three sisters curtsied in return, his focus centered upon Sarah. "Lady Delacroix," he said. "How do you do?"

"I am well, Mr. Locke. And you, sir?"

"Very well." He turned to the other women. "Miss Watson. Good afternoon."

"Do allow me to present our sister, Mary," Sarah said. "Mrs. John Heathhill."

"Mrs. Heathhill," Charles replied with another bow. "I am pleased to meet you."

"Oh, Mr. Locke, we are all so happy you have come!" Prudence exclaimed, skipping toward him. "Bamberfield is dreadfully dank and dreary in the rain, and nothing but your presence could enliven our spirits." She took his arm. "Do sit down, sir. The gentlemen will come to us directly."

"I shall call for tea," Sarah said.

Laying down her brush, she summoned the footman, who hurried away to fetch Delacroix and Mr. Heathhill. At Sarah's direction, Anne slipped out of the room to speak to the housekeeper. An additional guest would necessitate more tea, an extra place at dinner, and another bedroom opened and aired in the men's wing of the house. Sarah completed her orders and picked up her brush.

How could this have happened? Delacroix and her sisters must be conspiring to make her miserable! Or happy? She ventured a glance at Charles, who was answering a question put to him by Prudence but gazing all the while at Sarah. Disconcerted, she dabbed a large blue blob on the red apple she had so carefully painted only minutes before.

This was appalling! She did not want to see Charles. She had put him firmly out of her thoughts and centered all her attention on continuing her mission. While sorting through applications for funds from various places in England, Sarah also had received letters from her acquaintances in Burma, China, and India.

Gradually — and with much care — she was parceling out her fortune. The work had become a full-time occupation for her, and she enjoyed it immensely. Truly, she did, Sarah reminded herself. Mary and Prudence might accuse their sister of glumness, but they were wrong. Sarah knew she was laboring for God, and how could anything produce greater happiness?

"We understand you mean to become a barrister, Mr. Locke," Prudence was saying. "How very good. I am sure you will be wonderful at making laws."

Sarah gave an inward groan as Charles chuckled. "I shall do my best, Miss Watson."

"You ought to prohibit rain on weekends," Prudence suggested. "In such dreadful weather, no one can go outside, picnics are impossible, and everything is gray — most especially our humors."

"I fear not even the English Parliament has enough power to exercise control over the weather, madam. We must learn to be content with whatever God provides us. His will is perfect, after all; is it not, Lady Delacroix?"

At that, Sarah ran a blue streak right across the two pears that had so recently been a perfect shade of yellow. "Indeed," she managed. "Quite perfect."

"May I be so bold as to ask how you are getting on with your charitable occupations, madam? I have heard that you mean to stay here in England and carry on with your work."

Steadying herself, Sarah looked into his eyes. "Yes, sir. I do continue what I began on my journey to the Orient. I have had a letter from Miss Aldersey in China. Her school for blind girls at Ningpo continues to grow, and the Delacroix estate is assisting in the construction of new housing. Ink and paper are even now being shipped to India to assist in the printing of gospel pamphlets by Dr. William Carey. And three new missionaries travel to Burma soon with funds to assure their ministries for three years."

The blue in his eyes softened as she talked, and Sarah felt she could hardly keep speaking to him in so stiff and formal a manner. Mary and Prudence were clearly intent on every word that passed between them, and Sarah knew she must make every effort to show her sisters that she had no attachment to this gentleman.

"I am happy to hear this," Charles told her. "Surely you must be delighted as well."

"I am," Sarah agreed. "It pleases me greatly to —"

"You could never tell she is delighted by the sour expression she brings to the breakfast table each morning," Prudence observed. "Mr. Locke, was my sister this dreary aboard the *Queen Elinor*? If so, I am at a loss to imagine what you found to like in her."

"Prudence, please!" Sarah said.

"No, it is a good question, Lady Delacroix, for more than one source has provided me with alarming reports of your glum demeanor. Miss Watson, I assure you that aboard ship, your sister was the most delightful, charming, kind, and endearing young woman I have ever met in my life. I eagerly awaited her arrival each morning, and the sweet sound of her singing put me into peaceful slumber each night."

"But Sarah cannot sing!" Prudence blurted out. "None of us has any talent whatever in that regard."

"I beg your pardon, Miss Watson, but your sister sings like an angel." He smiled at Sarah, whose stomach turned an entire flip-flop at once. "Dear lady, have you deprived your sisters of the songs and hymns that so

216

encouraged those of us who endured the attack upon the *Tintagel*?"

"I truly do not sing well, sir," Sarah said. "You were ill, and I am sure you welcomed anything to distract you from your pain."

He laughed at this. "You are far too modest, Mrs. —" Catching himself, he shook his head briefly. "Lady Delacroix, only one thing could persuade me to come to Bamberfield House this weekend."

At this, Prudence brightened. "My letter! Why, Mr. Locke, how sweet of you to suppose that I should enjoy riding —"

"I came out of concern that a spirit of melancholy may have overtaken you, Lady Delacroix. Your sister's letter persuaded me to offer my assistance in doing anything that might cheer you."

"We are all overtaken by melancholy!" Prudence heaved an enormous sigh. "And you may do a great deal to cheer us. Tell me, Mr. Locke, how do you do at playing whist?"

"Tolerable, Miss Watson, but I have not come for card games. I bring a question for your sister." Again, he turned to Sarah. "Dear lady, what is your success at finding worthy charities here in England?"

For a brief moment, Sarah thought he must have come to beg money for himself.

His tea company might be called a charity, after all, for Charles must be as poor as a church mouse. But the sincerity in his eyes told her that he continued to be honorable and forthright with her.

"In the hope of securing funds, charities apply to every well-established English family," she informed him. "The Delacroix estate supports two orphanages and an almshouse."

"I see," he said. "In view of that, Lady Delacroix, may I ask you to accompany me this afternoon on a short excursion?"

"I want to go too!" Prudence trilled.

"Sit down, sister," Mary hissed. "You are not invited on the excursion, and the men will soon be here for tea."

"If you wish, you may all come." Charles stood and extended a hand toward Sarah. "Lady Delacroix?"

She rose tentatively. "Well, I —"

"Let us go together, the whole party," Prudence chirped, skipping forward and linking an arm through Sarah's. "Come, Mary."

"I intend to take tea and stitch my screen until dinner is called, thank you very much," Mary responded. "I am not one for impetuous excursions. You will excuse me, Mr. Locke."

"Of course." He took Sarah's other arm.

"Shall we?"

Without quite knowing why, Sarah stepped forward.

TEN

Charles had permitted himself the journey to Bamberfield only because of his certainty that Sarah needed him. Her sister had penned a letter filled with dire warnings. Sarah was consumed with dark moods, melancholy musings, and long hours of solitude, Prudence wrote. Nothing good could come of this bleak humor, and no one could cheer Sarah. None save Charles, whose recent visit had filled the young lady with joy and had brought about her resolution to stay in England at least until the new year. Would Charles please set aside his misgivings and come to Bamberfield? Prudence had pleaded. If he did not, she truly feared for her sister's health.

The letter had achieved its intended result, but now that Charles was seated across the carriage from the two women, he began to doubt his decision. Prudence Watson was surely the most determined flirt in the realm. Too young and silly to be taken seriously, she fluttered her long dark lashes at him, pouted her full lips, and made such laughable attempts to attract his attention that Charles could hardly keep a straight face.

Sarah was another matter. Wearing a simple white gown with puffed sleeves and a high waistline, she appeared almost angelic. So innocent and pure as to make his chest ache, she gazed out the carriage windows, her brown eyes soft and luminous. Her chestnut hair was swept up in a knot, leaving her neck bare except for the curled tendrils that floated like feathers against her silken skin. White kid slippers and white stockings seemed too delicate and fragile for the muddy floor of the old carriage, and Charles fretted that she might take offense.

He could hardly keep his thoughts on the matter at hand, for Sarah's presence distracted him from all his high-minded intentions. He had come to Bamberfield to talk sense into her. Now he wished for nothing more than to take her in his arms and shield her from every sensible and harsh reality the world had already laid upon her. He had hoped to make her smile and to occupy her hours with productive tasks. Now he longed merely to sit beside her and listen to the burdens of her heart.

In debating whether to make the journey, Charles had even gone so far as to imagine that Delacroix might make Sarah a good husband. Perhaps the golden-haired young man could bring her pleasure and ease. And perhaps Charles would, after all, attempt to incline her in that man's direction.

Though he found Delacroix's offer of financial support in exchange for match-making distasteful, Charles could not quite bring himself to deny the obvious. He needed money, and Sarah needed the security and stability of marriage. He had traveled to Bamberfield confident that he could help accomplish both.

Or so he had supposed until the moment he stepped into the drawing room and saw the young lady seated at a table, her easel and paints before her, and her lovely eyes settled upon him. He knew instantly that he could never urge her into any man's arms but his own. That he would support another match was impossible. Unthinkable.

"I declare that you are teasing us, Mr. Locke," Prudence said, lightly touching his arm. The girl had kept up such a chatter since leaving the house that her words took a moment to register.

"How do I tease you, madam?" he inquired.

"The carriage takes us to no known destination, and you speak not a single word along the way. Indeed, I begin to fear for my safety, for we are completely at your mercy."

"Nonsense, Pru," Sarah responded in a low voice. "Mr. Locke is a respectable man. I am sure his purpose in this journey is honorable."

"But of course," he concurred. "I keep our destination a secret merely that I may prepare you for it before our arrival. I sit in silence that I may ponder how best to reveal my purpose. At your request, Miss Watson, I shall now begin that task."

Lest he dismay Sarah by disclosing any of his most private thoughts, Charles turned his attention to the practical matter at hand. "From our conversations aboard the *Queen Elinor*, Lady Delacroix, I understood you to say you had been away from England for two years."

"Aye, traveling in the Orient."

"And in all that time, you received only a few letters from England?"

"I had a letter from Mary and two from Prudence. My solicitor wrote to me once, and on occasion I heard from various female acquaintances."

"I cannot believe that such correspondence gave much news of the political or economic situation of your homeland."

She smiled at this. "I became more familiar with the current fashion for sleeves than with British politics, Mr. Locke."

"I suspected as much." Her sweet expression lifting his spirits, Charles plunged ahead. "I wonder, madam, if you have heard of the Corn Laws — legislation that raised taxes on foreign grains. In order to stifle their competition, wealthy landowners supported the enactment of the Corn Laws. Sadly, these laws have penalized the poor of this country, who relied on less expensive imported grain for their sustenance."

"I am sorry to inform you, Mr. Locke," Sarah said, "that I heard nothing of this."

"Why should we write to our sister about the Corn Laws?" Prudence spoke up. "Such a dull subject would be a great waste of ink and paper. No, I had much better send Sarah copies of Lord Byron's darkly romantic poetry — and then tell my sister that Lady Caroline Lamb had openly pursued him for so long a time. Miss Pickworth wrote about it very often in her column in *The Tattler.* Do you read Miss Pickworth, sir?"

"I am acquainted with the piece."

"Miss Pickworth informed her readers that Lady Caroline cavorted with Lord Byron until the moment she published *Glenarvon.* That scathing novel satirized his poems as well as his relationship with Lady Melbourne and her husband! The book scandalized the whole of the *ton.*"

"Scandal?" Charles turned to Sarah again. "Is this what interests you, Lady Delacroix? I had thought it was the plight of the less fortunate."

Prudence gave a sniff of disgust. "While Parliament was enacting the Corn Laws, Mr. Locke, my sister was visiting the needy and making plans to join their ranks. I should rather she learn that Percy Shelley — who is yet another poet and nearly as infamous a cad as Lord Byron — abandoned his wife to run off with Mary Godwin, who is the daughter of Mary Wollstonecraft. Miss Pickworth has written that Mr. Shelley and the young lady went away to the Continent and will probably never be seen in England again."

"Thank you, Prudence," Sarah said. "I am sure I could not have been happier to receive such news."

"Miss Watson," Charles addressed the young lady, "I wonder if you have told your sister about Miss Pickworth's columns regarding the duke of Devonshire's renovations to his estate, Chatsworth, in Derbyshire."

Prudence's eyes lit up. "Oh, Sarah, he has spent thousands of pounds on Chatsworth. Miss Pickworth says that house now rivals the royal palace in majestic appointments. The duke is a most eligible bachelor, to be sure, and a favorite in our society. Mr. Locke, did you see him at the Marston reception? He was accompanied by —"

"But what of the fortune the prince regent has spent refurbishing the Royal Pavilion in Brighton and Carleton House in London?" Charles went on, determined to drown Miss Watson's gossip with his own more pertinent line of reasoning. "Parliament is outraged at the excessive expenditure, of course. Yet they stand in support of the construction of Regent Street and Regent's Park, which are merely the beginning of a grand plan for transforming that part of London."

"Oh, lovely Brighton," Prudence sighed. "Sarah, we must go down soon. There is little I like better than sea bathing. And as for Regent Street, let me tell you that Miss Pickworth writes —"

"May I ask the purpose of all these accounts, Mr. Locke?" Sarah cut in, her dark eyes pinning him. "Elopements and scandals mean nothing to me. And you surely know I am opposed to the expenditure of fortunes on grand houses."

"Then may we return to a discussion of the effects that these and other events have had upon England?"

"Of course, sir."

"I should like very much to inform you that while you were touring the Orient, Lady Delacroix, the gap between the aristocracy and the masses in this country widened. Our recent war with America and our ongoing troubles with the French have led to soaring prices and increased poverty. England now faces an enormous national debt that we have no way of repaying."

"Upon my word," Sarah exclaimed. "I am shocked. Can this be so?"

"Truly, it is so. Three hundred thousand soldiers have returned from the Napoleonic wars to find that their king is mad, and his obese and profligate sinner of a son has been made our prince regent. These thousands of soldiers seeking jobs have discovered that while they were away defending their country, many businesses closed or brought in machines to replace them."

"I do know something of this," Sarah said,

"for my lady's maid hails from Nottingham, and she has told me that city is greatly affected by lace machines. In fact, her father — a minister — was imprisoned with his parishioners for attempting to destroy the machines."

Charles nodded in sympathy. "Other firms stay profitable by hiring children, who are paid only a fraction of a man's salary. Wages of tenant farmers have fallen to half what they once were, while poor harvests have led to hunger and riots."

"Oh, dear," Sarah whispered. Even her sister appeared somewhat distressed by this information.

"Not only have the Corn Laws penalized the poor," Charles continued, "but other legislation now makes public gatherings illegal. Since you went away, madam, England has suspended habeas corpus and has made great efforts to curtail freedom of speech."

"Impossible."

"Yet all too true. Even as Parliament clamps down on liberties, our population is exploding. Of more than twelve million who now reside in this country, fewer than a quarter may be said to live above poverty."

"But Parliament must be addressing such problems," Sarah said.

"Our leaders protect their own, my lady. The landowners who control Parliament have little interest in easing the plight of the lower classes. They have actually raised taxes on tea, candles, paper, soap, and sugar. Newspapers are heavily taxed in order to restrict what is viewed as dangerous propaganda."

"This is dreadful!" Sarah exclaimed. "Pru, did you know of it?"

"I knew about the wars. But what have they to do with me?"

"You live here!"

"I did not cause the wars or raise the taxes. Honestly, sister, you turn on me as though all this is my fault — but I have done nothing."

"That is just it, Pru. You have done nothing. Nothing but flirt and shop and go to balls."

"Well, you sailed off to China and gave your money to blind girls! Why should they have it when people are starving here in England?"

"And just in time, we arrive at our destination," Charles announced. "Shepton."

Through the carriage window, he could see the small village that nestled at the edge of the Bamberfield estate. From white-washed wattle-and-daub cottages with thatched roofs rose thin wisps of pale gray smoke. Tiny windows covered with soot revealed nothing within the houses, but Charles knew what awaited him and his lovely companions.

As a boy, he had often raced Ruel and Alexander Chouteau down to this village that supplied their father's manor with produce grown by tenant farmers. For many years, he had thought the little hamlet was no more than houses, streets, and shops. The green featured a tiered marketplace, and the sun often shone brightly on the chestnut trees that surrounded it. And then one day, a little boy had invited the duke's sons and their companion to his house for tea. As Charles had stepped into this new friend's cottage, he was introduced to a foreign world, one he was eager to escape at the first opportunity.

"I have been to Shepton many times already," Prudence was lamenting as Charles stepped out of the carriage into the muddy street. He donned his top hat while his footman put up an umbrella for the ladies.

"Shepton has little to recommend it — a milliner's shop, a bakery, and the market," Prudence continued. "I am prodigiously chilled in this rain, Mr. Locke. I do hope we mean to stay only a few minutes, for I can guess your purpose."

"Can you indeed?" he asked.

"You mean to encourage my sister to use her money here — to help these villagers."

Charles smiled as he helped Sarah down from the carriage. "Miss Watson, I am of the opinion that your sister may give her money to whomever she wishes, as I have told her already."

"And you, sir?" Sarah asked as Prudence made a dash for the umbrella. "When you have earned your fortune, who will benefit from it?"

"My wife and children. I have told you that already, also."

"Your wife and children — and yourself, of course. You believe wealth will bring you happiness."

"It cannot harm my chances, can it?"

"It certainly can."

"I believe my only hope for great happiness was lost aboard the *Queen Elinor*," he said, speaking near her ear. Her eyes darted up at him, but he continued forward, instructing his footman as he led the ladies toward the nearest cottage. "Bring the baskets, please, Rochester. Three will be enough for now, I should think."

The footman handed large baskets to

Charles and to both women. They were filled with items Charles had purchased that morning before setting out from London. His father had thought him mad, of course. The journey to Bamberfield was a good idea, James Locke had agreed. But its object ought to be securing the affections of Lady Delacroix — or, failing that, those of her younger sister. Charles had a different aim in mind, and now he rapped on the door of the nearest cottage.

A small girl with large blue eyes opened the door and stared up at him. Her dirty cheeks were tearstained, her feet bare, and her gown nothing more than a brown rag. "Good afternoon, miss," Charles addressed her. "I am Mr. Charles Locke, and I bring Sarah Carlyle, the dowager Lady Delacroix, and her sister Miss Watson to call on your family. Is your father in?"

The blue eyes darted to the two fine ladies who stood ankle-deep in the muck and mire that flowed down the cobbled street. Without a word, the child pulled the door back to allow them inside. Charles removed his hat, ducked his head, and entered. Sarah and her sister slipped in behind him. The smoke-filled room contained nothing more than a rough table, three stools, an old chair, and a bed pushed up against the wall.

The open fire in the center of the room was encircled by stones around which sat three more children with tangled hair and dirty faces.

One of them, a gangly boy, stood. He stepped forward and made an awkward bow. "Good afternoon, sir. What do ye want of us?"

Charles held out his basket. "We come from Bamberfield to call upon the tenants in Shepton. Take this, lad. It is a gift."

At that magical word, the other children swarmed around, opening the basket's woven lid and pulling out a thick blanket, a box of tea leaves, two loaves of bread, a large pickled cow's tongue, and a packet of sweet lemon drops. It was not much, Charles knew, but considering his own financial straits, it was the best he could afford.

As the children danced about in joy, his eyes fell on a female figure lying on the bed. Instantly, memories of his mother assaulted him. How terribly ill she had been, unable to rise, unable to eat, and at the end, unable even to draw breath. He and his father had sat beside her bed for hours, days, weeks. James Locke had spent all he could afford on doctors and on medicines from the village apothecary. But it was not enough.

Maria Locke needed to go to London, they were told. She must see a surgeon and be given expensive emetics and treatments. Although Mr. Locke had earned a good salary as the duke of Marston's steward, by the time his wife fell ill, he had spent most of his savings in sending Charles to Eton and then to Cambridge. There was not enough money for transportation and surgeons and medicines. And so Maria Locke had died, and with her death, she took away the primary source of faith, love, and joy for both her husband and her son.

Awash in memory, Charles used the distraction of the children's excitement to cross the room and speak to the woman in the bed. "Good afternoon, madam," he addressed her, bowing. He introduced himself and the two ladies, both of whom hung back by the door, as if in shock at what they were seeing. "May I ask after your health?"

"I am not well, sir." The woman licked her dry lips. She was small and gray-haired, no doubt much younger than she appeared. "Me 'usband died in France two years ago. Kilt, he were, in the fightin'. I worked at the mill for a time, but me breathin' ain't good now. I cough too much, and they sacked me, for I were not puttin' in me hours. Consumption, they tell me, sir, though I

234

canna believe it."

"Have you seen a doctor?"

"Nay, sir. I ain't got no money for that. Me two eldest — girls, they is — work at the mill now. Eight and ten years old. But they don't 'ardly bring in enough to feed us all."

"I am so sorry to hear this news."

"Can ye come again, sir? And bring us more meat, I beg ye, for me wee ones is 'ungry."

"I live in London, madam. But I shall see that an apothecary visits you. Perhaps he may be of some use. You may direct the charges to me."

"Thank ye, sir. God bless ye."

Leaving his card on her bed, Charles turned back to the women at the door. "Shall we go, ladies?"

As they stepped out of the house into the rain, Prudence let out a cry of exasperation. "Oh, Mr. Locke, the odor in that room! I could hardly bear it. How can those children exist in such a filthy hovel? And that woman — was she their mother?"

"Aye, and very ill. I am sure she suffers from a cancer or consumption. She cannot live much longer." He spoke to his footman for a moment, sending the man to fetch an apothecary. Charles took the umbrella and shielded the ladies as they journeyed down the street.

"Please excuse me from this task, sir," Prudence said, coming to a halt near the carriage. "Putrid odors make me feel as though I must swoon. Sarah can go with you, for she has been to see the blind girls in China and the poor people in India."

"But I —" Sarah hung her head.

"Lady Delacroix?" Charles bent over to see her face beneath the deep brim of her bonnet. "Are you ill as well?"

She shook her head. "No, sir. It is just that I . . . I do not like this any more than my sister does. And I am ashamed of myself."

When she looked up, Charles saw that her eyes were swimming with tears. "But you assisted the ship's doctor," he said. "You went to Burma and —"

"Yes, but I did not have to smell such odors or see insects crawling across my slippers or touch . . . or touch . . . oh dear . . ." Drawing a handkerchief from her bag, she dabbed her cheeks. "In that horrid room, I realized that I should almost rather die than touch that woman. I am clean, you see, for I bathed this morning. My gown is new. And I should like to keep it white."

"Very well, then," Charles said gently. "This is not worth tears, dear lady."

"Indeed it is! For now I fear I may have been too pious. I can give away my fortune easily enough. But I cannot bear the thought of sullying myself through actual contact with that woman and her children. I see now that I somehow romanticized the idea of poverty, sir. But the reality of it is . . . untenable. I am a wealthy merchant's daughter. I was brought up with servants and clean gowns and good food. Oh, Mr. Locke, I am quite undone by my failings."

As Sarah pressed her handkerchief to her eyes, Prudence wrapped her arms about her sister. "It is all right, Sarah," she murmured. "You are not undone simply because you prefer to stand back and allow someone else to tend the poor. Give away your fortune — *some* of it — if you must. And know that you do very much good with your gift. You do not have to tread in the muck or sit in the midst of squalor and disease."

"But I do, Pru. Have you not heard what I have been telling you and Mary all this time? Christ said it was difficult for the rich to enter the kingdom of heaven — and it is! How very difficult it is! We love our good things. We might imagine ourselves able to give up all we have and follow Christ, but in the end, we cannot do it. *I* cannot do it!"

With a scowl drawing her pretty eyebrows

together, Prudence eyed Charles. "For heaven's sake, Mr. Locke, do something to repair this damage! You have needlessly upset my sister, and now we are damp and muddy and hopelessly chilled. And all for what? What did you hope to accomplish in this silly exercise?"

Charles stood in the mire, holding the umbrella over the two embracing sisters as he pondered the question. What *had* he hoped to achieve in Shepton? He had supposed that if Sarah saw England's poor, she might be more willing to stay here. She would understand how much good her fortune could do in her own country, and then she would feel little urge to wander the globe again. In England, she would be at home, comfortable and safe. And near *him.*

That was it then. He wanted her. As much as ever, he longed to keep her close. And in his effort to do that, he had distressed and discouraged her. The outing, he concluded, had been a colossal blunder.

Spying the footman, who was trotting back toward the carriage, Charles beckoned. "Come, man, open this door for us." He bundled the ladies toward the carriage. "We must return to Bamberfield at once."

"No!" Sarah pushed away from her sister and backed out from the umbrella into the rain. "I shall not go yet. I must give away my basket first."

"Sarah!" Prudence called out. "Do not be so stubborn! Let us go home and have a nice cup of tea!"

At that word, Charles envisioned the comfortable drawing room with its flickering fire and fine china teapot. He thought of dark leaves brewing in steaming water and of ships sailing for England, their holds filled with chests of those very leaves. He thought of rolling green hills in China and workers plucking buds and leaves to be fired and fermented into a tonic to be enjoyed by polite society. Warehouses and ships and gold. Coins flooding into coffers. All for himself. His own happiness. His health and wealth and welfare.

Hang the poor! Let them work their weary fingers to the bone. His ancestors had paid just such a price, and he was to be their champion. The first of their line — but certainly not the last — to partake of life's luxuries.

"Do something, Mr. Locke!" Prudence exclaimed, swatting him on the arm with her bag. "Look at my sister going off there in the rain! This is all your fault, sir. You are to blame if she catches some horrid disease. If she dies, it will be on your shoulders!"

"Let her go," Charles said, a morbid determination creeping across his chest. He would not feel sympathy for the needy. Nor would he plunge after a woman whose aims were so opposite his own. "Let your sister see the plight of England's poor, Miss Watson, and she will stay here. She will understand that she need not sail away to China in order to find charities enough to absorb every farthing she wishes to give."

"This is your plan, then?"

"Once her mind is settled upon remaining here, she must be urged to marry."

"Marry *you,* I suppose? A man who would toss her into the mud and force her to feel such guilt that she creeps from house to house with her ridiculous basket. Look at her now, going into that cottage! If she returns to us with lice, Mr. Locke, you will bear all the blame of it, I assure you."

Battling the urge to go after Sarah, Charles held open the carriage door for her sister. "Step out of the rain, Miss Watson; I beg you. And comfort yourself with the certainty that I do not intend to make another offer of marriage to your sister, now or ever. She would do better with Delacroix."

"Delacroix?" Prudence paused in gathering her skirts. "He is a roué. You would sentence Sarah to a lifetime of misery."

240

"She sentences herself to such a life." Charles climbed into the carriage after Prudence and took his seat across from her. "Your sister is determined to be a poor, miserable wretch, and I cannot understand why."

"My sister believes that happiness comes only after much suffering. She has been miserable all her life. Indeed, I do not suppose she has had a single day of utter bliss."

"How can this be? When I knew her aboard the *Queen Elinor* she was all lightness. I lived for her smile. Her voice enchanted me with the ring of joy in every word. I begin to wonder if the Sarah Carlyle I once knew is truly the same woman as Lady Delacroix. Perhaps they are twins, and I recall the happy one."

Prudence smiled. "There is just one of my sister, sir. You must have known her at a good time in her life. She has always been determined and courageous, but I have rarely seen her cheerful."

"Why is that? She was the eldest daughter of a wealthy merchant and then the wife of a respected and titled gentleman. What in that could have led to misery?"

"You must ask Sarah that yourself, Mr. Locke. I observed the causes of her sorrow, but I was powerless to help. It is not my place to reveal my sister's secrets."

"It is not my place to query her about them."

"Perhaps not. But she is lighter in your presence. While you are here this weekend, you might make some attempt to speak with her in private."

"I shall do nothing of the sort. It would be improper." The very thought of talking alone with Sarah sent a ripple of tension through Charles. As it was, he could hardly trust himself in the same room with her. In private, he would be helpless.

"You prefer she should be won by someone like Delacroix?" Prudence challenged. "Do you know that man's character?"

"He is penniless but titled. He owns two houses and an estate. He has many friends, one of whom was my boyhood companion. I cannot imagine his character is unredeemably bad."

Prudence gave a small laugh. "Perhaps he is a better man than I suppose. Certainly he is handsome and well mannered. If he were married to my sister, would he settle down and become respectable? At least, one would hope so."

Charles opened the carriage window and leaned out to peer down the road. What was taking Sarah so long inside the cottage?

Ought he to go after her?

His concern was tempered by the realization that he might use this opportunity to encourage Miss Watson as Delacroix had urged. She, and not her sister, should become the object of Charles's affections. And he must encourage her to incline Lady Delacroix in the direction of another man who wished to make her his wife.

A battle raging in his chest, Charles ducked back into the carriage and faced Prudence. "What of your sister and Delacroix?" he asked. "You might speak to her on his behalf."

The young lady's pretty mouth opened in surprise. "Has he told you to broach this with me?" She gave a high, tinkling laugh. "Upon my word, I am all astonishment! Delacroix wishes to attach himself to my sister? But this is too shocking!"

"Calm yourself, I pray. It would be a good match, and Delacroix is no fool." Again he looked out the window, fighting to make himself speak of a notion he could not endorse. "What is your opinion of such a match, Miss Watson?"

"You must ask my sister," she said coyly. "And now you have *two* reasons to speak with Sarah in private."

Taking out her fan, Prudence flipped it

open and began to flutter it before her face. Charles studied the muddy street. Next he examined the carriage floor. Then he observed the brim of his hat, which he held between his knees. Finally, he could bear it no longer.

"I am going after her," he announced.

A sly smile tipped the corners of Prudence's mouth. "I thought you might," she said.

ELEVEN

When the cottage door burst open, Sarah looked up in surprise. "Mr. Locke! I supposed you and my sister were returned to Bamberfield by now."

Seated in a chair beside the open fire, she cradled a baby in her arms. Two small children knelt beside her as she rocked their infant sister in an effort to calm the scene of hysterics in which she had found herself earlier. Now Charles Locke stood in the open doorway, rain dripping from the thatched roof outside and thunder rolling overhead. He studied Sarah for a moment. Then he doffed his top hat and shut the door behind him.

"Sarah, may I ask what on earth you are doing?"

"I am singing." She lifted her chin. "As you mentioned, I sang to you once — when you were as ill and troubled as these children."

His blue eyes turned to the little ones who had pressed smudged faces up against her white skirt and wrapped scrawny arms around her legs. "We are expected at tea," he reminded Sarah. "I believe Mrs. Heath-hill anticipates our return within the hour."

"Perhaps she does, but Mary can always find other ways to pass the time. If you wish, Charles, you may certainly go on to Bamberfield and take your tea. Send a carriage for me before dusk."

"But that is many hours!"

"Indeed, and I have many baskets to deliver."

He set his hands on his hips and exhaled a long breath. "My late mother often occupied herself in walking through our local village to distribute blankets and food. It was I who first informed her of the hungry cottagers, and she often took me along to carry the baskets for her. In this Christian deed, my mother discovered much joy and fulfillment. In bringing you here, I had hoped you might find the same."

"At this moment, I feel only dismay," she said, recalling the utter havoc she had observed upon first stepping into the room. "When I entered this cottage, baby Annie was wailing and the other two were in an uproar. Young Tommy had made every effort to comfort the baby, and having failed, he had become completely distraught and was threatening violence. Dear little Polly here was shrieking and weeping and racing about in an attempt to spare her sister from their brother's wrath. None of them had eaten since dawn, and their fire had gone out. I calmed the baby with a spoonful of treacle from the basket, while Polly and Tommy assisted me in lighting the kindling. We sliced the pickled tongue and the bread, and as soon as the kettle is hot, we shall all feel much better."

The small girl with a matted tangle of golden hair gazed up at Sarah. "Aye, Mrs. Carlyle," she said around a mouthful of bread. "And then we shall have lemon drops."

"Yes, we shall," Sarah confirmed. "You see, Charles? I certainly could not leave until calm had been restored."

"Why do you tell them your name is Mrs. Carlyle? You ought to —"

"Oh, Charles, they can hardly care about titles. All they want is a full belly and some tender care."

"But where is their mother?" he asked. "Surely they have a granny or an aunt to look after them?"

"They do not, for all their relations labor

at the village mill. Even the older children are employed. Tommy himself expects to begin working there next year. That will leave Polly to look after the baby by herself."

Charles frowned. "Children tending a baby? That is fraught with peril."

"I believe the family must have no other option." Sarah swung around and set the drowsy infant into a makeshift crib near the fire. As always, a mixture of anger and sadness poured through her when she thought about her past life. "It seems my late husband was not a very good landlord. Nor has his nephew been inclined to attend to the needs of his tenants. I intend to rectify that situation immediately."

Charles smiled. "This is the Sarah I once knew. High-minded and resolute, yet tender and kind. I believe Lord Delacroix must certainly fail at any attempt to defy you, madam."

Warming at the tone in his voice, Sarah observed Charles lifting the kettle from the fire. As he poured boiling water into the chipped teapot, the leaves swelled and spun about. Watching them brew, she recalled Charles discussing his plans to build a tea empire, and she wondered if he ever doubted them. Did he believe his aim of making a fortune in trade had some valuable purpose in the great scheme of things?

Of course he intended to honor his family name and lineage with this achievement — but his ancestors were dead men after all. He would make his father proud, but to what end? So that James Locke, like her own father, might purchase a house in Belgravia and strut among the *ton?* Vain men, to hold such empty ambitions!

Charles planned to have a large house and servants and money to spend on a fine education for his children and sumptuous parties at Christmas. But could he truly enjoy such pleasures knowing, as he did, that countless other children labored in mills and babies were abandoned by their mothers? Sarah had great difficulty reconciling her wealth with her faith in Christ. Would Charles fare any better, especially if his fortune was earned by the sweat of his brow?

"Here, Polly," Charles said, handing the little girl a mug. "And Tommy. You remind me of a lad I once knew aboard a fine merchant vessel named the *Tintagel.* I think of Danny very often. He was a strong, brave boy who became my friend as well as my protector. You must do your best to be patient with your sisters and look after them. They need your help, for they have no one else to guard and defend them. Do you understand me, young Tommy?"

"Aye, sir." The boy nodded. "I shall do me best."

"Very good. Take small sips, now, for the tea is hot. Sarah, will you have a cup?"

"Will you?" she asked. "Or does Bamberfield beckon?"

"Bamberfield is nothing to me." He drew a stool to the fire as he handed Sarah a mug of tea. "I should rather sit with you in a humble cottage than be anywhere else on earth. But you must recall that your sister waits in the carriage."

"It can do her no harm to linger. Pru is accustomed to idleness." Sarah took a sip and closed her eyes in pleasure. "Mmm. Charles, I do believe you make the best cup of tea I have ever tasted."

"It is the open fire," he said. "The smoke flavors the brew."

Looking across at him, she could not refrain from unburdening the concern that filled her heart. "How are you these days, Charles?"

"I believe I am about the same as ever. Making plans. Pressing on toward the goals I have set. And adoring you, dearest lady."

Always surprised at the openness with which he expressed his affection for her,

Sarah reached out and stroked little Polly's head. The children were engrossed in their meal, and the baby slept. Outside the rain fell, Pru waited in the carriage, and Mary took tea with her husband and Delacroix. But here . . . now . . . it was just Charles and she. The two of them. Together.

"And you?" he asked. "Are you happy, Sarah?"

"I have a measure of joy. I know I am doing what I must. My sisters provide me the comfort of family. I find it challenging and interesting to assist my attorneys and bankers in establishing endowments and trusts. It is pleasing to know that my fortune does good. And now, you have taught me how to step into the midst of poverty and find fulfillment. So, I am better prepared for the future that awaits me. I thank you for that, Charles."

"Sarah, you cannot mean you wish to live as these cottagers do."

"How else? Until I have been fully obedient to Christ, I cannot be at peace."

"Why have you no peace, dear lady?"

Sarah glanced at the sleeping baby and then at the two drowsy children who had satiated themselves on meat, bread, and sweets. How could she burden Charles with all that encumbered her? Dare she trust him? Would he understand?

She studied his eyes, filled with such tenderness that she could have no doubt whatsoever of his deep affection for her. And yet, she knew she *must* doubt him. His aim was wealth, and she could provide that so easily. Her fortune must surely be more alluring than she herself could ever be. Though his appearance gave every evidence of honesty and truth, she must never encourage Charles Locke in his designs on her. One false step, and she might be forever bound beneath a yoke of woe.

"I have told you enough of my past life to answer your question," Sarah told him. "My father's vain ambitions led me to marry a man with equally shallow aims. King Solomon in his wisdom wrote of man: 'As he thinketh in his heart, so is he.' I have learned that one's dreams give life to one's actions. My goal is peace and happiness, and my decisions must conform to that."

"Do you see no way to happiness other than giving away your fortune?"

"I do not, sir. And I believe my view is supported by every teaching of our Lord."

Charles ran his eyes from her face to the babe in the crib to the two children at Sarah's feet. Then he met her gaze again. "Sarah, why can you not find happiness in the prospect of marriage and children? Clearly you are meant for that purpose. Does our Lord not also teach of this? Is this not intended as the role of women?"

As greatly as Sarah desired to agree with him, she could not. "In the apostle Paul's letter to the church at Corinth, he instructed the believers that the unmarried and widows ought to remain as he was — alone and without attachment. Although Paul allowed that unmarried women should wed, bear children, and guide the house, he preferred that all Christians be alone and devoted entirely to the church."

"We should have great difficulty populating the world with new Christians in that case," Charles said lightly.

"New Christians are not created by being born into a Christian family, sir, no matter what you may have been taught. If we wish to enter the kingdom, we are to be born of the Spirit. That is a new birth altogether, and it is the only one that truly matters to God."

Charles shifted in the rickety chair. Observing his discomfort, Sarah could not refrain from adding a little kindling to the flame. "Do you read the Scriptures, Charles? You once told me you had searched them in an effort to better understand Christ's teachings on material gain. Pray, tell me, have you kept up your pursuit of spiritual enlightenment?"

He shrugged. "I am wholly employed reading English common law at the moment, madam. You have known from the beginning that I am not a pious man. I believe in the teachings of the Bible, but I do not make any great study of that book. I am not bound for the clergy but for the law and the trades. Can you abuse me on this account?"

"Indeed I can. If you do not study the Bible, how can you know what you believe?"

"I know very well what I believe." He stood. "I believe a woman ought to be the loving wife to her husband and the keeper of her home. If God should will, I believe she ought to bear children and be a godly, loving mother to them. I believe a man ought to work hard with his own two hands and the good mind that God has given him in order to provide for his family. And I believe that you, Sarah, were meant to marry me."

At her gasp, he paused for a moment. Then he went on, his eyes like blue flames that burned brighter with every word he spoke. "I believe you love me, Sarah — or you would if you permitted yourself to explore your own feelings instead of keeping them bottled away. And I know I love you. All my beliefs are firm, unchanging, and perfectly in tune with the teachings of Scripture. If you wish to continue challenging me, so be it. I shall duel it out to the finish, for I am resolute."

Unable to make any response at all, Sarah simply stared at the man. How many marriage proposals would he make to her? How often must he tell her he loved her before she could allow herself to believe him?

Observing her consternation, he tipped his head and held out a hand. "And now, dearest lady, it is time we left these children to their slumber and returned ourselves to Bamberfield. I shall send the footman back to Shepton to distribute the rest of the baskets."

Torn between flinging more Bible verses at him and falling into his arms, Sarah managed to collect her wits and let him escort her from the cottage. The rain had slowed to a mist, and steam rose from the thatched roofs around them.

As Sarah lifted her skirts to step into the carriage, she ventured a glance at Charles. "Mr. Locke, you are infuriating," she said in a low voice.

He smiled. "And you are delightful." Then

he leaned closer, putting his lips near her bonnet. "Marry me, my darling Sarah, and I shall make you the happiest woman on earth."

Lest she make some heedless response, she ducked her head and slipped into the carriage. Her sister then commenced such a harangue that neither Sarah nor Charles could say a word all the way to Bamberfield.

"Marry Lord Delacroix?" Sarah lifted her head from the blanket upon which she reclined and eyed her sister. "Now it is you who have gone mad. Why ever would I wish to marry such a man, Pru? He is a rake."

"He *was* a rake. But ever since your return from the Orient, he has been wholly devoted to you. Can you deny it?"

"I most certainly can. Delacroix has shown me no particular attention, and if he did, I should rebuff him at once."

Miffed, Sarah lay back and gazed up at the twining branches and bright green leaves of the large beech tree beneath which she and her sisters reclined. Unlike the previous dreary afternoon, Saturday had brought sunshine, a sapphire sky, and a fragrant breeze that brushed over the fells and made the dandelions dance. Delighted to leave the drafty old house at last, the ladies had enjoyed a lovely picnic of cold meats, cheeses, and fresh lemonade followed by a stroll down to the stream. After wading in the icy water long enough to turn their toes blue, they had climbed back to the beech tree and spread out their blankets in preparation for a long summer's nap.

And then Prudence had dropped her suggestion like a sudden squall.

"Besides, Lord Delacroix is my nephew," Sarah reminded her sister. "As the nearest relation to my husband, he is almost a son to me."

"Pooh!" Mary cried out. "Delacroix is older than you by at least three years. During your marriage to his uncle, he paid you little heed, and no one observed any motherly affection on your part. I think Pru is right in encouraging a union between you. It makes perfect sense that Delacroix should inherit his uncle's wife along with the houses and estates."

"Inherit me — as though I were an old chair or a candlestick?" Sarah gave a sigh of exasperation. "When will you and Pru ever accept that I have no intention of marrying again? I am far more content now than I have ever been, and I cannot see that taking another Delacroix for a husband would increase my chances of happiness at all."

"All you want is your own happiness," Prudence retorted. "I think it very selfish of you."

"I am not the least bit selfish," Sarah replied, her voice rising. "You know very well I am giving my entire fortune to those whose situations and living conditions are deplorable. How can you accuse me of thinking only of myself?"

"Because it is true. Why do you not consider poor Delacroix's unfortunate situation? He has no money and cannot marry for love. And he has been such a cad these many years that no woman in our society wants him for a husband."

"And so I make him the perfect wife?"

"Yes you do," Prudence confirmed.

"Aye, Sarah," Mary chimed in, "for Delacroix needs someone rich as well as forgiving. He has altered himself of late, and you ought to be religious enough to grant him atonement. Why, since meeting you again, he appears to have repented of his excesses entirely. I never see him flirting as he did before you returned from Asia. I believe you would do him very much good if you could get past your own selfish aims."

Appalled at the accusations of her sisters, Sarah stared up at the leaves fluttering like tiny green flags overhead. Clearly Prudence and Mary had conspired to broach this topic, for they had worked out their argument to perfection. But why did they think Sarah could ever be happy with Delacroix? And was she really being selfish in seeking to give away her fortune in a quest for happiness? Dreadful thought!

"I have already endured one marriage in an effort to do good," Sarah told her sisters. "I am not inclined to make the same mistake twice."

"Delacroix is not a bad man," Prudence insisted. "Even Mr. Locke agrees."

"Mr. Locke? When did you speak to him about Delacroix?"

"Yesterday in the carriage while we were waiting for you to return from the cottage. He brought up the subject himself. He suggested that you ought to marry Delacroix, for you would make a good match. Mr. Locke reminded me that although Delacroix is penniless, he is landed and has many friends. One of those friends was Mr. Locke's boyhood companion, and he places utmost confidence in this man's opinion."

"He must have been speaking of Lord Marston's son, the viscount. I believe Mr. Locke attended school with Sir Alexander and his elder brother, Sir Ruel." Sarah considered this news in light of the whispered marriage proposal Charles had extended the previous day. How dare he suggest she marry Delacroix in one breath and then ask for her hand himself in the next? What sort of impetuous and deceitful man was he to behave in such a way?

"If you marry Delacroix, Sarah," Prudence observed, "we shall always be near, for I mean to wed Mr. Locke."

At that, Sarah sat straight up. "Did he propose to you?"

Prudence giggled. "No, but I am thinking of encouraging him in that direction. You have said you want nothing to do with the poor man, and I find him enormously handsome. Since he has friends like Sir Alexander and Lord Delacroix, my husband and I shall be invited into your society quite often. In fact, Sarah, I think you ought to give us Trenton House as a wedding present, for then when we are in town, we shall be living directly across the square from you and Delacroix."

"Upon my word, Prudence Watson, you do run on!" Sarah reached across to grab her bonnet. "I have no plans to marry Delacroix, and you should give up all thoughts of wedding Mr. Locke, for that would be a terrible mistake!"

So saying, she tugged on her bonnet and

tied the ribbons in a hasty bow. As she struggled to her feet, she could see her sisters glancing at each other with brows raised and smirks on their silly faces. Why did they tease her like this? Calling her selfish and suggesting that she marry Delacroix. And the notion of Prudence marrying Charles was —

"Why should I not wed Mr. Locke?" the very girl cried out as Sarah started back toward the brook. "I like him! He is handsome and kind, and he is going to be a wealthy barrister some day! We shall have lots of children and live in Trenton House and be very happy!"

Gritting her teeth, Sarah hitched her skirt above her ankles and began to run. Dreadful girl! Abominable thought! Sarah would never marry Delacroix. And Prudence must not marry Charles. Though Sarah could not have him, yet he was hers. Hers by right. She had found him first, and he adored her. He loved her! Or did he?

Charles rubbed his eyes and yawned as he stood in an open window above the walled garden at Bamberfield on Saturday night. What a bore the weekend had become. He mused on the long hours that now seemed nothing but a waste. After taking Sarah and her sister to Shepton, he had returned them to the house, and they had joined the others for tea. Wanting to dress and refresh himself, Charles was shown to his rooms in a wing as far from the two unmarried ladies as possible — as was perfectly proper. Mr. and Mrs. Heathhill had taken a room near the center of the edifice, that they might chaperone the party.

Though the outing had gone well enough, dinner that evening proved tedious. Mary Heathhill took it upon herself to regale the company with a detailed accounting of all the events of the social season to date. This necessitated much recitation of various gowns, bonnets, jewels, and beaux. The latter topic excited Prudence Watson's enthusiasm, and she began her own review of London's most handsome and eligible bachelors — none of whom, it became obvious, were included in the current party at Bamberfield.

Throughout the meal, Sarah had sat quietly at the far end of the table from Charles, and Delacroix made it his object to entertain her with a running commentary on her sisters' discussion. He offered little jokes and told one or two ribald tales that caused the ladies to gasp in shock. Mr. Heathhill felt obliged to weigh in with anecdotes of his own, all of which revealed him as one of the most deadly dull gentlemen of Charles's acquaintance.

Today had proved hardly better. At breakfast, Sarah had informed the men that as it was a sunny morning, she and her sisters intended to walk into the country and enjoy a picnic. This was to be a ladies' outing, she told them, and the men must occupy themselves elsewhere. Delacroix usurped any discussion of possible activities to declare that he, Mr. Heathhill, and Charles would go fishing.

Although Charles enjoyed the sport, he soon found himself more engaged in hearing Delacroix's plans than in actually casting his fishing line. The lord of Bamberfield estate, it seemed, was intent upon marrying Sarah, and he felt sure he was making headway in the venture. He wanted to know how Charles had got along in urging the young woman in that direction on the previous day's outing to Shepton. Charles could hardly tell Delacroix that — against all his better judgment and in opposition to everything he intended — he had managed to propose a marriage of his own. Instead, he informed Delacroix that Sarah remained committed to her plan of divesting herself of her fortune, that she was as pious as ever, and she intended never to marry.

This evening's meal saw Sarah once again seated at a great distance from Charles and directly across from Delacroix. Miss Watson, who sat at Charles's elbow, amused the company by recounting her sister Mary's tumble into the chilly stream this afternoon. The women, it appeared, had enjoyed a fine day of frolic and dining *alfresco,* while the gentlemen had purported to fish while plotting marital schemes.

Exhausted by the tedium, Charles now made up his mind to depart the house the following morning after church. If possible, he would sit beside Sarah on the pew, for no one could orchestrate that event. The prospect of returning to London and his books pleased him greatly.

As he leaned on the rail outside the window of his bedroom, Charles wondered if Sarah had been correct in her assertions that the company of high society was empty and meaningless. Charles certainly had enjoyed his tea in the cottage with Sarah far more than anything else in the weekend at Bamberfield. Indeed, if the *ton* spent their days at hatching plans and their evenings attending receptions, balls, and dinners, he began to wonder if he truly wished to join that select rank. The gentlemen had little actual work to occupy themselves, for they employed stewards to oversee their finances and bailiffs to manage their tenants and estates. And the ladies . . . well, he could hardly blame Sarah for disdaining a life of embroidery, picnicking, and dabbling in watercolor paints.

The prospect of earning enough wealth to spend the rest of his days fishing, hunting, and dancing produced little interest in Charles's mind. He resolved to discuss the matter with his father. If the duke of Marston and his aristocratic companions were so despicable to James Locke, why was he determined to see his son join their ranks? Why would Charles wish such a fate upon his own sons and grandsons? No, his male progeny had much better employ themselves at some gainful labor than fritter away the hours playing whist and smoking cigars. As for his daughters, they ought to go to school and then take up writing plays and novels or traveling or some other useful occupation. Better yet, they could practice charity in earnest.

As his discomfort increased, Charles decided to take a walk in the garden below his window. The fresh, crisp air would clear his mind, and a stroll through the moonlight might dispel the lethargy that plagued him.

Wondering which door of the large house led into the garden, he studied the carefully plotted hedges and rose beds below. As he surveyed the walled enclosure, he spotted a lone figure emerging from behind the conical shape of a topiary yew.

Sarah. Her ivory evening gown had turned to silver in the moonlight that set a glow over the creamy rose blossoms and pale camellias. The long white gloves that slid up her arms and elbows almost to the poufs of her sleeves appeared ghostlike in the darkness. But Charles could not mistake the graceful way she strolled down the grassy alley between the low boxwood hedges that rimmed the flower beds. He knew the turn of her chin and the set to her shoulders. He knew the silken sheen of her skin. He knew the sweep of her dark hair and the glitter of the diamond tiara she had worn tonight at dinner. This was his Sarah. His beautiful, perfect lady. The desire of his heart.

Lest she leave the garden before he could join her, Charles abandoned his top hat and cane and hurried from the room. The corridor seemed endless, a long tunnel of doors and musty carpet and dripping candles. The stairs, too narrow for a man's boots, were determined to tangle his feet, so he took them two at a time until he reached the ground floor of the house.

Which doors led into the garden? Two wings housing countless rooms stretched out from either side of the grand foyer with its double staircase and marble floor. Charles pushed open the door to the spacious drawing room and crossed it at a trot. His leg was better, he realized with some surprise. Much better. He pushed open a pair of glass-paned doors and emerged on a portico a short distance outside the wall that surrounded the garden. Within that enclosure was the greatest treasure a man could desire.

But where did one enter? Nothing but the soaring stone wall met his eye from end to end. He considered calling her name, but he knew he would startle her. If he went back into the house, he might miss her entirely. Only one option presented itself, and Charles did not hesitate to take it.

As he dashed to the wall, he threw off his coat, yanked the links from his cuffs, and rolled his sleeves up each arm to the elbow. Pausing only a moment, he sized up the barrier. A stone jutted from the wall there. Another not far above it. An easy effort, drawing the thousand such ventures he had undertaken as a boy.

Forgetting his recent injuries, he reached

the first foothold, grasped a craggy rock with his fingertips, and began the ascent.

TWELVE

They were wrong. Prudence and Mary had no idea what they were saying. Sarah . . . *selfish?* Impossible!

Distraught at the very idea, Sarah had been consumed by their hurtful comments all the way from the picnic site back to Bamberfield this afternoon. She could hardly concentrate on Delacroix's prattle throughout dinner. Afterward, the silly chatter and games around the fire had nearly driven her mad. She had hardly been able to wait until Delacroix dismissed the ladies. As her sisters wandered off to bed and the men gathered in the billiards room, Sarah dismissed her lady's maid and fled to the walled garden where she had taken such solace during her marriage.

In anguish, she had walked up and down its pathways for what seemed like hours. How could it be selfish to give away her fortune? It was not selfish! Surely it was the height of generosity and charity. Such benevolence could only arise from a spirit of humility, selflessness, and godly kindness. How could anyone deny it?

Yet neither could Sarah deny some truth in her sisters' accusations. Although she had cared for the blind girls in China and the illiterate heathen hordes in India, Sarah's behavior at the cottage in Shepton had revealed the dark depths of her heart. She was willing to donate her money to the needy — but she hesitated to give of herself. What guilt she had felt as Charles stood talking to the ill woman while she and Prudence hung back by the door, too fearful of polluting themselves to enter and minister to that poor family.

Truly, Pru and Mary had spoken aright when they accused Sarah of selfish aims. She wanted peace, pleasure, and happiness — and she viewed the riddance of her fortune as the only path to that end.

Sarah knew she ought to do as Pru had suggested and wed Delacroix. Such a marriage made perfect sense. Equals in society, they would bring joy to all their friends and relations by reuniting title, fortune, and estate under that respected name. Delacroix himself was handsome and affable enough to please any woman, and unlike his uncle, he would want children. An heir would be vital to the success of his line, and who could deny his desire to continue it?

Though he had been a roué in his youth, Henry Carlyle, Lord Delacroix, was nearing thirty and must be thinking of his future. It was entirely possible, as both Sarah's sisters insisted, that he meant to reform himself, settle down, earn an honorable reputation, and become a gentleman of great esteem and moral principle. Mary and Pru liked him. Even Charles thought he would make Sarah a good husband.

At the thought of Charles and Pru conspiring together inside the carriage at Shepton, Sarah halted her steps and swallowed at the large lump wedged in her throat. How could the man be so wicked? And why was she such a fool as to believe every word he spoke? Within the space of five minutes, he had instructed Pru to encourage her sister to marry Delacroix . . . and then he had proposed to Sarah himself! What could he have meant by such irrational and impetuous behavior?

His goal was clear. Charles would ensnare Sarah if he could. If not, he would see that she married a man with whom he had influence. Delacroix and Charles shared the same friend in Sir Alexander, the future duke of Marston. The two men were now friends themselves! No doubt Charles hoped to involve Delacroix in his tea scheme. Oh, it was too much.

Sarah was nothing but a plaything. A puppet. Men toyed with her. Even God tossed her to and fro. How was she to bear another day of this torment? Why would God not lean down, pluck her out of the morass, and set her feet on solid ground?

"Sarah! Sarah, look up!"

At the voice from on high, Sarah nearly leapt straight out of her slippers. She gave a little cry and grabbed a trellis for support as she searched for the source of the call.

"Sarah, it is I. Upon the wall."

In the gleaming moonlight, she distinguished the crouched figure of a man perched above her on the stone parapet that surrounded the garden. At once, she recognized the broad shoulders and shock of unruly hair.

"Mr. Locke, what on earth — ?" she cried out. "Is it truly you?"

"The very man." So saying, he climbed down into the garden and vanished in the shadows beneath the wall.

Sarah gripped the trellis. "Charles Locke," she called in a soft voice. "Upon my word, you are a rogue, sir! What were you doing on the wall? How long have you been there? I declare, you must go back into the house at once, for I am unchaperoned."

"Impossible, dear lady. I have come to you precisely because you are alone."

Now he emerged into the moonlight, and she realized he stood no more than two paces away. Looking for all the world like a handsome prince come to rescue a maiden from her oppression, he was all dark hair and bare arms and white shirt unbuttoned at the collar. And blue eyes. Very blue eyes that captured the starlight and twinkled like candles as he gazed at her.

Holding tight to the trellis, Sarah squared her shoulders against him. She would not give way. Nothing he could say or do would soften her heart. She knew the truth. He was deceitful. Vainly ambitious. Heartless.

"I saw you when I was looking down from my room," he said now, advancing a pace. Too close. He lifted his head and pointed at the glow of the lamp from a window on the second floor. "It is just up there. I was thinking of a walk in the garden myself when I noticed you here."

"How convenient."

"Indeed, for I wished to tell you that I mean to take my leave of Bamberfield directly after church tomorrow morning.

Though I admire the house and grounds, I feel I cannot depart too soon." He held out his elbow. "Shall we walk, madam?"

"If you spied me from your window, sir, I am certain we may be seen by any number of the guests. I shall walk alone, thank you."

With that, she placed her hands behind her back, knotted her fingers firmly together, and stepped out into the grassy path. He would not sway her. Neither his friendly demeanor nor his honest air would topple her defenses. And she certainly would not believe a single word from his mouth.

"Delacroix had the best intentions in inviting me to his country house," Charles continued, as if unaware of Sarah's grim regard for him. "As did your sister, for her letter to me revealed great compassion for your well-being. But I have come to understand that I cannot be the means of easing your present distress, dear lady. I fear I only add to it by my presence."

"You do, sir. Very much so, and I pray you will not continue shouting our conversation to the world."

She could see him glance at her, but she kept her focus trained on the wall in the distance. "I was assigned," he went on, lowering his voice, "to join your party in the effort of accomplishing two objectives. Miss

Watson wished me very much to lighten your spirits. And Lord Delacroix hoped that I might encourage you to see the great benefit it would bring to you, to your family, and to himself, of course, were you to find it in your heart to marry him."

She paused and turned to him. "Then you admit that you plotted against me in this way?"

"If seeking to make you happy and to secure the contentment of your sisters may be called a plot against you, then, yes, I am such a scoundrel. But I beg to defend myself on that count."

Furious, Sarah swung away and started down the path again. "How can you expect me to accept any possible explanation for your effort to waylay my own aspirations? Were I to wed Delacroix, then I must hand over to him all my fortune, stay in England forever, and endure yet another unhappy marriage."

"Which is precisely why I am taking my leave of this place tomorrow. When I departed London yesterday, I believed I might bring myself to advocate such a match. I reminded myself that Delacroix is young and healthy and capable of providing you the security of a home and the joy of a family. He is your equal in rank, and your sisters admire him. Desiring to keep you in England and see that you are safe and well, I convinced myself that Delacroix might ensure that aim. And so I came to Bamberfield."

Sarah wished rather than believed Charles to be speaking the truth. Thus far, the explanation of his behavior toward her gave every evidence of honesty. Yet how dare he presume to the role of matchmaker? And what had prompted him to tease her with his own proposal of marriage?

No, he was a cad. There could be no other view on the matter.

"You are here," she said calmly, "and tomorrow you go. I cannot see that giving me this information necessitated a climb over the garden wall. Such valiant exertion might be better placed elsewhere."

Charles laughed as he leaned forward and tested his leg. "Perhaps. But I considered the opportunity of speaking to you alone as worth every effort I might put to the task."

"Thus far, you have told me what I knew already. My sister informed me that you had talked with her. She said you urged her to speak to me on Delacroix's behalf. I cannot think why you suppose I should ever want to marry a man whose sole aim in life is the accumulation of material riches. As you know very well, I have turned down an offer of marriage from one such man already." With that, she faced him directly. "Mr. Locke, may I speak frankly?"

"You always do, my dear Sarah. But I must ask that you first hear me out. After all, I did risk life and limb to talk with you."

"Well, I —"

"No, no, it is clear you think ill of me, and rightly so. I have behaved toward you in a most ungentlemanlike manner. Your presence elicits the basest impulses of my heart, I fear. I cannot be in the same room with you for even a moment before I begin to dwell upon your beauty, your gentle hands, your lovely eyes —"

"Mr. Locke, your flattery falls on deaf ears. Any man who could use my sister to press me toward an unwanted admirer is abhorrent to me. That the same man would propose marriage to me with his very next breath is —"

"Is evidence that he is hopelessly in love with you and can say or do nothing to contradict his own feelings. I have loved you from the moment I saw you aboard the *Queen Elinor*. Despite all my best intentions, despite the reasonable advice of my father, despite the obvious unsuitability of the match, I have been unable to prevent myself from loving you. I loved you when you were Mrs. Carlyle, and I love you now. I am convinced that nothing can end my love for you, nor can I advocate the aims of any man other than myself. Yes, Delacroix would be better for you. Yes, he would provide for you and secure your comfort. I am nothing. I have no money, no name, and no hope of a grand inheritance or a sudden elevation to knighthood. I certainly cannot afford to purchase a title for myself. I have nothing but my ambition — an aspect of my character that you clearly despise. And yet even the knowledge that you hate me cannot deter my love for you. I cannot conquer it, no matter how I try. This is why I must leave Bamberfield tomorrow, and this is why I shall never see you again."

He halted at the end of the path where a stone bench lay hidden in the shadow of the wall. Sarah stood so still, so unmoving that she felt as if a quiver of wind might topple her. She could not breathe. Could not will her feet to take another step. Could hardly even think.

She sank onto the bench and clasped her hands in her lap. Oh, for a bonnet with a deep brim to hide beneath! Could he see the turmoil she felt? Did he know the storm his words caused in her breast? And what was to be said? What could possibly be done?

For fully a minute, she sat staring at a clay pot in which a large topiary had been planted. She tried to think how to pray, but she could draw out nothing save the simple cry of her heart.

At last she lifted her head. "Why?" she asked the man who stood over her.

Dropping to one knee, Charles took her hand in his. "Why do I leave Bamberfield? Because I cannot bear to be near you and yet remain apart. Why did I at first support Delacroix's plan? Because I sincerely want your happiness. Why do I wish to keep you in England despite your dream of traveling the world? Because I must have you near me, even if you belong to another man. Why do I love you?"

"Yes, that," she choked out.

"Why not? You are everything I could want in a woman."

"Charles, I am plain, and you cannot deny it. My beauty is nothing to Prudence's. As Mary has pointed out, I cannot sing well. I paint badly. My embroidery is full of knots —"

"If I wanted a wife for painting and embroidery, I should be a shallow man indeed. And I confess, I am selfish enough to desire marriage to a woman with far greater qualities than your sisters' prettiness and pert opinions. Sarah, your eyes are filled with the kindness that wells from your heart. Your sweet lips hold the expression of softness that emanates from your soul. Your beauty approaches a level of holy serenity that I have never before seen in my life, and I daresay your inner spirit wells from the same source. Without and within, you are the most perfect creature I have ever beheld."

"Charles, this is false. . . . I am sure of it."

Rising, he seated himself beside her and kissed her hand. "Sarah, permit me to tell you of the woman who set the highest example of womanly worth I have ever known until I met you. Her name was Maria Wells, and she was the middle of seven children born to a miller and his wife. While riding in a coach to visit her aunt, Miss Wells met a fellow traveler, a young man employed as a footman in a great house near her village. The two were of equal social status, though he could boast a more formal education. That man, Mr. James Locke, wooed and eventually wed Miss Maria Wells."

"Your parents." Sarah's voice was barely a whisper.

Charles nodded. "Within two years of her wedding day, Maria Locke produced a healthy son. From that birth to the end of her life, she was unwell, suffering from a female malady that kept her in constant discomfort. She had no more children and might have become bitter but for her naturally cheerful demeanor. She doted upon her son, encouraged her husband — who rose to the position of steward of a great house — and dedicated herself to the poor and needy in the surrounding countryside. Her devotion to God was absolute and unshakeable. Perhaps a little too plump, always in pain, and certainly bereft of the brood of children she had desired, Maria Locke nevertheless managed to emerge as the most endearing, beautiful, and beloved of women."

"I am sorry I never knew her," Sarah murmured.

"At her funeral, more than a hundred people filled the village church and spilled outside to pay their respects. Her friends mourned her. Her husband never married again. Her son believed himself robbed of the gladdest reason for his existence. And then one day, he was hauled aboard a ship and cast into the arms of a woman so like his mother — and yet so supremely feminine and so infinitely desirable — that he lost his heart to her at once."

"Oh, no . . ." Sarah drew her hand from his. "I cannot believe —"

"In what way do I deceive you? I have told you my reasons for coming to Bamberfield. I tell you now why I must leave."

"Then go, sir," she commanded, standing. "Your presence distresses me, and I was under great duress already."

Without looking back, she started down the path again. He must go! Back over the wall and into the house and away forever. Never mind what he had said. His words could mean nothing to her. His avowal of love and his desire for marriage must be for naught. If she wed at all, her husband had to be someone like Delacroix — and she could not bear to marry such a man. Yet how could she fail to meet her sisters' wishes? How could she be as selfish as they believed?

"Sarah, what troubles you so on this night?" Charles asked, his shadow darkening the path behind her. "Why do you run from me?"

"You have no idea what I endure, sir, and truly it is none of your concern. Go home to London and become a barrister. Use the money you earn to start your tea enterprise.

Marry a good woman and give her children. I must take a different way."

"We were friends once, aboard the ship," he reminded her, falling into step. "Allow me to take that role again and hear your woes. I shall speak no more of my feelings or desires, but I do offer my friendship. Please, Sarah, speak honestly to me, for I cannot bear to see you so unhappy."

"Had you known me in any other place, you would have seen my unhappiness before now," she told him. "But what of it? If I am not happy, then let me bear my sorrows alone. I am not free to be who I was to you before. I never shall."

"Sarah, be reasonable; I beg you." He caught her arm and turned her to face him. "I know less of God and His character than you do, but I am certain He cannot mean for you to live in misery. Love, joy, peace — these are the fruit of the Holy Spirit. You tell me you are reborn of the Spirit. You say every true Christian must be born again as well. In every way, I am compelled to submit my life and all my ambitions to God. And yet your abiding unhappiness discourages me."

"Charles, do not lay this burden on me, too! Already, my sisters accuse me of selfishness. They say I seek my own happiness above all else. Now you tell me that my unhappiness keeps you from God! I am not responsible for their happiness or your salvation. Work it out on your own!"

As the tears she had been holding back began to well, Sarah grabbed up her skirts and ran from him. She was at the far end of the garden, but she knew her way through it without a stumble.

Did Charles love her? Could he be a true friend? Dare she bare her heart? No! It was all impossible. She was alone. Utterly and completely alone. And why did God cast her about in such a way? Dangling the possibility of true love before her, then snatching it away again; providing her with sisterly affection, then hurling their accusations at her; tossing her in the path of a man she disliked, then cornering her into marrying him!

"Sarah, I shall not be deterred." Charles stepped around her and stopped dead in the path, his hands catching her shoulders. "You must speak to me! I insist upon it. Tell me what weighs so heavily upon you. Allow me to ease your pain."

"You can do nothing for me, Charles! My path is set — as it has been from the day I was born a daughter instead of a son. From the moment I drew my first breath, I became my father's pawn. To this day I am nothing but a pawn. My life is laid out. Each move I make is directed already."

"By whom? If God is your master, then surely He desires the best for you."

"His will is greater than my own, Charles. He wants the best for me — but does that ensure my happiness?"

"Why not? How can God's love bring you anything but joy?"

"God loves those poor cottagers in Shepton, does He not? Yet look how they suffer! Am I so different for all my wealth and education? No, indeed, for I must bend to His plan for me. I must follow the path laid out, and I dare not complain of my woes."

"This God you depict is too severe. Why do you not feel His tender compassion, Sarah?"

"By Christ's sacrifice, I know of God's love. But *feel* it? No, I feel only His correction and reproof."

"But I believe God demonstrates His love daily — through others. You are an example of that yourself, Sarah. God showed His love for Shepton's poor through your tender compassion toward those children yesterday. My mother, in her kindness to others, acted out her faith. More than any other, she was my example of God's love. Though I have not been as faithful as you, I do feel God's care for me. How could I not, when He allowed me to survive the pirate attack? He loves you just as much, surely."

"Love? What do I know of that emotion? You were born in love and brought up in it, Charles. I doubt I would recognize love if I saw it."

"But you do see it. You see it in me."

"You do not love me, Charles. You are no different from my father and all the other men I have known, for you are determined to compress and shape me into some foreign idea of what you think I ought to be."

"That is a cruel indictment, and I must counter it. My love for you is honest and selfless."

"Selfless love? I cannot believe such a thing exists."

"But, Sarah —"

"Listen to *my* story, sir, and see how it stands up against your own sweet tale of a dear mother and an attentive father. Perhaps when I am done, you will understand me at last." She pushed his hands from her shoulders and lifted her chin. "Once upon a time, there lived an avaricious young apothecary who specialized in providing his clients with opium, laudanum, and other such soporific cures and tinctures. This man, Gerald Watson by name, seduced his wealthy landlord's daughter. Forced into marriage by her delicate condition, the woman despised her husband. Her father refused to grant a dowry and cut her off from the family. She gave birth to a daughter — a grave disappointment to Mr. Watson, who had placed all his hopes in having a son. Wishing to emulate the lifestyle of the aristocracy he so greatly admired, he took the baby from her mother and settled her with a wet nurse in the nearby village. There the little girl spent the first four years of her life and saw her own family but rarely. During his rise to wealth, Mr. Watson compelled his wife to forge social alliances for him using whatever means she could. Evidently, Mrs. Watson embraced the role, for she entertained many of London's wealthiest gentlemen and became courtesan to a prominent member of the House of Lords."

"Sarah, I had no idea. Please, you need not continue this, for my sympathy toward you is complete already."

Willing away her own revulsion, she held up a hand. But she could not hide the bitter tone in her voice as she continued. "Do not stop me now, Charles, for we are just to the interesting part. Another child was born to the scheming Watsons, again a girl. And then another daughter joined the first two. They named her Prudence — a little joke between them, perhaps. Mr. Watson's trade flourished. He sent his firstborn away to school at the age of five. There she lived in a cold attic and was taught her French, Latin, arithmetic, and grammar. Once a year, at Christmastime, she returned home. She and her sisters — who were taught at home — became warmly attached and wrote often to each other while apart. One summer, their mother went away to Brighton and suddenly died — the cause of death even now unknown to her three daughters. At thirteen, the eldest was sent to a new school to be trained in etiquette, painting, stitching, and other female accomplishments. At sixteen, she received the news that her father had sold his apothecary for a great deal of money. At seventeen, she was whisked from school and settled at Trenton House in London. Her father dressed her in new gowns and slippers, presented her at court, and saw to it that she was taken out into society."

"Such a change in circumstance. It must have been a shock. And the two sisters?"

"They were comfortable enough, for by that time they had formed friendships within the *ton* and knew how to enjoy the fine things their life offered. But then it was time for marriage."

"Sarah, I know your husband made you unhappy," Charles said. "You need not speak of him."

"Yet that marriage placed the final seal upon my character. You see, sir, my father decreed I should wed George Carlyle, Lord Delacroix, a man twice my age and utterly unknown to me. No more than a week into the marriage, I realized I was bound to a man devoted to dissipation and vice. Any hope of joy I had nurtured fled before the certainty that I would never bear a child, never know the loving arms of a husband, never enjoy even the slightest warmth of human kindness."

The expression on Charles's face told Sarah that he knew the reputation of her late husband. Taking her hand in his, he held it to his mouth and pressed his lips to her fingers. "Dearest Sarah," he murmured, meeting her steady gaze, "I had no idea that you had suffered so."

"I did not think it suffering then," she said, "nor do I now. It is all I have ever known. I am shaped as God meant to shape me, and I shall be used as He sees fit. Unlike my sisters, who are silly and romantic, I take my philosophy from Ovid, Aristotle,

Shakespeare, Milton, and the Bible. I believe in heaven and hell, passion and tragedy, love and hate. But I have never experienced such things. I know only how to exist . . . and not how to feel."

"I cannot believe this," Charles said. "Nor shall I accept it. Perhaps the past taught you to shun all hope of true affection, but your father and husband are dead now. You are released from their bondage."

"Released?" She forced a smile. "You have lived too far from my sphere, sir. At the death of my husband, I became the prey upon which every eligible male in London descended. My fortune . . . my title . . . why, I might as well be a sparrow in a sky filled with ravenous eagles, sir. You, perhaps, are one of those."

"I am not," he cried, his dark eyebrows drawing together. "How could you possibly think —"

"I have been wooed with professions of love and passion a hundred times. My beauty has been admired. My praises sung. My accomplishments applauded. Dear sir, your avowals of adoration are nothing new to me."

"But they are not lost on you entirely. I see what you feel for me, Sarah."

"You see nothing," she said. "I have only

one desire, and that is to obey God."

"The God who condemned you to such an unhappy life?"

"He has shown me a path to a new life. I must believe that. It is my only hope. Three years ago, at a time when I felt picked and plucked and torn nearly to pieces by the scavengers, I was sitting one Sunday in church. That is when I heard the lesson of the rich young ruler, as if for the first time. God Himself seemed to speak to me that day. A bright beam of light filled my heart as I finally understood. The enemy was not my father, not my husband, not the shallow admirers who fawned over me. My enemy was my fortune. Wealth prevented me from earthly happiness and would one day bar me from heaven. I knew at once that I must rid myself of my riches — and the sooner the better."

"And you were about that task when I met you." Charles lifted her hand again and pressed his lips gently to it. "My dearest lady, how completely I understand your actions."

"Understand me, yes, but approve?" Sarah tugged her hand away and turned her shoulder to him as she poured out the pain that stormed inside her. "Mary and Prudence insist I am cruel and heartless, giving my money away only to please myself and failing to think of my poor family. They want me to marry Delacroix! And how can I deny them this wish? My motive in giving away the fortune *is* selfish, after all, for I do seek my own happiness!"

"As do we all. Come to me, Sarah," he said, placing his arm around her shoulders and turning her into his embrace. "Do not weep; I beg you. Believe me when I tell you that I see your heart. I know your desires, and they are good. You are well intentioned in all you do, my darling, beautiful lady."

Sarah shivered as his warmth enfolded her, his breath heating her bare neck, and the scent of his skin filling her nostrils. As he spoke, his fingers spread wide, covering her back and pressing her closer against his chest. Though she tried to resist him, she could not. Every word he spoke rang true. His every caress drew and opened her to the possibility of love. Like a thirsty child, she slipped her arms around him and clutched his shirt, reveling in the solid mass of sinew, bone, and muscle beneath it as she drank in hope and promise and passion.

"You have provided for your sisters already." Charles spoke softly against her ear. "They cannot fault you, my love. But you must soften yourself if you wish to remove the barriers you have built so high around your heart. No matter how jealous your sisters may be, they adore you. Can you not see that? And I love you sincerely. I want what is best for you. Above all that I hope and plan for myself, I wish to make you happy. Please believe —"

"Lady Delacroix?"

"Sarah!"

"Oh, heaven help us!"

The cries of shock poured down Sarah's spine like cold water. Still clinging to Charles, she turned her head to see her two sisters and their host standing inside the garden gate. Delacroix held up a lantern, and the yellow beam that washed down the grassy pathway lighted her transgression for all to see.

THIRTEEN

"Oh, Sarah!" Prudence Watson rushed down the path, her arms flung wide. "What has he done to you?"

Charles stood back as the two women embraced. The shock of exposure had rendered him speechless, and he could only watch in dismay as Mary Heathhill now followed her sister's example in throwing her arms around Sarah. Weeping, crying out as though the world had come to an end, exclaiming in dismay, the three sisters made an indistinguishable rosette of white silks and muslins, pink arms, tearstained cheeks, and flowing hair.

"Locke, what is the meaning of this outrage?" Now Lord Delacroix strode toward the gathering, his boots eating up the length of the grass swath and his shoulders braced as if for battle.

Charles touched the small knife he wore at his waist, reassuring himself that he had some means of defense should the master of the house be inclined to challenge him. He had not intended to compromise the lady. But his love for Sarah had caused him to throw caution to the winds. Never in his life had he heard a more desolate tale, and it was impossible that he would refrain from offering her whatever comfort he could. Certainly, they ought not to have embraced. Even his chaste kisses must be regarded as suspect. But dash it all, his actions were defensible!

Drawing a deep breath, he faced Delacroix. "Sir, my deepest apologies to you for any offense you may have taken." He made a stiff bow. "I came upon Lady Delacroix in the garden this evening and sought to relieve her suffering. Any indiscretion in the foregoing incident is entirely my own, I assure you."

"You scoundrel!" Delacroix exploded. "You thief! You were to press *my* case — not your own! We had an agreement, sir. You pledged me your oath."

"I pledged you nothing," Charles snarled back. "I did not agree even to come here this weekend. But for Miss Watson's letter, I should be in London at this very moment."

"As well you should be! Sir, you are no longer welcome on my property."

"I am more than happy to depart this place." He glanced at Sarah, who was wedged tightly between her sisters. "Lady Delacroix, please forgive me any injury I have caused you. Mrs. Heathhill, Miss Watson, my apologies for your present distress. Excuse me."

Another brief bow and he made for the gate. But Delacroix started after him. "And how is this travesty to be explained to the general public, Locke? I ought to have you bound in chains and locked away forever! You are a cad to prey upon the lady in such a way!"

"You, sir, are the cad." Charles turned on his heel and jabbed a finger at the man. "My intentions toward Lady Delacroix are honorable. Can you say the same?"

"I am not the one who has just exposed her to such an infamous seduction! At all times I have behaved as a gentleman toward Lady Delacroix. But you —"

"I sought to comfort her in her distress — nothing more."

"You are the cause of her distress, sir!"

"No more than you. But what would you know of that, for all your attentions toward her have but one aim — the acquisition of her fortune."

"And your aims are more principled?"

"Infinitely. I seek only her happiness."

"But you came to Bamberfield at my request, did you not? Miss Watson's letter was written under my direction. Can you deny you knew that? Of course not, for you are too well aware that her sisters and I stand in agreement regarding Lady Delacroix's future. Both Mrs. Heathhill and Miss Watson share with me the goal of settling her into the security of home and family. Only you, sir — in whom we held such hope — have proven faithless. Your single duty was to urge her toward that happy future."

"Toward you and your own happy future, do you mean?"

Delacroix lowered his voice and turned his back on the ladies. "Indeed, and you would have been well compensated for your services. But you could not accept the portion due you, for you had in mind to claim the whole treasure! You want her for yourself — vain, proud man. You have nothing. You are no one. Yet you presume to everything! And seeing, as you surely do, that your suit is worthless, you attempt to seduce her. Seduce and ravish her in my garden!"

"Upon my word, you are rash," Charles growled. "I have neither seduced nor ravished any woman, nor should I undertake such reprehensible behavior. I am a gentleman, sir. My honor and reputation remain untarnished. The scene you witnessed may be easily explained. Lady Delacroix was in distress, and I asked after her emotional state. That is all. Your accusations are unfounded, and they serve you ill."

Fearful that Delacroix might try to draw Sarah into the argument, Charles strode toward the gate again. He could hear the man following, but he would not stop. In truth, Charles knew he had placed Sarah in a difficult position, and he was at fault. He had no defense for his behavior other than his love for her — and such justification would hardly stand with a man like Delacroix.

"Do you turn your back on me, sir?"

Charles kept walking. "You dismissed me from your house some time ago."

"Make certain you are not seen near the premises again." As they halted in the shadow of the arbor that arched over the gate, Delacroix dropped his voice to a whisper. "Does the lady love you, sir? Tell me the truth at once."

Biting off his retort that it was none of the man's business, Charles gritted his teeth. "She does not," he said finally.

"And you acknowledge that such a union may never be?"

"You know it cannot. Why do you hold the slightest doubt? Sir, you may speak to Sir Alexander on my account, if you will. He will vouch for my character and reputation. I cannot make her love me, nor would I compromise her in any way. The lady and I were friends once, and I believe we are still. What you witnessed was nothing more than an expression of that companionable affection, for she is most aware of her position . . . and of mine."

"I see. And what is her regard for me?"

"You were not the subject of our discussion."

"Should she contact you in the future, sir, you must swear to convey to me the content of any conversation. You owe me that much."

"I owe you nothing, Delacroix."

"I could have you locked up."

"And destroy the lady's reputation along with my own? I think not." Charles wrapped a hand around the cool iron of the garden gate. "Have no fear, sir. Your chances of winning her hand are as good as any man's. Maybe better. You hold her sisters in your palm already. Perhaps the three of you will win her fortune after all."

"If God is willing. But we have yet one obstacle in our path." Delacroix crossed his arms and let out a breath. "The lady clearly prefers your companionship above that of any other man. Why, I cannot say, for you are as small and unimportant as a louse."

"One louse in a man's hair can cause a great deal of woe, sir." Charles tipped his head in farewell as he stepped out of the garden. "And now, I wish you good evening, Lord Delacroix. May your itch be of short duration — though lice, I am told, can be abominably difficult to eradicate."

"Delacroix instructed you to write to Mr. Locke?" Sarah exclaimed, hearing her own voice close to hysteria. "He actually gave you the words to say? Oh, Pru, how could you conspire with that man in such a way? Do you care for me so little?"

"I love you dearly, Sarah," Prudence cried, sobbing into her handkerchief as she sat on the end of her sister's bed.

After the disastrous encounter in the walled garden, the three women had retired to Sarah's bedchamber to talk, while Delacroix and Mr. Heathhill went into the drawing room to smoke cigars, drink port, and discuss the evening's events. Mr. Locke, it must be assumed, had left Bamberfield House for London.

Though Sarah would have preferred to be

alone, she could hardly dismiss her sisters, who were nearly as distraught as she. The ornate bedroom, with its blue brocade curtains, cut-velvet bed hangings, gilded chairs, carved picture frames, and thick Persian carpet could do nothing to comfort any of them. Still fully dressed, Sarah lay back against the pillows and pulled the down-filled bedding to her chin. Prudence curled at her feet, her white hankie damp with tears. And Mary sat on the vanity stool, occasionally glancing into the mirror as if to make certain she displayed the proper expression for this somber and most worrying occasion.

"Delacroix told me he had not been able to persuade Mr. Locke to join us this weekend," Prudence explained to Sarah, "and I very much wanted him to come. That is why I wrote to him — I hoped he would cheer you."

"You hoped to flirt with him," Mary corrected. "You and Sarah are the two most foolish sisters any woman could ever have to endure. I thank God I am married and settled happily with my dear Mr. Heathhill. Sarah, your piety and melancholy will drive us all to distraction. And, Pru, your irresponsible trifling with men is abhorrent. You are the most audacious coquette in the kingdom, and you subject all of us to ridicule with your behavior."

"Well, you are a profligate spendthrift," Prudence whimpered over her damp hankie, "and you will squander every farthing in poor Mr. Heathhill's coffers."

"I shall not! I merely keep my proper place in society — though I should do a better job of it if Sarah would stop clinging so tightly to her purse strings. Honestly, sister, you proclaim yourself a missionary with one side of your mouth and kiss Mr. Locke with the other!"

"I did not kiss Mr. Locke," Sarah insisted.

"How can anyone kiss a man with one side of her mouth, Mary?" Prudence tossed out. "Really, you are too ridiculous to be believed."

"I saw her in the garden! I saw what she was doing with that man. Oh, Sarah, what a shock you gave us all. He was holding you, and you were kissing him —"

"I was *not* kissing him!"

"If it had been me in the garden, I should have kissed him straightaway." Prudence folded the wet hankie and tucked it into her sleeve. "I believe Mr. Locke is the most dashing, the kindest, and certainly the handsomest of men."

A soft knock on the door drew the attention of all three sisters. As a head emerged into the room, Sarah recognized her lady's maid. The young woman stepped inside, curtsied, and drew her night robe more closely to her throat. Her brown hair done up in curl papers, Anne was panting a little, as though she had been running.

"Beg pardon, my lady," she said, glancing at the other women. "Lord Delacroix's valet woke me and said there was a to-do in the garden just now, and I must hurry to you at once. May I be of assistance?"

"Thank you, Anne," Sarah told her. "All is well. I was speaking to Mr. Locke when my sisters and the baron happened upon us. Now we are discussing the matter at hand in order to draw some conclusions. Your services are not needed, but I thank you for —" She paused. "Anne, your father is a minister, is he not?"

"Yes, madam. A rector."

"And you are a Christian?"

"I am, indeed. Very much so."

"Come and sit with us, then. Perhaps you will have some valuable advice to contribute." Sarah pointed to a chair. "Mary, Prudence, this is Miss Anne Webster from Nottingham. She knows the particulars of my current situation, for I have not attempted any secrecy. I have found Anne to be more than a lady's maid. She is a friend."

Flushing bright pink, Anne perched on the edge of the chair and folded her hands in her lap. Sarah felt as though the young woman had been sent by God and not the valet. If Anne would speak her mind — as she very often did — the communication would be one of good sense born of a solid education and well-founded religious instruction. And that could only bode well for Sarah.

"Now, then, Pru," Sarah addressed her youngest sister, whose expression betrayed her dismay at this unexpected violation of their privacy, "you were telling us that you find Mr. Locke exceedingly handsome."

"I do," Prudence returned. "I cannot think what he sees in you, Sarah, for you are quite determined to be dull on every occasion. But he does like you; that much I know. He only came to Bamberfield because of you, for I truly believe he did not know Delacroix had asked me to write that letter."

Sarah tried to swallow her anger. "I can hardly accept that you and Delacroix plotted against me to bring Mr. Locke here. How devious of you! And Delacroix intended to pay Mr. Locke to promote his suit!"

"Why should Mr. Locke not accept such an offer?" Mary asked. "He has your friendship, but he stands to gain nothing by it. Delacroix no doubt promised Mr. Locke a handsome sum should he press you into accepting a marriage offer."

"Pay him for such a service? No, that cannot be true. Neither man would stoop so low. But Delacroix claims that Mr. Locke's kindness to me is born of a desire to have my fortune for himself." Sarah glanced at her sister. "Do you think that is true, Mary?"

"Of course it is true! What reasonable man thinks of anything but money? You told us yourself that Mr. Locke has dreams of establishing a tea company, and clearly he intends to have it by whatever means possible. He may be poor and untitled, but he is not stupid. My husband informed me that he had spoken to Mr. Locke during their fishing expedition this morning, and that the plan for the tea company is a good one. Mr. Locke will be able to use his influence with Sir Alexander of Marston to make many useful associations."

Mary paused a moment, considering the situation before continuing. "He cannot have done himself any good tonight by offending Delacroix. My husband will have to distance himself from Mr. Locke as well —

at least for a time. Even so, the Marston connection is a strong one, and it will serve him well enough. When he has become a barrister, Mr. Locke can further associate himself with influential men and build his fortune. Once established as a gentleman of means, he will use his connections to apply to investors. From then, it should be quite easy to move into the tea trade."

Sarah could not deny what her sister was saying. Surely Mr. Heathhill had heard the plan from Charles himself. "But why would Mr. Locke risk all good opinion by attempting to seduce me?" she asked.

"Lady Delacroix's question is a good one," Anne spoke up suddenly. "Mr. Locke would not behave in such a way. The danger to his reputation would be too great."

"Thank you, Anne," Sarah said, gratified to have an advocate. "Mr. Locke is a sensible man. He values his standing in society too much to jeopardize it."

"Oh, Sarah, your fortune is far greater than any risk to Mr. Locke's reputation," Mary said. "If he can win you over — if he can convince you to throw off your family and friends in favor of an ill-conceived marriage to him — then his future is assured. He will hardly care what anyone thinks! And why should he? He will have enough money to build an entire tea dynasty and see to the future of his heirs for generations to come."

"But I am sure Mr. Locke truly cares for Sarah," Prudence insisted.

"He is well liked below stairs," Anne added. "All the staff find him most agreeable. He is a kind man. A generous man. And I believe he is an honorable man."

"The material word in that, Miss Webster, is *man*." Mary stood and smoothed down her skirts. She had rushed out to the garden in her dressing gown and mobcap, but the white cotton and lace headwear had fallen off in her haste. Now her hair flowed down onto her shoulders, making her look younger and sweeter than her tone implied.

"Mr. Locke may care for Sarah," she continued, "but he cares far more for her fortune. I am sorry to be the one to give you such disappointing information, ladies, but I must assure you that men do not fall in love. Not with women, anyway. They love pounds, guineas, and pence. They love horses and strong drink. And they love dallying with pretty girls. But they marry for rational reasons. Woe betide the man who would let his fondness for a woman overcome his good sense. No, indeed, men are very measured in their thinking. They rank us, you know, each one of us on a scale of usefulness to their aims. Sarah is not a great beauty, but she rates the top position on any eligible man's list of desirable women. Prudence, you *are* beautiful, but you must fall far lower than Sarah, because you have not even half her fortune. I was lucky to win Mr. Heathhill, who both admires my appearance and appreciates my dowry, such as it was. Miss Webster, despite her father's position as a clergyman, has little hope of making a profitable marriage. I am sorry to say that ladies' maids may marry only other members of a household staff. Or peddlers who come to the back door to sell their wares."

"I cannot believe all men are such schemers," Prudence protested. "After all, what of Shakespeare's sonnets and John Donne's professions of passion —"

"Shakespeare wrote sonnets to his mistress, and Donne was a minister!"

"Yes, but Milton —"

"He was blind."

"Alexander Pope —"

"Essays and epitaphs. Come, Pru, you cannot toss any more poets at me without drawing the same response. No man actually loves his wife — not in the way he might love God or his mistress or his own cherished philosophies. Mr. Locke came to

Bamberfield to accomplish one of two ends. He planned to press Sarah to marry Delacroix — by which he could enrich his own coffers. Better yet, he hoped to win Sarah and her fortune for himself. Can either of you deny it?"

Sarah stared down at her hands, so ardently kissed by Charles Locke not an hour before. How sweet his words had been. How loving his embrace. How perfect and gallant his behavior toward her. Nothing he had said or done had been truly ungentlemanlike. In every way he had appeared the honorable friend he claimed to be.

But Mary could not be wrong. The enormity of Sarah's wealth once again weighed too heavily to be discounted. Charles did want it. Not even he would deny that. How could she even be sure of his motive in climbing over the garden wall? Had it been to inform her that he meant to leave her forever . . . or to lure her into an alliance from which he would accomplish everything to which he aspired?

"I have a very decided opinion on what ought to be done after tonight's events," Mary announced. "Will you hear me out?"

The women nodded. Although her sisters could never fully know her heart, Sarah had to trust that they did care for her. Through their many years apart, the letters had flowed — always a flurry of information about joys and woes from Mary and Pru, and a return of the details of her studies and schoolmates from Sarah. At Christmastime, the three had slept in the same room and stayed up far too late each night engaged in discussions much like this one. Each girl had taken her own path into adulthood, but the bond among them remained strong.

Now Mary stood to impart her wisdom, the proud and knowledgeable married sister. Sarah could not deny that Mary knew more about men, more about society, more about real life than either she or Prudence. They might not agree with her, but certainly they would listen.

"It is my judgment," Mary proclaimed, "that you, Sarah, ought to marry Delacroix. He knows you are a valuable prize, and he will treat you accordingly. He owns two good homes and an estate of considerable size here at Bamberfield. He is well connected in society, and he will have to behave himself properly or risk endangering his lucrative marriage. In exchange, you will have comfort and security. Despite your humble origins, your reputation will be perfectly established. And most important, you will bear children to give you joy and care for you in your old age. You cannot object to Delacroix, as you might have your first husband. Delacroix is handsome enough and certainly should be able to provide for you amply in the bedroom."

"Mary!" Prudence let out a squeal. "How can you talk so calmly about such delicate matters?"

"This is hardly delicate, Pru. It is among the most practical considerations a woman ought to make before taking a husband. She must be certain that her spouse is healthy and strong enough to put her into the breeding way."

Anne cleared her throat. "Mrs. Heathhill's point is well-taken. With children, a house, and enough money at hand, a woman may spend her days in contented association with friends and family."

"Contentment — no matter what her husband chooses to do," Mary confirmed.

"You are more than practical, Mary," Sarah said. "You are cynical."

"I think not. I watched our father maneuver his way through the pitfalls of society, and I know how it is properly done." She shrugged her shoulders. "The climb to wealth and status is not so difficult as one might imagine. As for you, Prudence, I am convinced that you ought to marry as well. In the past year or two, you have become rash and heedless. Your flirtations are likely to get you into trouble — and to bring all your relations under undue scrutiny. You will need a man who is handsome enough to please your eye, but one who is not too rich to permit you the freedom to go off and be entirely silly. You need a husband with valuable connections in society. And you need someone with the education, the sober demeanor, and the more advanced age to ground you in reality. I believe the man to fit the bill is Mr. Charles Locke."

"Oh, lovely!" Prudence cried out. "But can you be serious about this? And what of Sarah? Mr. Locke wants her, not me!"

"No matter what he may want, he cannot have Sarah, for she is far too wealthy to marry him. You have just enough money to make the match a good one for him, Pru, and despite his rash behavior in the garden tonight, I think he is perfect for you. When he has become a barrister and has established his tea trade, he may very likely be able to use his connections to purchase a title. He has a good head on his shoulders, and he is old enough to know what he wants in life. His association with the Marston name is an excellent advantage, and you will bring your Delacroix connection to the marriage. You think he is handsome, and he certainly cannot object to you. So it seems perfect."

"But should Miss Watson not perhaps aim higher than Mr. Locke?" Anne inquired. "There are a great many men who must admire her beauty. She might be able to win a baronet. Or even a baron."

"Aye, or a viscount," Prudence added.

"Men will always admire you until you lose your beauty, Pru. They will court you and fawn over you, but they will not wed you. Not the rich or titled ones, anyway. I am sorry to say, but unless Sarah suddenly decides to settle a great deal more money on you, you will have to accept someone very like Mr. Locke."

"I admire this plan," Prudence announced. "You have turned down Mr. Locke's proposal, Sarah, so you cannot be too angry with me for marrying him, can you?"

Sarah tried to force a smile to her lips. "No, of course not."

"But you do not look pleased, sister. I think you do like Mr. Locke. After all, you were kissing him —"

"I was *not* kissing him! He had come to the garden to tell me he meant to leave

Bamberfield after church tomorrow. He saw that I was distressed, and he comforted me. That is what you witnessed, nothing more."

"May I inquire what had upset you so, madam?" Anne asked. "When you returned to your room after dinner, I saw that you were greatly troubled, and it pained me to leave you."

"In truth, I was distraught over my conversation with my sisters at our picnic today," Sarah told her. "They accused me of being selfish by seeking my own happiness. I do not wish to be thought of in such a way. And yet I can think of no better means by which to bring myself joy than to be rid of my fortune."

"Why not turn it over to us?" Prudence asked brightly. "I am sure Mary and I should be very happy to have it."

"If I cannot bear such a plague myself, how could I even think of visiting it upon the two I care for most in the world? No, indeed, I have given each of you enough money to see that you are secure, but not so much that it might grieve you, as it has me."

Mary tossed her head. "Oh, Sarah, how can you claim to suffer from your fortune?"

"You know the price our dear sister has paid in life," Prudence spoke up. "We both saw how our father used Sarah to accomplish his ends. And then her husband took advantage of her wealth without giving her anything but his title in return."

"A title is worth a great deal. It is one's ticket into good society."

"Still, Mary, I begin to sympathize with Sarah in this. If she keeps the fortune, she must remain a pawn. She could never be sure her husband truly cared for her."

"All her friendships would be suspect," Anne put in.

"That is true. Even Mary and I — who have always loved her — seem always to be clamoring for a greater share in her legacy. Although it is difficult not to think of the benefits of wealth, we must remember it has its drawbacks."

"Thank you, Pru," Sarah said in relief. "More than all that, in keeping the money, I cannot be obedient to the teaching of Jesus. Christians are not to seek riches. The Bible clearly teaches this. If we wish to enter the kingdom of heaven, we must sell all we have, give the proceeds to the poor, and follow Christ."

"My father often preached from that passage in the Gospel of Mark," Anne told the others. "Jesus spoke those words to a man for whom money was a barrier to heaven.

315

The rich young ruler loved his money more than he loved Jesus."

"But you are not like that, Sarah," Prudence said. "You have got things the right way round — loving God at the top and your fortune after."

"Indeed," Mary said. "Sarah does not like her fortune at all."

Anne glanced at Sarah. "I do believe Jesus knew that rich and poor alike would follow Him, my lady. Surely He did not expect all His disciples to be fishermen or tentmakers."

"Besides," Prudence said, "do you really wish to live like those cottagers in Shepton, Sarah? Too poor to have wood on your fire? Too sick to care for your children? What good can you do for God if you must struggle simply to exist?"

Sarah closed her eyes and let out a breath. "I do not know."

"Well, I know," said Mary. "If you are poor, you can do nothing useful at all. The right thing for everyone to do is to become as rich as possible, give tithes to the church, and enjoy the rest of one's money as much as one possibly can. And, Sarah, the best way for you to be successful in that aim is to marry Lord Delacroix. Let Pru have Mr. Locke, for then you and he may continue your warm friendship in the ease and comfort of our family gatherings."

"That is quite true, Sarah," Prudence put in. "If I were married to Mr. Locke, you could remain his dear friend without causing any undue speculation."

Mary set her hands on her hips. "That is exactly what I am proposing. Sarah and Delacroix will take their proper place as kind and generous patrons of the poor — a celebrated couple devoted to charity as well as to the well-being of their own family and friends. Mr. Heathhill and Mr. Locke will benefit from associations with Delacroix, as will Pru and I. We shall all rise in society, enjoy happy lives, and do our Christian duty by the needy. There. What do you think?"

"It is a brilliant plan," Prudence cried, stepping off the bed and hurrying across the room to throw her arms around Mary. "And I think you are the dearest, wisest, and cleverest of sisters. Let us all see the good in this! We shall have homes in Belgravia — if Sarah will be kind enough to give Trenton House to Mr. Locke and me — and we can all come to Bamberfield for riding and picnics whenever we wish, and Mary will plan wonderful parties and balls for us every weekend, and everything will be absolutely marvelous. We shall be a family again, even better than we were long ago in Cheapside, because Sarah will be with us every day and not sent away to school. And our children will grow up together with proper mothers and fathers and governesses. And we shall all have love and happiness and contentment and joy! Oh, my darling sisters, what a happy, happy night!"

As she and Pru spun around and around in giddy pleasure, Mary laughed and clapped her hands. "Please say yes, Sarah!" she cried. "Please be happy along with us!"

Her heart welling with an unbearable mixture of longing and pain, Sarah slipped out of the bed and embraced her sisters. More than almost anything, she wished to fulfill their dreams. She wanted to be faithful to God and not a selfish, willful woman.

Yet somewhere in the farthest recesses of her soul, a blue-eyed man's words whispered to her: *I loved you when you were Mrs. Carlyle, and I love you now. I am convinced that nothing can end my love for you.*

Truth? Or lies? Sarah clung to her sisters and allowed her tears to spill over at last. As Prudence pulled a damp hankie from her sleeve and began to dab, Sarah softly kissed each girl on the cheek.

"Give me tonight," she said. "Allow me the time to think and pray. Tomorrow I shall give you my answer."

With fond hugs and warm wishes for a peaceful sleep, Mary and Prudence at last left the room.

Anne rose quietly to bid her mistress a brief farewell. "My prayers will join yours," she added; then she whispered a Bible verse: " 'All things, whatsoever ye shall ask in prayer, believing, ye shall receive.' "

"It is the believing that is difficult," Sarah confessed.

Anne smiled in acknowledgment, took her mistress's hand, and squeezed it briefly before crossing the room. As the door shut behind her lady's maid, Sarah went to the window and gazed down on the garden where Charles had held her in his arms. She could almost see him, almost hear him. But he was gone now, back to London and his father and his studies. Back where he belonged.

Stepping away from the window, Sarah released the ties that held the curtains apart and watched as the heavy brocade swung down into place.

FOURTEEN

Charles sat at the window, its diamond-leaded panes pushed open to admit the afternoon light. No matter how often the maid cleaned the glass, the soot from London's many coal fires quickly blackened it again and made reading almost impossible. As he tried to absorb the book of English law in his hands, Charles shivered. The house felt cold and musty as the bustle of London rattled by on the streets outside. He had lit a fire in the book-lined library, but he could not find warmth in its merry glow.

Charles knew he would never see Sarah again, and he must accept it. The evening he had climbed over the garden wall at Bamberfield and had been exposed by Delacroix had sealed his expulsion from her life. But he had intended to separate himself from her the next day after church anyway — so why did he feel so bereft?

They had conversed. He had told Sarah everything on his mind. She had confessed her own thoughts. And, despite their discovery and the ensuing fracas, the event had ended with no loose end left untied.

Sarah knew he loved her. He knew she did not love him. She would never choose him. She hardly trusted him. Nothing he could say now might change that. Her faith, her wealth, her sad childhood, her unfortunate marriage, her sisters, and even Delacroix all stood in the way.

Men, she believed, meant to make use of her. She was right. Even Charles, who had adored her on board ship when he fancied her a lady of common means, would happily unite himself not only to Sarah but to her money. But that was a moot point now, and he must accept his destiny.

"I go to call upon my cousin, Mr. Brampton," Charles's father said as he stepped into the library. James Locke wore a black frock coat and black trousers. Together with his white cravat and somber gray vest, they made him appear as bleak as his outlook. "Perhaps Brampton will have some advice for us upon this woeful turn of events. His son is a banker, you know, and he hears many things. He may be able to give us information on the damage done to your reputation last weekend. I confess, I never thought I should live to see the day when my only son — in whom my dear wife and I had such hopes — would be expelled from society."

Charles set the law book upon the stack of reading matter at his side. "Father, I was not expelled from society. Delacroix asked me to leave Bamberfield House; that is all."

"All? That is as good as a discharge from the *ton.* You will never be asked to another ball or reception; I am sure of that. And I sincerely doubt that even Sir Alexander will want to be associated with you. You have ruined yourself entirely."

"Why should I care what I have done?" Charles asked in exasperation. Over the past week, they had discussed the situation too many times to be endured. "You despise the aristocracy with their airs and prejudices, Father. Why would you wish me to join them?"

"You know the answer to that question very well, and yet you continue to taunt me with it. No man can enrich himself in this country without the proper connections. And by your unseemly behavior toward Lady Delacroix, you have severed yours."

"Good connections are not the only key to a successful life, sir. Lady Delacroix's father made his fortune as a middleman in the opium trade. His beginnings were far more unfortunate than my own, and he had no associates in society whatsoever. He ended by owning a house in Belgravia and wedding his eldest daughter to a peer."

"I am sure he had not offended half of the *ton* with his boorish behavior prior to his elevation into their ranks." James strode across the room toward the foyer. "You have done yourself and me a great harm, Charles, and I cannot think how you will repair it."

"I have written apologies to Lady Delacroix and her nephew. Beyond that, I begin to care very little for my involvement in their society."

Eyes narrowed, James turned on his son. "You should care! You will never be rich without it — neither as a barrister nor as a tea trader. I am sure an opium merchant could earn a fortune peddling Dover's powder, Sydenham's laudanum, and sedative nostrums for children to every doctor, apothecary, and household in the country. But the law? No, you will need Marston's backing if you want to take on the really lucrative cases. And as for tea, a flourishing enterprise will require the support and investment of Sir Alexander, as well as his acquaintances. I begin to fear you will take the Locke name straight back to its beginnings and end as a gate warden or a blacksmith."

"Would that be so wrong?" Charles asked, rising. "Would you despise your only son if he failed to advance the lineage in which you take such pride?"

"I shall never despise you. But I should be sorely disappointed in you. You are intelligent, handsome, and well educated. Why would you consider doing less than your utmost to achieve the goals to which you aspire?"

Letting out a hot breath, Charles gazed out the window. "Perhaps I no longer aspire to the goals I once held so dear, Father. Perhaps the acquisition of money, land, and standing in society does not appeal to me as it once did."

"How can you say such a thing?"

Charles snatched the Bible from the pile of books near his chair. "Day and night, I read the pages of this volume in search of true guidance. The more I study the Scriptures, the more I begin to believe that my purpose on this earth may be something more significant than defending criminals or building a trade in tea leaves."

James stared at the heavy black book in which his dearly adored late wife had immersed herself. Charles knew his father could not dismiss its power. The greatest joy, the strongest bulwark, the deepest love in both their lives had come from a woman who took literally every word that had been printed on the pages of the Bible.

"Charles, do you mean to become a clergyman?" James asked in a low voice. "Is the church now your aim?"

"I cannot tell you my aim, for I hardly know it myself. My mother believed the Scripture was the guide to an abundant life on earth and a future in heaven. Lady Delacroix, for whom I have great admiration and affection, assures me my mother was correct. And as I search the passages contained within this book, I can find nothing to support a life spent in the accumulation of wealth. Nor do I find any indication that an association with the aristocracy leads to happiness. Treasures are to be amassed in heaven, Father, not on earth. Our dearest companions are to be our brothers in Christ, not the most influential members of the *ton.* If we hope to find fulfillment and joy, we are not to abide by society's rules but to follow the teachings of Jesus Christ. Our true lineage derives not from a key maker named Locke, but from our heavenly Father, who has adopted us into His holy kingdom."

James stared as though his son had been speaking Greek. "Do you mean this, Charles? Do you truly believe what you tell me?"

"I do, sir. My words are not my own. They are written on the pages of this Bible."

"Then we must resign ourselves to ruin."

Before Charles could respond, the bell at the front door jingled. Without waiting for the servant to answer, James strode into the foyer. "I shall see to this," he said. "As it appears I must see to everything in this house."

As the door opened and his father spoke to a messenger outside it, Charles crossed to the fire in hope of drawing some warmth from its flames. He had told James Locke he believed what he had said. But did he truly? Enough to surrender his dreams? And if he did, what then? Must he and his father descend to poverty and disgrace? Or did a true Christian have the right to honest labor and the resulting income? What was the answer to this apparent dilemma, and how might he ever discover it? Bowing his head in distress, Charles prayed that the God of the Bible he held in his hands would hear his cry and answer him.

He felt as though the man once known as Charles Locke had been slowly unraveling from the moment he awoke in Sarah's arms aboard the *Queen Elinor*. In the hour preceding his rescue from the waves, he had lost his young friend, his father's gold, and nearly his own life. The pain that remained in his leg served as an ongoing reminder of the nearness of death. Charles had managed to cling to life — and yet he had begun to surrender it as well. Bits and pieces of himself seemed to fall away each time he saw Sarah, each time he searched the Scriptures, each time he heeded the cry of his own heart.

He must let go of everything, he began to realize. Hope. Dreams. Even love. He must be willing, as Sarah was willing, to give up everything. And he was.

"A packet has come for you by post," James said, stepping back into the library. "I suppose it is some text you have ordered." He tossed a box wrapped in brown paper onto the chair by the window. James regarded his son for a moment, disappointment in his eyes and regret etched in the lines on his face. "Do you mean to continue your studies in the law, Charles?"

"I intend to do what is necessary to provide for you, sir." Charles summoned what scraps remained of his once-glorious dreams. "I hope to please you with my deportment, to advance my connections with everyone I may be privileged to call friend, and to earn a living in a manner that satisfies you and does honor to the name of Locke."

"I am happy to hear it. You are much altered since your misadventure at sea, Charles. I daresay your mother would worry about you."

Charles smiled sadly. "I daresay she would make me a matter of earnest prayer — as she always did. And I believe I should benefit greatly from her entreaties on my behalf. Yes, I am altered, Father. And I do hope it is for the better."

"We shall see in time, I suppose. Good day." With that, the older man settled his hat on his head and left the room.

As the front door shut, Charles studied the old Bible in his hand. It was a great treasure, this book. Greater than any law text he might ever own. Setting it on the oak mantel, he glanced at the stack of volumes and then at the parcel that had come by post. Although he did not recall ordering a book recently, it was possible that something had slipped his mind. He would investigate it later. For now, he needed to concentrate on his current studies.

Charles returned to the window, moved

the parcel from his chair to the table, seated himself, and turned the pages of his law book to the place where he had left off. The legal case under consideration was a difficult one, though for some reason on this day it reminded him of a letter that might be printed in Miss Pickworth's gossip-and-advice column in *The Tattler.* "The Dreadful Dilemma of the Multiple Mates," it might be titled.

A smile tickling his lips, Charles read that in Cornwall in the last century, a rich woman had married a man who soon afterward went to sea. Not long following his departure, a letter came to the woman from the captain of the ship on which her husband had sailed. It reported that the man had died of a fever. She then married a second husband, only to learn that the first was hale and healthy and on his way back to England. Both men subsequently claimed the woman as their lawfully wedded wife — whose fortune was, of course, the true object of the suit.

As Charles began to read how the high court determined which man was the lady's rightful spouse, his amusement vanished. The woman's situation brought Sarah immediately to mind. How difficult her lot in life. Everyone envied her, yet Charles now understood that the destiny of a rich woman was not all happiness and ease, as many supposed. Even a wealthy young widow, whom most would imagine to enjoy the very best of situations, could not always count herself blessed.

Poor, darling Sarah. Recalling her beautiful brown eyes, Charles turned toward the window and his glance happened to fall upon the packet that had recently arrived. Oddly, the paper-wrapped container was not in the shape of a book. Nor — now that he thought of it — had the parcel carried the weight of a volume of legal proceedings. He picked it up again. In fact, the package was light. And soft.

Curious, he set the parcel on his lap and tugged apart the twine that held it closed. Then he broke the wax seal and tore away the brown paper. Lifting the lid of a box, Charles recognized his own coat — the frock coat he had torn off in his haste to climb over the wall at Bamberfield House and speak with Sarah in the garden. He lifted the garment and saw a smaller box tucked in its folds. Inside it, his cuff links lay nestled in a bed of cotton.

Who had found them? Who had packed his things so carefully and sent them to this address? Lord Delacroix knew the location of the Locke residence. Did anyone else?

As Charles stood, a sheet of paper slipped from the inside of the coat and drifted like a leaf to the floor. Though he had never seen Sarah's writing, he knew it was hers before he even picked up the letter.

" 'Sir,' " he murmured as he scanned the words, " 'please meet me at once in Leadenhall Market on Gracechurch Street. Come to the west side of the Green Yard where the fishmongers' shops are located. S.C.' "

His heart hammering, Charles tugged on his coat and started across the room. *Sarah Carlyle,* he thought as he grabbed his hat from the hall tree and settled it on his head. She needed him.

Sarah waited, trembling, in the deep shadows beneath an eave of the great market that fronted on Gracechurch Street. Located in central London, Leadenhall Market was the largest in England and in fact, in all of Europe. It had arisen centuries before around a lead-roofed manor house. Rebuilt after the Great Fire of London in 1666, the market now consisted of three crowded courts.

Sarah knew the place intimately, for her childhood home stood not a half mile away.

She and her sisters often had roamed the market's narrow lanes during the Christmas holidays. In the beef court, vendors hawked meat, leather and hides, and baize and wool. The Green Yard, where Sarah now waited, featured a central area for shops selling veal, mutton, and lamb, while on the south and west sides were houses and shops for fish-mongers. At the east end of Leadenhall stood a market house erected upon columns, with vaults beneath and rooms above. Inside this house were the butchers' stalls. A bell tower and a clock rose above the old house, and Sarah kept her eyes trained upon it.

Nearly an hour had passed since she had sent the parcel by messenger to the Locke house on Threadneedle Street, but Charles had not come. Within fifteen minutes, her carriage would arrive at the church of St. Peter-upon-Cornhill near the market and stand ready for her return. During Sarah's childhood, the Watson family occasionally had attended services inside the large structure with its redbrick tower, dome, and obelisk. The church stood on the site of an ancient Roman place of Christian worship, but the present structure had been built by Sir Christopher Wren not long after the Great Fire. Citing a desire to return to the familiar church to pray, Sarah had taken leave of her sisters not long after their luncheon.

After dismissing the carriage, she had prayed inside the vaulted church — but not for long. A side door had let her out into the tiny graveyard, through which she had hurried toward Leadenhall Market. Anxious and filled with trepidation, she had paid a messenger boy to take the parcel to Charles Locke's house. Then she had lingered there until it was almost too late to start back to St. Peter-upon-Cornhill. If she did not emerge through the church doors near the hour she had instructed her carriage driver to return, the footman would no doubt send someone inside to look for her. So she must be there.

Though the fish market was busy even at this late hour, its powerful odor made it an unpopular area to loiter. Sarah hoped no one would recall the presence of a lone woman in a dark cape and deeply brimmed bonnet. Oh, where was Charles? Did he not know what a risk she took to be seen in this public place?

Perhaps he had not been at home when the packet arrived. It was possible his father had opened it, even though she had addressed it to Charles. What if they had argued about her? Or what if Charles had failed to open the box at once? Or worse — what if he had opened it, read her note, and chosen not to come?

Wringing her gloved hands beneath her cape, Sarah peered out from under the brim of her bonnet. Then she looked up at the clock. Another five minutes had passed. Soon she must hurry back to the church.

Surely Charles would come if he had received her note. But perhaps he had not seen the letter. What if he had opened the box to find his coat but had not bothered to remove it from the box? Or what if the note had been too well hidden beneath the folds of the heavy fabric? Oh, why had she bothered to try to see him again? God must not mean for them to meet. She knew it was already too late to alter the course of events in her life anyway.

But what if Charles had fallen ill? Perhaps his injured leg was bothering him after the climb over the garden wall. She should not suppose his absence had anything to do with her, Sarah reminded herself. He might simply wish to get on with his studies in law as she had urged him to do.

Oh, dear, she fretted as a young man pulled a cart heaped with silvery mackerel past her. This was all a very bad idea. She would return home smelling of fish and —

There! Charles stood just across from her near a barrel of fresh eels. He wore the coat! The brim of his top hat was pulled low, and he seemed to be searching for her. What should she do now? And look at the time!

Swallowing down her trepidation, Sarah lifted her skirts as she crossed the muddy lane between them.

He spotted her at once. Without speaking a word, he stepped to her side, took her arm, and escorted her deep into the winding maze of lanes that crisscrossed the market. Though fear of discovery left her hardly able to breathe, the firmness of Charles's stride and his solid presence gave her comfort.

"Mrs. Carlyle," he addressed her in a low voice when they were safely hidden from the main road. "You wished to speak to me?"

She could not bring herself to look at him as she talked quickly, breathlessly. "Yes, sir. I must clarify something you said to me during our last encounter."

"Every word I spoke in the garden at Bamberfield was true, madam."

"Then you did love me aboard the *Queen Elinor*?"

"With all my heart."

"And you did not know at the time that I was Lady Delacroix?"

"I did not. As I have told you, I believed you were Mrs. Sarah Carlyle, a widow who had inherited a sum of money from her father and intended to disburse it to the needy. That is all I knew or cared to know. The essential aspects of your character were more important to me than your financial status. You had tenderly cared for the victims of the attack upon the *Tintagel.* You sang hymns and read Scriptures in testimony to your deep faith in God. Most important, perhaps, you believed in my ability to overcome all that beset me."

They paused near a stall where mutton chops lay in neat rows on a table and freshly dressed veal carcasses hung from hooks above it. A woman was haggling with the shopkeeper about prices, while a young boy clung to her skirts and whimpered in exhaustion. Nearby, an old man whistled as he trimmed a leg of lamb.

Despite her nervousness, Sarah allowed herself to meet the blue eyes she had held so dear. Instantly, she regretted it, for Charles was no different now than he had been upon their first meeting. He was the same man — kind, gentle, sincere, honest. She could find nothing in his words to doubt. Nothing in his character to dislike. And oh, how lovingly he gazed at her!

Sarah turned away. "You must know that I have told my sisters I will marry Lord Delacroix," she told him, barely able to make herself speak the words. "I believe you were correct in pressing his suit, and my sisters agree that it is for the best."

Charles said nothing for fully a minute. Now they were too deep inside the market for Sarah to see the clock, and she had no desire to root through the small bag beneath her cape in search of her watch. She would be late — and face the consequences.

When Charles still did not speak, she glanced at him again. His face wore an expression of solemn resignation as she attempted to continue the message she had determined she must give him. "Mrs. Heathhill," she continued, "has suggested that . . . she thinks it appropriate — and certainly it is acceptable . . . that you ought to . . . that perhaps you might wish to become attached to Miss Watson."

"Marry Miss Watson?" Now his tone grew angry. "Why should I be at all inclined to marry your sister? It is you I love. You alone." He let out a growl of frustration. "If you wish to marry Delacroix, I cannot stop you. But I certainly have no interest in Miss

Watson beyond a brief acquaintance. Without you, she is nothing to me."

"Think what you say, sir. Prudence is both beautiful and good. I have settled far more than a comfortable living upon her. Her connection with the Delacroix name is a good one and will bring her husband influential friends. With these advantages, you may certainly resurrect your plan to launch a tea enterprise."

"Are you now converted from benefactress into conspirator, madam?" he demanded, his voice hard. "I had thought the very idea of marriage for the sake of social and financial advancement abhorrent to you. Yet now I see that you mean to wed yourself to a man you do not love, and you hope to attach your sister to one who cannot love her. All for the sake of convenience and security."

"You advocated such an arrangement not a sennight ago!" she argued. "At Bamberfield House, *you* were the conspirator — scheming with my sister to press me to wed Delacroix. Despite your profession of affection for me, you showed no inclination to abandon your own plan to establish a tea enterprise. You were unaltered from the man you were aboard the *Tintagel* — the one who refused to surrender his goal of a financial

338

empire for a life of charity and poverty. Are you now converted into someone who prizes love and compassion above all else?"

"Perhaps I am converted," he replied. "Perhaps I have been converting all along."

Sarah stared at him. "What do you mean, sir? Do not trifle with me — I must know your meaning."

"Your example . . . your words . . . your sweet spirit . . . all have taught me what I was unwilling to accept — until now. Oh, indeed, I continue to study my law books. I dwell on the possibility of enterprise. I behave in all ways like the man my father educated me to become. And yet my spirit . . . I believe the Spirit within me revolts against it."

"Charles . . . ?"

"Do not gaze at me with those brown eyes, Sarah. Do not write to me and ask to meet in secret. Do not even think of seeing me again — and certainly not as your sister's husband — if you truly will wed Delacroix."

As she hesitated, hovering on the cusp of hope, the clock in the bell tower above the market struck the hour. She was late. Fifteen minutes, at least. The carriage driver and footmen would be searching for her at the church.

"Charles, I am expected at Trenton House," she breathed out. "My carriage awaits me at St. Peter-upon-Cornhill, and I cannot delay."

"Does Miss Watson know you intended to speak to me today?"

"No."

"Then tell her nothing of our meeting. I would not have her waste a moment's thought upon me."

"She adores you."

"She hardly knows me. You know me, Sarah. Your opinion is all that matters. What do you feel for me? Can you see beyond the harsh treatment of your father and husband, beyond the clamoring of false friends, beyond the scheming of your sisters? Do you yet know the meaning of love, Sarah? I shall ask you once and never again — do you love me?"

She lowered her head, unwilling that he should see her face as tears welled in her eyes. "I do, Charles," she whispered. "I do love you."

"Sarah!" He caught her around the waist and pulled her close. "Sarah, marry me. If you love me, be my wife; I beg you!"

"I must go! I have agreed to wed Delacroix, and you should marry Prudence. She is very pretty! This was not to be the outcome of our meeting. I only wanted to be sure that you had truly . . . on the ship . . . oh, Charles, let me go!"

"Sarah, how can I stand back and —"

"Now then, not in the market, eh?" the old man in the next stall cried out, waving his carving knife at them. "Save your love-makin' for the street corners and public 'ouses, man!"

"I must go, Charles," Sarah gasped, pulling away from him. "My footmen will be looking for me. Please do not follow me! Please do not write to me or call on me! This cannot be. It cannot!"

As her tears spilled down her cheeks, Sarah turned from him and fled.

FIFTEEN

"Here you are at last, Charles!" James Locke looked up from his book as his son stepped into the library. "I returned home from my cousin's house in time to take tea with you, but you were away. Now it is quite dark, and I had become concerned. Please tell me you are all right!"

"I am well enough, Father." Charles tossed his hat and gloves onto the settee near the fire and sank into the soft cushions. Discouraged, still unsettled by his encounter with Sarah, he raked a hand through his hair and leaned his head against a doily his mother had crocheted many years before. "Forgive me, sir. I did not intend to distress you by my absence."

"But where were you? Did you not take your tea at home?"

"No, sir. I confess, I did not think of tea at all this afternoon."

"Not think of tea?" James blinked at his

son. "Then did you go to Lincoln's Inn to speak with one of your instructors? Or were you drinking ale in a public house?"

"Father, you know me better than to suppose I would stop at a pub. Nor did I give any thought to my studies. I have been walking."

"Walking? To exercise your leg?"

"I needed to think."

"Oh, dear me. I knew I had upset you with my stern words this afternoon. I never should have encouraged you to go away on that dreadful ship in the first place. Your mother would not have permitted it. It was rash of me — selfish. Hang that dashed chest of gold! You might have lost your life, and then where would I be?"

"Do not trouble yourself so, Father," Charles said wearily. "Our conversation was exactly as it should have been. I needed to be urged to decide upon my future course . . . and, in fact, I believe I have."

"You will go into the church!" James exclaimed, grinning in triumph over the certainty of his conjecture. "Nay, do not give me such a look, my boy. I have seen you reading that Bible of your mother's morning and night. I know you faced death aboard the *Tintagel,* and I understand that such an event can divert the course of a man's life. Well, if you wish to join the clergy, Charles, I shall accept it with my whole heart. I spoke to my cousin upon the matter this afternoon, and he has thoughtfully reminded me that the duke of Marston's lands encompass two parishes. I believe if you speak to Sir Alexander, he may be very likely to prefer you to one of them. Life as a curate can be more than profitable, and certainly your mother would approve."

"I do not mean to go into the church, Father," Charles said. "I shall continue my studies in the law."

"A barrister then! Well, this is fine news!" James beamed. "I had not thought this to be the outcome of your —"

"I shall not become a barrister, sir. I intend to aim no higher than solicitor. Cases in the lower courts involve debtors, petty thieves, drunkards — in short, the dregs of the city. Upon examination of my conscience, I have determined that these are the ones who most need my assistance. Men too poor to pay their debts, women compelled by poverty to sell themselves in the streets, children so hungry they resort to picking pockets . . . such indigents have need of a compassionate solicitor. More important, in handling their defense before the court, I shall have opportunity to speak to them about what is truly important in life."

"And what is that, Charles? Do not tell me you wish to preach to those wastrels and molls. Those ne'er-do-wells need food in their stomachs and coats on their backs — not sermons."

"I shall try to give them both, sir. A man cast into debtors' prison cannot work to pay back what he owes. A woman thrown into gaol for prostitution can hardly hope to rise above her circumstances in that setting. If I can spare these people such a sentence and assist them in finding legitimate work, they may be more likely to hear the truth of Jesus Christ."

"Upon my word, son, you are altered!" James pushed himself from his chair and stalked to the fire. Taking the poker, he gave the charred logs a firm jab. "What has brought about this change in you? Was it your brush with death? or your encounter with a young lady equally lethal?"

"I am sure both have played a part in the changes you observe. But it has been Lady Delacroix's influence that fixed my heart upon this new course. By her words and her example, I have been taught the futility of my previous aims. Oddly enough, it appears that she and I have reversed roles. I have decided to abandon my striving for wealth and social standing in favor of a life spent in the service of the needy. She has chosen to surrender her goal of disbursing her fortune to the poor in favor of embracing both affluence and society. I learned today that she means to wed her late husband's nephew, the present Lord Delacroix."

"That is it, then." James set the poker back into its rack. "You are distressed at this news, and your thoughts are befuddled."

"On the contrary, Father, my clarity of mind has increased since learning of the intended marriage. In succumbing to the pressure of her sisters and her nephew, Lady Delacroix actually has surrendered everything most dear to her. She has sentenced herself to a life she longed to escape. Though her action in accepting the proposal — along with the security, lands, and social status it ensures — would appear to be selfish, it is, in fact, quite the opposite. She wanted to be rid of all the trappings of property and society. But in order to bring happiness to her sisters, she now sacrifices her own pleasure and condemns herself to misery."

"Balderdash!" James exploded. "Rot!

Infamous lies! That woman has bewitched you! For what reason, I cannot say, but there is no question in my mind that she has totally bedeviled you. Under her spell, you will give up everything you might achieve in life — fortune, fame, position, security — all of it! While she — wicked vixen that she is — will dance away with her new husband and enjoy twice the social success she had before!"

"You are wrong, Father," Charles said, standing. "You do not know her as I do."

"You are a besotted fool!"

"I am in greater control of my senses than ever before in my life. It pains me to disappoint a deeply respected father, but I shall not be waylaid from this course. I shall become a solicitor, assist the needy, and speak the truth of Christ to those whose lives are empty of it."

"Then preach to the aristocracy! By heaven, they are as bereft of Christian morality as any moll who walks the streets of Cheapside. Marston was a schemer, a cheat, and a lazy glutton! Lady Delacroix's first husband was worse. Everyone knew his affinity for gaming and drink! He married her only to enrich his coffers."

"You do not know that, Father."

"It was obvious to all who knew him.

Everyone said so."

"Father, I beg you to refrain from repeating malicious rumors. Delacroix is dead and certainly cannot defend himself against such charges."

"Oh, Charles, I should not be as fastidious as you for a kingdom! Be a man. Earn your way in life. Make yourself and all who know you proud."

"I am a man, sir. I shall earn my way and provide for you as well. But I have no intention of acting in any fashion that might lead me to take pride in myself. I mean to bring glory to God and Him alone. If you find such behavior repulsive and weak, perhaps you ought to have paid greater attention to your wife."

"Upon my honor, I have never known you to be so insolent!"

Charles let out a hot breath. "I apologize, Father. That was uncalled for. Do you suppose I welcome this new life? Can you believe I wish to consort with the lice-ridden, pox-afflicted, unwashed criminals of this city? Do you think it has been easy to relinquish my dreams of building a tea trade? No, indeed. Worst of all is the knowledge that the woman I love will wed herself to another man. I must live out my days under the sentence that society has imposed upon me. No matter how much Lady Delacroix may have loved me, we could never marry."

"But if you worked your way up —"

"I can never ascend to her social stratum. She is beyond me, and I must accept that."

"But why punish yourself further? Why demean your character and reputation by aspiring to nothing higher than the lot of a common solicitor?"

"Because that is the only way I know to be at peace." Charles reached down to pick up his hat and gloves. "Lady Delacroix taught me that this life is not to be spent in amassing earthly treasures. Every true Christian must be bent on heaven. For where a man's heart is, there will his treasure be also."

"And you believe that by aiding these miscreants you will earn yourself a place in heaven?"

"No, sir. My destiny there became secure during these past few days — as I gradually surrendered my own will and placed myself into the hands of Christ. But I do believe heaven awaits me, Father, and I intend to spend my time on earth preparing for that better life. Your wife was wise in loving the Bible as she did, you know. It is a book well worth the reading, for who can deny its description of the futility of amassing a fortune that must be left behind upon one's death? It is much better to build a fortune in heaven. And that, my dear father, is done with good works."

As he started for his room, Charles could hear his father harrumphing and blustering behind him. "Well, of all the . . . upon my word . . . I cannot believe this . . . what has come over the boy . . . utterly besotted . . ."

Returning to the fireside, Charles picked up the Bible and held it out to his father. "Read this, please," he said. "Begin with the first chapter of the Gospel according to St. John, and continue through the third chapter. Then peruse the epistle of James. Salvation is a gift of God, and it cannot be earned. But a man's true faith in Christ is revealed by his works done on this earth. It is all there, Father, and very clearly explained. Do give it a try, sir. My mother would approve."

Sarah sat beside the window of the drawing room at Trenton House and watched the rain slash against the panes. All afternoon, she had been trying to finish embroidering a screen depicting a forest replete with maidens, unicorns, and pear trees. But her thoughts would not stay with the tranquil scene nor with the thread and needle, and finally it became such an effort to untangle the knots that she gave it up entirely.

Laying her work on the settee beside her, she studied her lady's maid, who was patiently putting the skeins of colored wool back into the sewing basket. Despite her unfavorable condition in life, Anne possessed a serenity that Sarah envied. How could such a young woman be so happy — a poor creature whose father had been put into prison, who had been compelled to travel far from home to find work, and who labored at tasks demeaning to one with her education and training?

Only once had Sarah witnessed evidence of Anne's distress. The day after the private conversation among the women in the bedroom at Bamberfield, Mary had recommended that Anne be sent to another house far from Cranleigh Crescent and those who called Belgravia their home. The maid knew too much, Mary reasoned, and she might inadvertently mention personal information about the family. Anne had heard every word of Mary's argument, of course. In the presence of her newfound confidante, Sarah had rebuked her sister and had flatly refused to consider dismissal.

That evening, Anne had come with tears

in her eyes and had told Sarah more about her dire situation. Without her income as a lady's maid, the family had no hope of paying for her father's legal defense. Sarah had reassured the young woman that she would not be sacked, and Anne's pleasant demeanor returned. The two women had become such fast friends, in fact, that Sarah hardly hesitated to tell her anything, and Anne had been a willing accomplice in Sarah's rendezvous with Charles at the Leadenhall Market.

"Prudence will be home for tea soon," Sarah observed as she rolled up the unfinished screen and tied a ribbon around it. "No doubt she will be all achatter about the bonnets she has seen in the shops today. Mary has sent a message across the Crescent to say that she wishes to join us here at Trenton House for tea. I understand she possesses some information she believes will bring great joy."

"I wonder what news she has heard," Anne offered. "Perhaps it is political in nature."

Sarah chuckled. "No doubt she has winkled some tidbit of gossip out of one of her friends and can hardly wait to tell it. I have pointed out the Bible's teachings against spreading gossip, but my sisters continue to pursue the salacious details of every rumor they hear. I confess, I have no hope of quelling their ardor for scandal."

With a sigh, Sarah propped her chin on her hand and frowned at the drumming rain on the panes. Ever since her secret meeting with Charles in the Leadenhall Market, her heart had been rocked by emotion. But her sisters had no idea that she was at all distressed. Once they had learned of her willingness to marry Delacroix, they could talk or think of little else. Though Sarah had forbidden them to mention a word of it to anyone — including the man himself — Prudence and Mary considered the marriage all but settled.

"Wedding gowns and churches and invitation lists are all my sisters can think about these days," Sarah said. "Pru went visiting millinery shops today, you know."

"She will have gathered pictures of various hats to show you." Anne closed the sewing basket and leaned back in her chair. "I am told that quail feathers are quite the fashion on turbans these days."

Sarah had to smile at the image of such frippery. "No doubt once Mary has regaled us with her gossip, our teatime discussion must revolve around the endlessly fascinating topic of headwear."

"Can it be so unpleasant to talk of such things? When I was a girl, our fireside conversations often centered on lace patterns. I quite enjoyed it, for I can think of little that pleases me more than to sit with my lace pillow on my lap and my bobbins flying."

"You have a skill with lace unlike any I have ever seen, Anne. The collar you gave me last week was exquisite. If I do marry — as it appears I must — I shall be happy to wear it on my wedding day."

"Thank you, madam. You are too kind." Anne set the basket on the floor between them. "I do wish you could take joy in the life God has given you, my lady."

"As do I. But I am not accomplished in lace making or painting or anything that brings me such pleasure as your own. The only true happiness I can recall was on my recent journey." Sarah looked out the window. "How long ago it all seems now . . . those days of happiness aboard the *Queen Elinor*. I was filled with my mission . . . so certain I was obeying God's directive."

"And those hours spent with Mr. Locke as he recovered," Anne added. "They were happy times, too."

Sarah nodded. Why had she not appreciated every minute as a golden chalice of opportunity? How could she have failed to know at once that she loved him? Now, when it was too late, love seemed the most obvious and easily discerned emotion in the world!

As a child and a young woman, Sarah had never been able to imagine love. What was it? Where did it come from? What did it mean? How could one even recognize it?

But one look into Charles Locke's blue eyes should have been like opening the Bible directly to that wonderful passage in First Corinthians . . . love was long-suffering, kind, utterly lacking in envy and pride. It was virtuous, unselfish, rarely angry, and altogether without evil. Love did not rejoice in sin but in truth. It bore all things, believed all things, hoped all things, endured all things. Though God Himself was the essence of true love, on this earth the closest Sarah was likely to come to witnessing human love made flesh was in a gentleman named Charles Locke.

"He is a wonderful man," she murmured. "How could I have failed to see it at once? What did it really matter that he wanted to build a tea enterprise?"

"That was not a sin," Anne said softly. "It was, in fact, a most honorable aim."

"I see now that you are right. To work

hard, to provide for a family, to become the best husband and father possible. . . . This is all that God asks of any man." She shook her head. "Yet I chastised and berated him for it."

Sarah closed her eyes in humiliation. Oh, she was a fool. Now she knew beyond any shadow of doubt that she loved Charles. And despite all her harsh words and cruel rejections, he still loved her. Yet they could never be together.

"I have told my sisters I shall marry Delacroix," Sarah said, "and I must keep my word."

"Does he know? Have you spoken to him about your intent?"

"No, but I have no doubt he will favor the attachment at once. Clearly, a union between us is his aim. Though he has not made me a proposal, he gives me his entire attention whenever we are together."

"He calls upon you here at Trenton House at least once a day." Anne's voice held a wistful tone. "I should not be surprised if Lord Delacroix will come again this afternoon."

"Aye, smiling and telling little jokes and posturing before me. I shall laugh and be polite and accommodating."

Sarah gazed out the window, imagining

the effort such an act would require. Though she might feign interest and pleasure in the company of her sisters and friends, she was heartbroken at the turn her life had taken.

"Hello the house!" Prudence sang out from the foyer. "I am home at last, and whom do you suppose I should find coming up the stairs just as I arrived? It is Mary! Sarah, are you there?"

Both women stepped into the drawing room just as Sarah turned from her perch beside the window. "Dear sisters — how happy I am to see you looking so well. Anne, will you send for our tea at once?" As her maid hurried away, Sarah left the settee. "But you are both very wet. Pru, your skirts are six inches deep in dirt."

"Upon my word, the streets are a veritable river!" Prudence skipped to the table near the fire and dropped a portfolio upon it. "There! What do you say to that?"

"Are these the pictures of new bonnets?" Sarah asked.

"The bonnets are there, but atop them is something of far greater importance!" She swept up a damp copy of *The Tattler* and displayed it for her sisters. "Miss Pickworth has printed my letter — and she has given me an answer!"

"No!" Sarah and Mary cried at once, both

rushing for the newspaper. Prudence whisked it away and motioned them to be seated. Opening to the pertinent page, she cleared her throat.

" 'The Wealthy Widow and her Affectionate Adversary,' " she read aloud. "I shall not trouble you with the details of my letter though, I flatter myself, it was very well written. I cannot think why Miss Pickworth cut away half of it and summarized the rest. At any rate, here is her answer:

"While lasting love is rare in this world, it is not impossible. Clearly, the wealthy widow has lost her heart to this proud and principled pauper. She adores him. More meaningfully, he loved her long before he learned of her reservoir of riches. His love is genuine.

"While Miss Pickworth is loath to discard the stringent strictures of society, she believes there must be exceptions to every rule. Let our wealthy widow wed her worthy wooer. Let our affectionate adversary abandon all his ambition.

"May her riches become his. May his aims in life become hers. And may the ton turn warm welcomes and wholehearted best wishes upon this praiseworthy pair."

"Miss Pickworth believes I should marry Mr. Locke?" Sarah asked.

"You must have written your letter in a very opinionated manner," Mary said. "Did you mention Lord Delacroix?"

"I did. But she says nothing about him at all." Prudence handed the newspaper to Sarah. "Miss Pickworth, who never hesitates to point out the slightest flaw in anyone, approves of Mr. Locke. Can you credit such a thing?"

"I am all astonishment," Sarah said. She passed the column to Mary. "Miss Pickworth has admonished the *ton* to accept such an unbalanced match."

" 'Proud and principled pauper,' " Mary read. "Well. That makes Mr. Locke sound almost romantic. As though he were some sort of Robin Hood."

"He *is* romantic. He is as handsome as anything, and if he did not love Sarah so dearly, I should try even harder than I have to win him for myself. Indeed, I am quite taken aback by her answer, for were Sarah and Mr. Locke to follow Miss Pickworth's advice, I should be left with no one." Prudence snatched the newspaper and folded it up again. Recovering her aplomb, she waved the paper in front of Mary's nose. "I told you Miss Pickworth would publish my letter."

Sarah had to laugh. "Surely this day cannot provide any greater surprises! Pru, we must study your bonnets as soon as may be. But you ought to go upstairs first and put on a dry gown."

"Nonsense! I want to hear Mary's news. Do tell us everything, dearest! Is it about Delacroix? or Sarah? Or do you have some news of Charles Locke, our 'principled pauper'?" Prudence glanced at her eldest sister. "I have heard nothing at all about him since we left Bamberfield, and that is nearly two weeks! I am thinking of calling on him."

"Prudence!" Mary scowled at her younger sister. "You will do nothing of the sort."

"How are we to 'warmly welcome' the man if he supposes our whole family has turned against him? You ought to send your husband to make amends. Mr. Heathhill has the perfect demeanor to mollify the situation."

Mary flushed with pride. "I shall speak to my dear husband this very evening. We have discussed the situation at length, and you must know . . . he agrees with me that Mr. Locke ought to be more than willing to marry Prudence. Both of you would benefit greatly from the arrangement."

"Miss Pickworth would not agree on that account." Prudence turned to Sarah. "And what about you? Will you allow Mr. Heathhill to tell Delacroix of your willingness to wed? Or do you change your mind on this?"

Sarah knotted her hands in her lap. "I shall speak to Delacroix about a marriage myself when the time is right."

"You? Propose to him?" Prudence gaped at Sarah.

"It is not unheard of," Mary informed her. "Sarah is above Delacroix in title and fortune, and it is her place to decide whether she will marry or not. Indeed, she is actually condescending to wed Delacroix, for if she chose, she could set her sights upon someone of higher rank."

"Or I could remain unattached." Sarah laid out the possibility like a silk shawl, a thing to be studied and examined but treated with great delicacy. "It is not so long ago that I had planned to live out the rest of my life alone, and that situation could hardly hurt either of you."

"But to be put on the shelf forever?" Prudence asked.

"I shall hardly be on a shelf, dearest. I am in a most enviable position."

"But what about children? heirs?"

"You and Mary can see to that."

"Do you mean this, Sarah?" Mary asked. "Do you now reverse your previous statement to us that you would wed Delacroix?"

"I am considering it — that is all I can tell you."

"It is Miss Pickworth," Prudence said. "Her advice is always on the mark."

"I had been thinking of this long before I heard Miss Pickworth's pert counsel."

"But what about the money?" Prudence blurted out. "Will you also go back to your plan to give it all away?"

"I have come to believe that you and Mary were correct in your estimation of my former aims. Though it seems odd to say it, I *was* thinking selfishly when I planned to give away my fortune. I see now that I cannot deprive you of my company or my money without compromising your own contentment. And so I must assure you that I shall stay in England and provide for both of you and your families."

"But you need not provide for Delacroix? Is that what you are saying?"

"I am not certain on that account, Pru. Marriage to him might be best for me. I should very much like to know the love of a husband and children. But . . ." She reached out and laid her hand over Mary's. "We are delayed too long on this. What is your exciting news, sister? Prudence and I are all eagerness to hear it."

Mary pursed her lips, turning pinker than ever. Then she began to blink rapidly, and at last, when Sarah feared Mary might begin to swoon, she burst out, "I am in the increasing way!"

"A baby!" Prudence exclaimed. "Oh, Sarah, do you believe it? We soon shall have a niece or a nephew!"

"This is wonderful news!" Sarah cried out. "I am delighted for you! Dearest Mary, how could you not have told us the moment you came in the door? This is too, too delightful!"

As the three sisters embraced, Anne directed two maids and a footman into the drawing room; they were bearing trays of tea and cakes and other small dainties. By now, Mary was weeping, while Prudence kept exclaiming in joy, thus informing all the servants in the most inappropriate manner.

But who could not rejoice at such news, Sarah thought as she dabbed her handkerchief on Mary's damp cheeks. The Heathhills had been married more than three years with no sign of a baby. Mary had confessed in her letters that she began to despair of ever becoming a mother, while Pru had fretted that Mary grew more and more despondent over this serious shortcoming in her happy marriage. And now it was all come to this delightful result.

"Mr. Heathhill is beside himself with joy," Mary told her sisters. "He treats me as though I am a china doll, tenderly assisting me in every way. And, of course, I have had to order new clothes and undergarments, but he has made not a single objection. Instead, he goes about the house whistling and fancying himself the very luckiest of men."

"As he is," Sarah assured. "Have you any idea of the month when we may hope to be blessed?"

"April, I believe." She looked at her sisters and burst into tears again. "Oh, do you believe it? Next spring I shall present my dearest Sarah and Prudence with the beginnings of a new family! We shall all be as one — here together in London. It will be better than we ever dreamed possible in our former life, for we three shall be mothers, and our dear husbands will be fathers, and our children will be rich with such happy, happy relations."

"We shall all be good mothers," Prudence announced, her own tears falling. "I mean to be the kindest, the most attentive, and certainly the most loving parent any child could wish for. And I shall not send my babies away to wet nurses, no matter what my husband may wish. I shall keep them at home with me and see to the task myself."

"Aye, as shall I," Mary pronounced. "I have told Mr. Heathhill already that if he has any intention of sending our children off to boarding school, he must abandon it at once. They will all be taught privately at home, or they may go to a day school in town. I have vowed never to repeat the terrible situation that was foisted upon us, with our dear Sarah put away in an attic while Pru and I learned our alphabet and numbers at home."

"Never!" Prudence concurred, turning to Sarah and wrapping her arms around her. "Never will such a thing be done to my children as was done to you. Oh, Sarah, please say you will always live near us. Let us all be loving mothers and the dearest of sisters and the very happiest of —"

"Excuse me, Lady Delacroix." Sarah had not been aware of her maid's presence nearby until Anne spoke up. "I am sorry to interrupt, madam."

Sarah drew back from her sisters. "Yes, Anne? What is it?"

"A gentleman has come to call upon you, madam." A footman stepped forward and held out a silver tray. Anne glanced at Mary and Prudence. "Forgive me for disrupting your glad tidings," she said, "but we have kept him waiting for some time."

"It is all right, Anne. In our joy, we have ignored you entirely; I am sure. Please send Lord Delacroix in, for he will be happy to hear our news."

"I beg your pardon, but your caller is not Lord Delacroix, madam," Anne informed her. "The gentleman is Mr. Locke. Will you see him?"

Sarah glanced at Prudence and then at Mary. Both her sisters had stiffened and sucked down gasps, as if stricken by a chill wind. Taking the card from the tray, Sarah read the name. It was indeed Charles. He had come.

"Yes, Anne," she answered. She smoothed down her skirts. "Do send Mr. Locke in."

Sixteen

"Mr. Locke," the footman announced as Charles entered the main drawing room at Trenton House. Because only Sarah and Miss Watson lived in the home their father had purchased shortly before his death, Charles was surprised to find all three sisters present. Gowned in white day dresses, they stood near the tea table that had been drawn up before the fire.

"Lady Delacroix," Charles said, bowing. "Good afternoon, madam. Mrs. Heathhill, Miss Watson, how do you do?"

"We are all well, Mr. Locke." Sarah stretched out her arm to indicate an empty settee. "Will you not join us at tea, sir? You are most welcome."

"Indeed, you are, sir," Miss Watson concurred, stepping out from the cluster of chairs near the table. "Do come and rejoice with us, for we have just had the happiest news of our lives! And you cannot guess what else! I have had a letter printed in *The Tattler,* and Miss Pickworth has answered me. Have you seen it?"

"I have not," he told her. "I am much occupied with my studies."

"We are all aflutter, and you must be told everything." Miss Watson glanced at her sisters. "You cannot mind if Mr. Locke knows your news, can you, Mary? He is our dear friend, and he will be as pleased as we."

Mrs. Heathhill appeared considerably less than pleased at her younger sister's gush of information, but she gave Charles a polite smile. "Of course, Mr. Locke. Do sit down with us."

"Our sister Mary has just informed us that she is in the increasing way!" Prudence whispered, leaning close to Charles and enveloping him with the scent of heliotrope and roses. She wore a gown with a deeply scooped neckline, and her fingers were warm as she took his hand to lead him toward the gathering. "We expect our new niece or nephew to be born in the spring. As you can imagine, we are beside ourselves with joy."

"My heartiest congratulations, Mrs. Heathhill," Charles said, hoping his expression did not reveal the extreme discomfort that news of such a delicate and private matter engendered. He had been taught that polite society never mentioned the sensitive condition in which women often found themselves. But perhaps this confidential information indicated that the family had forgiven him for the indiscretion at Bamberfield House and intended to embrace him as a friend after all. If so, he was pleased — especially considering the objective of his current mission.

"Thank you, Mr. Locke," Mrs. Heathhill told him. "I shall convey your kind words to my husband. Do be seated, and make yourself comfortable among us. We have not seen you for some time, and we hope you are well."

"Thank you, madam. I am in the best of health. My studies at Lincoln's Inn progress admirably, and my father continues to enjoy his retirement. Now all I lack is the certainty that my letters to your family and friends achieved their intended purpose."

"Yes, they did," Miss Watson declared. "All is forgotten. Sarah's account of the events that night in the walled garden at Bamberfield concurred perfectly with your own, and your letters further mollified the situation. Lord Delacroix speaks well of you and has mentioned how very much he enjoyed fishing with you that weekend at his lake. I believe he would welcome another opportunity to engage in sport with you. He is a great fox hunter, you know."

"Thank you, Miss Watson, but as I am currently much occupied with the law, I fear another weekend away from town is out of the question."

Thus far, Sarah had said nothing beyond her greeting. She hardly glanced at Charles as she poured him a cup of tea and spoke to her lady's maid to send away for another pot. Her sisters, on the other hand, were all attention and solicitous welcome. Though Charles was not quite certain what had brought about their happy demeanor, he was grateful.

"It must require a great deal of effort to become a barrister," Miss Watson was saying now. "Are there many years of study before one can be called to the bar?"

"About five years are required to attain the rank of barrister. But I must inform you all that after careful consideration and much prayer, I have decided no longer to strive toward that position. I am resolved upon the lower courts, where I shall undertake the practice of law as a solicitor."

The stunned silence that followed this announcement was broken by the timely arrival of the fresh teapot and a new round of savories and sweets. Charles focused on Sarah, who carefully attended to the distribution of the tea things and gave him not a glance. Her sister, Mrs. Heathhill, posted a decided frown upon her visage, while Miss Watson appeared to be in shock.

"A solicitor?" she exclaimed as the footman retreated once again. "But solicitors are very low. They cannot present cases before the House of Lords, nor do they obtain clients of any prestige whatever. Solicitors defend . . . well, they defend . . . the refuse of the streets."

"If by *refuse* you refer to the commoner who cannot pay his debts or the woman of ill repute who has been cast into gaol, you are correct. But I am a man of common descent, Miss Watson, as you know. I am not ashamed of my ancestry, nor can I consider myself above the task of promoting the legal rights of my fellow man."

"But they are thieves and prostitutes! And debtors! And pickpockets! And murderers! And highwaymen! And gypsies!"

"Enough, Prudence," Sarah cut in firmly. "If Mr. Locke has chosen to become a solicitor, I am certain he has good reasons."

"I do," Charles said, capturing Sarah's eyes and willing her to look at him. "You see, Lady Delacroix, I once met a woman who imparted to me some wisdom that greatly affected my life. May I share with you the story of that encounter?"

"Please do," Miss Watson insisted on her sister's behalf. "I should like to know what could convince a man of good sense to undertake so unhappy a course. Especially one who is clever and well educated and has friends who might support his advancement."

"Then I shall tell you," Charles replied, never taking his focus from Sarah. "This particular woman — for whom I have great respect — told me that if I wished to set the course of my life in a manner that would bring true peace of mind, I ought to seek the will of God by making a thorough study of the teachings of Scripture. Furthermore, she insisted that a life spent in the accumulation of wealth and position was a wasted life, and that —"

"It was Sarah!" Miss Watson exclaimed. "She is the woman of whom you speak, for I can hear her in your message."

"You are correct, madam," Charles said. "Although I once rejected your sister's instruction, I now believe she was right. I have studied Scripture. I have asked God for guidance. And I am resolved to follow a course quite different from the one that I first set. I no longer have any desire to accumulate earthly wealth. I hope to provide a living for myself and my father, and that is all. On Judgment Day, I shall lay my labors on behalf of London's destitute and criminal element before the throne of God. If He chooses to reward me with heavenly treasures, then I shall be grateful. And I shall be content in the knowledge that I undertook to please Him above all else. That is all I ask."

"Then you do not plan to start a tea company after all?" Miss Watson asked, an expression of dismay on her face. "Nor do you mean to mingle in our society?"

"I do not. I am sorry if my decision distresses you in any way, madam, but I shall not be moved from it. I am resolute."

"Is this why you came to Trenton House today, Mr. Locke?" Sarah asked him. "To inform us of this?"

"I hoped to inform *you,* my lady. I knew your sisters would learn the information in time." Pausing, Charles summoned his resolve before speaking again. "But I came also with a second objective, and I shall be frank. I wish most humbly to present my suit before you one last time. Lady Delacroix, you know now that I am in complete agreement with all that you hold most dear.

I have no interest whatsoever in your fortune, and I willingly encourage you to disburse it in any manner you see fit."

He turned to Prudence and Mary, while continuing to address Sarah. "I admire your sisters and enjoy their company, and I should be happy to meet with them on any occasion — but I have lost all desire to ascend to a social stratum above the one in which I currently reside. In fact, I shall be quite pleased to descend, as did my Lord and Savior, to consort with the so-called publicans and sinners of the streets. As I assist these people in their legal defense, it is my hope to proclaim Christ's salvation that their hearts may be changed as well as their lot in life."

Charles shifted to face Sarah again. "And now, in view of all I have just stated before you, Lady Delacroix, I wish to beg once again — and most respectfully — for your hand in marriage."

As if a barrel of gunpowder had exploded, leaving a disturbing calm in its wake, a profound silence fell over the room. Sarah stared down at her hands, knotted and white-knuckled in her lap, as though she were trying to prevent them from moving. Mrs. Heathhill stared unblinkingly at Charles. Miss Watson let out a small gasp and clapped her hand over her mouth.

"May I expect any answer at this time, Lady Delacroix?" Charles ventured. "I realize my proposal is unusual in its public nature, but I am pleased that your sisters may know exactly where I stand. I should be very happy to learn your own feelings on the matter."

Sarah opened her mouth to speak, but at that moment, Henry Carlyle, Lord Delacroix, strode into the drawing room without introduction. "I am told that Locke is here!" he bellowed as he stepped toward the gathering. "Aha! I see that my information is correct, and I am —"

"Oh, Lord Delacroix, you are come just in the nick of time!" Miss Watson cried out and leapt from her seat. "We have such a to-do here, for Mary expects a baby in the spring, and Mr. Locke proposes marriage to Sarah instead of to me, which may be well enough, but you and I are left with no one but each other!"

Mrs. Heathhill and Sarah both stood along with Charles as their sister hurtled into the newcomer's arms.

"Upon my word, you must calm yourself at once, madam." Delacroix took the young lady's shoulders as she sagged into him. "You are all at sixes and sevens, Miss Watson, and . . . dear Lady Delacroix, whatever is the matter with your sister?"

"I am undone!" Miss Watson exclaimed. "I shall be utterly abandoned by all my friends and family!"

By this time, Mrs. Heathhill was hurrying to assist Delacroix in the suppression of Miss Watson's hysterics. Sarah, too, helped return her youngest sister to the fireside, draped her across a chaise longue, and began to fan her with great ardor.

Charles found himself earnestly wishing to make his departure as swiftly as possible. He had stated his intentions upon calling at Trenton House, and he could do nothing but add further duress to this current state of panic to which he had inadvertently contributed.

Before he could determine how best to escape, Delacroix turned on him. "Marry *you?*" he demanded of Charles. "You again asked Lady Delacroix to marry you? I believed we had an agreement, sir! You were to press my suit to her. You were to inform me if she contacted you."

"I never agreed to anything of the sort, sir," Charles insisted. "My love for Lady Delacroix precludes such a pact. I have presented my case to her, and I am now prepared to depart the premises."

"On the contrary, sir, you will remain precisely where you are." Running his hands over his golden curls, Delacroix gave his head a shake. "Allow me to gain some understanding of the crisis at hand. Mr. Locke has gotten Mrs. Heathhill with child, *and* he wishes to wed Lady Delacroix?"

"No!" all three sisters cried out at once. Miss Watson's eyes rolled back in her head, and her sisters called the maids to fetch the smelling salts.

"Certainly not!" Charles sputtered. "Mrs. Heathhill expects . . . well, she anticipates . . . dash it all, she bears her husband's progeny, of course. Mr. Heathhill is the father of the child."

"Mr. Locke had nothing to do with *that!*" Miss Watson called out, her eyelids fluttering. "But . . . he loves Sarah as he always did . . . and she loves him —"

"She what?" Delacroix squared his shoulders at Charles. "Has she accepted your offer, sir? Answer me at once."

"Ask her yourself, for the lady stands beside you."

"I have not accepted any offers of marriage," Sarah spoke up. "Mr. Locke and Lord Delacroix, if you will both be so kind as to sit down and be quiet, I shall attempt to make some sort of sense of this entire muddle. And, Prudence, please do not speak another word until I say."

"But —"

"No!" Sarah covered her sister's mouth with her hand. "You have said too much already, you silly ninny. Now then . . . Mary, will you please inform Lord Delacroix of your happy news."

Mrs. Heathhill swallowed. "I am . . . increasing."

"How very pleased I am to hear this news," Delacroix replied. "And even happier to learn that Mr. Locke has refrained from involving himself in our lives at least to that extent."

Here he glared at Charles, who raised his eyebrows and picked up his teacup. By now, Miss Watson had managed to revive herself enough to sit up. The smelling salts were not needed after all, and Sarah waved away the maid who had raced into the room with the small silver bottle. The three sisters, each bearing a fan and sporting a pair of bright pink cheeks, leaned back in their respective chairs and let out a collective sigh.

"I have asked Lady Delacroix to marry me," Charles informed the gentleman. "I continue to await her answer in the hope that she will agree to become my wife."

"And Miss Pickworth approves of this," Miss Watson spoke up weakly. "But now Mr. Locke aspires to become a solicitor, not a barrister. He does not wish to join our society, but he plans to defend publicans and sinners, because Sarah told him to."

"Your sister did not tell me what to do," Charles corrected. "She merely demonstrated the truth with her own life. My decisions are my own."

Delacroix crossed his arms over his chest. "This is a fine plate of eels. I find the house all in an uproar caused by Mr. Locke, the very gentleman for whom I have been searching these past three hours. I have important news to deliver."

"Speak plainly, Delacroix," Sarah said. "What do you have to tell Mr. Locke?"

"I shall . . . but I believe a prior issue yet remains before us on the table. Dear lady, how can I relate my own information until you have answered Mr. Locke's proposal?"

"Perhaps your news may affect my answer, sir. You must give it to him at once."

"I beg your pardon, madam, but I shall hold my tongue — for it is your turn to speak."

"But I am not prepared to give Mr. Locke an answer. I have only just —"

"Oh, come, Sarah, he has proposed marriage to you before," Miss Watson reminded her sister. "If you wish to marry this . . . this proud and principled pauper . . . and give away all your fortune . . . and live on the streets . . . and beg with the blind girls in China . . . and leave Mary and me and our new baby niece or nephew all alone, then how shall we stop you?"

"I have assured you, sister, that I do not mean to leave this country again. Not permanently, anyway."

"Then marry Mr. Locke and live in Cheapside and preach to the doxies and pickpockets."

"Pru, for heaven's sake, do stop these ridiculous theatrics."

"Dear Sarah," Mrs. Heathhill spoke up, "you will put us all at ease if you can finally set your mind upon a course and refrain from any more wavering. I am queasy enough as it is. You recently informed Prudence and me that you meant to remain in England, retain your fortune, and wed Lord Delacroix. We agreed that Mr. Locke is much better suited to Prudence. God gave you the role as the eldest of three sisters, He permitted our father to train you for an elevated position in society, and He means for you to make yourself and all your family happy by choosing a wise and profitable path."

Pausing, she turned to Charles. "Mr. Locke, I cannot doubt that you feel some surprise concerning the plans my sisters and I made. Clearly, your preferences lie in another direction. Yet our offer can be seen in a prudential light. Prudence is by far the prettiest of the three of us, and she brings to her marriage ten thousand pounds — enough to pay for your studies and see you to the bar as a solicitor. But why be content with such a menial lot? While it is true that our Lord consorted with publicans and sinners, do the wealthy not require salvation as well?"

"Indeed they do," Miss Watson answered her sister. "Everyone requires it — rich and poor alike."

"It is my observation," Mrs. Heathhill observed, "that our society is rife with every sort of immorality — adultery, greed, covetousness, laziness. The rich, as our dear sister Sarah reminds us all too often, will have a harder time getting into heaven than anyone else. Why should you not put your piety to use in ministering to them on behalf of God?"

"Well, I — ," Charles began.

"You have surely heard," she continued,

"of our regent's reproachable and dissipated life. In short, the seven deadly sins may as well be the motto for his coat of arms."

"Mary," Miss Watson admonished her, "you should not speak of the regent in such a way."

"I may speak as I please. The regent is as immoral and ungodly as the most brazen harlot to walk the streets of London. Let Mr. Locke rise to barrister and preach to the refuse of the grand salons of this city. I daresay he will find as many sinners there as he would in all of Cheapside."

"I beg your pardon, Mrs. Heathhill," Delacroix spoke up, "but may I clarify one point in your previous discourse? Did you say *all three* sisters agreed that the eldest should marry me?"

"Of course," the woman replied. "And I cannot see that Mr. Locke's impetuous proposal should change Sarah's mind. Sarah, you will wed Lord Delacroix as you promised us; will you not?"

His heart slamming against his chest, Charles clenched his fists. Though every fiber of his being called out to her to deny that man and accept his own offer, he knew that nothing he could say would influence Sarah.

Her sister was wise. Surely Sarah would

not opt for love over reason. No matter how she may have felt aboard the *Queen Elinor,* she would no longer choose a life of poverty when she had seen the value of security, stability, and the constant presence of family and friends. No matter the love she may have professed for Charles in the shadows of Leadenhall Market, she could not refuse her sisters when she had made them a promise.

He would lose her. He must surrender her. He must accept his loss and continue in his plan to follow God's leading.

Closing his eyes, he gritted his teeth in anticipation of Sarah's answer. And then she spoke.

"I thank you very much, dearest sisters, for the kind advice you have given me, but I cannot abide by it. And, Lord Delacroix, although you have not made me an offer of marriage —"

"I do so now!" he cried out, leaping to his feet. "I was waiting . . . I was calling on you . . . courting —"

"Do not trouble yourself, sir. I knew your intent. I am sorry if my answer gives you pain, but I shall not be able to marry you. My heart, you see, was lost to Mr. Locke some time ago, and I do not wish to have it back again."

She halted, and when Charles lifted his head, he could see that her lips were trembling. "Dearest Sarah," he said, hardly able to believe what he had just heard. "My darling, beautiful lady. Will you . . . ? Can it be true that . . . ? Do you, at last, accept my offer of marriage?"

She smiled through her tears. "I do, sir. I do."

"Oh, dear me!" Miss Watson exclaimed as Charles rose from his chair and knelt at Sarah's knee. "Mary, look at her! Delacroix, what is to become of us? Do something!"

"I shall do something, indeed," Delacroix announced. "Mr. Locke, it is now time for me to relate to you some very important information."

Unable to make himself care in the least what this news might be, Charles took Sarah's hand and kissed it. "My love, how happy you make me," he murmured. "I assure you that I shall do all in my power to bring you happiness and peace. You cannot know how —"

"Mr. Locke," Delacroix cut in, "I bring a report that may change all your strategies, and thereby may influence Lady Delacroix's decision to become your wife."

"I adore you, Charles," Sarah whispered as tears trickled down her cheeks. "I do not know how I could have failed to see it all this time. Love is the simplest thing in the world, and you are the best and dearest man I have ever known."

"My passion for you has never wavered," he told her. "Not for a moment. Nothing can change my feelings for you, my darling Sarah. I vow that I shall protect and cherish you all the days of my life. I shall make every effort to honor your wishes and heed your —"

"Mr. Locke!" Delacroix interrupted loudly, clapping his hand on Charles's shoulder. "I beg you to refrain from this display of ardor until you have heard me out."

"Upon my honor, sir," Charles retorted, "I am hardly disposed to listen to you when this dear woman has made me the happiest man in the world. Please allow me a moment of peace in which to thank God and pledge myself to my future bride."

"I believe your joy must be postponed, sir. For what I have to present to you may take precedence over it." So saying, Delacroix motioned to one of the footmen who stood beside the drawing-room door. Then he turned and addressed the group around the fire. "Lady Delacroix, Mrs. Heathhill, Miss Watson, and, of course, Mr. Locke — may I introduce a young man whose arrival at my gentlemen's club this morning stirred a greater interest than I have observed there in some time. Do come in, sir."

Into the room stepped a thin fellow clad in a slightly overlarge suit — a black frock coat and matching breeches, a gold vest, a ruffled cravat, and a tall top hat, which he removed at once. Making a deep bow, he stepped forward and spoke. "Good afternoon to ye, Mr. Locke. I reckon ye gave me up for dead, sir, as I did ye. And yet here we both be, sound as whistles."

Charles stared for a moment, hearing a voice he knew quite well, but unable to believe his eyes. "Danny Martin?" he asked. "Is it you?"

"The very lad, sir," the youth said, his face breaking into a familiar grin. "We've come back from the grave, eh? Both of us! I were stole away by them pirates, sir. Chained up and shipped off toward Malabar to become a slave to some rajah or pirate king. But what do ye suppose happened along the way? A British naval vessel brought down the pirates and carried me back home to England. Me . . . and something ye might be wantin', sir."

As he spoke, Danny stepped aside to allow a footman to carry a small locked chest into the room. Danny burst into laughter at the look on Charles's face. "Aye, sir," he cried, throwing out his hand toward the chest, " 'tis exactly what ye think! I brought ye back your gold!"

SEVENTEEN

As though a drop of melting snow had fallen from a roof down the back of his shirt, Charles knew a sudden, thrilling chill of realization. It was true. This boy was indeed Danny. And the black chest at his side contained enough gold to finance an entire tea enterprise.

Feeling as if the world might suddenly tilt away from him and spill him down a long dark tunnel, Charles rose gingerly from the carpet on which he had knelt to profess his love to Sarah. How could this be? Danny had drowned along with many others on the *Tintagel.* Pirates had stolen the chest. The gold was gone. The tea company had vanished in the puff of smoke from a cannonball.

"Are ye not pleased to see me, sir?" Danny wondered, his face sobering. "The admiral wanted to turn in the gold with the rest of the loot they took off the pirate ship. Said he could surrender it to the naval authorities at Portsmouth, and it would add to the credit he'd get for bringing down the enemy. But I told him I knew who the chest belonged to, and I said that even though ye were dead — which is what I thought — ye had told me about your father and the tea company, and it weren't right to take the gold from its proper owner. So he give me a set of new clothes and an armed escort and a letter with a seal and sent me to London to look for your father. I went to the gentlemen's club to inquire, and that man there, Lord Delacroix, told me ye were not dead, and so here I be. Mr. Locke, ye were a friend to me aboard the *Tintagel,* and I hoped to make ye happy by returnin' the chest."

His head clearing at last, Charles broke from his trance and strode quickly across the room. "I am happy to see you, Danny!" he said, taking the boy's hand, pumping it for a moment, and then giving up all formality by throwing his arms around the scrawny fellow. "By george, you are a brave lad! Stood up for me before the admiral, did you? Came here with an armed escort? Well, well, well! I am as astonished and pleased as I have ever been in all my life."

Laughing, the boy fairly danced a jig. "I

saw ye go over the side of the ship, sir! I knew ye could never survive! But here ye be — and me, too. Both of us together again, just as we was!"

"The last I saw you, Danny, a pirate was coming after you!"

"Aye, and he got me, too, but he didn't kill me. No sir, for by that time, they was finished with their attack and was beginnin' to take slaves and loot. I thought I was done for. I thought we both was!"

"So did I," Charles cried, a surge of joy filling his chest. "Look, Sarah! This is the fine lad of whom I told you so much. Lady Delacroix, Mrs. Heathhill, Miss Watson, may I present Danny Martin?"

"At your service, ladies." With another gallant bow, the young man bent himself nearly in half. "And pleased to meet all of ye."

Beaming as if the boy were his own son, Charles turned to Sarah. But the look on her face sobered him instantly.

She stepped forward and curtsied. "Mr. Martin, I am pleased to welcome you to Trenton House." She motioned to the fire. "May I offer you some tea, sir?"

Danny blushed bright pink. "No, thank ye, milady, but I would be very pleased if Mr. Locke would open up this chest and let us all have a look at the gold! The locks be sealed and fixed, and the admiral said 'tweren't proper that any should open the box save its rightful owner."

Charles thought for a moment, trying to read the significance of Sarah's ashen face, wondering if he should send for his father, searching his mind for the location of the key and concluding that the most important thing was the woman he loved. "Madam," he said, turning to Sarah, "I wish to assure you that nothing —"

"Here is your key, sir," she spoke up. She held out her hand. "The captain of the *Queen Elinor* gave it to me during your funeral service. Thinking it of no use to you, I kept it as a memento of our friendship. But I see now that it does have a purpose after all."

Charles felt as though somehow he was being handed the key to the gates of hell itself. Gold. Riches. Mammon. Filthy lucre. He took the slender object from her palm. "Sarah, I —"

"Please, sir, do open the chest. I am sure everyone is eager to see inside it."

"Oh, yes, do!" Miss Watson exclaimed. "Is the gold in coin or bars? Were you intending to purchase tea, Mr. Locke? chests of tea? Or does it come in bags?"

"Be quiet, Prudence," Mrs. Heathhill

ordered. "Mr. Locke will open the chest in good time."

His heart in his throat, Charles stepped to the iron box and fitted the key into the first lock. It turned smoothly. The second lock snapped open easily as well. And then he broke the seals his father had set upon the chest so many months ago and lifted the lid.

A gasp ran through the group as he reached a hand into the chest and lifted one of the small gold coins. "It is all here," he said.

"Beautiful!" Mrs. Heathhill murmured, her voice husky. "Utterly beautiful."

"My goodness!" her younger sister cried. "I have never seen so many coins all at once, have you, Delacroix?"

"I should wager not. May I be so bold as to ask how much you have there, sir?"

"Enough," Charles said, shutting the lid and locking the chest once again. "This was the sum given to my father by the duke of Marston. 'The workman is worthy of his meat,' Christ taught His disciples, and my father certainly deserved this reward upon his retirement from a lifetime of service as the duke's steward."

"I should guess it at five thousand pounds," Miss Watson announced.

"More than that," Mrs. Heathhill said. "Nearer to ten."

"It is a mighty treasure!" Danny crowed. "And ye be a rich man again, Mr. Locke. I hope ye may find it in your heart to grant me employment at your tea company, sir, for I believe I have had all I want of the sea and pirates and even admirals."

Charles laid a hand on the lad's head and rumpled his hair. "You will have more than employment, Mr. Martin. You will have a fine reward for your loyalty and service. A more faithful or better friend than you, I cannot imagine. I am deeply grateful."

Danny grinned. "Thank ye, Mr. Locke. I know ye would have done the same for me had our places been reversed."

"And so you will establish your tea company after all?" Miss Watson asked Charles. "If you do, Sarah will not have you, but anyone else would be delighted, and you surely will find a very good wife. I, for one, am not opposed to riches at all. Quite the contrary, for I should like to buy a country house and keep horses. Indeed, I think a tea company is a very good enterprise on which to build a family and a name."

Charles hardly heard her as he searched the faces of those gathered around the chest of gold. Where was Sarah? He looked at the tea table. The settees and chairs around it were empty. The doors to the drawing room were shut. But she was nowhere to be found.

"Where is Lady Delacroix?" he asked her sisters. He turned to a footman. "My man, have you seen the lady of the house?"

"She has retired to her room, sir," the footman replied. "Her lady's maid requested that her mistress not be disturbed."

Letting out a groan, Charles raked a hand through his hair. "I am doomed," he said. "I may win her love, but I cannot keep her."

"Keep who, sir?" Danny asked. "That fine lady who 'ad your key? Is she to become your wife?"

Charles surveyed the solemn faces before him. "You knew this would ruin all my hopes, Delacroix; did you not?"

"You are hardly ruined, sir. You have a tidy sum here, and certainly your friendship with Sir Alexander will ensure you a fair number of willing investors in your tea company. I shall be pleased to speak to my friends. Many of them would be eager to put their assets to profitable use. Your father, too, will be delighted with this turn of events, for all his efforts on your behalf will now come to fruition. You may purchase a fine house one day — perhaps even something in Belgravia — and you may even become wealthy enough to buy yourself a title. If you will agree to wed Miss Watson, I assure you that she will make you very happy, and I have no doubt that you must be welcomed into her society with opened arms."

"I agree with Lord Delacroix, of course," Mrs. Heathhill spoke up. "Let me assure you from experience and observation, Mr. Locke, that in the great scheme of life, passion is fleeting. A wise man would do better to marry well than to give up everything for love. You wish to serve God, Mr. Locke, and clearly He wishes to make you a wealthy man. Will you turn away this heavenly gift in the name of misguided piety and a romantic zeal for a woman who cannot become your wife?"

"Why not?" Danny spoke up bluntly. "If the lady loves Mr. Locke, she should wed him, for never will she find a better 'usband."

"That is exactly what Miss Pickworth said," Miss Watson observed. "But I think —"

"My sister is a baroness, Mr. Martin," Mrs. Heathhill told the boy. "Her late husband was a baron, as is his heir, Lord Delacroix." She gestured to the man who stood beside her. "Your friend, Mr. Locke, though certainly a fine and now a wealthy gentleman, is a commoner. A commoner cannot marry a baroness. It is not done. She must wed a peer, someone whose rank and place in society are nearer to her own. Should she marry so far beneath herself, she would be ridiculed. My sister may love Mr. Locke, but she will not become his wife."

Danny scowled. "Beggin' your pardon, madam, but if two people love each other well enough, they ought to get married, for that is 'ow God intended it to be."

"Thank you, Danny," Charles said. "I believe you are the bravest and wisest of all gathered here. And now if my hosts will be so good as to excuse me, I must see that the gold is secured and my father informed of the news of its return as soon as may be. I thank you for the tea, and I beg you to extend my best wishes to Lady Delacroix. Please tell her that I shall call upon her as soon as I am able, that we may discuss this situation and make our plans accordingly."

Without waiting for any more of Lord Delacroix's protests, Miss Watson's hysterics, or Mrs. Heathhill's sober lectures, Charles bowed and beckoned Danny. "Do accompany me, Mr. Martin, for I shall be very pleased to introduce you to my father."

"Yes, sir! At once!" With a little hop-skip,

Danny followed Charles out of the drawing room. Charles instructed the naval guard to fetch the chest and accompany him to the Bank of England.

"What are you doing, Sarah?"

Mary and Prudence had just burst into their sister's bedchamber without knocking. At the sight of Sarah bent over an open trunk, Prudence let out a squeal.

Mary marched straight to her. "You are not leaving us, are you?" Mary demanded. "Do not run away from your troubles, sister; I beg you. Your past torment is behind you, and only happiness awaits. Please stop . . . stop packing!"

"Put that down at once!" Prudence jerked a gown from Sarah's fingers and grabbed another from the half-full trunk. "Do not leave us, Sarah! Just because Mr. Locke has recovered his gold —"

"I am not going far," Sarah said, taking her gowns from her sister's arms and laying them carefully into her trunk. "I mean to go away to Brighton for a holiday. You may both come along if you wish. I believe a month of sea bathing would set us all up very well."

"Sea bathing!" Mary exclaimed. "In my condition, Sarah? How can you even suggest such a thing!"

"The sea air will do you good in such a circumstance. And I am sure Mr. Heathhill cannot object. Indeed, I hope he will join us."

"But today?" Prudence snatched the gowns back out of the trunk and tossed them on a chair some distance from her sister's reach. "You are leaving today? We have only just learned of Mr. Locke's change in circumstance, and you have had two proposals of marriage, and Mary is increasing, and you cannot go away today!"

"Why not? I am in no humor to give consequence to anything but sun and wind and salt water. Let Mr. Locke enjoy his gold and build his tea empire. He will find another wife easily now, and I shall soon forget him. Let Delacroix set his sights on some other rich woman, for I am sure he is handsome and clever enough to barter his title for a fortune — as did his uncle before him. No, sisters, I am quite finished with men. I shall enjoy Brighton until the season is over, and then I shall return to London."

Mary and Prudence stared at her as if she had said the most unreasonable thing in the world. But she had not. Sarah's plan had come into her head the moment she saw the look in Charles's eyes as he fastened them upon his chest of gold. She knew exactly what she needed to do. And the more she acted upon her decision, the more peace and certainty eroded the panic, fear, and dread in her heart.

"Pru," Sarah went on, "I have been thinking that I ought to purchase a country house. I am keen on Hampshire, for the weather there is amiable, and we can keep horses. Mary, you may come and visit us there as often as you wish. And do bring all your children, for I have no doubt there will be many."

"But — ," Mary sputtered.

"In time, Mary, you and I shall find a suitable husband for Prudence. He must be a sensible man with a good heart and high morals — a gentleman of good breeding, neither too rich nor too poor. Pru, I shall make you a wedding gift of Trenton House, where you will entertain us all when we are in town. How is that for a jolly scheme?"

Without waiting for an answer, she crossed to the chair where Prudence had tossed her gowns and returned them to the trunk. Her lady's maid was gathering up toiletries and packing them in a bag. The silence in the room spoke volumes, for Sarah knew she had satisfied her sisters' every desire. For herself, she could not leave the city fast enough. She wanted no more unexpected calls from Charles, and she could not bear the sight of Delacroix. Her heart, she had to believe, would mend in time.

She could never marry Charles, Sarah thought as she tried to swallow her tears. Too easily, he had returned to his former ways. The merest glimpse of his gold had lit a fire in his eyes and set a brilliant glow on his face. He loved it. That gold represented his dreams, his hopes, everything he had wanted in life until he met her. But until the moment she saw Charles's expression, she had not understood how very deeply — and with what passion — he adored his treasure.

Certain he had lost the gold, Charles had transformed himself. He had fallen in love with her. He had surrendered all his dreams. He had given his life to God. But the instant he had wealth again, he reverted to someone she had never known but had caught glimpses of from the start. Driven, ambitious, determined, he would build his empire. Perhaps he would continue to love Sarah as much as he thought he did now. But she could not live a life so far removed from the values she held dear. Money, esteem, and society all must be secondary to faith in God. Even human love must bow before a passion for obedience to the will of the Almighty. This was all Sarah knew, and all she could accept of herself or anyone close to her.

"I think it is a good plan," Prudence offered at last. "I should very much like to go sea bathing and then buy a house in the country. With horses. Although I must say I am quite devoid of hope for a marriage of my own. I should so much prefer to love my husband than to unite with a man for whom I have no like. I do not care sixpence for Delacroix, you know."

"Perhaps we shall find a husband for you in Brighton," Sarah suggested. "Miss Pickworth reported last week that Sir Alexander Chouteau and several of his friends mean to holiday there in the coming month. You could not object to a duke's son, could you?"

"Certainly not!" Prudence said, brightening. "Though the duke of Marston's son is said to be as great a cad as Delacroix."

"You are thinking of the elder Chouteau. The marquess of Blackthorne had a terrible reputation. But he died in America."

"Or so Miss Pickworth reports," Prudence clarified.

"No matter who is in Brighton, I cannot think of going there with you," Mary observed. "I have at least a month of balls and receptions on my calendar. Besides, Mr. Heathhill has business in town. He could not come with me, and I should not like to be without him."

"Even though 'from experience and observation, you have learned that in the great scheme of life, passion is fleeting'?" Sarah asked, imitating her sister's moralizing tone of voice. "I believe you and Mr. Heathhill belie your own sage advice, Mary."

The young woman blushed. "Perhaps we do. I cannot deny that we are warmly attached. And marriage does benefit from an affable and obliging friendship between the two partners."

Prudence snorted with laughter. "*Affable* and *obliging*! Oh, Mary, you adore your boring old husband, and you might as well admit it. As for Sarah, if she wishes to put herself on the shelf and live out her days as an auntie to our children, why not? Only, dear Sarah, do not go sailing away to India or China and giving away your fortune left and right; I beg you."

Sarah smiled. "I have made ample allowance for charities, missions, almshouses, and hospitals. Our earthly father would not be pleased, but our heavenly Father must take great joy in the good that those talents He gave me will do. My bankers and barristers advise me well, I believe, and you may rest in the knowledge that as hard as you may try, neither of you is likely to drain us dry in a lifetime."

"Oh, Sarah, I am pleased to hear this," Mary said. "I know you mean well, and I agree that the money cannot all be spent upon our pleasures. But neither should it all go to charity and mission work."

"Moderation," Anne Webster spoke up from the table she had cleared of toiletries. "Moderation, I think, is the key to all things."

"Thank you, Anne," Sarah said, rewarding her maid with a smile. "Perhaps there is more than one key to living a godly life."

But Sarah could not make herself feel happy as she thought of another key — the small gold one she had worn on a chain about her neck these many months. How could she have known that it represented the end of all she had loved and held most dear? Even now, she wondered if she had misread the look in Charles's eyes when he opened his chest. But no . . . he was a changed man, and no longer would she have him.

"I shall pack my trunks too!" Prudence said, all but singing as she skipped out of the room. "Anne, will you help me, for Sarah is nearly finished?"

"Of course, madam," Anne said as she closed the toiletries bag.

"I cannot wait to go to Brighton!" Prudence sang out. "I believe I should very much like to have a better look at Sir Alexander. And what if he should add a handsome friend to his party? Would that not be delightful?"

"Yes, dearest," Sarah said as the door fell shut on her sister and the maid. "Mary, will you go down and send for a carriage? And please do not tell Delacroix where Pru and I have gone. Allow us a week or two of peace before we must be faced with his attentions once again."

Mary chuckled. "As you wish, Sarah. And may I say that I think you are wise to forgo your love for Mr. Locke, no matter how it may pain you to separate yourself from him. He was never meant for you."

"I appreciate your sentiment, Mary." As her sister left the bedroom, Sarah shut the lid of her trunk and leaned upon it while recalling another chest, the one filled with gold. Charles, she felt confident, would have a good life. And perhaps her influence would serve him well. Maybe he would be more thoughtful, more generous, more pious than most men in his position. Mary had been correct in her observation that the upper class was as much in need of Christian morality and surrender as commoners.

Well done, Charles, she thought. *Well done, Danny.*

At the memory of the lad and his eager joy, it was all Sarah could do to hold back her tears. Everyone who knew Charles intimately, it seemed, could not help but love him. Such depth of feeling had brought a young boy all the way across the ocean. It had brought Sarah to a place of utter surrender. How she would dispel that love she did not know, for memories had a disturbing way of lingering — sometimes forever.

EIGHTEEN

James Locke drew a large white handkerchief from the pocket of his greatcoat and gave his nose a loud, window-rattling honk. Nodding to acknowledge that he was weeping, he held up a hand to silence any condolences his son might attempt to offer. He blotted his cheeks, blew his nose a second time, and finally managed to swallow.

"You make me very . . . very happy," he choked out. "Dear Charles, your action pleases me greatly and would . . . would of course have pleased your . . . your moth . . . moth . . . mother."

Lest the outpouring of emotion wash both father and son right out the door of the small house on Threadneedle Street, Charles clapped his hand on his father's shoulder and gave it a strong shake.

"Well, then!" he said, fighting his own feelings. "I am delighted that you approve of my plan, Father. Mr. Martin and I shall pay a visit to the bank directly. After that, we shall call upon Sir Alexander. And, of course, we shall speak to Lord Delacroix as well. I am convinced that you and I shall set forth upon our enterprise with a cadre of investors. And this time, we shall not fail to achieve our aims."

"No, indeed," his father mumbled. "No, we shall not fail. You are too good a son. Too loyal a friend. Too amiable and educated to be anything but a great success. I have said it all along, as did your . . . your dear . . . your dear late mother —"

"I must be going," Charles said, rising from his chair before his father could sink them both into the sea of nostalgia. "We have spent three days in our planning and discussion of what to do with the gold, and I believe all London must be awaiting our decision. I am told that the gentlemen at Lord Delacroix's club can talk of little else, and even the duke of Marston's letter of enquiry displays a rather impertinent interest in the matter."

"Aye, that it does!" James chuckled through his tears. "The old cabbagehead himself is eager to know how we mean to make use of his gold now that we have it back. We shall send him a chest of our finest tea when it comes into port, shall we?"

"Compliments of Locke & Son," Charles said, grinning at the image of the duke's reaction to such a gift. He motioned to Danny, who was waiting rather impatiently near the library door. "Come, Mr. Martin; shall we be on our way?"

"Aye, sir." Danny's habit of hop-skipping had not deserted him despite his small sack of gold, two fine suits of clothing, and comfortable residence in his own bedroom inside the Locke house. "To the bank first, then, sir?"

"No, Danny, my lad," Charles replied, as he donned his top hat, picked up his cane, and stepped through the front door into Threadneedle Street. "I have a prior commitment."

Attempting to match the youngster's brisk pace down to the lane where their carriage was kept, Charles reveled in the glorious afternoon sunshine. "This quest supersedes all others," he informed Danny. "You may recall that I am engaged to be married to the most delightful, most beautiful, and most amiable Mrs. Carlyle — better known to London as Lady Delacroix."

"Ye have reminded me quite regular, sir."

"That dear lady accepted my proposal of marriage three days ago. Her sister, Mrs.

Heathhill, writes to me that my lady keeps company with their youngest sister, Miss Prudence Watson, and that all concerned are eager to hear the outcome of my decision regarding my future. It is time now to enlighten them and, if need be, to reassure my fiancée that nothing in the world can alter my commitment to God, my devotion to her, or my determination to make her the happiest woman on earth."

Danny laughed. "I daresay she has been eager to see you these three days, sir. No lady likes to be kept waitin'."

Charles stepped up to the carriage he had summoned and followed Danny into it. "She has waited, aye, but through her sister, I have communicated with her each morning and evening."

As he seated himself beside the lad, Charles mused upon the unsettling fact that Sarah had failed to reply to any of his missives. Might she be having second thoughts now that he had regained his wealth? He hoped not. Mrs. Heathhill had assured him that his beloved was in good health and was happily occupied with her younger sister. He trusted the two were engaged in some female activity, perhaps pertaining to the wedding or to the furnishing of a future home.

"Lady Delacroix lives a far piece from Threadneedle Street, eh?" Danny observed.

"She does. As London grows, it seems the wealthy want less and less to do with the old city and her winding streets, alleys, and open markets. They now congregate around Grosvenor Square and Berkeley Square in the Mayfair District or Belgrave Square in Belgravia."

"Will ye buy a 'ouse in one of them places when ye be rich enough, Mr. Locke?"

Charles studied the familiar streets of the city in which he had spent all his adult life. "I have found my father's house a cheerful enough place, small though it is. I should very much dislike to leave it. Society, however, may dictate otherwise."

Again, a tingle of discomfort tightened Charles's chest. He hoped Sarah's decision to depart the drawing room upon the presentation of his gold reflected her desire to be alone with her happy thoughts of his love and her future with him — and not some other, less pleasurable, emotion.

"I am glad ye do not mean to go to sea again, sir," Danny spoke up. "Although if need be, I would go with ye."

Charles glanced across at the young boy's eager smile. "I know you would, my friend. And I should be glad of your company. But

I cannot risk the loss to my father and to my wife were I again to encounter such travail as we did upon my first journey. No, I shall endeavor to secure an investor — indeed a full partner — who is willing to risk his life upon our enterprise. He must be a man of adventure, and he must be entirely trustworthy. I cannot say, at this moment, to whom the task will fall, but I am convinced that God will provide."

"Ye believe God means ye to be a tea merchant, Mr. Locke? Even though ye were nearly killed by them pirates? The old bo's'n aboard the *Tintagel* would have called that a sign that ye were not meant to take the gold to China. Signs and omens was what he was always tellin' us about. And he were never wrong."

"Sometimes difficulties may be seen as God's way of diverting us to another, better path, Danny. And at other times, they may be seen as barriers intended to be sur-mounted with God's help — as we carry on in the same path. 'The trying of your faith worketh patience,' as the apostle James explained. We must be patient, slow, careful, and deliberate as we overcome the obstacles in our way along the straight and narrow road God has laid out for us."

"But how can we tell whether a difficulty

411

be meant to lead us to a new path or whether it is to be attacked and gone over as we stay on the same path?"

Charles pondered the insight behind the simple question. "That is an excellent query, Danny, and the answer is not an easy one. Do you know that in the very ancient days of the Bible's history, priests used to cast lots in order to determine God's will? But we no longer abide by that old method, for as Christians we have been given the Holy Spirit. This Spirit is our guide, our counselor. He leads us to discern the will of the Father. In my attempt to hear the whisperings of the Spirit, I have prayed, spoken to my father, searched my heart, and read my Bible. And I believe — most firmly — that I am, after all, meant to surmount all obstacles, marry my dear Sarah, and become a tea merchant."

Danny's face broke into a wide grin. "I am pleased to hear it, sir, for ye shall be the best 'usband and father, and the most honest of all traders near and far."

"Thank you for your faith in me, young Mr. Martin. I shall do my best always to live up to it." He let out a breath as the carriage slowed before the large house on Cranleigh Crescent. "And now I must ask you to pray for me in silence as I speak of these matters with my dear Sarah. She loves me as I love her, but the course of our affection has not run smoothly. I should very much hope to find her in agreement with all my own feelings. But be assured that if she is not, we shall strive to come to a place of joint communion."

"I shall wait for ye in the carriage, sir," Danny said. "And ye shall have me prayers, for whatever they be worth to ye."

"They are worth a great deal."

So saying, Charles stepped out onto the street and climbed the steps to the door of Trenton House. A footman answered and took Charles's card. "Mr. Locke," he said, "I regret to inform you that the family has departed town for the remainder of the season."

Charles took a step back. "Gone? Lady Delacroix and her sister both?"

"Yes, sir. Excuse me, please." The footman made to shut the door.

Charles stuck out his hand to hold it open. "But where? Where have they gone?"

"I am not at liberty to reveal their present abode. Forgive me, sir, but the house is closed until winter."

As the footman stepped back and pushed the door to, Charles turned on his heel and raced down the stairs. "Across the Crescent!" he called to the carriage driver. "Meet me at the Heathhills' house!"

Without pausing to explain, he took off running across the large expanse of green grass toward the imposing façade of the two-story home. He was still sprinting up the steps when a liveried footman stepped through the door to greet him.

"The master and mistress of the house are not in, sir," he said.

"But where are they? My good man, I am looking for Lady Delacroix. I have just learned that she and her sister are away from town. Can you tell me where they have gone?"

"No, sir. I beg your pardon, sir."

"Upon my word, I am a close friend of the family. I must know where . . ." He stopped his words. It would do no good. Servants were never at liberty to disclose the comings and goings or other private information regarding their masters. As his carriage rounded the crescent-shaped park onto which all the homes faced, Charles pointed in the direction of Delacroix House.

A dash down the street took him to the steps of that grand domicile, which he took two at a time. "Lord Delacroix," he blurted, flipping his card at the footman who answered the door. "Charles Locke to see him.

Do not tell me he is out, man, just fetch him forthwith."

The footman's eyes widened. "Do come in, sir. I shall inform my master that he has a caller."

"Excellent. And see that he makes haste; I beg you. I must speak to him at once."

The footman regarded the visitor with a suspicious glance over his shoulder as he carried the silver tray down the corridor. Charles took off his hat and tapped it against his leg. How could she have gone away without telling him? Her sister had lied! They were all out of town, and he had lost her again. Blast!

Grinding his teeth, Charles paced the black-and-white marbled floor. This was unthinkable. Why had she left him? They had declared their love — in public. She had agreed before her sisters to become his wife. What had undone everything?

"Locke?" Lord Delacroix's voice echoed down the hall. "I say, my good man, how pleased I am to hear from you at last. Capital to see you! Capital!"

"Delacroix," Charles burst out. "Where is she? Where have they gone?"

"Who?"

"Lady Delacroix. Her sisters. I am told they have left town for the season."

"Upon my word, they have not. I saw Mrs. Heathhill only two hours ago. She said she intended to lie down, for she is tired in the afternoons these days. It is the way with women in her delicate condition, you know. But you are very distressed, sir. Come, who told you the women were away?"

"The manservant. Trenton House is closed for the season. He would give me no further information and shut the door on me. I have not spoken to Lady Delacroix these three days, but as was proper, I wrote to her sister, and Mrs. Heathhill informed me that she was well. She said that Lady Delacroix and Miss Watson were occupying themselves pleasantly and that all were awaiting word regarding my future plans. I have elected to use the money as it was originally intended —"

"You will establish your tea company then? Excellent! I have good news for you, sir. Several men who heard about the fortunate recovery of your chest of gold are most eager to meet with you to discuss that venture. Your tea company is quite the talk —"

"Hang the tea company! Where is Sarah?"

Delacroix's brows lifted for a moment before he spoke again. "Mr. Locke, you are again a man of some means, but you cannot think her sisters will permit Lady Delacroix to marry you. No matter what she said."

"I think that decision belongs to the lady herself, and if she has been taken away —"

"She is not taken away. Calm yourself, man. Mrs. Heathhill informs me that her two sisters have gone off on a holiday."

"A holiday?" Charles bellowed. "Where?"

"She would not say. They are to rest and refresh themselves. I should imagine they have gone to Bath or Brighton. But you never know. I am told that Lady Delacroix fancies Hampshire and may purchase a property there. And the entire family is fond of the Lake District. So it is quite possible —"

"Delacroix!" Charles said, grabbing the man's shoulders. "You will tell me where she is . . . now!"

"Upon my honor, I do not know!" He jerked free of Charles's grasp. "Come, we shall call upon Mrs. Heathhill. If she is resting, we shall wait for her to arise. Perhaps she will agree to tell us where her sisters have gone."

As Charles accompanied Delacroix back out into the summer afternoon, he knew the end of all the promise of the day. She had left him. Whether convinced by her sisters to leave or gone away of her own accord, Sarah had left him. She did not want him. Her love was not strong enough to overcome her fear. She could not trust him to honor her beliefs and to act upon his own conscience as a Christian.

The two men walked the short distance back to the Heathhill residence. Charles's carriage, with Danny still inside, followed at a discreet distance. Delacroix clearly wished to dismiss the matter of the missing women. His mind was on the tea company, and he made no attempt to disguise his interest in the scheme. Friends, acquaintances, business relations — all had been told of the chest of gold that had been delivered from the hands of cutthroat pirates by a lad of twelve. Young Danny Martin had become a veritable angel sent from heaven, while Charles himself appeared as a hero bent on glory and fortune.

What tripe. Charles could hardly bear to listen to the man's gushing narrative as they mounted the steps to the Heathhill residence. Suddenly, the tea company looked to him exactly as it had to Sarah upon Charles's first description of it to her. Empty. A great mound of nothingness. A dream with no foundation. A hollow hope built on misguided priorities.

"Do come in, Lord Delacroix," the footman said. This time, he took Charles's card and placed it on his tray. "Mr. Locke. I shall see if Mrs. Heathhill is disposed to greet callers."

"At least we know she is in," Delacroix murmured to Charles as the footman hurried up the stairs leading from the foyer. The two men entered the reception room at the front of the house, but neither was inclined to sit. Charles paced the floor, trying to think how to find Sarah and change her mind. But what if he was unable? Had he chosen wrongly? Was Sarah not meant to become his wife? In the carriage it had been so easy to explain the workings of God's divine plan to Danny. Now Charles felt as much confusion as he had ever known in his life.

"Tea, you know, will never go out of fashion," Delacroix was saying. "Coffee may wane, but not tea. A man will always want his morning brew. And a lady must have her afternoon cup. Indeed, one can hardly escape tea wherever one goes these days. The East India Company deserves credit for introducing that great beverage to us, but Parliament was right to end their monopoly. Open the sea-lanes to free trade, I say. Competition will infuse healthy blood into the economy of this country. Nothing better than men vying for business. Money is to be made in tea, and why not us, sir? Why not?"

Charles leveled a stare at the golden-haired young lord who had never lifted a finger to labor at anything in his life. What did Delacroix know about tea or business or competition?

"Ah, Lord Delacroix!" Mrs. Heathhill stepped into the room and smiled at the gentlemen awaiting her. "Mr. Locke, how do you do? I am so pleased to see you both. Do sit down."

"I hope you are well, madam?" Delacroix began. "You are looking rather —"

"I beg your pardon," Charles cut in, "but I can no longer delay upon the subject that consumes me. Mrs. Heathhill, I must know where your sisters have gone. I am told that Trenton House is closed for the season."

She smiled at Charles. "They are away, sir, but I fear I am not at liberty to —"

"Mrs. Heathhill, you must tell me where Lady Delacroix has gone. You heard her declaration of love for me, and you know very well that she accepted my proposal of marriage. I expect to make your sister my wife, and I beg you to tell me where she is."

"Dear, dear Mr. Locke." Mrs. Heathhill

sighed as she sat down and drew out a letter, which she extended toward Charles. "My eldest sister left London shortly after you departed Trenton House with your gold, and she wishes not to be contacted by you or Lord Delacroix or anyone else, for that matter."

"Not by me?" Delacroix said in astonishment.

"No one." Mrs. Heathhill leaned back as Charles took the letter from her hand and broke the seal. "My sister finds company tedious at present. She is eager to rest and refresh herself. I am sure you understand."

Charles scanned the short note written in Sarah's careful hand. *Dear Mr. Locke,* he read.

Please forgive me for any surprise or pain my sudden departure may bring, but I find I am unable to remain in London at present. I am sure you will understand that my statements to you this afternoon were made in haste and without careful consideration, and I feel certain you will agree that they were not meant to be taken seriously. I do thank you for your friendship. I shall pray for your health and for the well-being of your tea company.

Sincerely,
Sarah Carlyle, Lady Delacroix

Charles folded the letter and studied Mrs. Heathhill. "She wrote this of her own volition, did she?"

"She did. Mr. Locke, you must see that while my sister values the acquaintance she made with you aboard the *Queen Elinor,* she understands too well that you and she are from different worlds. Her purposes are not your own. And while your present happy situation makes you welcome in our society, you cannot reasonably expect to form an attachment to a lady whose circumstances are so far above your own."

"As you have reminded your sister and me very often, Mrs. Heathhill." He looked down at the note in his hand. "And this is all I am to have from her? This letter? These few words?"

She shrugged. "What else can you expect? Sir, be content. You have been given much. Do not ask for more; I beg you."

With that, she claimed that she was feeling extremely weak, made her farewells to Delacroix and to Charles, and drifted from the room like a dandelion seed upon the wind. Charles stared after the woman, unable to accept all that had transpired. He had left his home in every certainty of joy and contentment. And now he stood clutching the ruination of all he held most dear.

"Excuse me, Lord Delacroix," Charles said, making for the foyer. "I beg your pardon, but I must go."

"May I call on you, sir?" the man cried after him.

Charles hurried down the steps without answering. The footman held the carriage door open for him, and Charles climbed into the welcome shadows of the leather-lined cocoon.

As the coachman set the horses in motion and the carriage moved forward, he crumpled the letter. Lost. Gone. He must accept it. All was finished. Done.

"Be ye well, sir?" The voice beside him startled Charles. "Ye were runnin' back and forth as if the devil hisself were after ye."

"Ah, Danny —" Charles let out a breath — "I believe he has been after me, and he has captured me in his foul grip."

"What has 'appened, Mr. Locke? Some terrible misfortune, I fear."

"My love . . . my dearest Sarah . . ." Charles bit off the words. "It is too much to explain, lad. I have lost her. That is all you need to know."

"Lost her, sir? Be she dead?"

"No, Danny. But she has left London . . . left me . . . gone away forever."

The boy sat in silence for a moment. " 'Tis a terrible trial, sir."

"It is, Danny. I am undone."

"Undone? After ye told me not an hour ago the lady were meant to be your wife?"

"I thought she was, Danny. But now —"

"Now ye must climb over this obstacle and stay on the same path the Holy Spirit told ye to follow, Mr. Locke. Ain't that the way of it, sir?"

Charles looked up from the haze of sorrow that had clouded his vision. "What do you mean, lad? Speak plainly."

"This, sir." Danny took the crumpled letter from Charles's fist. " 'Tis nothin' more than a trial. Ye said the Holy Spirit told ye to marry that lady and be a tea merchant. Now ye have been given a trial to grow ye."

"But she has rejected me, boy. That is not an obstacle I can surmount."

Yet even as he said the words, he heard the distant echo of a woman's sweet voice as waves lapped the side of a ship: *"No, Mr. Locke, I shall not marry you. Please do be reasonable."*

Sarah had rejected Charles before. Ten times. Maybe fifteen or twenty. How often had he asked for her hand aboard the *Queen Elinor*? Again in the cottage in Shepton? And in the walled garden at Bamberfield? Each time, in her gentle way she had told him the same thing: *"No, Mr. Locke, I shall not marry you. Please do be reasonable."*

Now he had another rejection. An obstacle. A trial. To lead him onto another path? Or to grow him as he made his way along the same path?

Charles took the letter from Danny's hand, held it up, and tore it in half. "Lad," he said, "I believe it cannot be many years before I must make you a partner in Locke & Son Tea Company, Ltd. You learn quickly. You are loyal to a fault. And you are far too wise."

Danny grinned. "Aye, sir, but what lad could ask for a better teacher than the one I found when I were naught but a ship's boy aboard the *Tintagel*?"

NINETEEN

Sarah dipped a silver spoon into her tea and gave it a stir. As she gazed from her deck chair upon the fair scene of lapping waves and sapphire sky that stretched out before her, she could hardly imagine herself any happier.

Hardly.

But no matter how her heart might ache, she believed that her new quest was off to an admirable beginning. After a month of bathing, strolling the beach, and reading countless novels, Sarah had sent her sister back to London to stay with Mary and her husband. Prudence remained unattached, but not for any lack of flirting. To Sarah's dismay, the young woman had trifled with every cad in Brighton, thus making it imperative to put her back under Mary's thumb for the remainder of the summer.

The lady's maid whose wisdom and friendship meant much to Sarah had departed too. On learning of Sarah's plan to go to sea, Anne Webster had requested not to be asked to leave England while her father remained in prison. Though Sarah missed the companionship, she was pleased to have found Anne a position with one of Sir Alexander Chouteau's sisters. Someone as bright, pretty, and well educated as Anne could not fail to advance herself — and what better place to do it than in the house of the duke of Marston?

And so Sarah was alone at sea again. This time, she would not go all the way to India, Burma, or China. France was her destination. After her ship docked in Dieppe, Sarah planned to make her way to Paris and then down to the Mediterranean. By winter, she would have rented a house near the sea, where she would write letters to her sisters, bask in the sunshine, and eat olives.

Of course, no one in England needed to know that she also intended to have a look at the orphanage in Italy, the hospital in Greece, and the small Christian mission in Cairo where God was using her father's money to minister to the least of His people. And if she happened to wander a bit farther after that, well . . . at least she would not have to listen to Pru's hysterics or Mary's sermons beforehand.

Sipping her tea, Sarah paged through her copy of the most recent issue of *The Tattler*. She recalled Pru's letter to Miss Pickworth and the surprising advice printed for all of London to see. This day's column contained the usual recitation of attendees at various receptions and balls, Sarah noted. As she scanned the names and smiled at the witty barbs and accolades dished out by the anonymous writer, her eye fell on a surprising note.

Rumor is rife, Miss Pickworth had penned. *An alarming and astonishing account has reached our ears. Can it be that the dead do descend upon us? Dare death deliver up a reportedly deceased duke?*

A duke? Sarah thought. What could this mean? As usual, Miss Pickworth was coy.

Our grave gossip goes like this, Sarah read on. *A future duke whom all deemed to have been bludgeoned, beheaded, and buried may be bound for home. Will Duke Marston make merry at the prodigal's return? Or will Chouteau call "cheat!" at the taking of a transitory title? Only Miss Pickworth can deliver the details.*

Good heavens. Sarah read the cryptic gossip again. The columnist seemed to be referring to the Duke of Marston's elder son, Ruel. Known as the marquess of Blackthorne, Ruel Chouteau had gone to America and was rumored to have been brutally murdered there. His brother, Sir Alexander Chouteau — Charles Locke's friend — thus stood to inherit his father's title and the duchy.

But perhaps the marquess was not dead after all. What would the return of the heir mean to Sir Alexander? and to Charles?

Shaking her head to clear it of all thoughts of the man she had dismissed from her life, Sarah folded the newspaper, placed it on the table, and set her teapot on top of it. The respite in Brighton had done her good. Prudence's love of the outdoors had meant the two sisters enjoyed picnics, long walks, and an occasional outing on horseback.

Mary would be delighted to have Prudence staying with her at Heathhill House, where they might more easily confer and scheme. Mary's "confinement" had not confined her in the least, Sarah realized, for she had written of parties, dinners, receptions, and balls — listing every attendee, details of all the gossip, and a general commentary on gowns, manners, and puddings. Puddings, it seemed, had become as important to Mary as slippers and bonnets these days. She was rounding out very nicely, she reported.

No mention was ever made of Charles Locke. Sarah thought it very kind of her sisters to avoid discussing the man. She herself hardly thought of him.

Only when she chanced to look at the sea did she recall their long conversations and his whispered words of admiration and commitment so long ago aboard the *Queen Elinor.* Only while strolling in Brighton's endless gardens did she think how he had climbed over the wall at Bamberfield to profess his passion for her. Only when browsing in shops did she remember their ardent avowals of love beneath the awnings of the Leadenhall Market. And only at night, alone in her bed, would Sarah allow herself to dwell upon how very lonely she felt, how bereft of him, how quietly the years stretched out before her.

But enough. Now she was on her way again. A new course. A quest worthy of her time and energy. She reached for her teapot and lifted it to pour out another cup. Charles was probably halfway around Africa by now — on his way to buy tea and begin his new life as a successful tradesman. Or perhaps he was still in London, purchasing a warehouse and establishing his investors. He might go to sea in springtime, when the weather was better and the winds more favorable. Either way, Sarah was not likely to see Charles again for another year or two — by which time she would have forgotten him altogether.

As she took a sip of tea, Sarah gazed out at the receding strip of white shoreline. Dear England. Such a blessed isle. She would be grateful to return here in time. But God had other work for her to do now that she had calmed her sisters and settled them even more comfortably than before. For the first time since she had walked away from Charles and left him standing over his gold in the drawing room at Trenton House, Sarah could honestly say she felt happy.

"Excuse me, madam, is this seat taken?"

Sarah glanced up to find an elderly gentleman with a curled white mustache. She smiled as he tapped the empty chair at her table. "No, sir, I have no use for it. Do feel free to take it away."

"Thank you, my dear." He lifted the deck chair. "May I inquire . . . do you go to France?"

"I do, sir. To Paris."

"You are welcome to join my wife and our daughters at our tea table, if you wish. We are on our way to see our son who was injured in battle. We plan to take him home to England with us when he is well enough to travel."

"I do hope you find him much improved." She looked over her shoulder at the three women who were waiting expectantly at the next table. "I thank you for the invitation, sir, but I am truly very happy to be alone."

"Are you, indeed?" The voice from the other side of her chair drew Sarah's breath out of her lungs. She swung around to find Charles Locke standing before her, his top hat in his hand. He tilted his head, one brow raised quizzically. "You are *very* happy to be alone, Lady Delacroix? Or may I join you?"

"Oh . . ." She bit her lip.

"I beg your pardon, madam," the older gentleman said with a bow. "I believe you may need this chair after all. I see another there at the far side of the deck. Good afternoon."

"But I —"

"It has taken me a very long time to discover you, Sarah," Charles said, settling into the chair. "Your sister is quite protective. Very admirable of her, I must say. Poor Delacroix was most distressed to be kept in the dark."

"How did you find me?"

"I looked. Everywhere." His mouth tipped into the hint of a smile. "I even applied to Miss Pickworth, who was kind enough to mention in a recent column that Sir Alexander Chouteau had danced with Miss Prudence Watson while both were on holiday in Brighton. Come now, Sarah . . . you did not think I would let you go so easily, did you?"

"You have your gold. Your tea enterprise. Your father . . . I thought —"

"Did I not tell you how I felt about you? I am sure I did. But perhaps you were not listening carefully enough." He leaned forward, his blue eyes searching. "I love you, Sarah. I have loved you always, and I shall love you forever. God brought you into my life, and you opened my eyes to Him. Never mind about chests of gold and boxes of tea. Never mind about money and status and lineage and title."

"But you do mind."

"I mind that I obey God. That is all. You taught me the importance of looking about to discover what really matters. I have done that, and I see that God has given me certain things. Gifts. And, you see, I am meant to use them."

He drew a small locket from his coat. As he pressed open the clasp, Sarah saw two miniature portraits. "My father and my mother," Charles said, setting the locket on the table. "God gave them to me, and they, in turn, gave me the education and the guidance to become the man I am."

Now he pulled a gold coin from his pocket and laid it beside the locket. "God permitted me this living, Sarah. In Christ's teachings, I am not the rich young ruler who walked sadly away from Jesus because he could not part with his treasures. I am, rather, the servant whose master gave him five talents. That servant traded with what he had been given and made five more talents. When his master returned and saw the increase, he said, 'Well done, thou good and faithful servant: thou hast been faithful over a few things, I will make thee ruler over many things.' Sarah, I have been given this money to use in the most responsible and godly way I can. And I mean to do so."

Now he took a sheaf of paper from his coat pocket and spread it on the table beside the coin and the locket. There were several pages, and he set his hat atop the stack to keep them from blowing into the sea. "Here I have been given something more. These are promissory notes, letters of intent, and other documents from investors committed to the establishment of Locke & Son Tea Company, Ltd. And here I have the first letter from my partner, the man I have entrusted with the responsibility of taking my gold to China to purchase the first shipment of tea — Henry Carlyle, Lord Delacroix."

"Delacroix!" Sarah exclaimed, nearly as shocked at the mention of that name as she was at the sight of the man who sat beside her. "Delacroix has gone off with your coins? You trusted him?"

"I did. I do. He very much wishes to restore the financial security of his estate, and I have agreed to assist him. He writes to me from Casablanca, saying that brisk winds and amiable seas make his journey a pleasure. I shall expect his return within two years. In the meantime, I have purchased the property adjoining my father's house on Threadneedle Street, and we begin the plans for our warehouse and shop. I shall build my enterprise, tithe from the increase, see that my employees are treated well and fairly paid, do all in my power to ease the lot of those who suffer, and — yes, Sarah, your sister Mary and my father were wise in what they suggested — I mean to use my position to influence the wealthy, the aristocracy, politicians, all with whom I meet, to benefit the kingdom of God."

"Oh, Charles," Sarah managed, her eyes swimming. "I must tell you that . . . that I am very happy for you. I truly am. So much has happened since our first meeting. I was certain I understood God's intention for the rich, but I have come to see . . . oh, I am ashamed at how carefully I read the Scriptures but failed to understand . . . even now. I confess I am not quite sure I fully comprehend how it is all meant to be."

" 'We see through a glass darkly,' " Charles reminded her. "I, too, find it difficult to fathom the workings of our Father. He unfolds His will rather slowly . . . and with an odd sense of humor . . . and to purposes I cannot always discern. I have had to be reminded that God sees the world from quite a different place than I do. Thankfully, to assist me in this, I have been given another gift."

Now Charles turned and motioned to a table at the farthest edge of the deck. Sarah's eyes widened. "It is Mr. Martin," she whispered as the lad doffed his hat at her. "Your Danny."

"Young Danny Martin has quite a future before him. I believe he may become the rudder by which Locke & Son is guided, for his loyalty and wisdom continue to astonish me. Sarah, Danny is the one who helped me to see that God has been leading me along a path blessed by these gifts."

He touched each item he had laid upon the table — his parents' portraits, the gold coin, the letters of commitment — and then his hand covered hers. "I believe," he said, "that God brought you into my life too. I believe that He opened my heart to love you before I knew anything about your title or your fortune, and that He taught you — who were so sure she could never love — how to love me. And I am certain, Sarah, that no matter what your sisters might think or what London's *ton* might whisper or what —"

"Wait! Charles, please, I beg you." Drawing her hand from beneath his, Sarah pushed back from the table and stood. He did not move as she walked to the edge of the deck and leaned on the damp rail. Closing her eyes, she breathed deeply of the sea air and felt the sun's warm rays heat her cheeks. Overhead a seagull cried, and below, the waves splashed against the hull of the ship.

Charles had loved her . . . searched for her . . . found her . . . loved her still. He would not give up; she understood at last. She could no more run from Charles than she could run from God, who loved her far more. Yes, she had been hurt, abandoned, mistreated, used. She had known the underbelly of the world — the attic of a boarding school, the chill of an empty marriage bed, the flattery of shallow acquaintances, and the poverty and anguish of the blind and starving who suffered far more than she could ever comprehend.

But God had laid out a path for her, just as He lays one out for every Christian. She had been given parents, sisters, a fortune, widowhood . . . what next? Where was she to go? How was she to use the life she had been handed?

Knitting her fingers together tightly, Sarah opened her eyes and studied the lapping waves and the distant shoreline of England. Then she turned and crossed the deck to the table where Charles sat waiting for her.

Taking her chair, she looked into his eyes. "Mr. Locke," she said with a gulp. "Mr. Locke, will you marry me?" She blurted out the words in a rush of breath. "Please do be reasonable."

Throwing back his head, Charles laughed out loud. "Oh, no, Mrs. Carlyle, that will never do! Never, never — for I have asked far too many times to have you turn the tables on me at the last moment." Leaving his chair, he dropped to one knee and took her hand. "My darling Sarah, will you marry me?"

"I have already answered you, sir. At Trenton House."

"Answer me again."

"Yes, Mr. Locke. I shall marry you. I shall marry you every day of my life from now on. But —" she winked at him — "will you marry me?"

He chuckled. "Yes, Lady Delacroix, I shall marry you. Every day of my life from now on."

"Good. Then I suggest we dispense with it at once, before I can be persuaded otherwise." Taking the gold coin, she stood and lifted Charles to his feet. "Let us find the captain and see if this will suffice for the fee."

"What, get married here? now?"

"Absolutely," she said. "Unless you mean to change your mind, sir?"

"Absolutely not!"

Laughing, she led him across the deck toward the table where Danny now was rising awkwardly to his feet. "Mr. Martin," Sarah addressed him. "I have proposed marriage to Mr. Locke, and he has kindly accepted. Will you be so good as to fetch the captain of this ship and ask him if he can take the time to perform a wedding?"

Danny's mouth dropped open as he gawked at Charles. "She proposed? to you?"

"Aye, and I proposed back, and we have both accepted each other — which means we are desperately in need of a wedding. At once, lad!"

Charles tossed the coin through the bright blue sky, and Danny caught it with one hand. Hop-skipping away, he flipped the gold up and down as if it were nothing more than a tuppence.

"My beautiful Sarah," Charles said, turning her toward him and taking her into his arms. "You have made me so very happy."

"Do you know, sir," she whispered, standing on tiptoe to reach his ear, "I have done nothing but think of you day and night since first we met aboard the *Queen Elinor*. When you opened your eyes and I looked into them, I was lost to you at once."

Drawing her close, he kissed her cheek. "Lost to me?" he murmured as his lips brushed softly across her mouth. "Dearest lady, it was at that moment we both were found."

MISS PICKWORTH'S
PONDERINGS

After reviewing the tale of the affectionate adversary and the wealthy widow, please peruse Miss Pickworth's ponderings. She has a quantity of questions, and she wonders if you, dear reader, may come to any clever conclusions.

1. Why did Sarah's father treat her as he did? Did he see her only as a tool to accomplish his own aims? Or did he believe he was actually going to help her in the long run?

2. What do you suppose happened to Sarah's mother? Why did she cooperate with her husband in his mistreatment of their daughters? Do women ever do this kind of thing today?

3. Do women today use marriage in the same way they did during England's

Regency period? How do we look at marriage in contrast to the way Sarah, Mary, and Prudence viewed it?

4. Was Charles just trying to please his father in starting the tea company — or was that really his own ambition? Is ambition always a bad thing? Can it be good? How?

5. Do you think God puts people like Charles and Sarah together in unexpected circumstances — or are such meetings simply coincidence?

6. What do you think of the way Charles explained God's will to Danny Martin? Does God have a set path for our lives? What should we do when a barrier drops in front of us — especially when we think we're doing God's will?

7. Charles considers several different plans for his life. Do you think he finally chose the best one? Do you believe this was what God wanted for him — or did he manipulate the circumstances to fit his own desires?

8. Sarah felt sure that money was the source

of all her unhappiness. Can money bring true joy? Why or why not? Had money made Sarah unhappy — or was it something else entirely?

9. What did Prudence believe about money? What did Mary believe? Did they have their focus in the right place? Did Sarah influence them . . . or did they influence her?

10. Read the following several Bible passages that speak about money and riches. What does God say about wealth?

Listen to this, all you people! Pay attention, everyone in the world! High and low, rich and poor — listen! For my words are wise, and my thoughts are filled with insight. . . . Why should I fear when trouble comes, when enemies surround me? They trust in their wealth and boast of great riches. Yet they cannot redeem themselves from death by paying a ransom to God. Redemption does not come so easily, for no one can ever pay enough to live forever and never see the grave. *(Psalm 49:1–9)*

Look what happens to mighty warriors who do not trust in God. They trust their wealth instead and grow more and more bold in their wickedness. But I am like an olive tree, thriving in the house of God. I will always trust in God's unfailing love. I will praise you forever, O God, for what you have done. I will trust in your good name in the presence of your faithful people. *(Psalm 52:7–9)*

Choose a good reputation over great riches; being held in high esteem is better than silver or gold. *(Proverbs 22:1)*

Wisdom is even better when you have money. Both are a benefit as you go through life. Wisdom and money can get you almost anything, but only wisdom can save your life. Accept the way God does things, for who can straighten what he has made crooked? Enjoy prosperity while you can, but when hard times strike, realize that both come from God. Remember that nothing is certain in this life. *(Ecclesiastes 7:11–14)*

Is anyone thirsty? Come and drink — even if you have no money! Come, take your choice of wine or milk — it's all free! Why spend your money on food that does not give you strength? Why pay for food that does you no good? Listen to me, and you will eat what is good. You will enjoy the finest food. *(Isaiah 55:1–2)*

This is what the LORD says: "Don't let the wise boast in their wisdom, or the powerful boast in their power, or the rich boast in their riches. But those who wish to boast should boast in this alone: that they truly know me and understand that I am the LORD who demonstrates unfailing love and who brings justice and righteousness to the earth, and that I delight in these things. I, the LORD, have spoken!" *(Jeremiah 9:23–24)*

On their arrival in Capernaum, the collectors of the Temple tax came to Peter and asked him, "Doesn't your teacher pay the Temple tax?"

"Yes, he does," Peter replied. Then he went into the house.

But before he had a chance to speak, Jesus asked him, "What do you think, Peter? Do kings tax their own people or the people they have conquered?"

"They tax the people they have conquered," Peter replied.

"Well, then," Jesus said, "the citizens are free! However, we don't want to offend them, so go down to the lake and throw in a line. Open the mouth of the first fish you catch, and you will find a large silver coin. Take it and pay the tax for both of us." (Matthew 17:24–27)

The Kingdom of Heaven can be illustrated by the story of a man going on a long trip. He called together his servants and entrusted his money to them while he was gone. He gave five bags of silver to one, two bags of silver to another, and one bag of silver to the last — dividing it in proportion to their abilities. He then left on his trip.

The servant who received the five bags of silver began to invest the money and earned five more. The servant with two bags of silver also went to work and earned two more. But the servant who received the one bag of silver dug a hole in the ground and hid the master's money.

After a long time their master returned from his trip and called them to give an account of how they had used his money. The servant to whom he had entrusted the five bags of silver came forward with five more and said, "Master, you gave me five bags of silver to invest, and I have earned five more."

The master was full of praise. "Well done, my good and faithful servant. You have been faithful in handling this small amount, so now I will give you many more responsibilities. Let's celebrate together!"

The servant who had received the two bags of silver came forward and said, "Master, you gave me two bags of silver to invest, and I have earned two more."

The master said, "Well done, my good and faithful servant. You have been faithful in handling this small amount, so now I will give you many more responsibilities. Let's celebrate together!"

Then the servant with the one bag of silver came and said, "Master, I knew you were a harsh man, harvesting crops you didn't plant and gathering crops you didn't cultivate. I was afraid I would lose your money, so I hid it in the earth. Look, here is your money back."

But the master replied, "You wicked and lazy servant! If you knew I harvested crops I didn't plant and gathered crops I didn't cultivate, why didn't you deposit my money in the bank? At least I could have gotten some interest on it."

Then he ordered, "Take the money from this servant, and give it to the one with the ten bags of silver. To those who use well what they are given, even more will be given, and they will have an abundance. But from those who do nothing, even what little they have will be taken away. Now throw this useless servant into outer darkness, where there will be weeping and gnashing of teeth." *(Matthew 25:14–30)*

Jesus sat down near the collection box in the Temple and watched as the crowds dropped in their money. Many rich people put in large amounts. Then a poor widow came and dropped in two small coins.

Jesus called his disciples to him and said, "I tell you the truth, this poor widow has given more than all the others who are making contributions. For they gave a tiny part of their surplus, but she, poor as she is, has given everything she had to live on." *(Mark 12:41–44)*

It was nearly time for the Jewish Passover celebration, so Jesus went to Jerusalem. In the Temple area he saw merchants selling cattle, sheep, and doves for sacrifices; he also saw dealers at tables exchanging foreign money. Jesus made a whip from some ropes and chased them all out of the Temple. He drove out the sheep and cattle, scattered the money changers' coins over the floor, and turned over their tables. Then, going over to the people who sold doves, he told them, "Get these things out of here. Stop turning my Father's house into a marketplace!"

Then his disciples remembered this prophecy from the Scriptures: "Passion for God's house will consume me." *(John 2:13–17)*

Look here, you rich people: Weep and groan with anguish because of all the terrible troubles ahead of you. Your wealth is rotting away, and your fine clothes are moth-eaten rags. Your gold and silver have become worthless. The very wealth you were counting on will eat away your flesh like fire. This treasure you have accumulated will stand as evidence against you on the day of judgment. *(James 5:1–3)*

There are many more teachings in the Bible about money. Do you think you treat money the way God wants you to? If not, why don't you ask God to forgive you right now — and then make a fresh start. That's what forgiveness is all about!

MISS PICKWORTH POSES PROBLEMS

Regular readers may recall that trifling tidbits need to be tidied:

What is to befall our pretty Prudence? Will she wed or be stranded on the shelf of spinsterhood?

What of maternal Mary and her humdrum husband? Will they be blessed with a boy . . . or will they dote upon a daughter?

Dear dapper Delacroix . . . sailing the seas in search of tea. Will he return safe and sound? Or will storms, shipwrecks, and savages undo him?

Amiable Anne, the prisoned parson's poor daughter. Will she find happiness doting on a duchess in the Chouteau clan? Can she earn enough to ensure her father's freedom?

And what of this rampant rumor about Ruel

Chouteau? Has he returned from the dead? What will befall his beloved brother — the ambitious Alexander — who so happily hoped to inherit the duchy?

The duke and duchess of Marston . . . James Locke . . . young Danny Martin . . . a cast of characters currently left languishing.

Miss Pickworth recommends that her readers rush to gather all the gossip in the next tempting tale of *The Bachelor's Bargain.*

A NOTE FROM THE AUTHOR

Dear Friend,

I truly hope you enjoyed *The Affectionate Adversary.* My prayer is that God will use this series to provide you with respite from the cares of the world and challenge you to keep your focus always on Jesus Christ. It is only through Him that we can surrender ourselves and live in a way that pleases God.

Several years ago, the Holy Spirit opened my eyes to the possibility of writing novels with a Regency setting. I've always loved that period in England (1811–1820), when chaos reigned among England's royalty, Napoleon was wreaking havoc on land and sea, and the writer Jane Austen — delightfully oblivious to the pandemonium — was penning her charming books.

You may be wondering what the Regency period was all about and why it fascinates me so. Please visit my Web site at www .catherinepalmer.com to step further into this wonderful world of lords and ladies, tea parties and pirates, grand manor houses and wee cottages, and of course, true love!

This new series introduces my favorite character, Miss Pickworth, London society's witty tattler and advice dispenser. Who is this cleverly cunning columnist? Well, my dear friend, you'll just have to keep reading to find out!

Blessings,
Catherine Palmer

ABOUT THE AUTHOR

Catherine Palmer's first book was published in 1988, and since then she has published more than thirty books. Total sales of her books are more than one million copies.

In 2005, Catherine was awarded the Career Achievement Award for Inspirational Romance by *Romantic Times Bookclub* magazine. Catherine's novels *Sunrise Song, The Happy Room,* and *A Dangerous Silence* are all CBA best sellers. Her book *A Touch of Betrayal* won the 2001 Christy Award for Romance, and *Wild Heather* was a finalist for the 2005 Christy Award. Her novella "Under His Wings," which appears in the anthology *A Victorian Christmas Cottage,* was named Northern Lights Best Novella of 1999, historical category, by Midwest Fiction Writers.

Catherine lives in Missouri with her husband, Tim, and sons Geoffrey and Andrei. She has degrees from Baylor University and Southwest Baptist University.